PUZZLES OLD AND NEW.

© L.E.Hordern and Martin Breese Limited, 1988

Martin Breese Ltd, 164 Kensington Park Road, London W11 2ER, England

See p. 75.

PUZZLES

Old and New.

BY

PROFESSOR HOFFMANN,

Author of "Modern Magic," "Tricks with Cards," "Conjurer Dick," etc.

WITH ILLUSTRATIONS

LONDON
FREDERICK WARNE AND CO.
AND NEW YORK.
1893

Printed in Great Britain

FOREWORD TO THIS EDITION

BY L.E.Hordern

The year 1893 was a milestone in the history of puzzle literature. Until then few, if any, books had been devoted to any great extent to mechanical puzzles. Over the previous century or two, many books had contained parts that dealt with mathematical problems and/or scientific experiments. Any section that covered mechanical puzzles was nearly always limited to a few pages. There was good reason: before 1878 there was little interest in puzzles. The best known was the *Tangram*, which almost certainly originated in the Far East and which was brought to England by 1809.

But in late 1878 or early 1879 an event occured that took the world by storm. A little puzzle — called the "Fifteen" or "Boss" puzzle — with its 15 numbered square blocks that had to be slid into their correct order in a box, captured the imagination of the public. The resulting craze was well documented in the press of the day.* It is said that hundreds of thousands, or perhaps millions of this little puzzle were sold, and that people became so engrossed that all kinds of things happened: "Pilots are said to have wrecked their ships and engineers rush their trains past stations". [Almost exactly a hundred years later, there was a similar craze in the form of the Rubik's Cube.]

Whilst the "Fifteen" puzzle craze died down after a few years, it spawned a whole variety of mechanical puzzles, and interest in them has continued to a greater or lesser extent ever since. The first era of interest in puzzles, started in 1878, seems to have lasted until about 1907. This period could best, perhaps, be described as the "Golden Age" of puzzles. It is the time during which Henry Dudeney in England and Sam Loyd in America did so much to promote the knowledge of puzzles.

It is an interesting insight into the life of the times that

Foreword

Professor Louis Hoffmann was only a pen name. His real name was the Reverend Angelo John Lewis. It was not so common to use pen names for books of this kind (it still isn't) and it is more than likely that he chose to use one because of his occupation. It could have been thought at the time that writing books on *puzzles* was incompatible with his profession!

Professor Hoffmann's achievement was twofold. He was the first to describe in the minutest detail *mechanical* puzzles available commercially at the time and his aim was to make it as complete as possible. He was able to combine this with a wealth of accurate drawings, from which it must be assumed that he either possessed or had access to the puzzles he was describing. For some 80 years or more (until the advent of modern colour printing techniques), his book stood alone, head and shoulders above the rest. For this reason, collectors of mechanical puzzles often refer to *Puzzles Old and New* as the "Bible" of the industry, and the puzzles described as "Hoffmann" puzzles.

The book gives just over 400 puzzles, and it is interesting to establish just how many of these can have been commercially produced prior to 1893. [Of course, some puzzles continued in production many years after.] For example, it is evident that all of the puzzles in Chapter I — except the last two — and all those in Chapter II must have been manufactured. On the other hand, many of the arithmetical puzzles in Chapter IV and the "Quibble" or "Catch" puzzles in Chapter IX are pure pencil and paper exercises and are unlikely to have reached any shop. I have calculated that, at most, 190 of the 400 may have been produced. In my collection of some 12,000 mechanical puzzles, I possess 125 "Hoffmann" puzzles, all of which were manufactured between 1850 and 1910. On this basis it might be worthwhile to produce a "colour supplement" showing in photographic detail the actual puzzles. But that will depend on demand ...

OXFORDSHIRE, ENGLAND   EDWARD HORDERN
March 1988

---

* A history of the "Fifteen" puzzle and a detailed description of other sliding block puzzles from 1880 to the present day, can be found in *Sliding Piece Puzzles* written by L.E. Hordern and published by Oxford University Press in 1987.

PREFACE.

The Natural History of the Puzzle has yet to be written. It is a plant of very ancient growth, as witness the riddle of the Sphinx, solved by Œdipus, and the enigma wherewith Samson confounded his Philistine adversaries. Homer is said by Plutarch to have died of chagrin at being unable to guess a riddle; and folklore abounds in instances where the winning of a princess, or the issue of some perilous adventure, is made to depend upon success in solving some puzzle, verbal or otherwise. In more modern times grave mathematicians, like Cardan and Euler, have not disdained to employ their leisure in the fabrication of "posers" for the puzzlement of their less erudite compeers.

The chief difficulties I have found in compiling the present collection have been nomenclature and classification. In view of the varieties of taste, some preferring a mathematical, some a mechanical problem—one person a trial of skill, another an exercise of patience—it seemed desirable to have as many categories as possible. On the other hand, the more numerous the divisions, the more difficult does it become to assign a given puzzle definitely to one or another. In many instances the same item might with equal propriety be classed under either of several categories.

Nomenclature presents even greater difficulties. The same title is often applied, with more or less appropriateness, to two or three different puzzles. For example, there are some half-dozen "cross" puzzles, more or less unlike, yet all having a fair claim to the title, and being scarcely distinguishable by any other. Again, a mechanical puzzle is frequently described in the price-lists of different dealers by different names, the "Arabian Mystery" of one being, say, the "Egyptian Paradox" or the "Ashantee Difficulty" of another. Others are of necessity nameless, it being impossible to devise any short title which shall give any idea of the nature of the problem.

The very wide class of verbal puzzles, comprising conundrums, enigmas, charades, etc., is here, from considerations of space, omitted. With this exception, it has been my endeavour to make this little book as complete as possible, and I have to acknowledge a substantial debt of thanks to the many friends (notably Messrs. Paul Perkins and Edward Montauban) who have lent helping hands to make it so. The field is, however, very wide, and it is almost a matter of course that many "good things" should have been, through ignorance or inadvertence, omitted. Should any reader note such omissions, or have private information as to items of special merit, I shall be glad, with a view to future editions, to be made acquainted with them.

LOUIS HOFFMANN.

TABLE OF CONTENTS.

CHAPTER I.

PUZZLES DEPENDENT ON DEXTERITY AND PERSEVERANCE.

		PAGE
I.	The "Pick-Me-Up" Puzzle	1
II.	The Planet Puzzle	2
III.	The i Dotting Puzzle	3
IV.	The Spider and the Flies	,,
V.	The Tower Bridge Puzzle	4
VI.	In the Soup	5
VII.	The Matrimonial Chair	6
VIII.	The "Tire 'Em Out" Puzzle	7
IX.	The Electric Ball	8
X.	The "Hang Him" Puzzle	9
XI.	Bouci-Boula	,,
XII.	The Switchback	10
XIII.	The Five Horse-Shoes	11
XIV.	The Two Horse-Shoes	,,
XV.	The Maze	12
XVI.	The Pitfall Puzzle	,,
XVII.	The Fifteen Pellets Puzzle	13
XVIII.	The Cross Puzzle	,,
XIX.	The Hand of Cards	14
XX.	The Pig Puzzle	,,
XXI.	The Four Colours Puzzle	,,
XXII.	The Amphitheatre Puzzle	15
XXIII.	The Persian Shah	,,
XXIV.	The Balance Puzzle	16
XXV.	The Fish Puzzle	,,
XXVI.	The Marksman	17
XXVII.	The Snake and Bird	18
XXVIII.	The Coin and Card Puzzle	19
XXIX.	The Egg and Card Puzzle	,,

CHAPTER II.

MECHANICAL PUZZLES DEPENDENT ON SOME TRICK OR SECRET.

		Problem PAGE	Solution PAGE
I.	The Barrel and Ball	20	48
II.	The Dice Box	21	49
III.	The Churn	,,	,,
IV.	The Cannon and Ball	22	,,
V.	The Cage and Ball	,,	50
VI.	The Castle Money-Box	23	,,
VII.	The New Castle Money-Box	,,	,,
VIII.	The Brass Money-Box	24	51
IX.	The Captive Sixpence	,,	52
X.	The Cannon and Cord	25	,,
XI.	The Heart Puzzle	26	,,
XII.	The Alliance (or Victoria) Puzzle	,,	53
XIII.	The Two Balls	27	,,
XIV.	The Ariel Puzzle	28	54
XV.	The Pen and Wheel	,,	,,
XVI.	The Balls and Rings	29	,,
XVII.	The Chinese Ladder	30	55
XVIII.	The Staff	,,	56
XIX.	The Imperial Scale	31	,,
XX.	The Sceptre	32	57
XXI.	The Balls and Chain	,,	58
XXII.	The Four Keys	33	,,
XXIII.	The Screw Box	34	59
XXIV.	The Ball and Three Strings	,,	,,
XXV.	The Lighthouse	35	60
XXVI.	The Jubilee Puzzle Box	,,	61
XXVII.	The Jubilee Penny	36	,,
XXVIII.	The Invisible Gift	,,	62
XXIX.	The Arabi Gun	,,	,,
XXX.	The Psycho Match-Box	37	,,
XXXI.	The "Touch-me-not" Match-Box and Tobacco-Box	38	63
XXXII.	The Magic Drawer Match-Box	,,	,,
XXXIII.	The "Unique" Match-Box	39	64
XXXIV.	The Surprise Match-Box	,,	,,
XXXV.	The New Brass Puzzle Match-Box	40	,,
XXXVI.	The Ne Plus Ultra Match-Box	,,	65
XXXVII.	The Sphinx Match-Box	41	,,
XXXVIII.	The Puzzle Snuff-Box	,,	66

Table of Contents.

PUZZLES DEPENDENT ON SOME TRICK OR SECRET—*continued*.

	Problem PAGE	Solution PAGE
XXXIX. The New Puzzle Snuff-Box.	42	66
XL. The Puzzle Ball.	,,	67
XLI. The Ebony Puzzle Ball	,,	,,
XLII. The Puzzle Purse	43	68
XLIII. The Puzzle Pocket-Knife	,,	,,
XLIV. The Automatic Knife.	44	69
XLV. The Double Barrel and Ring	,,	,,
XLVI. The Wedding-Ring Box	,,	,,
XLVII. The New Money-Box.	45	70
XLVIII. The Zulu Box	,,	71
XLIX. The New Persian Puzzle	,,	,,
L. The Magic Handcuff.	46	,,
LI. The Key and Ring Puzzle.	,,	,,
LII. The New Egg of Columbus.	47	72

CHAPTER III.

DISSECTED OR COMBINATION PUZZLES.

The Dissected Puzzles of fifty years ago.—The Richter Building Stones	74	
Hints for the readier solution of Dissected Puzzles		111
The Richter Puzzles—		
I. The Anchor Puzzle	77	,,
II. The Tormentor Puzzle	80	115
III. The Pythagoras Puzzle	81	117
IV. The Cross Puzzle.	83	118
V. The Circular Puzzle	85	120
VI. The Star Puzzle.	87	122
VII. The Zigzag Square	91	124
VIII. The Extended Square	,,	,,
IX. The Octagon Puzzle.	92	125
X. The Patchwork Square	,,	,,
XI. The Two Squares	93	,,
XII. The Latin Cross Puzzle	,,	126
XIII. The Greek Cross Puzzle	94	,,
XIV. The Protean Puzzle.	,,	127
XV. The Caricature Puzzle	96	128
XVI. The Chequers Puzzle.	97	129
XVII. The "Spots" Puzzle.	98	130
XVIII. The Endless Chain	99	131

DISSECTED OR COMBINATION PUZZLES—*continued.*

	Problem PAGE	Solution PAGE
XIX. The Hexagon	100	132
XX. Eight Squares in One	,,	,,
XXI. The Five Squares	,,	,,
XXII. The Geometrical Square	101	133
XXIII. The Dissected Square	,,	134
XXIV. The Twenty Triangles	,,	,,
XXV. The New Triangle Puzzle	102	135
XXVI. The Japanese Square	,,	,,
XXVII. The Chinese Square	,,	,,
XXVIII. The Yankee Square	103	136
XXIX. Another Cross Puzzle	,,	,,
XXX. The Carpenter's Puzzle. No. 1.	,,	,,
XXXI. The Carpenter's Puzzle. No. 2.	,,	137
XXXII. The Cabinet-Maker's Puzzle	104	,,
XXXIII. The Bonbon Nut Puzzle	,,	138
XXXIV. The Rattle Puzzle	105	139
XXXV. The Cross Keys (or Three-piece) Puzzle	106	,,
XXXVI. The Nut (or Six-piece) Puzzle	,,	,,
XXXVII. The Fairy Tea-table	107	141
XXXVIII. The Mystery	,,	,,
XXXIX. The Diabolical Cube	108	142
XL. The Chinese Zigzag	109	143
XLI. The Man of Many Parts	110	144

CHAPTER IV.

ARITHMETICAL PUZZLES.

Elementary Properties of Numbers		174
I. The "Forty-five" Puzzle	145	181
II. A Singular Subtraction	,,	,,
III. A Mysterious Multiplicand	,,	182
IV. Counting the Pigs	,,	,,
V. Another Pig Problem	146	,,
VI. A Little Miscalculation	,,	,,
VII. A Simple Magic Square	,,	,,
VIII. The "Thirty-four" Puzzle	,,	183
IX. The "Sixty-five" Puzzle	,,	186
X. The "Twenty-six" Puzzle	,,	191
XI. An Unmanageable Legacy	147	,,
XII. Many Figures, but a Small Result	,,	192
XIII. Can you Name It?	,,	,,

	Problem PAGE	Solution PAGE
ARITHMETICAL PUZZLES—*continued.*		
XIV. Squares, Product, and Difference	148	192
XV. A Peculiar Number	,,	,,
XVI. A Novel Century	,,	193
XVII. Another Century	,,	,,
XVIII. Another Way to Make 100	,,	,,
XIX. The Lucky Number	,,	,,
XX. The Two Ages	149	194
XXI. The Graces and the Muses	,,	,,
XXII. The Graces and the Muses again	,,	,,
XXIII. Just One Over	,,	,,
XXIV. Scarcely Explicit	,,	,,
XXV. Making Things Even	,,	195
XXVI. A Rejected Proposal	150	,,
XXVII. The Market-woman and her Stock	,,	,,
XXVIII. The Captives in the Tower	,,	196
XXIX. Father and Son	151	,,
XXX. A Complicated Transaction	,,	,,
XXXI. A Long Family	,,	197
XXXII. A Curious Number	,,	,,
XXXIII. The Shepherd and his Sheep	,,	,,
XXXIV. A Difficult Problem	,,	198
XXXV. Well Laid Out	152	200
XXXVI. The Two Travellers	,,	201
XXXVII. Measuring the Garden	,,	202
XXXVIII. When Will They Get It?	,,	,,
XXXIX. Passing the Gate	,,	,,
XL. A Novel Magic Square	153	203
XLI. Another Magic Square	,,	204
XLII. The Set of Weights	,,	205
XLIII. What Did He Lose?	,,	,,
XLIV. A Difficult Division	154	206
XLV. The Hundred Bottles of Wine	,,	,,
XLVI. The Last of her Stock	,,	207
XLVII. The Walking Match	,,	,,
XLVIII. A Feat of Divination	155	,,
XLIX. A Peculiar Number	,,	208
L. Another Peculiar Number	,,	,,
LI. The Three Legacies	,,	209
LII. Another Mysterious Multiplicand	,,	,,
LIII. How to Divide Twelve among Thirteen	156	,,
LIV. Tenth Man Out	,,	210
LV. Ninth Man Out	,,	,,

xiv   *Table of Contents.*

		Problem PAGE	Solution PAGE
ARITHMETICAL PUZZLES—*continued.*			
LVI.	The Three Travellers	157	211
LVII.	The Wolf, the Goat, and the Cabbages	,,	212
LVIII.	The Three Jealous Husbands	,,	,,
LIX.	The Captain and his Company	,,	213
LX.	The Treasure Trove	158	,,
LXI.	The Row of Counters	,,	214
LXII.	A Loan and a Present	159	,,
LXIII.	Eleven Guests in Ten Beds	,,	215
LXIV.	A Difficult Division	160	,,
LXV.	The Three Market-Women	,,	,,
LXVI.	The Farmer and his Three Daughters	,,	216
LXVII.	How Many for a Penny?	,,	,,
LXVIII.	The Magic Cards	,,	,,
LXIX.	The "Fifteen" or "Boss" Puzzle	161	217
LXX.	The Peg-away Puzzle	163	218
LXXI.	The Over-polite Guests	,,	,,
LXXII.	The "Royal Aquarium" Thirteen Puzzle	164	219
LXXIII.	An Easy Creditor	165	,,
LXXIV.	The Three Arabs	,,	220
LXXV.	An Eccentric Testator	,,	,,
LXXVI.	Another Eccentric Testator	166	221
LXXVII.	An Aggravating Uncle	,,	222
LXXVIII.	Apples and Oranges	,,	,,
LXXIX.	The Two Squares	,,	,,
LXXX.	A Curious Division	167	223
LXXXI.	A Curious Multiplication	,,	,,
LXXXII.	The Two Schoolmasters	,,	224
LXXXIII.	Nothing Left	,,	,,
LXXXIV.	The Three Generations	,,	,,
LXXXV.	The Two Brothers	168	,,
LXXXVI.	The Two Sons	,,	225
LXXXVII.	The Two Nephews	,,	,,
LXXXVIII.	The Reversed Number	,,	226
LXXXIX.	Another Reversed Number	,,	227
XC.	The Shepherd and his Sheep	,,	,,
XCI.	The Shepherdess and her Sheep	169	228
XCII.	A Weighty Matter	,,	229
XCIII.	The Three Topers	,,	,,
XCIV.	The False Scales	,,	,,
XCV.	An Arithmetical Policeman	,,	,,
XCVI.	The Flock of Geese	170	230
XCVII.	The Divided Cord	,,	,,

Table of Contents. xv

ARITHMETICAL PUZZLES—*continued*.

	Problem Page	Solution Page
XCVIII. The Divided Number	170	230
XCIX. The Two Numbers	,,	231
C. The Horse and Trap	,,	232
CI. The Two Workmen	,,	233
CII. Another Divided Number	171	,,
CIII. The Three Reapers	,,	,,
CIV. The Bag of Marbles	,,	234
CV. The Expunged Numerals. A.	,,	,,
CVI. The Expunged Numerals. B.	,,	,,
CVII. A Tradesman in a Difficulty	172	235
CVIII. Profit and Loss	,,	,,
CIX. A Curious Fraction	,,	236
CX. The Menagerie	,,	,,
CXI. The Market-Woman and her Eggs	173	237
CXII. The Cook and his Assistants	,,	,,

CHAPTER V.

WORD AND LETTER PUZZLES.

I. A Puzzling Inscription	239	253
II. An Easy One	,,	,,
III. Pied Proverbs	,,	,,
IV. Scattered Sentiment	240	,,
V. Dropped-Letter Proverbs	,,	254
VI. Dropped-Letter Nursery Rhymes	241	,,
VII. Transformations	,,	,,
VIII. Beheaded Words	242	255
IX. Anagrams	243	,,
X. Word Squares	244	256
XI. Word Diamonds	245	,,
XII. A Cross of Diamonds	247	258
XIII. Knight's Tour Letter Puzzles	248	259
XIV. Knight's Tour Word Puzzle	250	262
XV. Hidden Proverbs	251	263
XVI. The Five Arab Maxims	252	,,

CHAPTER VI.

PUZZLES WITH COUNTERS.

I. With 11 Counters, to make 12 rows of 3	265	275
II. With 9 Counters, to make 10 rows of 3	,,	,,
III. With 27 Counters, to make 9 rows of 6	,,	276

xvi   *Table of Contents.*

		Problem PAGE	Solution PAGE
PUZZLES WITH COUNTERS—*continued.*			
IV. With 10 Counters, to make 5 rows of 4.		265	277
V. With 12 Counters, to make 6 rows of 4.		,,	,,
VI. With 19 Counters, to make 9 rows of 5.		,,	278
VII. With 16 Counters, to make 10 rows of 4		266	,,
VIII. With 12 Counters, to make 7 rows of 4.		,,	,,
IX. With 9 white and 9 red Counters, to make 10 rows of 3 white and 8 rows of 3 red		,,	279
X. The Blind Abbot and his Monks.		266	,,
XI. With 10 Counters, to make 8 rows of 4.		267	280
XII. With 13 Counters, to make 12 rows of 5		,,	,,
XIII. The Eight-pointed Star Puzzle		,,	,,
XIV. The "Okto" Puzzle		268	281
XV. With 21 Counters, following the lines of a given figure, to form 30 rows of 3		,,	,,
XVI. The "Crowning" Puzzle		,,	282
XVII. The "Right and Left" Puzzle		269	,,
XVIII. The ,, ,, (Improved).		,,	284
XIX. The "Four and Four" Puzzle		270	,,
XX. The "Five and Five" Puzzle		271	,,
XXI. The "Six and Six" Puzzle.		,,	285
XXII. The "Thirty-six" Puzzle		,,	,,
XXIII. The "Five to Four" Puzzle.		272	,,
XXIV. No Two in a Row.		,,	286
XXV. The "Simple" Puzzle.		,,	,,
XXVI. The "English Sixteen" Puzzle		273	287
XXVII. The Twenty Counters		274	,,

CHAPTER VII.

PUZZLES WITH LUCIFER MATCHES.

	Problem	Solution
I. Of Eleven Matches, to make Nine.	288	293
II. Of Nine Matches, to make Three Dozen.	,,	,,
III. Of Nine Matches, to make Three and a half-dozen.	,,	,,
IV. Of Three Matches, to make Four.	,,	,,
V. Of Three Matches, to make Six	,,	,,
VI. The Bridge of Three Matches.	,,	,,
VII. The Bridge of Four Matches.	289	294
VIII. From Twenty-four Matches, forming Nine Squares, to take Eight, and leave Two Squares only	,,	295
IX. The Bridge of Two Matches.	,,	,,
X. From Seventeen Matches, forming Six Squares, to take Five, and leave Three Squares only.	,,	296

	Problem PAGE	Solution PAGE
PUZZLES WITH LUCIFER MATCHES—*continued*.		
XI. From Seventeen Matches, forming Six Squares, to take Six, and leave Two Squares only	290	296
XII. Twelve Matches being so placed as to fo m Four equal Squares, to remove and replace Four so as to form Three Squares only.	,,	,,
XIII. From Fifteen Matches, forming Five Squares, to remove Three, and leave Three Squares only	,,	297
XIV. With Five Matches, to form Two Equilateral Triangles	,,	,,
XV. With Six Matches, to form Four Triangles of equal size	,,	298
XVI. To Lift Three Matches with One	291	,,
XVII. To Lift Nine Matches with One	,,	299
XVIII. The Magnetised Matches.	,,	,,
XIX. The Fifteen Matches Puzzle	292	300

CHAPTER VIII.

WIRE PUZZLES.

I. The United Hearts	302	309
II. The Triangle	,,	,,
III. The Snake and Ring	303	,,
IV. The Hieroglyph	304	310
V. The Five Triangles	,,	,,
VI. The Double Bow and Ring	305	311
VII. The Egyptian Mystery	,,	,,
VIII. The Ball and Spiral	306	312
IX. The Unionist Puzzle	,,	,,
X. The Eastern Question	307	313
XI. The Handcuff Puzzle	,,	,,
XII. The Stanley Puzzle	308	,,

CHAPTER IX.

"QUIBBLE" OR "CATCH" PUZZLES.

I. A Remarkable Division	315	323
II. Subtraction Extraordinary	,,	,,
III. Two Halves Greater than the Whole	,,	,,
IV. A Distinction and a Difference	,,	,,

Table of Contents.

"Quibble" or "Catch" Puzzles—continued

	Problem PAGE	Solution PAGE
V. The Family Party	315	323
VI. A Sum in Subtraction	316	324
VII. Another Sum in Subtraction	,,	,,
VIII. Three times Six	,,	,,
IX. A New Way of Writing 100	,,	,,
X. A Seeming Impossibility	,,	,,
XI. Multiplication Extraordinary	,,	,,
XII. A Question in Notation	,,	,,
XIII. The Miraculous Herrings	,,	,,
XIV. Two Evens make an Odd	,,	325
XV. Six made Three	317	,,
XVI. A Singular Subtraction	,,	,,
XVII. A Sum in Addition	,,	,,
XVIII. The Flying Sixpence	,,	,,
XIX. The Last Thing Out	,,	,,
XX. The Three Gingerbread Nuts	,,	,,
XXI. The Mysterious Obstacle	318	326
XXII. The Bewitched Right Hand	,,	,,
XXIII. The Invisible Candle	,,	,,
XXIV. The Draper's Puzzle	,,	,,
XXV. The Portrait	,,	,,
XXVI. The Charmed Circle	319	,,
XXVII. The Egg and the Cannon-ball	,,	327
XXVIII. A Curious Window	,,	,,
XXIX. A Queer Calculation	,,	,,
XXX. An Arithmetical Enigma	,,	,,
XXXI. A Short Year	,,	,,
XXXII. The Mysterious Addition	320	,,
XXXIII. Arithmetical Enigma	,,	,,
XXXIV. A New Valuation	,,	,,
XXXV. Easy, When You Know It	,,	328
XXXVI. Necessity the Mother of Invention	,,	,,
XXXVII. A Singular Subtraction	,,	,,
XXXVIII. A Vanishing Number	,,	,,
XXXIX. A Queer Query	321	,,
XL. The Mouse	,,	,,
XLI. The Fasting Man	,,	,,
XLII. The Family Party	,,	,,
XLIII. A Reversible Fraction	,,	329
XLIV. The Three Counters	322	,,
XLV. Magic Made Easy	,,	,,

CHAPTER X.

MISCELLANEOUS PUZZLES.

		Problem PAGE	Solution PAGE
I.	The John Bull Puzzle.	330	357
II.	The Pig in Sty	331	358
III.	Hide and Seek	332	359
IV.	The Brahmin's Puzzle	333	361
V.	Cardan's Rings	334	364
VI.	The Knight's Tour	335	367
VII.	The Knotted Handkerchief.	337	374
VIII.	Crossette	,,	,,
IX.	Single-Stroke Figures	338	375
X.	The Balanced Egg (Another method).	,,	376
XI.	Solitaire Problems	339	,,
XII.	Skihi	340	377
XIII.	A Card Puzzle	342	378
XIV.	Another Card Puzzle	,,	,,
XV.	The Floating Corks	,,	379
XVI.	The Obstinate Cork	,,	380
XVII.	Fixing the Ring	,,	,,
XVIII.	The Treasure at Medinet	343	381
XIX.	The Four Wine-Glasses	344	,,
XX.	One Peg to Fit Three Holes	,,	,,
XXI.	The Balanced Pencil	,,	382
XXII.	To Balance an Egg on the Point of a Walking-Stick	345	,,
XXIII.	The Ashantee Horseshoe	,,	383
XXIV.	A Feat of Dexterity	,,	384
XXV.	The Divided Square	346	,,
XXVI.	The "Oval" Problem	,,	385
XXVII.	The Floating Ball	,,	,,
XXVIII.	The Cut Playing-Card	,,	,,
XXIX.	The Mitre Puzzle	347	386
XXX.	The Five Straws	,,	,,
XXXI.	The Three Fountains	,,	387
XXXII.	The Two Dogs	348	,,
XXXIII.	Water Bewitched	,,	388
XXXIV.	The Balanced Hal'penny	,,	,,
XXXV.	The Balanced Sixpence	349	389
XXXVI.	Silken Fetters	,,	390
XXXVII.	The Orchard Puzzle	350	,,

Table of Contents.

MISCELLANEOUS PUZZLES—*continued.*

	Problem PAGE	Solution PAGE
XXXVIII. The Cook in a Difficulty	350	390
XXXIX. The Devil's Bridge	351	391
XL. The Two Corks	,,	,,
XLI. The Divided Farm	352	,,
XLII. The Conjurer's Medal	353	392
XLIII. The Maze Medal	,,	,,
XLIV. The Puzzle Key-ring	354	,,
XLV. The Singular Shilling	355	393
XLVI. The Entangled Scissors	,,	,,
XLVII. The Penetrative Penny	356	,,
XLVIII. The Packer's Secret	,,	394

PUZZLES OLD AND NEW.

CHAPTER I.

PUZZLES DEPENDENT ON DEXTERITY AND PERSEVERANCE.

In this first section we propose to describe a class of puzzles which do not depend upon any secret, or intellectual process, but upon some knack, only to be obtained by repeated persistent effort of the "try and try again" kind on the part of the operator.* Of these a very good example is—

No. I.—The "Pick-Me-Up" Puzzle.

This puzzle was brought out by the proprietors of the well-known serio-comic weekly of the same name, and en-

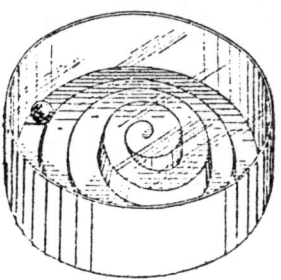

FIG. 1.

joyed for some time widespread popularity. It consists of a cylindrical pasteboard box, four inches in diameter by two in depth, with a glass top, as illustrated in Fig. 1.

---

* There will accordingly be no KEY to the present Chapter. Any hint likely to assist the operator will be incorporated in the text. Beyond this, he must work out the solution for himself.

The base is occupied by a shallow cone in plaster of Paris, with an inclined plane in the form of a spiral (but diversified by sundry irregularities and depressions) leading to the top, where there is a minute "crater." At the bottom lies a marble, and the puzzle is to get such marble to the top and down again. The marble must not be *jerked* into the required position (this being a comparatively easy feat), but worked steadily up and down the inclined plane.*

To an unpractised hand the feat seems almost impossible; but we have seen an expert work the ball to the top and down again with the greatest apparent ease.

No. II.—The Planet Puzzle.

This very pretty puzzle also emanated from the *Pick-Me-Up* Office. It is a shallow tray five inches in diameter by three-quarters of an inch in depth, and, like the puzzle last described, closed at top with a fixed glass lid. (See Fig 2.) On the bottom are traced concentric rings, re-

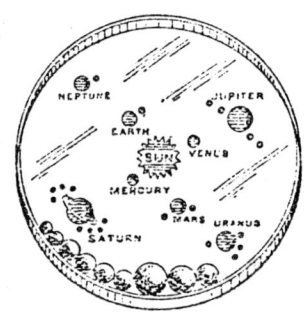

Fig. 2.

presenting the orbits of various heavenly bodies, with the sun as centre. At a given point in each such orbit is a minute depression, marked with the name and a pictorial representation of the corresponding planet, the list com-

---

* There is a miniature form of the "Pick-Me-Up" Puzzle made in brass, about the size of a crown-piece, a swan-shot taking the place of the marble.

prising (in addition to the Sun and Earth) Mercury, Venus, Mars, Jupiter, Saturn, Uranus, and Neptune. The heavenly bodies themselves are represented by minute marbles, of various sizes and colours, corresponding with the representations of the various stars; and the task of the experimenter is to coax each marble into its proper position on the chart—a by no means easy matter. Indeed, by the time he succeeds, the aspirant should have acquired a very fair idea of the sizes and positions of the more important members of the Solar System.

No. III.—The **i** Dotting Puzzle.

This is a shallow cardboard box, with glass top, in which are enclosed five leaden pellets. The central space (see Fig. 3) is surrounded by vertical cardboard partitions, the only access to the centre being by means of sundry minute

Fig. 3.

archways, cut in the lower halves of such partitions. In the centre is printed, in "script" type, the word *Indivisibility*, and the task of the experimenter is so to manipulate the five pellets that they shall each rest on the dot of one of the *i's*, each of which has a minute depression to receive it.

No. IV.—The Spider and the Flies.

This is a puzzle on the same principle, but with a difference which renders it one of the prettiest of its kind. It is a little wooden tray with glass top. (See Fig. 4.)

On the piece of cardboard which covers the bottom is delineated a spider's web, with a depression in the centre for the reception of the "spider," which is represented by a globule of mercury, **A**. At different points of the web are spots of colour, two blue and two red, while the "flies" are

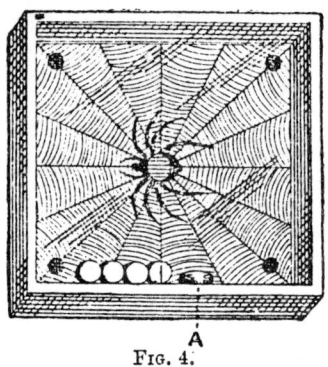

A
Fig. 4.

represented by four circular wads of felt, a quarter of an inch in diameter, these also being two of each colour.

The puzzle is, by means of the globule of mercury, to coax the four flies to their proper positions, red on red, and blue on blue; and finally to leave the "spider" in the centre of the web.

No. V.—The Tower Bridge Puzzle.*

An unusual amount of imagination has been expended over the surroundings of this puzzle. The bottom of the box (see Fig. 5) represents a moat, professedly dividing Tooley Street from Great Tower Street. An inclined plane leads from the bottom of the moat to a gallery or quay on the Tooley Street side. This side is connected on the gallery level with a balcony on the opposite side, the intervening space being crossed by a narrow bridge of a somewhat peculiar construction. The bridge is divided in the centre, each half working on a very light spring-hinge, so that it rests normally in a horizontal position, but the moment any weight is allowed to rest upon it, it drops, and the unwary passenger

---

* Manufactured by Messrs. Feltham & Co.

is precipitated into the moat below. The floor space of the balcony is divided into five squares, coloured white, black, blue, pink, and green respectively, and at the bottom of the moat lie five marbles of corresponding colours.

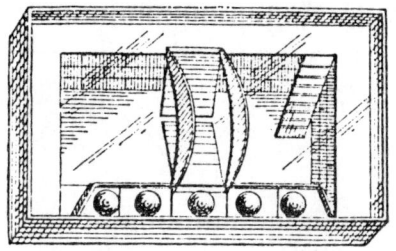

Fig. 5.

The puzzle is to get the marbles one by one up the inclined plane, across the bridge, and into the balcony, each on its proper colour. By a knack acquired by practice, the marbles can be shot across the bridge so quickly that they have not time to drop into the moat below. Beyond this, the only key is patience and perseverance.

No. VI.—In the Soup.

The appliances for this puzzle (introduced by Messrs. Perry & Co.) are a little red earthenware bowl, three inches in diameter by two in height, a glass marble, and a "spoon,"

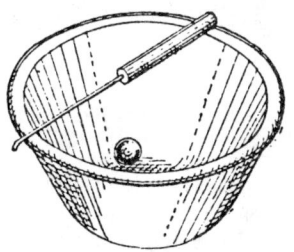

Fig. 6.

consisting of a bit of wire set in a wooden handle, and slightly curved and flattened at the opposite end. (See Fig. 6.)

The bowl is placed on a table or other flat surface, and the puzzle is to get the marble out with no other aid but that of the spoon. It must not be tossed or flirted out, but gently coaxed up the side and over the edge.

This is by no means a puzzle of the most difficult kind, but demands a steady hand and a considerable amount of patience, the ball having a provoking way of escaping from the spoon and falling "in the soup" again, just at the very moment when the neophyte thinks that he has at last succeeded. With juveniles it is invariably popular, and affords a good deal of amusement even to older members of the community.

No. VII.—The Matrimonial Chair.

This again depends upon the manipulation of a marble, but after a different fashion. Within a cardboard box, in

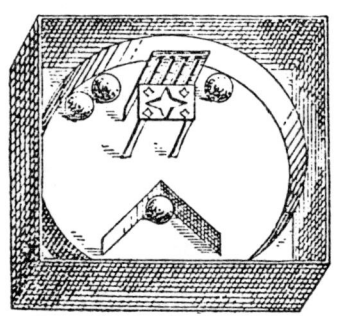

Fig. 7.

this case not glass-covered, but open, and five inches square by one and a half deep, is constructed a sort of miniature circus. At one point of the circle is fixed a little chair of sheet brass,—the "matrimonial chair,"—and facing it (see Fig. 7) an angle-piece of the same material, of the same height as the seat of the chair, and with its apex about an inch distant from it. Loose in the box are four small marbles of different colours, representing four different characters: a blue marble standing for the gay young bachelor; a red marble for the old maid; a green marble appropriately representing a bashful young man; and a yellow marble (not quite so appropriately) a giddy young girl.

The experimenter is invited to select whichever of these he pleases, and, without touching it, so to manipulate it as to seat it in the chair.

Both dexterity and perseverance will be needed to achieve success, but there is a definite method to follow, apart from which neither dexterity nor perseverance will be of much avail. Having chosen a given marble, get it singly within the angle-piece, and depress the "chair" end of the box very slightly, so that the marble may run down into the angle. Then, holding the box in the left hand, with the chair facing you, give a little fillip with the right thumb against the bottom of the box, just below the marble; when, if your degree of force and angle of inclination have been discreetly calculated, the marble will jump over the screen and rest on the seat of the chair.

No. VIII.—The "Tire 'Em Out" Puzzle (L'Enervant).

This is a puzzle of French origin. It consists of a little circular salver about four and a half inches in diameter, rising gently towards the centre, at which point there is a slight depression. (See Fig. 8.)

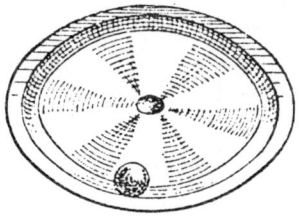

Fig. 8.

A marble, half an inch in diameter, is laid upon the salver, and the operator is required to work it into the pit in the centre.*

---

* Our young readers can construct a home-made version of this puzzle in a rough and ready way, by gluing a ring of stout cardboard (say one inch in external, and half an inch in internal diameter) in the centre of an ordinary cheese-plate.

The easiest method of getting the ball into position is to work it close up to the centre, and then drop the salver with a slight jerk to a depth of half an inch or so. With a little dexterity the ball may easily be caught and retained in the centre. This method is, however, scarcely legitimate. The ball should be rolled, and not jerked, into the desired position.

No. IX.—The Electric Ball.

This also is a French importation. It is more of a game than a puzzle, though it may be presented in either shape. It consists (see Fig. 9) of a hollow elbow piece, *A B B*, to which is attached a sort of miniature gallows, *C C*. From the

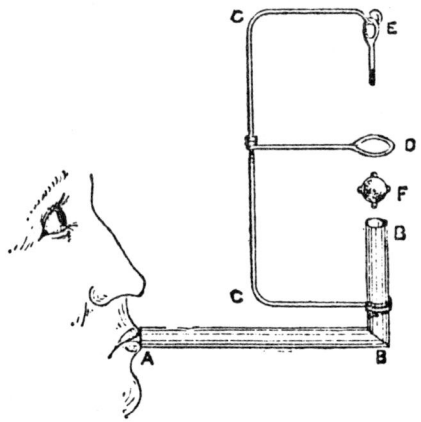

Fig. 9.

middle of this projects a ring, *D*, and suspended from its upper arm swings a little piece of strongly magnetized iron wire, *E*. A gilt cork ball, *F*, into which are thrust six little iron pins with their heads projecting, completes the apparatus.

The ball being placed on the open end of *B B*, the operator brings *A* to his lips and blows through the tube, endeavouring to force the ball upwards through the ring, and bring one or other of the pinheads into contact with the magnetized wire, *E*, when the ball will remain suspended

Some little skill is required in order to blow in the right way. The force must be gentle, but continuous. A novice generally endeavours to blow the ball into position by a succession of quick puffs, a method which inevitably results in failure.

No. X.—The "Hang Him" Puzzle (Le Pendu).

This is a variation of that last described, and is productive of even more amusement. The apparatus is in this case of wood instead of metal. The little magnet is replaced by a circular loop of fine wire, about an inch in diameter, and the ball (which is somewhat smaller than the "Electric") is traversed by a thin wire, not quite two inches in length, terminating at its upper extremity in a little hook. The straight portion of the wire projects about an inch in the opposite direction. This is placed on top of the vertical tube corresponding to BB in Fig. 9, the straight portion of the wire passing down the tube. The experimenter then blows through the mouthpiece, just as in the last case. The little ball hovers in the air for a while, hook upwards, the weight of the straight part of the wire keeping it pretty nearly erect, and if the neophyte is fortunate, ultimately hooks itself on to the little loop, and remains suspended.

The blowing, as before, should be gentle, but sustained, when the ball will flutter in the air, after the manner of the larger ball sometimes seen on the top of a fountain, with extremely pretty effect.

No. XI.—Bouci-Boula.*

This again is a puzzle of French origin. It consists (see Fig. 10) of a double bulb of blown glass about three inches in length, in which are contained some fifty minute pellets

Fig. 10.

(resembling the sweets known to children as "hundreds and thousands").

---

* Presumably an abbreviation of "*Boule-ci, Boule-là,*" (a ball to this side, a ball to that side).

Half of these are red, and half white, and the puzzle is to separate them, getting all the white pellets into the one bulb, and the red into the other.

At first sight, one would be disposed to declare the task impossible, but the puzzle is really an easy one of its kind. The first step is to tilt all the pellets into one bulb, then shake them till three or four of one colour, say red, lie together near the neck. Tap the full bulb on the under side with the finger-nail till these are one by one worked into the opposite bulb. Then give the puzzle another little shake, till a few more reds lie next to the red side; work these over, and so on, till all the reds have crossed the bridge. If, as will occasionally happen, a pellet of a wrong colour should find its way into the opposite bulb, it must be worked back again before proceeding further.

With a steady hand and light touch, five or six minutes should suffice to complete the separation.

No. XII.—The Switchback.

This is a bent glass tube, about seven inches in length by half an inch in diameter, closed at each end. (See Fig. 11.)

Fig. 11.

At each of the points A, B, C is a little hollow or depression. Enclosed within the tube are three swan-shot, and the puzzle is to get one of these into each of the three depressions.

Success depends mainly upon dexterity and perseverance; but the task of the operator becomes very much easier if he sets about it in the proper fashion. The expert begins by turning the tube *upside down*, so that A, B and C shall, for the time being, be uppermost. There is now below each of the three points named a much larger depression, into which it is comparatively easy to get one of the three balls. He then gradually turns the tube round until A, B and C are again undermost; and if his hand is steady enough, the trick is done, each pellet resting at its proper point.

Puzzles of Dexterity and Perseverance. 11

The series of puzzles next described is for the most part only made in a very small size, suitable for the waistcoat pocket. They are usually of stamped sheet brass with fixed glass top, enclosing one or more leaden pellets (taking the place of the marble in the larger puzzles), which the operator is required to work into certain specified positions. We will begin with

No. XIII.—The Five Horse-Shoes.

Five horse-shoes are stamped in relief on the bottom of the box (see Fig. 12) and five pellets are enclosed, one of which is to be worked into each of the horse-shoes.

A very moderate degree of perseverance will in this case ensure success; but there is another and more difficult form

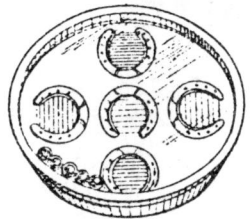

Fig. 12.

of the same puzzle, in which the space enclosed by each horse-shoe is differently coloured, say red, green, blue, black, and white respectively. The five pellets are of corresponding colours, and each must be coaxed into the space bearing its own colour.

No. XIV.—The Two Horse-Shoes.

Fig. 13.

This is very nearly identical with the last item, save that there are in this case *two* horse-shoes only (see Fig. 13), and

that their points face inwards, instead of outwards, while the space on either side is occupied by three raised partitions. There are eight pellets, and the experimenter is required to work four of them into each horse-shoe.

No. XV.—The Maze.

(See Fig. 14.) Here five pellets are enclosed, and the operator is required to work them all into the central com-

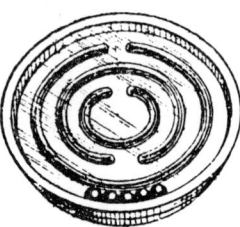

Fig. 14.

partment of the "maze." This is a more difficult puzzle than that of the horse-shoes, but still well within the reach of a patient operator.

No. XVI.—The Pitfall Puzzle.

The puzzle to which, for want of a better, we have given the above name is another variation of the same idea. (See Fig. 15.) It has a circular enclosure in the centre,

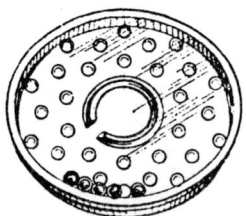

Fig. 15.

with a single narrow opening. Half a dozen pellets are to be worked into this enclosure: in itself no easy matter, but the difficulty is enhanced by the fact that the surrounding space is indented with some twenty or thirty minute depressions or pitfalls, which seriously impede the pellets in their journey to the centre.

No. XVII.—The Fifteen Pellets Puzzle.

This is the same idea reversed. In this case (see Fig. 16) there are fifteen pellets and a like number of indentations to receive them, but there are five larger depressions, not to

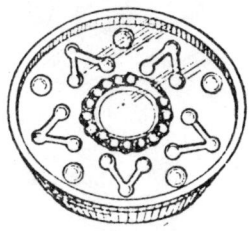

Fig. 16.

mention a circular channel or moat in the centre of the puzzle, into which the balls have an awkward knack of rolling, rather than to their intended destinations.

No. XVIII.—The Cross Puzzle.

This is a puzzle very simple in appearance, but demanding considerable skill for its successful manipulation. It has (see Fig. 17) four pairs of raised partitions, arranged in the

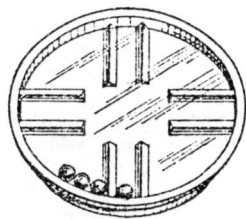

Fig. 17.

form of a cross, with their opening towards the centre. There are four pellets, and these are to be worked one into each compartment.

No. XIX.—The Hand of Cards.

This is on the same principle, but the figure occupying

Fig. 18.

the central space (see Fig. 18) represents a hand of cards. There are five pellets, one of which must occupy each angle.

No. XX.—The Pig Puzzle.

We have here (see Fig. 19) a pig in bas-relief, with a ring growing out of the middle of his back. There are three

Fig. 19.

pellets, which are to be so manipulated as to rest, one between his fore-legs, one between his hind legs, and one in the ring aforesaid.

No. XXI.—The Four Colours Puzzle.

The ground plan of the puzzle is in this case as shown in Fig. 20. There are four spaces or stalls, each distinguished

by a letter, R, W, B, M (in the actual puzzle stamped in
the space itself), standing for red, white, black, and mauve

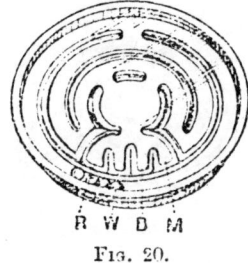

R W B M
Fig. 20.

respectively. There are four pellets, one of each colour; and
the aspirant is required to work each pellet into its proper
compartment.

No. XXII.—The Amphitheatre Puzzle.

This (see Fig. 21) is, after a fashion, the converse of the
"Pick-Me-Up" Puzzle, described at page 1. It has a series
of grooved channels, with openings at various intervals, and

Fig. 21.

the experimenter is required to work the pellets, of which
there are seven, down the inclines into the central space.
It is one of the easiest of this class of puzzles.

No. XXIII.—The Persian Shah.

In this case a little cardboard box with glass top encloses
the pictorial representation of the head of a handsome cat,

the "*chat*" referred to (see Fig. 22). A couple of pellets, representing the pupils of the eyes, are to be worked into

Fig. 22.

their proper positions, slight indentations being made to receive them.

No. XXIV.—The Balance Puzzle.

This (see Fig. 23) is a puzzle of a rather novel kind, and, of its class, of more than average merit. It consists of a little brass dish, a couple of inches in diameter, with glass top, enclosing two leaden pellets. Revolving freely on a

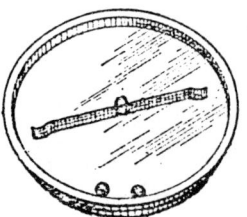

Fig. 23.

pivot in the centre is a tiny brass bar, stamped into a minute cup or hollow at each end, and forming a balance.

The task of the experimenter is to get the two pellets to rest one in each scale, a work of considerable difficulty, inasmuch as the merest touch disturbs the equilibrium of the bar.

No. XXV.—The Fish Puzzle.

This is a variation of the same idea. The balance is in this case replaced by the representation of a stamped metal

Puzzles of Dexterity and Perseverance. 17

fish, in tolerably high relief, with open mouth. This revolves freely on a central pivot, like the balance in the puzzle last described (see Fig. 24). Enclosed with the fish are some twenty very minute pellets, and the experimenter is required to get such pellets one by one into the fish's

Fig. 24.

mouth, till all have found a resting-place in his belly. The task is not easy, for the mouth is only just large enough to allow the passage of one pellet at a time, and any slight accidental movement of the fish will cause him to spin round on the pivot, and consequently to disgorge all those already swallowed.

No. XXVI.—The Marksman.

The place of the "fish" is here taken by a little figure of a kneeling soldier, with his gun to his shoulder, as if in the act of firing (see Fig. 25). This figure is not, like those of

Fig. 25.

the pig and fish, pivoted in the centre, but slides about freely between the glass top and metal bottom of the box. There are four pellets, and the aspirant is required to get

c

three of them on to the barrel of the gun, and one on the bent knee of the marksman.

No. XXVII.—The Snake and Bird.

This may be regarded either in the light of a game or of a puzzle, though there is an element of chance about it which to some extent bars its claim to rank as a puzzle proper.

It consists of a cardboard medallion or counter representing a bird, and a snake, of many convolutions, of the same material, chopped up into ten segments, more or less curved, and in length ranging from three to six inches (see Fig. 26).

The "bird" is laid upon the table, and the tail segment of the snake placed hap-hazard a couple of feet or so away from it. The experimenter is then required, beginning from

Fig. 26.

the tail, to reconstruct the snake by adding segments one by one, till the head is reached; his object being so to place the head at the finish that the "bird" shall be just within the open jaws. His prospect of effecting this will, of course, depend upon the arrangement of the successive segments, the choice of a wrong segment, or the selection of an upward instead of a downward curl (or *vice versâ*) at a given point, making just the difference between success and failure.

The various segments (which are coloured on both sides, and may therefore be used with either side uppermost) must be so placed as to butt fairly one against another, no overlapping being permissible.

No. XXVIII.—The Coin and Card Puzzle.

Balance a playing-card horizontally on the top of your left forefinger, and on it lay a coin, say a half-crown or a penny, so that both shall be in equilibrium. You are now required to remove the card without touching the coin.

Any one not in the secret usually endeavours to draw away the card by slow degrees, when failure is the inevitable result. The proper method is as follows: give the corner of the coin a smart "fillip" with the second finger of the right hand. If this be done exactly in the plane of the card, the latter will be shot away with a sort of spinning motion, the coin remaining undisturbed.

No. XXIX.—The Egg and Card Puzzle.

This is the same puzzle in a slightly altered form. Fill a wine-glass half full of water, and over its mouth lay a playing-card. On the centre of the card place a wedding-ring (or other fairly stout ring of similar dimensions), and with the aid of this balance an egg, small end upwards, upright on the card. You are now required to remove the card, and let the egg fall into the water, without touching egg or ring.

The *modus operandi* is the same as above described. The coin being neatly flicked away with the second finger, the egg and ring will fall into the glass. The water prevents any injury to the egg.

CHAPTER II.

MECHANICAL PUZZLES DEPENDENT ON SOME TRICK OR SECRET.[*]

We will commence this section with a few examples of the pretty extensive class of puzzles in which the *crux* propounded is to extract a marble or other small object from some outer receptacle which has no visible opening large enough to allow of its passage, or which cannot be opened without the knowledge or discovery of some secret.

Fig. 27.

No. I.—The Barrel and Ball.

This is a small barrel of boxwood. There is a hole in the

---

[*] There are but few London dealers who make a speciality of Puzzles. The largest assortment is probably that of Messrs. Hamley, of 231, High Holborn, whose stock is peculiarly varied and extensive. Good selections will also be found at Bland's, 35, New Oxford Street; Jaques & Son's, 102, Hatton Garden; and Passmore's, 124, Cheapside. The above are the only firms, within the writer's knowledge, that go in at all extensively for this class of goods.

Where the publisher or manufacturer of a particular puzzle is known, he has been duly credited with it. The name of the ac'ual inventor is, in most cases, unfortunately unascertainable.

Puzzles Dependent on some Trick or Secret. 21

upper end, wherein rests, quite loosely, a little ebony pestle. (See Fig. 27.)

The barrel contains an ordinary marble, considerably larger than the hole (the only visible opening), and the task of the experimenter is to get the marble out.

No. II.—The Dice Box.

This also is in the shape of a miniature barrel (see Fig. 28),

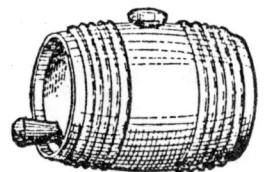

Fig. 28.

the bung and spigot being represented by movable plugs of ebony. The barrel contains three little dice, and the puzzle is to get them out.

No. III.—The "Churn."

This is another boxwood puzzle. It is in the shape of a little churn (see Fig. 29). There is a small hole in the top,

Fig. 29.

from which projects the handle of the plunger. Closer inspection, however, discloses the fact that the handle is a handle only, being a mere plug of ebony, as shown at *a*, quite unconnected with anything in the interior.

The churn contains a bone or wooden counter, which the experimenter is required to extract from it.

No. IV.—The Cannon and Ball Puzzle.

The receptacle in this case takes the form of a cannon (see Fig. 30). It contains a small marble, which the aspirant is

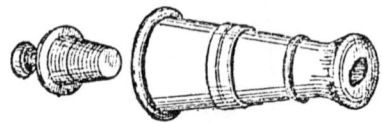

Fig. 30.

required to extricate. The only visible opening is a small oval hole at the muzzle.

The breach is movable, as shown in the diagram, being screwed into the cannon, but the cavity revealed by its removal is only just large enough to receive it, and has no connection with the portion containing the ball.

No. V.—The Cage and Ball.

In this case the experimenter is again required to extricate a ball, but under different conditions. The ball (a glass

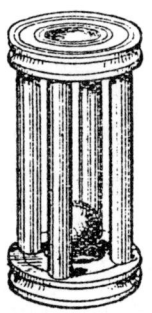

Fig. 31.

marble) is enclosed in a little boxwood cage (see Fig. 31) consisting of a cylindrical top and bottom, united by four upright pillars, between which the ball is confined.

Puzzles Dependent on some Trick or Secret. 23

No. VI.—The Castle Money-box.

This is a neatly turned box in the form of a castle or tower (see Fig. 32), with a slit across the top large enough to admit a shilling. The coin actually in the box is, however,

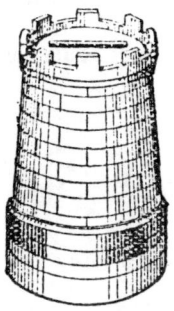

Fig. 32.

a penny (which is too large to pass through the slit), and the box has no other visible opening.

The aspirant is told that the box contains money, which he may keep for himself if he can get it out; but he is very unlikely to do so without a knowledge of the secret.

No. VII.—The New Castle Money-box.

This (see Fig. 33) is very much like the last puzzle in

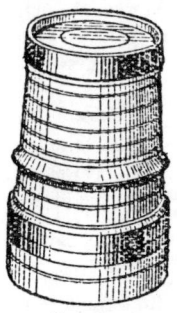

Fig. 33.

appearance, taking the shape of a little boxwood castle or

tower, about two and a half inches in height. It differs from it, however, in one important particular—viz., that it has not any slit at the top, nor indeed any visible opening whatever. A coin is placed in the box, and the puzzle is to extricate it. To an outsider the task seems hopeless, but any one in the secret can extract the coin with perfect ease.

No. VIII.—The Brass Money-box.

This also is a money-box, but of brass, and of more elaborate construction. It is somewhat smaller than the last

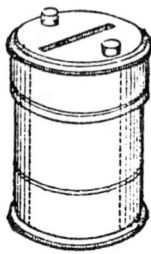

FIG. 34.

described, and in outward appearance as depicted in Fig. 34. A coin is dropped in through the slit at top, and the puzzle is to extract it.

No. IX.—The Captive Sixpence.

This is a puzzle of American origin. It is a neat little nickel-plated box, of very small size, being only an inch in

FIG. 35.

height, and in diameter just large enough to admit a sixpence (see Fig. 35). On the top, shut in by an overlapping edge of metal, is seen an actual sixpence. The top, with the sixpence upon it, is depressible to the extent of a quarter of an inch. Just below this point is a horizontal slit, a sixteenth of an inch wide, and extending half-way round the circumference; but the opening is closed by an inner tube of metal, forming one with the movable top.

The puzzle is to extricate the sixpence. The experimenter can see at a glance that if he could depress the top *below* the level of the horizontal slit, the slit would be left open, and would afford an exit for the coin. But the top stops just short of this point, and the coin remains imprisoned until the "open sesame" is discovered.

There is a large class of puzzles in which the task to be performed consists of the removal of a ball or ring from a silken cord, passed backwards and forwards through openings in a piece of wood or bone in a more or less complicated manner. One of the simplest examples of these is—

No. X.—The Cannon and Cord.

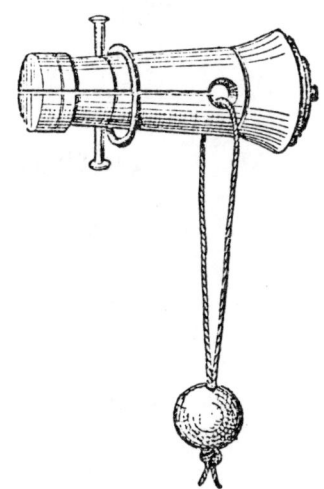

Fig. 36.

This is a miniature boxwood cannon, a couple of inches in

length. There is a perpendicular slot, starting at the "touch-hole" and traversing the whole length of the gun. A loop of cord, with a small ball on its opposite end, is threaded through the touch-hole. To prevent the cord being drawn out through the slot above-mentioned, the cannon is encircled by a brass ring, and this is in turn kept from coming off by a couple of brass pins, as shown in Fig. 36.

The puzzle is to detach the cord and ball from the gun.

No. XI.—The Heart Puzzle.

This is a very easy puzzle. It consists of a heart-shaped piece of boxwood, through which is threaded a silken cord

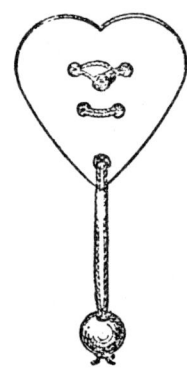

Fig. 37.

terminating in a glass ball, as shown in Fig. 37. The problem to be solved is the detaching of the cord and ball from the heart.

No. XII.—The Alliance (otherwise known as the Victoria) Puzzle.

This is composed of two pieces of boxwood, attached together by a cord, on which is strung a bone counter with two holes in it (see Fig. 38, giving a front and back view of the puzzle).

Puzzles Dependent on some Trick or Secret. 27

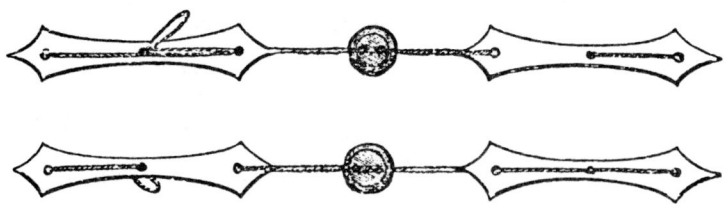

Fig. 38.

The problem is to remove the counter from the cord.

No. XIII.—The Two Balls.

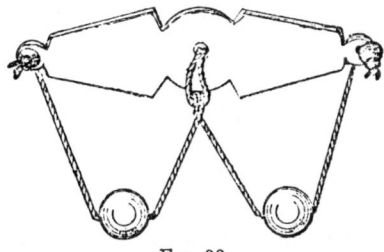

Fig. 39.

This consists of a flat piece of ivory or bone, from which, by means of a silken cord, two glass balls are suspended, one on each bight of the cord, as shown in Fig. 39.*

The puzzle is to get both balls on the same bight of the cord.

---

* Fig. 39 represents the puzzle, as sometimes sold, with the two end knots coming *from the back to the front*, in the same direction as the central loop. This introduces a needless element of complexity. If the loop comes from back to front, the cords at the ends should pass from front to back. If the neophyte chances to come across the puzzle in the shape shown in our illustration, he is recommended to untie the end knots, and retie them with the cords passed through in the opposite direction.

No. XIV.—The Ariel Puzzle.

The puzzle to which this name is given is composed (see Fig. 40) of a flat wooden base with two turned pillars rising from its upper side. Through the head of each is a hole. Through these holes are threaded a couple of silken cords, drawn taut, passing through other holes at the four corners

FIG. 40.

and secured on the under side by glass beads, the upper part forming a sort of bridge between the two pillars. Over this bridge is looped a third cord, which passes down through a hole in the base between the two pillars, thence through a glass ball, and then up, through a second hole, again to the bridge, above which the two ends are tied in a knot. The ball, therefore, hangs suspended below the base, and the puzzle is to take it off the cord, of course without untying the knot.

No. XV.—The Pen and Wheel.

The Pen and Wheel (brought out by Messrs. Perry & Co.) is another ingenious application of the same principle. It consists of a little iron wheel, with six spokes, and a hole in the centre (see Fig. 41). A double cord, about twenty inches in total length, is looped over one of the spokes, then laced in and out between the remaining spokes, and finally brought through the hole in the centre. It is then passed through a bit of stamped brass in the form of a pen, and secured by a double knot on the opposite side.

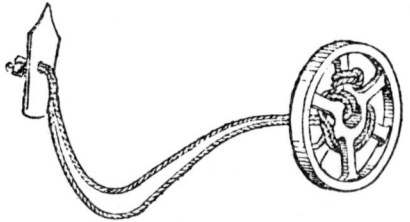

Fig. 41.

The puzzle is to detach the cord and pen from the wheel without unfastening the knot.

No. XVI.—The Balls and Rings.

We have here a flat mahogany ring, $3\frac{1}{2}$ inches in diameter, and $\frac{1}{4}$ inch thick, in appearance not unlike a miniature lifebuoy. In this are a number of holes, through which passes

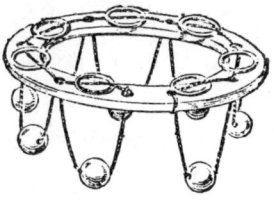

Fig. 42.

a silken cord threaded through glass balls (usually six) on the one side, and through a like number of bone rings on the other. (See Fig. 42.) The puzzle is to *reverse* the balls and rings—*i.e.*, to bring the balls into the place of the rings, and *vice versâ*.

No. XVII.—The Chinese Ladder.

This is a puzzle of a different kind, the "loop" element being in this case wanting. It is said to be a genuine importation from China. It consists of a small wooden ladder of four steps (see Fig. 43). Each step has two

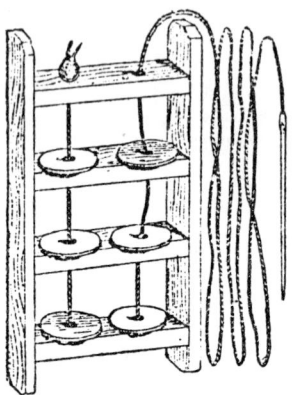

Fig. 43.

holes in it. A silken cord, a yard in length, secured at top with a knot and glass bead, is threaded through each hole in succession (down one side and up the other). Between each pair of holes it is also threaded through a hole in a bone counter, so that there are two counters in each compartment. To the free end of the cord is attached a stout needle.

The puzzle is to bring the whole of the counters *together* on the cord.

No. XVIII.—The Staff.

This (see Fig. 44) is a miniature staff or truncheon—sometimes shaped like that carried by a police-constable; some-

Puzzles Dependent on some Trick or Secret. 31

times of the plainer pattern shown in our illustration—with a hole running from end to end through the centre. Through this is passed a double cord, knotted in four places, with a

Fig. 44.

ball at either end. Notwithstanding the knots, the cord can be drawn backwards and forwards freely through the staff.

The puzzle (a very easy one) is to remove the balls and cord from the staff.

No. XIX.—The Imperial Scale.

This is a puzzle of a more difficult character, though, like many others, easy enough when you know it. It consists (see Fig. 45) of a flat piece of boxwood, three inches square,

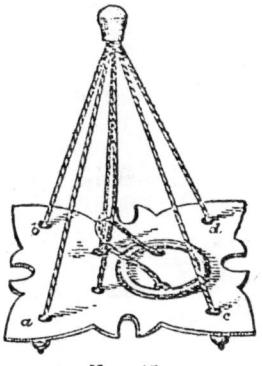

Fig. 45.

with eight holes in it, four in the centre and one at each corner. Through each of the corner holes passes a silken cord, about four inches in length, secured by a glass bead on the under side, and united with the rest in a knot at top. A fifth cord, of rather more than double length, is passed downwards through two of the centre holes, then up again through the other two and through the loop formed by the passage of the cord through the first pair of holes, the two ends then being made to form part of the general knot at top. Between the loop and the standing part of the central cord is secured a ring, of bone or metal.

The problem is, without untying either of the knots, to detach the ring from the cord, and again to restore it to its position.

No. XX.—The Sceptre.

This (see Fig. 46) is a little wooden rod, a fanciful representation of a sceptre, with a couple of rings upon it, pre-

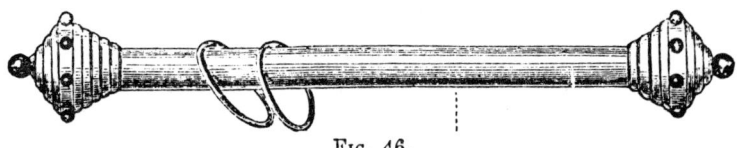

Fig. 46.

vented from coming off by an ornamental knob at each end Round each knob are a number of little bosses.

The puzzle is to remove the rings from the rod.

No. XXI.—The Balls and Chain.

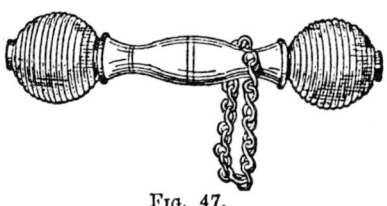

Fig. 47.

This is somewhat similar in general idea, but the principle is different. Two wooden balls (see Fig. 47) are here united by a turned bar, on which they revolve freely. Round the bar is an endless chain, too short to be passed over the ball at either end.

The puzzle is to remove the chain.

No. XXII.—The Four Keys.

This is a puzzle of a different variety. It consists of a boxwood disc (2 inches in diameter by ¾ inch in thickness) with a cross-shaped opening in the centre, as *a* in Fig. 48.

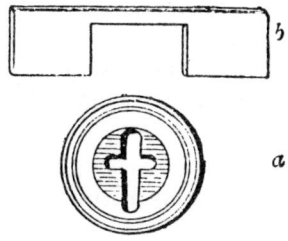

Fig. 48.

Through this disc (the "lock") are passed four boxwood "keys," each consisting of a narrow slip of wood uniting two broad, flat ends (see *b* in the same figure). When all are inserted, the effect is as shown in Fig. 49. The puzzle is to

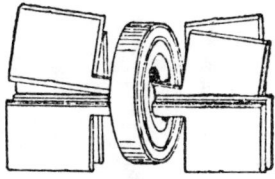

Fig. 49.

disengage the keys from the lock; no easy matter, for when once inserted they instantly fall crosswise in various directions, each blocking the others when you endeavour to extricate them.

No. XXIII.—The Screw Box.

This is a little box a couple of inches in height, and shaped as shown in Fig. 50. The lid moves round and round

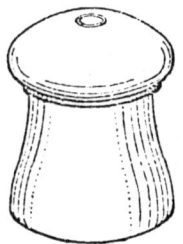

Fig. 50.

with the utmost freedom, but cannot be removed without a knowledge of the secret.

No. XXIV.—The Ball and Three Strings.

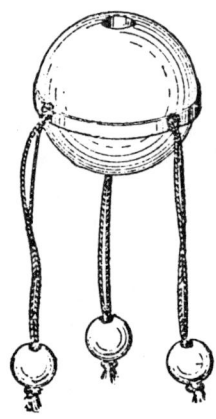

Fig. 51.

This is a very pretty puzzle. It consists of a boxwood ball, not quite two inches in diameter, with a cylindrical opening down the centre (see Fig. 51). At equal distances

Puzzles Dependent on some Trick or Secret. 35

apart, round the circumference, are three smaller holes, converging to the centre, and through these pass three loops of cord, interlaced in the centre. The opposite ends of each pair of cords are secured by a knot, and further prevented, by a glass bead, from being pulled through the ball.

The puzzle is to detach the beads and string from the central ball.

No. XXV.—The Lighthouse.

This is a miniature representation in boxwood of a lighthouse, with a ring of *lignum vitæ*, b, loosely encircling its centre (see Fig. 52). The "lantern" at top and the base at bottom are both larger than the inner circumference of the

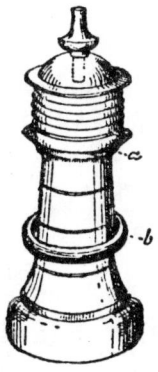

Fig. 52.

ring, which it is the object of the puzzle to remove. The solution which naturally suggests itself is to screw off the lantern; but this is found to revolve freely at the point a, and the only other movable portion of the puzzle is the little pinnacle at top, which may be taken out at pleasure.

No. XXVI.—The Jubilee Puzzle Box.

This is a little cylindrical box, fashioned as shown in Fig. 53, with a little movable pin at top. The experimenter is informed that it contains, somewhere or other, a portrait of Her Majesty, and the puzzle is to find it.

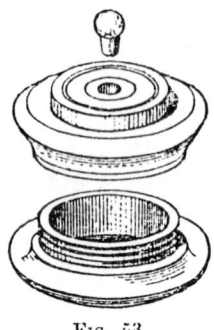

FIG. 53.

No. XXVII.—The Jubilee Penny.

This is a French penny of the Second Empire, and bearing accordingly the effigy of Napoleon III. The puzzle is to find the Queen's head on it, a somewhat difficult thing to do. And yet the likeness of Her Majesty, when found, is unmistakable, and the ingenuity of the puzzle will deservedly elicit high praise.

No. XXVIII.—The Invisible Gift.

This is a small box, very similar in appearance to that depicted in Fig. 53. The Queen's head is in this case represented by a concealed coin, a sixpenny or threepenny piece, and the puzzle is to extract it, the box being to all appearance empty.

No. XXIX.—The Arabi Gun.

This is a neatly-turned boxwood cannon, with the ball peeping out at the muzzle (see Fig. 54). The ball is not a fixture, but is held in position by the pressure of an internal spring. It may be forced inward to a limited extent, but the muzzle is too small to allow of its exit in that direction. Some other means must, therefore, be found of effecting its extraction, which is the problem required to be solved.

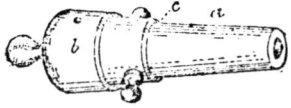

Fig. 54.

It should be mentioned that b and c are in one piece. The chase, a, is independent, revolving freely on c.

It is curious what a large amount of ingenuity has been expended over the construction of puzzle match-boxes. It would almost seem as if human nature took a malignant pleasure in offering a friend a match from a box which he cannot open, and which in some cases even does him a mild personal injury by unexpectedly pricking his fingers. One of the oldest, and at the same time one of the cleverest, of puzzle match-boxes is now known as—

No. XXX.—The Psycho Match-box.

This is an oblong box of wood or metal, of the shape indicated in Fig. 55. When made of wood it is usually about 3 inches in length by $1\frac{1}{4}$ inch in width, and $\frac{3}{4}$ inch in depth; in metal, about half that size. In either case its principle

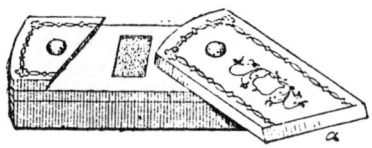

Fig. 55.

is the same. A portion (a) of the top works on a pivot, as shown in our illustration, and any one taking up the box for the first time naturally imagines that on pushing this aside he will have access to the interior. But such is not the case, nothing but a plain wooden surface (with or without a striking plate for the matches) being visible below. This under portion of the top—the true lid—is apparently a fixture. The problem is to open it.

No. XXXI.—The "Touch-Me-Not" Match-box.*

This is on a totally different principle. It is a nickel-plated box shaped as depicted in Fig. 56, and bearing on the top the word "Precaution." The warning is justified by the fact that any one endeavouring to open the box in the ordi-

 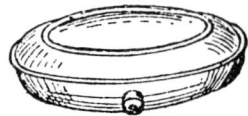

Fig. 56.   Fig. 57.
THE "TOUCH-ME-NOT" MATCH-BOX.   THE "TOUCH-ME-NOT" TOBACCO-BOX.

nary way (by pressing the little stud in front) produces no result, save that a hidden needle in the stud pricks his finger, and suggests the desirability of trying again in some other quarter.

There is a puzzle tobacco-box, as illustrated in Fig. 57, made on the same principle.

No. XXXII.—The Magic Drawer Match-box.

This is again a new departure. The box in this case takes the form of a little drawer, working in an outer case (see

Fig. 58.

Fig. 58). There is not the least difficulty in pulling out the drawer, but any one unacquainted with the secret finds

---

* This name is applied to boxes of two or three different patterns having as a common element the finger-pricking stud in front, this being a rather favourite device of puzzle fusee-box makers.

Puzzles Dependent on some Trick or Secret. 39

it empty, though the owner may only the moment before have shown it full of matches, as it will again appear when the secret is discovered.

No. XXXIII.—The "Unique" Match-box.

This is a box of the upright pattern, with hinged lid (see Fig. 59). It has the customary stud in front, but such stud

Fig. 59.

is in this case a mere make-believe, the true "open sesame" lying in another quarter, and being very ingeniously concealed.

No. XXXIV.—The Surprise Match-box.

This (see Fig. 60) is much like the last-mentioned in appearance, though quite different in its working. It re-

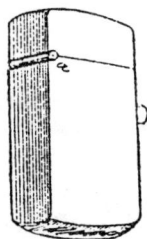

Fig. 60.

sembles the "Touch-Me-Not" in the fact that any one incautiously pressing the stud in front pricks his finger.

No. XXXV.—The New Brass Puzzle Match-box.

This, sometimes described as the "Egyptian" Match-box, is fashioned like Fig. 61, being a ribbed cylinder of brass,

Fig. 61.

and having on the top a copper coin, with two holes in it. This coin revolves in its centre, being rivetted to the top of the box, which has no visible opening.

No. XXXVI.—The Ne Plus Ultra Match-box.

This is, in our own opinion, one of the best of puzzle match-boxes. It is a flat box of plain metal, nickelled. It has no visible hinges, and the lid, instead of overlapping,

Fig. 62.

is sunk within the box all round (see Fig. 62). The Ne Plus Ultra is of the simplest possible construction, having neither stud, spring, nor catch about it; but, save by accident, a stranger will puzzle in vain to open it, though any one in the secret can do so with almost magical ease.

No. XXXVII.—The Sphinx Match-box.

We mention this next in order, the principle being very nearly identical, though with some difference of detail. In

Fig. 63.

appearance the box is as shown in Fig. 63. It bears on the lid the head of a sphinx, from which it takes its name.

No. XXXVIII.—The Puzzle Snuff-box.

This is a very old puzzle, but as good as it is old. It is a neat little box, of the appearance shown in Fig. 64; air-tight, and in every respect a capital snuff-box. Its only drawback to the uninitiated is that there is no apparent way of opening it. A keen eye can just trace what might

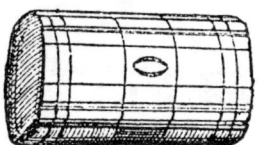

Fig. 64.

be the outline of a lid, but it sinks flush with the surface of the box, and the neophyte, after pulling and pressing in every conceivable direction, is half inclined to believe that he is the victim of a "sell," and that the box never was intended to be opened at all. The owner, however, opens it with perfect ease.

No. XXXIX.—The New Puzzle Snuff-box.

This, though very similar in appearance, is a box of a different kind. It is of the orthodox snuff-box shape, and can be opened without difficulty, but no one can "take a pinch," for the snuff lies below an inner slab, or false bottom. There are two circular openings, each about the size of a sixpence, through which the snuff is visible; but any one inserting his thumb and finger only pinches the woodwork between the holes, and not the snuff.

The puzzle is, notwithstanding this obstacle, to take a pinch of the snuff. This, of course, to be done in the legitimate manner, and not by emptying the snuff out of the box.

No. XL.—The Puzzle Ball.

This is a boxwood ball, not quite two inches in diameter, ornamented with six ebony bosses, with raised centres (see

FIG. 65.

Fig. 65). A threepenny-piece or bonbon being inserted in the ball, the experimenter is invited to extract it.

No. XLI.—The Ebony Puzzle Ball.

This, sometimes known as the "Indian" puzzle ball, is somewhat larger, of unpolished ebony, ornamented with rose-cutting in various directions (see Fig. 66). To the eye it appears to be absolutely solid, the keenest eye failing to detect any sign of an opening. And yet it can be opened by any one having a knowledge of its secret, and will be found to contain a receptacle for a dozen shillings or sovereigns.

Fig. 66.

No. XLII.—The Puzzle Purse.

This (see Fig. 67) is a bag or purse of roan or morocco leather, with two flaps, the inner one scored with longitudinal slits. What would ordinarily be the mouth of the

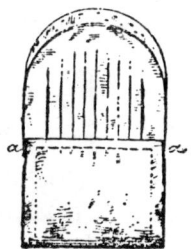

Fig. 67.

purse, *aa*, is stitched right across, so that it has no visible opening. A coin is placed in the purse by some one in the secret, and the puzzle is to extract it.

No. XLIII.—The Puzzle Pocket-knife.

This is a very ingenious puzzle. It is a small single-bladed knife with buckhorn handle, in appearance of the simplest possible kind; indeed, just such an article as a schoolboy would buy for sixpence. But it has a peculiar quality in the fact that no one, save with a knowledge of its secret, can succeed in opening it. We have known hours expended, in vain, over the endeavour, though by the initiated it is as easily opened as any other pocket-knife.

No. XLIV.—The Automatic Knife.

This is an elegant little knife, with oxidized silver handle, and of the appearance shown in Fig. 63. The puzzle is to

Fig. 63.

open it, the blades being unprovided with the customary notch for the nail, or, apparently, any substitute for it.

No. XLV.—The Double Barrel and Ring.

This (see Fig. 69) has a superficial resemblance to the Balls and Chain (No. XXI.), but is wholly different in principle. It consists of a substantial boxwood stem, with

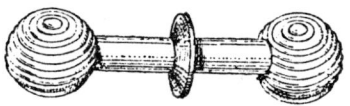

Fig. 69.

a turned ball at each end, not revolving, but secured firmly to it. On the stem slides an ebony ring, which it is the object of the puzzle to remove.

No. XLVI.—The Wedding-ring Box.

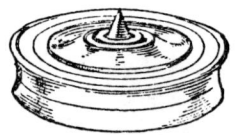

Fig. 70.

This is a small box of hard wood, neatly turned and polished, and fashioned as shown in Fig. 70, alike, top and bottom.

It contains a wedding-ring, which can be heard to rattle within, and which it is the object of the aspirant to extract.

No. XLVII.—The New Money-box.

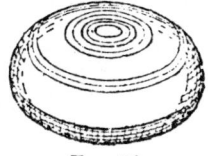

Fig. 71.

This is a box of different shape, being as depicted in Fig. 71. A coin is placed within, and the neophyte is invited to extricate it, which he will find some difficulty in doing.

No. XLVIII.—The Zulu Box.

This has a considerable resemblance to the Screw Box (No. XXIII.). It is slightly different in shape, but has the same peculiarity—viz., that the lid revolves freely on the box, though without any nearer approach to the desired consummation of removing it. The expedient which in that case was found to be successful is here quite useless.

No. XLIX.—The New Persian Puzzle.

The puzzle to which this name is given is a little box with a shaft running through the centre, and is professedly intended to contain rings (see Fig. 72). The shaft termin-

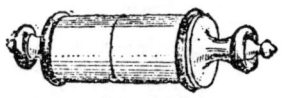

Fig. 72.

ates at each end in a little ornamental knob. The remainder is in three separate parts—the cylinder in the middle and the moulded portions at either end of it. All these revolve freely on the central shaft, and the puzzle is to open the box.

No. L.—The Magic Handcuff.

This is really more of a practical joke than a puzzle. It consists of a woven tube, seven inches in length by half an inch in diameter, made of some kind of very strong and pliable grass. The victim is invited to insert his (or her) little fingers one into each end of the tube (see Fig. 73). He does so without suspicion, but when he again endeavours

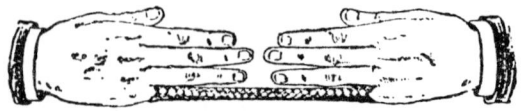

Fig. 73.

to withdraw them, he finds it impossible to do so, the internal friction holding the tube tight to the fingers, and every additional "pull" causing the tube to contract more and more in diameter, and so to grip the fingers the tighter.

In the case of a lady, the tube will probably be too large for the little finger. If so, the second or third finger may be inserted instead.

No. LI.—The Key and Ring Puzzle.

We have in this case a neatly finished brass key, of the appearance shown in Fig. 74, with a wedding- or other finger-ring upon its stem.

The aspirant is invited to remove the ring. The puzzle

Fig. 74.

may also be propounded in the converse manner—viz., the key and ring may be handed separately to any person, and he may be invited to pass the ring over the stem of the key —an equally impossible task without a knowledge of the secret.

No. LII.—The New Egg of Columbus.*

Every reader is, as a matter of course, acquainted with the somewhat heroic expedient whereby Christopher Columbus managed to make an egg stand upright. If the great navigator were to try the same experiment with the new egg that bears his name, he might not succeed so easily, and would probably have to appeal to some one in the secret to show him how to do it.

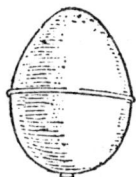

Fig. 75.

The egg (see Fig. 75) is in this case of metal, with a little raised disc or stud, a quarter of an inch in diameter, at its base. The experimenter is required to make the egg stand upright on this. If the egg were empty, the task would be easy enough, but some kind of weight is heard to roll about within, and the continual shifting of this displaces the centre of gravity. In spite of this, however, it is quite possible to balance the egg, if the experimenter is acquainted with the proper way to set about it.

---

* Perry & Co.

KEY TO CHAPTER II.

MECHANICAL PUZZLES DEPENDENT ON SOME TRICK OR SECRET

No. I.—The Barrel and Ball. Solution.

For the explanation of the secret of this puzzle see Fig. 76, representing a section of the barrel and its contents. It will be observed that the lower end consists of a plug *screwed* into the body of the barrel, the difficulty of the puzzle consisting, first, in discovering this, and, secondly, in getting any hold on the movable part, which when in position is sunk flush with or below the lower edge of the barrel.

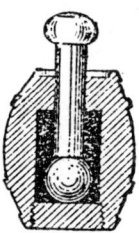

Fig. 76.

To unscrew the end, hold the barrel with the second finger on the top of the pestle, and the thumb on the bottom, and press vigorously. This binds all together, and makes the three (pestle, ball, and plug) practically one piece. Now nip the barrel between the thumb and two first fingers of the opposite hand, and screw from left to right. The body of the barrel revolving round the movable portion, while this latter remains stationary, the effect will be that after a few turns the bottom is screwed out of the barrel, and the ball is released.

No. II.—The Dice Box. Solution.

This is a puzzle of a much simpler character. The bottom of the barrel is made slightly tapering, and retains its position by force of friction only. To release it, all that is needful is to tap the barrel (holding it perfectly perpendicular) smartly on a table or other flat surface, and after a few attempts the bottom will fall out and the dice with it.

The bung and spigot have nothing to do with the solution, but are doubtless added in order to lead the experimenter in a wrong direction, and so increase the difficulty of the puzzle. The spigot, however, is not without its use, for it may now and then happen that the bottom is driven in too tightly to be got out in the orthodox manner. In such case it may be forced out by thrusting a piece of stout wire, or some other convenient implement, through the spigot-hole.

No. III.—The Churn. Solution.

On examination of the churn (Fig. 29), it will be noted that there is in front, midway between top and bottom, a black spot a quarter of an inch in diameter, being apparently a piece of ebony let into the boxwood. A similar circle, a shade less in diameter, is found on the opposite side. These two black spots, though apparently designed for mere ornament, are in reality the key to the puzzle. The churn is made in two parts, the one fitting tightly into the other, and the point of division being just below the third hoop. The two supposed black spots are in fact the opposite ends of a tapering plug of ebony, which passes through corresponding holes in the two parts of the churn, and so locks all together.

To force out the plug, press with the end of the plunger *a* on the smaller of the two black spots. The plug once removed, the two portions of the churn may be pulled apart without difficulty.

No. IV.—The Cannon and Ball. Solution.

The cannon is very ingeniously contrived. On closely examining the muzzle, it will be seen that the small oval opening is surrounded by an incised circle, apparently placed there for mere ornament. This is, however, in reality the dividing line of a circular plug screwed into the muzzle.

The movable breech is in two portions, the one screwing into the other (see Fig. 77). On the removal of the inner portion, it will be found that its smaller end is fashioned

Fig. 77.

into a square stud, slightly tapering, just fitting the opening in the muzzle, and serving as a key to screw out the plug above-mentioned.

No. V.—The Cage and Ball. Solution.

Of the four upright pillars, though seemingly all fixtures, one is in reality movable. On turning such pillar partially round on its own axis, it will be found, when it reaches a certain point, to sink about a sixteenth of an inch deeper into the socket at one end. This draws it in the same degree out of the socket at the opposite end, and it may then be withdrawn altogether.

No. VI.—The Castle Money-box. Solution.

The secret lies in the fact that the top of the box is *screwed* into the main portion. To extract the concealed coin, take a shilling or halfpenny, and inserting it half way into the slot at top, use it screw-driver fashion to screw out the movable portion.

No. VII.—The New Castle Money-box. Solution.

It will be observed (see Fig. 33) that near the base of the box is a black band. The opening of the box is midway in this band, the lower part screwing into the upper (see Fig. 78). So far there would be no difficulty in opening it. The secret lies in the fact that at one point of each portion is bored a little cylindrical hole, that in the upper, *a*, being a quarter of an inch deep, and that in the lower, *b*, an eighth of an inch; so that when the two holes are brought the one over the other they have a joint length of three-eighths of an inch. In this cavity is a little brass bolt, a quarter of an inch in length, working freely up and down within it.

Key to Trick or Secret Puzzles. 51

When the lower part of the box is screwed into the other, (which is done with the "castle" bottom upwards) the final turn of the screw brings the two holes opposite one another. The "castle" being then turned right end upwards, the little bolt drops partially into the lower hole, thereby locking the two portions together.

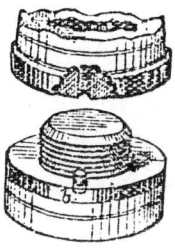

Fig. 78.

To open the box, invert it, and give it a rap on the table or some hard substance. This drives the little bolt back into the upper hole, and the bottom may then be unscrewed without difficulty.

There is a mark on the black band, above and below, which shows when the box has been screwed up tightly enough to bring the two holes into apposition.

No. VIII.—The Brass Money-box. Solution.

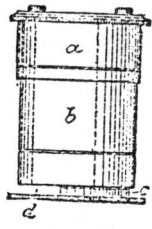

Fig. 79.

It will be found on close examination of this box that it consists externally (see Fig. 79) of two brass cylinders, the upper one, a, being a shade larger in diameter than the lower, *b*. This is in fact a tube, working within the larger tube, *a*, with an upward and downward play of nearly a quarter of an inch. *a* is attached, by means of an inner tube, *c*, to the brass disc which forms the bottom. The lower part of such inner tube is partially cut away, leaving a slot, *d*. By pushing *b* upwards within *a* this slot is exposed, as shown in the figure, and the coin contained in the box can be let fall through it. A downward movement of *b* closes the opening, and the box is again as shown in Fig. 34.

With a little practice it is quite possible to open and close the money-box with one hand, the coin being in the meanwhile invisibly extracted. To do this the box should be held with the first finger on the top and the third on the bottom of the box, when the thumb and second finger will be in the right position to grip *b*, and move it upwards or downwards, as may be necessary.

No. IX.—The Captive Sixpence. Solution.

To release the sixpence, turn the box *upside down*, holding it as vertically as possible. A little ball, which normally prevents the depression of the movable portion beyond the slot, will then drop into a central cavity provided for it; and the movable portion, being no longer impeded by the ball, may then be lowered beyond the slot, when the sixpence will slide out through the opening.

No. X.—The Cannon and Cord. Solution.

Draw the cord down the slot towards the muzzle, as far as the brass ring will permit. Slide the ring back again. Take hold of the loop now formed on the cord, draw it completely out of the slot, pass it over the brass pin on either side, and it may then be drawn away altogether.

To replace the ball, pass the loop of the cord through the ring, from the breech towards the muzzle. Pass it over the pin on either side, and into the slot. You can then draw it back again into the breech portion.

No. XI.—The Heart. Solution.

On closely examining this puzzle it will be seen that in the centre the cord forms a loop, which passes round the opposite portion. Draw the ball close up to the heart; then by means of the "slack" thus gained draw out the loop as far as possible. Pass it down through the centre hole, then through the next two holes, and back again to the front through the bottom hole. Finally slip the loop over the ball.* Draw back the loop, which is now disengaged from the rest of the cord, and all will come off together.

To replace the cord, pass the loop first from the front through the bottom hole, up through one of the adjoining pair of holes, and back again through the other, then through the next pair in like manner. You now have the loop brought to the front. Pass it down through the centre hole and up through the bottom hole, then over the ball, and draw it back again. Pull down the ball as far as the cord permits, and all will be as at first.

No. XII.—The Alliance Puzzle. Solution.

It will be found on examination that the cord is secured at each end by a loop passing round the other portion. To remove the counter, draw up either loop, and pass it through the hole nearest the counter, then over the counter and the opposite piece of wood. The cord is now free, and may be drawn away altogether, when there will no longer be any obstacle to the removal of the counter.

To reinstate the cord and counter reverse the process.

No. XIII.—The Two Balls. Solution.

Hold the puzzle with the central loop passing through the hole to the front. Draw down this loop to its full extent, pass the right hand ball through it, and then pass the loop (with due precaution against twisting) through the right hand hole (from the side opposite to that on which the knot is), over the knot, and draw it back again. Repeat at the opposite side, and the loop will be free. Draw it through the centre hole, and you will have the cord hanging in a

---

* In all puzzles of this class, wherever a loop has to be passed over a knot, ball, or other obstacle, special care must be taken that the loop is clear—*i.e.*, that the two cords constituting it are not twisted. If the loop be passed in a twisted condition over the ball, the result is "confusion worse confounded," and the difficulty of the puzzle proportionately increased.

single bight, with the two balls side by side upon it. Run them along the cord to either end. Re-form the loop in centre, and pass it through the middle hole, then (from the front) through one of the end holes, over the knot, and draw back again. Repeat at the opposite end, and the trick is done.

No. XIV.—The Ariel Puzzle. Solution.

To detach the ball, first draw up the "loop" end of the cord, and pass it through the hole in the top of the pillar nearest to it, then down one of the corner holes on the same side, and over the bead; back again inside the inclined cord, down the other corner hole on the same side, over the bead, and back again, then back through the hole in the pillar. It will be found that the loop is now clear, and the ball can be drawn off it without difficulty.

No. XV.—The Pen and Wheel. Solution.

To detach the pen, draw this latter close up, or nearly, to the wheel, so as to make the "loop" as long as possible. Pass this under and over the spokes, side by side with the portion already wound, finally passing it through the hole in the centre and over the pen, then draw it back again in the same direction and the cord will be free from the wheel.

The caution given on page 53, as to not twisting the loop, is especially necessary in the case of this puzzle, the successive passages under and over the spokes rendering such twisting a very likely occurrence. In such case the cord, when drawn back again, will be found rather more entangled than it was in the first instance.

To reinstate the cord and pen, reverse the process.

No. XVI.—The Balls and Rings. Solution.

It will be observed, on close examination of the larger ring, that two of the holes are very close together. These form the starting-point of the solution. Taking the puzzle in the left hand, with, say, the rings uppermost, and these two holes next towards you, you will observe that in the case of one of them the cord passes through a loop, and *round* the wooden ring from the one side to the other. Draw the loop up through the hole, and through it pass the nearest ring, which will then fall below the wooden ring, though still suspended by the cord. Draw up the second loop through its hole, and pass the second ring through both this and the first loop. Proceed in like manner with the remaining rings (each having one additional loop to pass through). When you have got thus far, the rings will hang side by side on the same bight of the cord.

Turn the wooden ring over, and go through the same process with the six balls, passing them one by one through the six loops in succession. You will now have the balls

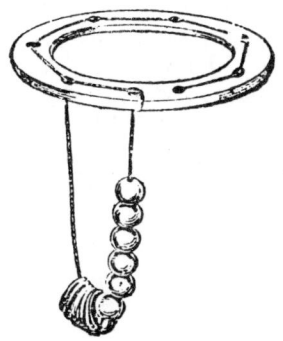

Fig. 80.

hanging side by side with the rings, as shown in Fig. 80. Now pass the balls through the rings so that they shall lie to the left, instead of the right.

Having done this, turn over the wooden ring again, and work the rings back through the loops. All six rings must pass through the first loop, *five* through the second, *four* through the third, *three* through the fourth, *two* through the fifth, and *one* through the sixth.

Turn over the wooden ring once more; pass the balls through the loops in like manner, and the deed is done, the puzzle remaining ready for use again.

No. XVII.—The Chinese Ladder. Solution.

This, though at first sight it appears somewhat formidable, is in reality a very simple puzzle. Take the ladder in the left hand, with the small bead and knot undermost at the same side. Drawing the cord moderately taut, twist it twice round the lower right-hand end of the ladder. Then pass the needle up through the lower hole on the same side, through the first counter, and so on till you reach the top; then, in the same way, down the holes and through the counters on the opposite side. You have now exactly reversed the process by which the counters were threaded into position, and if you were to release the hitch you made round the lower end of the ladder, and pull on the cord in its now doubled condition, it would be drawn clean out, and the counters would fall off it. You are, however, required to keep the counters still on the cord. To effect this, you must hitch the end, still drawn tightly, round the other foot of the ladder, and then thread the remaining portion, with the aid of the needle, through each counter in succession (this time *not* passing through the holes in the ladder). This done, unfasten your two hitches, and draw away the doubled cord. It will now come clear away from the ladder, but the counters will be left upon it, according to the conditions of the puzzle.

No. XVIII.—The Staff. Solution.

The cord is in two parts, each terminating in a loop. Of the four knots, one is a sham, being, in fact, merely the junction of the two loops, which are interlaced, the one

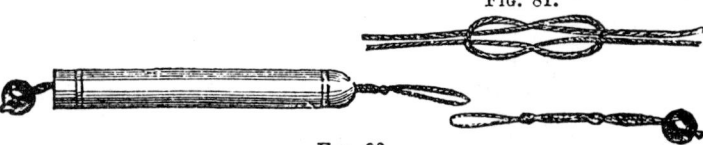

Fig. 81.

Fig. 82.

within the other, as shown in Fig. 81. Loosen this, and draw the nearest ball through the loop. This frees this ball, as shown in Fig. 82. The remaining portion of the cord may then be drawn through the staff, and both will be free.

No. XIX.—The Imperial Scale. Solution.

To get the ring off, draw up the central loop a couple of inches; pass it through the hole a; pass it under the bead at that corner, and draw it back again *outside* the cord. Repeat the same process at the *b* corner, and the loop will be outside both cords. Draw it up a little further, and pass it *over the central knot*, then down through the holes *c* and *d* in succession (*over* bead, and draw back *under*). The loop will now no longer embrace the standing part of the central cord, but will lie loose on the scale, and the ring will be free.

Care must be taken not to twist the loop during either of the foregoing operations.

To work the ring on again, draw the loop through the ring, then down through the hole *a*, under the bead, and up again outside the cord. Repeat at the corner *b*. You will now have the loop outside two of the cords. Pass it over the general knot at top, down through *c*, outside the cord, over the bead, and up again inside. Repeat at *d*, and the ring will be secure.

If the puzzle be home-made (and it is a very easy matter to make it), it will be found an improvement to have the centre cord of a different colour from the four others. By adopting this plan there is much less risk of getting the cords "mixed" in passing the loop through the corner holes.

No. XX.—The Sceptre Puzzle. Solution.

It will be observed, on inspection of Fig. 46, that the two knobs, with which the rod terminates, are surrounded with small black studs, apparently for the purpose of ornament.

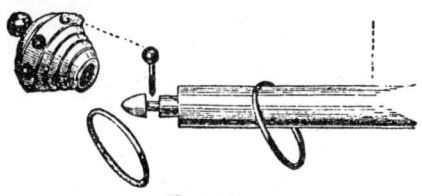

Fig. 83.

One of these studs is *screwed* in, its opposite end fitting into a groove at the end of the rod, and thereby securing the knob. (See Fig. 83.) On unscrewing this the rod and knob come apart, and the rings may be removed.

No. XXI.—The Balls and Chain. Solution.

The secret lies in the fact that one of the balls is in two portions, the smaller portion being attached to the central rod or stem by an ordinary carpenter's screw, on which it revolves, and the larger portion screwing on to this, as shown in Fig. 84. The concentric grooves on the balls in a great measure mask the join, but it will be discoverable on minute inspection.

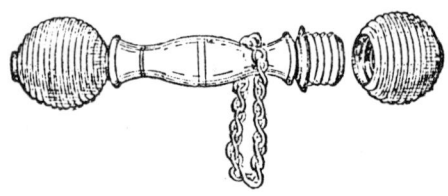

Fig. 84.

Having ascertained which is the "trick" ball, grasp the rod firmly in the left hand, with the point of the thumb and forefinger pressed hard against the base of the ball. The ball being thus prevented from revolving, the other hand screws off the upper portion, when the state of things will be as shown in the diagram, and the chain can be removed.

No. XXII.—The Four Keys. Solution.

On careful examination of this puzzle it will be found that the "web" (or broad portion) of one of the "keys" is a shade narrower than those of the others. It will further be discovered that one of the longer arms of the cross is of slightly extra width, allowing just room for two of the keys to lie in it, side by side.

To solve the puzzle, hold the "lock" horizontally in the left hand, letting the keys hang perpendicularly. Arrange the stem portions of two of them in the shorter arms of the cross, and a third in the broad part of the longer arm above-mentioned. The narrow key may now be pressed out through the longer arms of the cross, passing beside the key already there. The removal of one key renders the removal of the others a very easy matter.

To replace the keys, reverse the process, beginning with the three broader keys. Get these into their proper positions, and then insert the narrow key.

No. XXIII.—The Screw-box. Solution.

The secret lies in the fact that the lid screws, not into the visible box, but into an inner lining, prevented from being withdrawn by an overlap of the upper edge of the box (see Fig. 85). The lining fits loosely within the box,

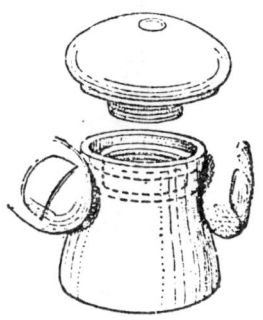

Fig. 85.

and so in inexperienced hands moves round and round with the lid, which cannot under such circumstances be unscrewed.

To open the box, pinch its sides smartly between the thumb and finger while endeavouring to unscrew the lid. The outer shell, which is very thin, is thereby pressed against the inner lining, and holds it fast. The lid may then be unscrewed without difficulty.*

No. XXIV.—The Ball and Three Strings. Solution.

The secret lies in the fact, not perceptible save to the closest inspection, that one of the three "knots" which apparently unite the ends of the three pairs of cords is in reality *two* knots, one on each end of the cord, but made to look like one by the bead which holds them together.

---

* There is another version of the Screw-box, known as the "Profane" Box, from the fact that there is a hidden needle-point in the lid, which, picking the unwary finger, is apt to elicit some more or less forcible ejaculation.

Having discovered the two knots, pull out the bead to which they belong as far as possible. This will bring out the two loops of the other strings. Then push back the bead beyond these loops, as shown in Fig. 86, and the cord

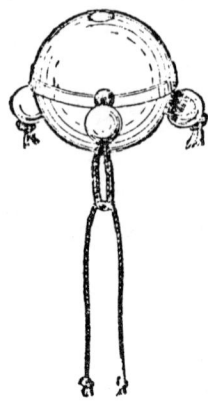

Fig. 86.

thus set free may then be drawn out through the loops, thereby releasing the other two. It is best not to pull out these latter completely, as it will be found a rather troublesome matter to thread them through the holes again.*

No. XXV.—The Lighthouse. Solution.

On close examination of the little lighthouse it will be found that there are four holes on its under side, and on looking through these holes and at the same time turning round the lantern portion, it will be seen that an inner core revolves with it. At a particular point of its revolution a small cavity, hollowed out in this core, is brought into juxtaposition with one of the four holes. By removing the little pinnacle at the top of the puzzle, and thrusting it into this hole, the core is made a fixture, and the top may then be unscrewed at the point *a*, and the ring released.

---

* This is best done with a piece of bent wire.

No. XXVI.—The Jubilee Puzzle Box. Solution.

The Queen's head is hidden in the lid, just under the raised portion in centre. To find it, unscrew the lid, and remove the little ornamental knob and top. Then take the lower portion of the box, turn it upside down, and press it down over the raised portion of the lid (see Fig. 53), which it will be found to fit pretty tightly. This is then used as a key to screw out this raised portion, when a photograph of Her Majesty will be revealed.*

No. XXVII.—The Jubilee Penny. Solution.

Most people, on making the acquaintance of this very clever puzzle for the first time, are apt to seek for some fanciful resemblance to Her Majesty among the various lines on the coin. In this endeavour they are necessarily disappointed, for the secret of the coin is mechanical, as will be seen by an inspection of Fig. 87. The centre of the coin is cut away, and a photographic portrait of Her Majesty

Fig. 87.

pasted in the centre. The central portion of a second coin is then fitted to the cavity, and held in position by an ingeniously constructed pin-hinge, *a*. Pressure on this hinge, from the "head" side of the coin, lifts the cover. The fact that the penny, with the amount of skilled workmanship that must have been expended upon it, can be sold (as it is) for a shilling, is by no means the least surprising part of the "puzzle."

---

* There is another box on the same principle, known as the "Diplomacy" puzzle. The box differs slightly in shape, and the portrait of her Majesty (on a farthing) is visible through a glass disc in the top of the lid. In other respects the two are identical.

No. XXVIII.—The Invisible Gift. Solution.

It will be noticed, on examining the interior of the box, that both box and lid are scored with one or more lightly cut circles, apparently for the purpose of mere ornament. In one of these, however, sometimes box, sometimes lid, lies the secret of the puzzle. A small circular space has been excavated in the centre, and then filled up again with a little wooden disc, beneath which lies the hidden coin. To extract it, tap the portion in question with the inside downwards smartly on a table or other hard flat surface. After you have tapped for a minute or two, the wooden disc will begin to work itself out, and a little later will drop out altogether, releasing the coin.

No. XXIX.—The Arabi Gun. Solution.

This is on the same principle as the "Lighthouse" puzzle described on pp. 35, 60—viz., the fixing of the revolving portion of the gun (*a* in Fig. 54), so that it can be unscrewed and taken apart.

The first step is to unscrew the knob at the breech. This knob is in reality in two portions, the one, *c*, screwed

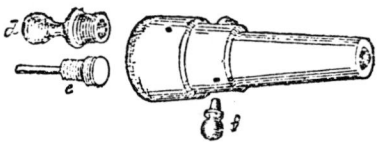

Fig. 88.

into the other, *d* (see Fig. 88). Having separated them, remove the trunnion *f*, and through the hole thus left thrust the pin *e*, moving *a* round until the pin finds a deeper hole (in an inner core), into which it sinks. The core being now held fast, the portion *a* may be unscrewed from *c*, and the ball extracted.

No. XXX.—The Psycho Match-box. Solution.

As we have already indicated, the box has an upper and a lower lid, the latter being the true one. The former, as we have seen, can be moved aside at pleasure, but the lower remains a fixture, save when the box is turned *upside down*, when an internal "bolt" drops out of position, and releases it.

To open the box turn it *upside down*, then push aside the movable portion a, as shown in Fig. 89. You will find that

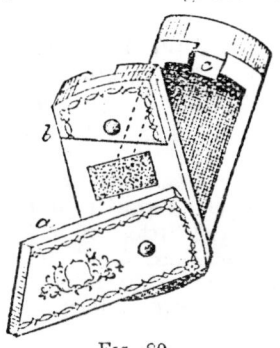

Fig. 89.

you can now push the lower lid, b, forward a quarter of an inch in the direction of the pivot at the opposite end, on which it moves. In this new position it just clears the tongue or stop, c, which previously held it fast. Again turn the box right side uppermost, and turn b to right or left, when the box will be open.

No. XXXI.—The "Touch-Me-Not" Match-box.
Solution.

To open this box, press strongly with thumb and finger on its *two ends* simultaneously, when the box will fly open. The metal yields to the pressure and makes the box "bulge" to a minute extent in front, thereby releasing the catch.

The same method opens the "Touch-Me-Not" Tobacco-box.

No. XXXII.—The Magic Drawer Match-box.
Solution.

The secret here lies in the fact that the "drawer" portion is double, the true or inner drawer, which contains the matches, working within a shell or dummy drawer. In the normal condition of the box the inner drawer is held back by a spring, and only the "shell" or empty drawer comes out. By pressure on a particular part of the bottom of the box the catch is lifted; and if the box be then opened, the true drawer comes out with the dummy, and the matches are exposed.

No. XXXIII.—The "Unique" Match-box. Solution.

The opening is in this case effected by means of the striking plate seen at the bottom of the box. This, being drawn forward with the finger-nail, releases the catch, and the box flies open.

To open the box without disclosing its secret, take it between the forefinger and thumb of the left hand. Then make believe to press the little stud in front with the thumb of the right hand, when the second finger of the same hand will be brought underneath the box in just the right position to draw the striking plate forward, and so release the spring.

No. XXXIV.—The Surprise Match-box. Solution.

To open this box, take it in the right hand, with the little projecting stud resting against the lower joint of the forefinger. Then with the thumb-nail press the nearer end of the supposed "hinge," marked a in Fig. 60, and the box will open at that point. The real hinge is at the opposite side, immediately above the little stud.

No. XXXV.—The New Brass Puzzle Match-box. Solution.

The secret here is of the simplest, but very few persons discover it; the experimenter being usually led astray by the revolving coin on top, with its two holes, which he naturally assumes to play some important part in the solution.

The coin in question is, however, simply intended to mislead, the actual fact being that the box *unscrews* at about one-fourth of the way down; but the screw is a left-handed instead of a right-handed one, so that any one attempting to unscrew it in the ordinary way only fixes it the tighter. If, on the other hand, he makes the usual movement of *screwing*, the lid comes off without difficulty.

No. XXXVI.—The Ne Plus Ultra Match-box. Solution.

It will be observed that one side of the box bears a striking plate. This indicates the front, which would be otherwise undiscoverable, there being no visible hinge. To open the box, press down the opposite edge of the lid in the

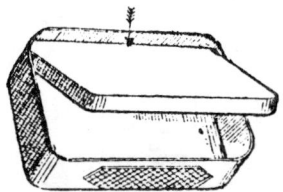

Fig. 90.

direction shown by the arrow in Fig. 90. The secret lies in the fact that the lid works on a *pin* hinge, pivoted between the two ends of the box, though the pins do not come through, and are not perceptible from the outside. The lid therefore forms, in fact, a lever, pressure on whose shorter arm raises the opposite end, and thereby opens the box.

No. XXXVII.—The Sphinx Match-box. Solution.

This is the "Ne Plus Ultra" over again, with an addition— viz., that the striking plate, which is in this case at the back,

Fig. 91.

is movable, being hinged to the bottom of the box, with the striking surface on its inner side. Open this, as shown in Fig. 91, and then press down the edge of the lid, thereby

F

left exposed, and the box will open as depicted in our illustration.

When the striking plate is closed the lid is "locked," and the box cannot be opened.

No. XXXVIII.—The Puzzle Snuff-box. Solution.

The decorative markings of the box serve to conceal the fact that the portion of the front marked *A* (see Fig. 92) is movable, sliding up and down between the adjacent portions.

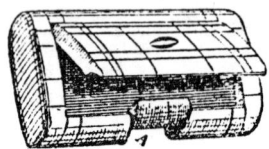

Fig. 92.

On pushing this up with the thumb, the lid is forced up with it, and the box may then be opened without difficulty. The sliding piece should be quietly pressed down again before inviting any one to take a pinch, when there will be nothing to disclose the secret.

No. XXXIX.—The New Puzzle Snuff-box. Solution.

There are in point of fact *two* lids to this box, opening in opposite directions (see Fig. 93). The smaller is the

Fig. 93.

normal lid, and is the one first opened. This done, the second can be opened, as shown in the figure, and the snuff is then accessible.

No. XL.—The Puzzle Ball. Solution.

The secret here lies in the fact that one of the supposed ornamental bosses is continued, in a tapering shape, right through

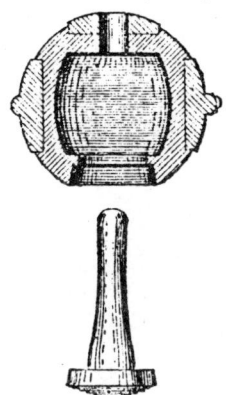

Fig. 94.

the ball, its smaller end forming the centre of the boss on the opposite side (see Fig. 94). By tapping this centre, which must be discovered by experiment, the boss is forced out and the ball opened.

Fig. 95.

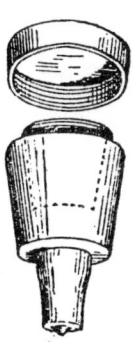

Fig. 96.

No. XLI.—The Ebony Puzzle Ball. Solution.

On minute inspection of the ball, it will be found that

close beside one of the little bosses is a minute depression, scarce bigger than a pin's head. This serves to indicate the position of the opening, of which the next boss (looking from the boss above-mentioned *across* the indicating mark) forms the centre. Rap the side of the ball *diametrically opposite to this* on the table, and the broad end of a tapering plug will be forced out, as shown in Fig. 95. This plug, shown in detail in Fig. 96, is hollow, with a screw-lid, and forms a receptacle for coins or any other small object.

The mechanism of the ball is so perfect and the opening so cleverly masked by the rose-cutting that its secret is hardly ever discovered.

No. XLII.—The Puzzle Purse. Solution.

The back of the purse, like the front, is in two portions, and is in like manner divided across the line *a a* by a line of stitching. The lower portion of the back forms part of the same piece of leather which is seen scored in front, and by nipping this lower portion with the forefinger and thumb of the right hand, at the same time holding the hinder flap with the left hand, the slit portion may be pulled down till it comes below the stitched line *a a* at back, and access may then be obtained through the slits to the interior. The stitches are of such a size as just to allow the passage of the strips of leather.

To close the purse again, take hold of its lower edge, and pull up the slit portion, when all will be as at first.

No. XLIII.—The Puzzle Pocket Knife. Solution.

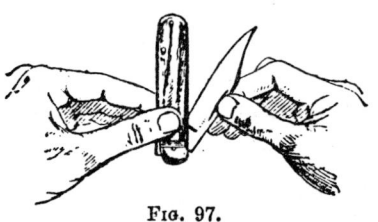

Fig. 97.

The reader is probably acquainted with the ordinary dagger knife, in which the blade is kept from closing by a catch on the spring, which catch drops into a notch at the back of the blade, and so holds it fast until, by the raising of the spring, the catch is again withdrawn. The puzzle pocket knife is on the same principle, but the manner of its application is here concealed. There is, in this case, one notch to receive the catch when the knife is closed and a second to receive it when open. One of the buckhorn sides is attached to the free end of the spring. By drawing this back with the left thumb, as shown in Fig. 97, the catch is withdrawn, and the knife can be opened without difficulty. When it is opened the blade is again held fast, and the operation must be repeated to close it.

No. XLIV.—The Automatic Knife. Solution.

On minute examination it will be observed that there is at either end of the knife (see Fig. 68) a little projecting tongue of white metal, flat on one side and convex on the other. By pressure on the flat side of either of these tongues, the corresponding blade is made to fly open to a small extent, assuming an angle of about 30° to the handle. From this point it may be fully opened without difficulty.

The knife is closed in the ordinary manner.

No. XLV.—The Double Barrel and Ring. Solution.

This is somewhat on the principle of the Puzzle Ball (No XL.). It will be observed that the ball at each end is cut in circles, parallel to the central stem and growing smaller and smaller as they pass higher or lower from the central circle; the final circle being a little boss, in pretty strong relief. By rapping one of these (the right one must be ascertained by experiment) on a table or other hard surface a little plug which binds the ball to the stem is forced out of position. The ball may then be unscrewed from the stem and the ring released.

No. XLVI.—The Wedding-ring Box. Solution.

This is a very clever puzzle, for the uninitiated invariably take it for granted that the box must unscrew or otherwise open at the mark round its centre, whereas the actual opening must be sought in quite another direction. To open the box, press firmly on one of the central bosses, and a

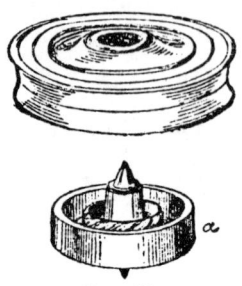

Fig. 98.

circular wooden piece, *a*, will be forced out below, as shown in Fig. 98. The ring lies around the central plug.

No. XLVII.—The New Money-box. Solution.

This is on the same principle. The circular groove round the larger circumference of the box is a mere blind, but by pressing the central portion of the top (see Fig. 99) an inner

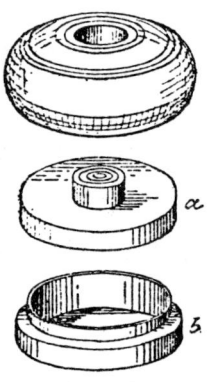

Fig. 99.

receptacle (after the manner of that in the Ebony Puzzle Ball, No. XLI.) is forced out. The top, *a*, of this lifts off, and in the lower part, *b*, is found the concealed coin.

No. XLVIII.—The Zulu Box. Solution.

The revolving loose lid is, in this case, in two portions, the one screwing into the other. To open the box, take it in the left hand, as shown in Fig. 100, and with the thumb and

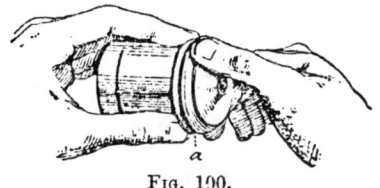

Fig. 100.

fingers press the lower portion of the lid vigorously upwards. This will make it, for the time being, a fixture, and the upper part may then be unscrewed at the point a, as shown.

No. XLIX.—The New Persian Puzzle. Solution.

The secret here lies in the fact that the central rod or shaft is in two portions, the one screwed into the other. To open the box, take hold of the little knob at each end simultaneously and screw them in opposite directions, when the one knob will come off, and the box will come apart in three portions.

No. L.—The Magic Handcuff. Solution.

To obtain your release, bring the imprisoned fingers as near together as possible, thereby enlarging the diameter of the tube. Then, with the thumb and forefinger of the right hand take hold of the *opposite* end of the tube and draw it off the finger, which in this manner you can do without difficulty.

No. LI.—The Key and Ring Puzzle. Solution.

The secret here lies in the fact that the point of the key, which, it will be observed, projects some threequarters of an inch beyond the "web," can be unscrewed, as shown in Fig. 101. With the key in this condition the ring can be passed over the web, and on to the stem, without difficulty.

This puzzle is sometimes introduced in the guise of a conjuring trick. For use in this case, a little thumbscrew, shown at *a* in Fig. 101, is supplied with the key. By the aid of this the movable point of the key may be screwed up so tightly that no one, save a Japanese dentist, could

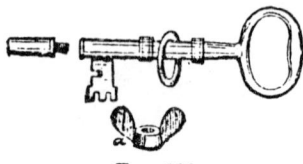

Fig. 101.

possibly hope to remove it with the unassisted fingers, though the wizard, armed with the "fake," can do so at pleasure. It is hardly necessary to remark that, for puzzle purposes, the use of such an appliance is illegitimate, it being an understood thing that every "fair" puzzle contains within itself all the elements necessary to its complete solution.

No. LII.—The New Egg of Columbus. Solution.

The secret of this excellent puzzle lies in the fact that the base of the egg is occupied by a hollow cone, with an opening on one side of its apex, and a shallow groove leading up to such opening. The weight heard rolling about within the egg is a leaden bullet. When this is once fairly within the cone, it naturally settles down in the centre, and the egg can be made to stand upright without difficulty; but so long as the bullet is outside the cone, its weight throws the egg to the one side or the other, and makes it absolutely impossible to balance it. The difficulty, therefore, resolves itself into the getting the ball inside the cone. To do this, it is necessary to know on which side the opening lies, and the guide as to this is a little mark, a mere dent, on one side of the smaller end of the egg. Holding the egg smaller end upwards, and with the mark facing you, turn the point of the egg over towards your own body. This brings the bullet on the same side as the opening. Then turn the egg over, very slowly and steadily, till it lies horizontal, with its point away from you, and, if you are lucky, the bullet will roll along the groove into the cone, and you will have no further difficulty.

The entrance to the cone is purposely made somewhat narrow, in order to diminish the likelihood of an accidental discovery of the secret. The neophyte must, therefore, not be discouraged if he finds that he has to repeat the above process once or twice before he succeeds in lodging the bullet in the proper quarter.

CHAPTER III.

"DISSECTED" OR COMBINATION PUZZLES.

The number of these is legion. We all remember the "dissected maps" of our early youth, whereby we learnt geography (and very thoroughly as far as it went), while we fondly imagined we were only amusing ourselves.* With these, however, we have for our present purpose nothing to do. The present chapter will be primarily devoted to the large class of puzzles in which, a given geometrical figure having been cut up into various segments, the experimenter is required to re-arrange such segments so as to form another figure, or figures, of a different character.

Foremost among these may be named the series of puzzles issued by Messrs. Richter & Co., the inventors and manufacturers of the admirable "Anchor" Stone Building-blocks, the *ne plus ultra* of Toydom, and delight of every kindergarten and schoolroom which is fortunate enough to possess a set of them. The Anchor building blocks may indeed themselves be regarded as a puzzle, and one of a very interesting kind. They are a modern and scientific development of the old-fashioned "box of bricks." Dr. Richter's blocks are not of wood, like their prototypes, but of a mineral composition compressed to the hardness of stone. They are of three different colours: cream-colour, to represent sandstone; red,

---

* We are sorry to note that in these later days the dissected map has fallen into comparative disfavour, being replaced by dissections of fairy tales, scripture histories, and the like, which have no natural aptitude for being so dealt with. In the case of maps, on the other hand, if the dissections are properly made—*i.e.*, so as to follow the outlines of the provinces, counties, or other divisions of the region represented—the shape and position of such divisions are impressed upon the memory in a manner almost unattainable by any other method. The course of rivers, situation of chief cities, etc., are unconsciously taken note of, and, once thoroughly learnt in this manner, are never forgotten.

"Dissected" or Combination Puzzles. 75

for bricks; and slate-colour, for roofing material. The boxes range in price from sixpence up to five guineas, and in weight from fourteen ounces to nearly threequarters of a hundredweight. Each block is shaped with mathematical

Fig. 102.

accuracy; and this fact, combined with the extra weight of the material, gives buildings constructed with them a degree of stability, as well as elegance, in which the old-fashioned wood-brick structures were wholly wanting.*

---

* So perfect are the Richter blocks in point of accuracy and finish that they are now largely used by professional architects to form temporary models of intended structures. Our illustrations (Figs. 102 and 103) give a notion of what may be attempted with the higher-priced boxes. The handsome castle depicted in the Frontispiece represents a still higher flight; and it must be remembered that this is not a mere fanciful design, but can really be constructed to the minutest detail by a sufficiently skilful operator. The box used in this case is No. 23, which contains 1549 stones, and eight books of designs. This is one of the most expensive sets, costing £4 6s. Of course, the construction of

By an ingenious system of "supplements" a person originally buying a box, of however small size, may by subsequent purchases, singly of small amount, so increase his store of material as ultimately to bring it up to the level of one of the largest sets, and for the same total outlay. Each new acquisition enables the purchaser to attempt a further and more ambitious series of designs, plans of which accompany his purchase accordingly. The ample supply of

FIG. 103.

building designs is one of the most valuable features of the boxes. The multiplicity of these designs may be imagined from the fact that two skilled architects, with half a dozen draughtsmen under them, are employed all the year round producing new ones. Each stone of the elevation is clearly shown, duly drawn to scale, a front and back view being given where necessary; where from the nature of the case some portion of the stones are not visible, or their arrangement offers any special difficulty, a horizontal section is

---

a building of this magnitude demands not merely more than average lightness of finger, but a very considerable amount of intellectual effort. The endeavour to build a very much less ambitious structure (using a box costing, say, ten or twelve shillings) will be found amply to justify our assertion that the Richter building stones not only come within, but hold a very high place in the province of Puzzledom.

added, giving a ground plan of the particular "course" in question.*

Passing from the Richter building blocks to the Richter puzzles proper, we have, in the first place—

No. I.—The "Anchor" Puzzle.

This consists of a square slab of the "Anchor" building-block composition, divided into seven segments, of the shapes shown in Fig. 104 (viz., two large triangles, *a, a,* a smaller one, *b,* and two still smaller, *c, c,* a square, *d,* and a rhomboid, *e*), neatly packed in a flat box, three inches square.

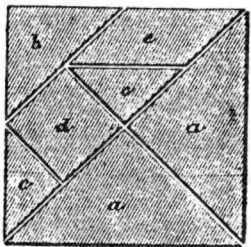

Fig. 104.

Even the replacement of the pieces in the box, when once fairly mixed, will be found a matter of some little difficulty, but this is the smallest of the problems presented by the puzzle. The box contains, in addition to the seven "stones," a little book, containing over 150 different designs, which may be formed by combining them in different ways. Space only allows of our giving a few examples (see Figs. 105–115. It is to be noted that the whole seven stones must be employed in the formation of each design; and it is a curious fact that some of those designs which are simplest in appearance are the most difficult to work out. The letters of the alphabet, each one of which can be formed (in more or less grotesque shape) by means of the seven blocks, give far less trouble

---

* The building stones are manufactured at Rudolstadt, in Thuringia, but may be procured through any high-class toy-dealer. The London branch of the firm is at 12, Jewin Street, E.C., where any desired information can be obtained.

than simpler forms. No more aggravating, and at the same time fascinating, puzzles have come under our notice than this series.

Fig. 105.

Fig. 106.

Fig. 107.

"Dissected" or Combination Puzzles. 79

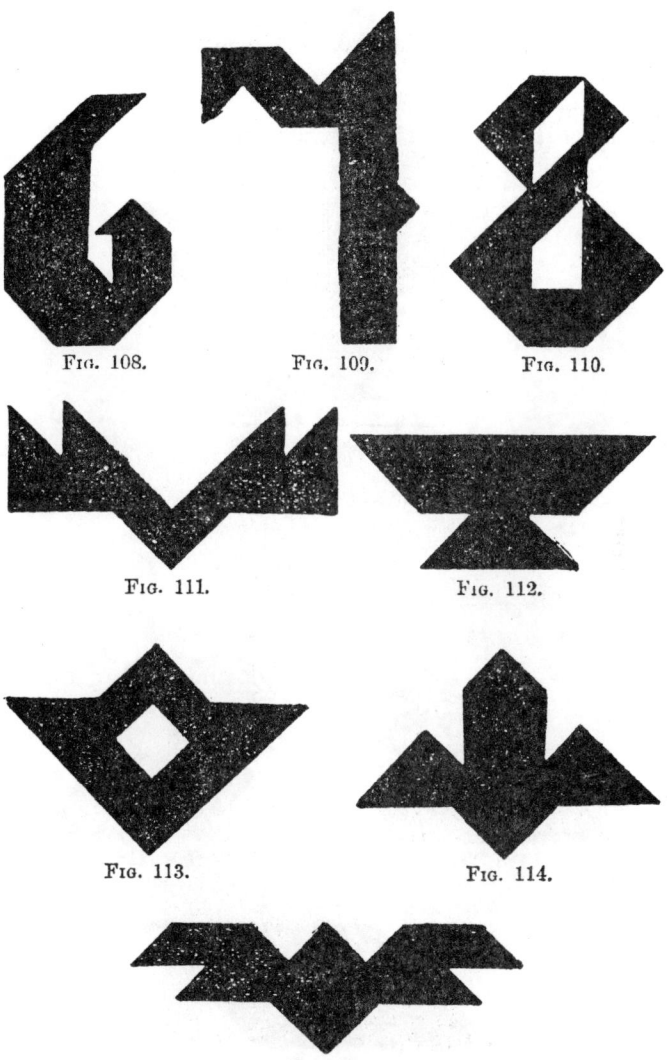

Fig. 108. Fig. 109. Fig. 110.

Fig. 111. Fig. 112.

Fig. 113. Fig. 114.

Fig. 115.

No. II.—The Tormentor Puzzle.

This, the second of the series, consists of a square divided into eight pieces, of the shapes depicted in Fig. 116. Here again we have over 150 designs which can be formed by

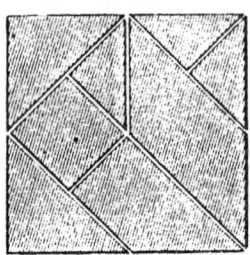

Fig. 116.

combination of the several segments. We append (Figs. 117–124) a few of the possible combinations.

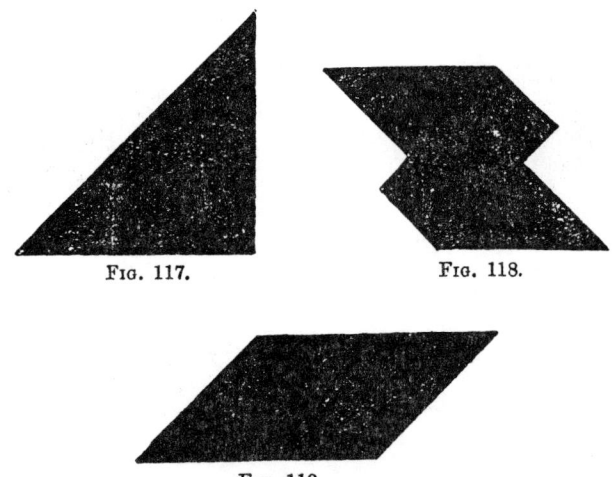

Fig. 117.   Fig. 118.

Fig. 119.

"Dissected" or Combination Puzzles. 81

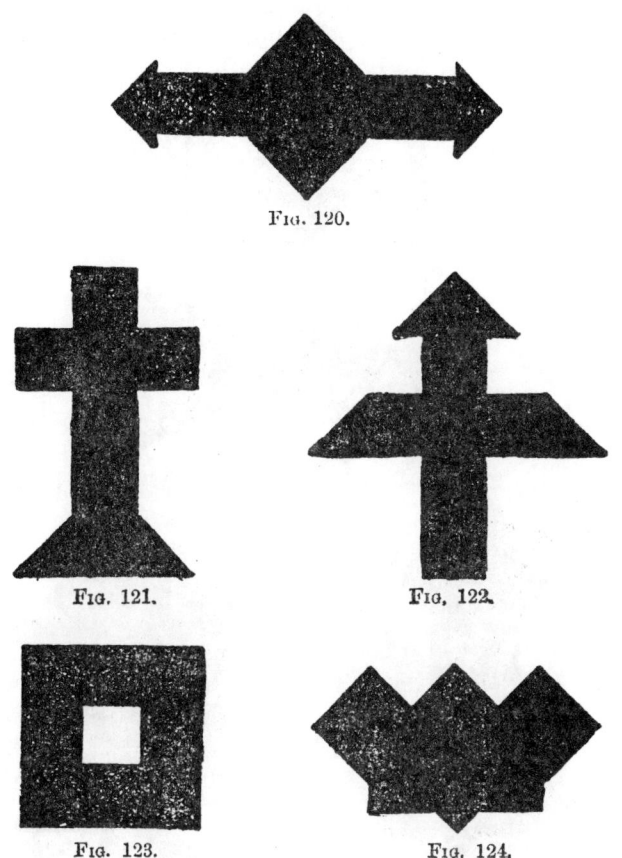

Fig. 120.

Fig. 121. Fig. 122.

Fig. 123. Fig. 124.

No. III.—The Pythagoras Puzzle.

Here we have again (Fig. 125) a square, divided into *seven* segments, and a selection of 181 figures which may be formed by their re-combination. We append a few specimens (Figs. 126-134).

G

82 *Puzzles Old and New.*

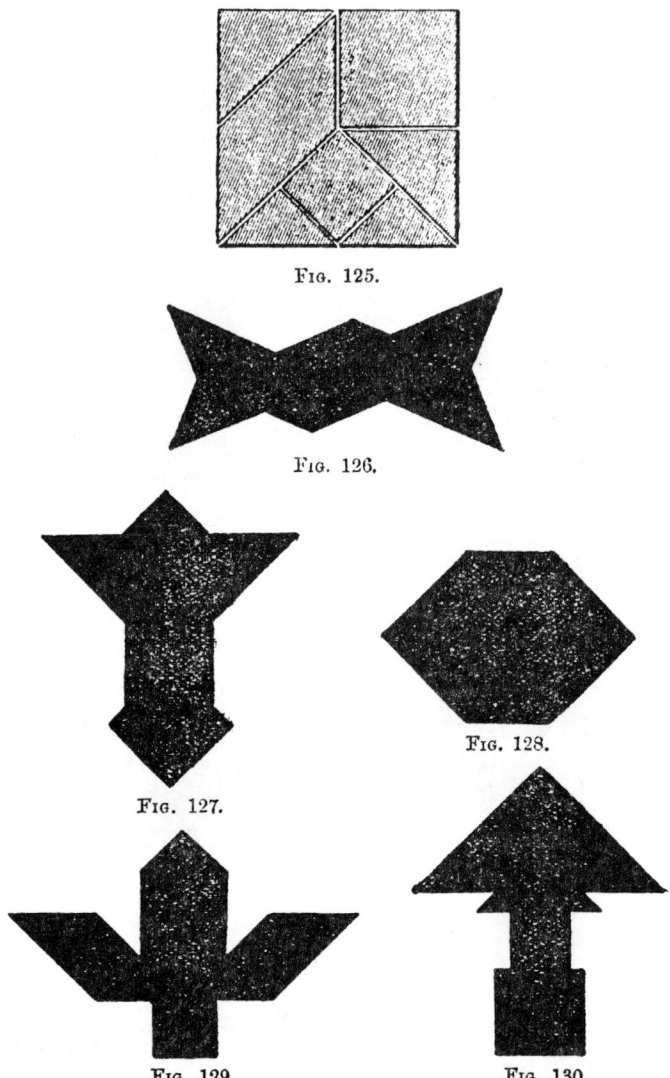

Fig. 125.

Fig. 126.

Fig. 127.

Fig. 128.

Fig. 129.

Fig. 130.

"*Dissected*" *or Combination Puzzles.* 83

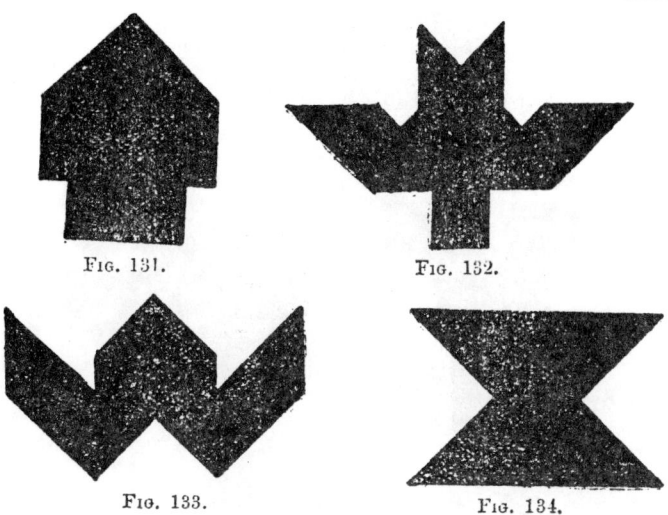

Fig. 131.   Fig. 132.

Fig. 133.   Fig. 134.

No. IV.—The Cross Puzzle.

This is so called from the fact that the first of the figures which the experimenter is invited to form with the

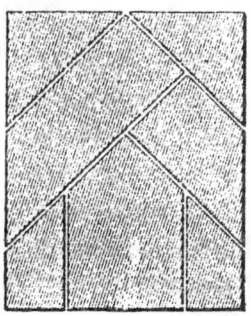

Fig. 135.

several segments is a cross. The rectangular slab of which the puzzle is composed is not in this case a perfect square, but slightly oblong, being 3½ inches in length by 3 in width (see Fig. 135). Over 130 designs are given, which may be composed by the aid of the seven segments. Of these examples will be found in Figs. 136-144.

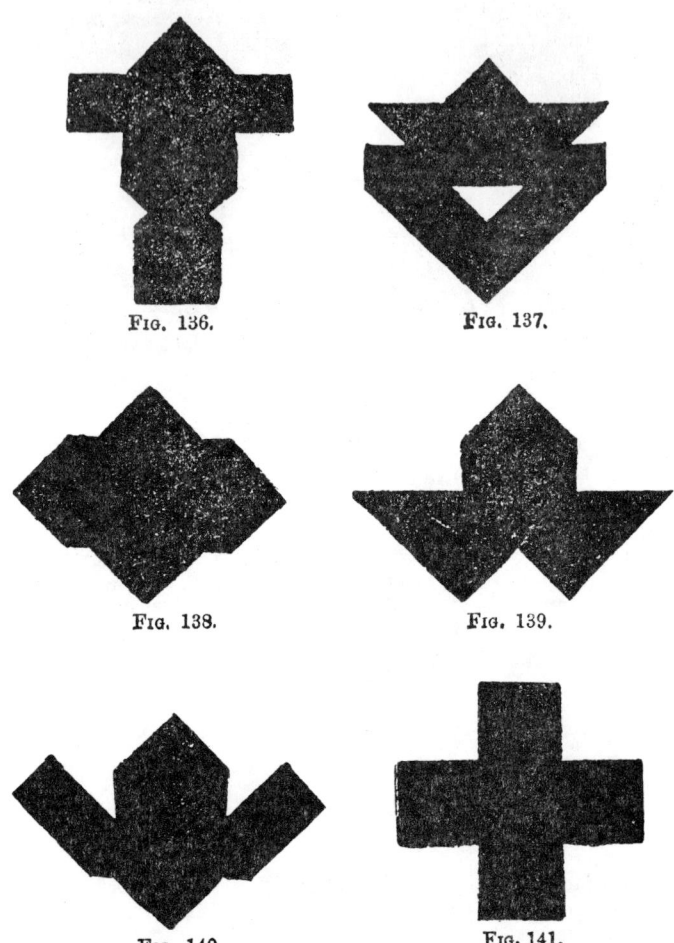

FIG. 136.

FIG. 137.

FIG. 138.

FIG. 139.

FIG. 140.

FIG. 141.

"*Dissected*" *or Combination Puzzles.*

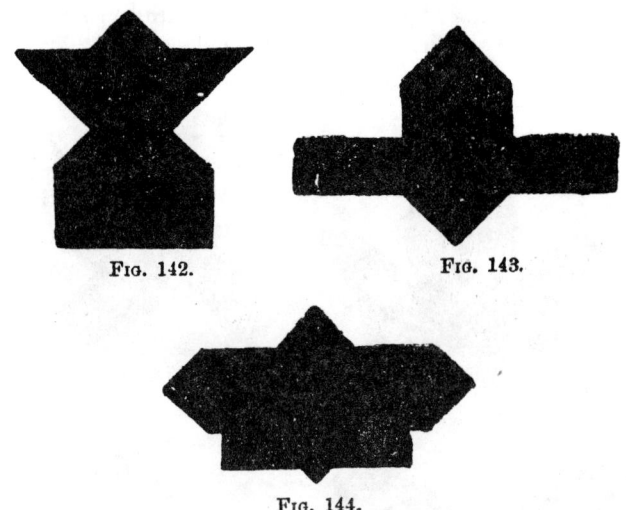

Fig. 142.   Fig. 143.

Fig. 144.

No. V.—The Circular Puzzle.

This is a new departure, the slab out of which the several segments are formed being circular, instead of rectangular. The number of segments is in this case *ten* (see Fig. 145).

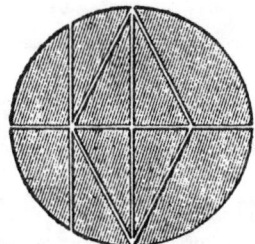

Fig. 145.

These facts lend greater plasticity to the resulting combinations, some of which, as may be gathered from an inspection of the diagrams appended (Figs. 146–154), are very artistic, and, with the aid of a little imagination, may be taken to

86 *Puzzles Old and New.*

represent familiar objects—as, Fig. 146, a crown; Fig. 149, a fool's cap; Fig. 150, a lobster; and so on.

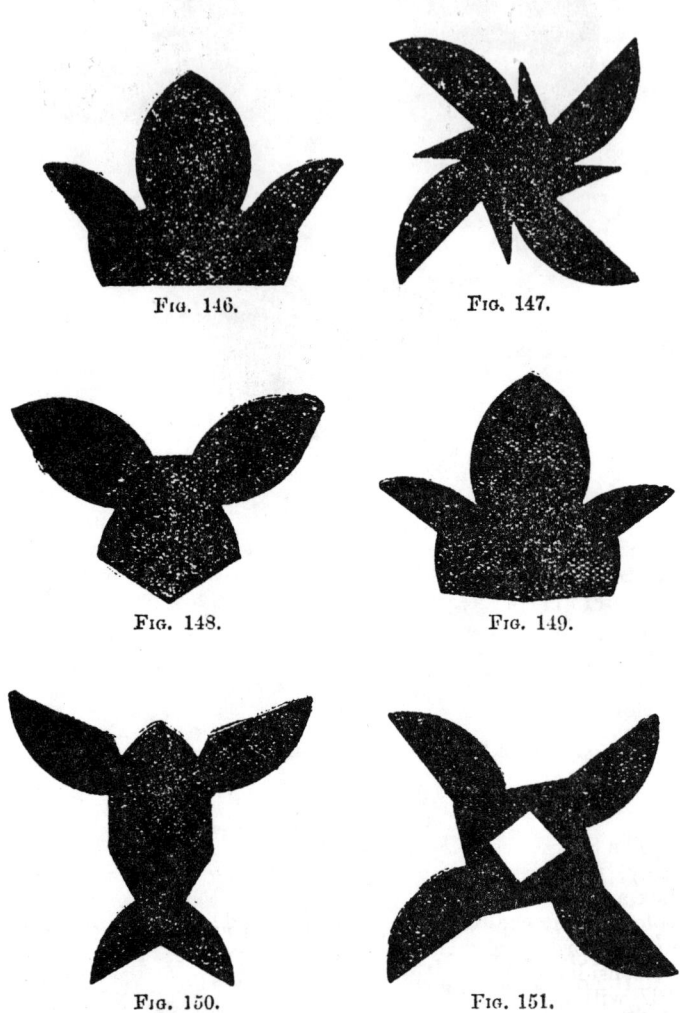

Fig. 146.

Fig. 147.

Fig. 148.

Fig. 149.

Fig. 150.

Fig. 151.

"Dissected" or Combination Puzzles. 87

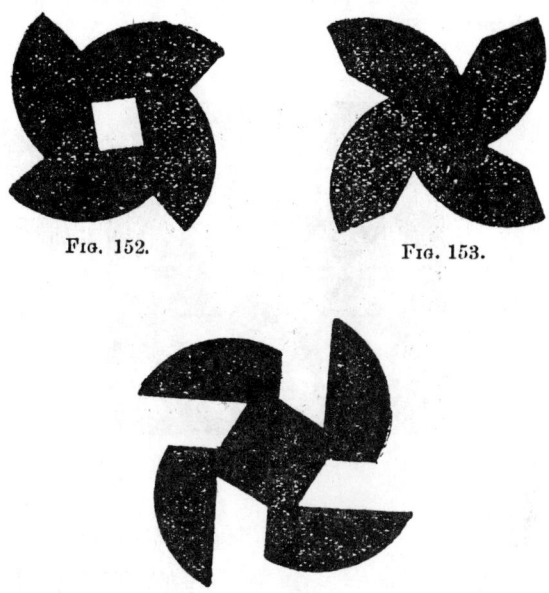

Fig. 152.   Fig. 153.

Fig. 154.

Over a hundred such figures are given in the little book which accompanies the puzzle, but this number might be largely increased, as indeed is the case with the whole of the series.

No. VI.—The "Star" Puzzle.

The Star Puzzle consists of 48 segments, 24 black and 24 grey, the grey forming in their original positions in the box a star. (See Fig. 155). This, from the use of the two colours, and the larger number of pieces used, is capable of an extraordinary variety of effect, and will by most persons be considered the prettiest puzzle of the series. Figs. 156–167 will give some faint idea of the almost kaleidoscopic effects which can be produced by combination of these simple elements.

Fig. 155.

Fig. 156.

Fig. 157.

"Dissected" or Combination Puzzles. 89

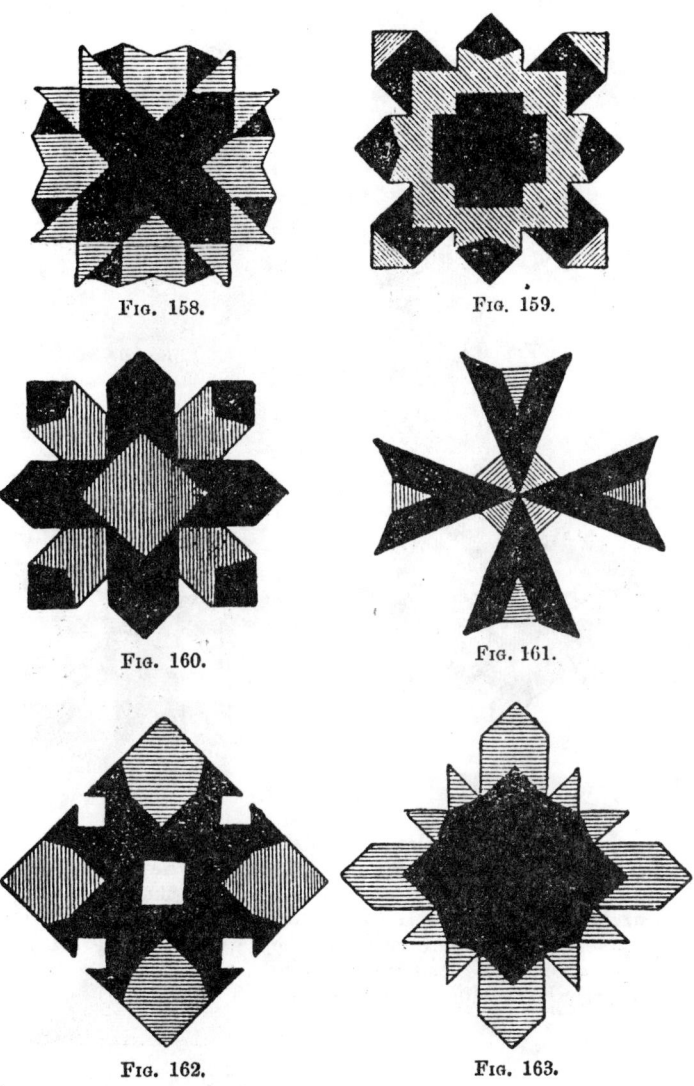

Fig. 158.

Fig. 159.

Fig. 160.

Fig. 161.

Fig. 162.

Fig. 163.

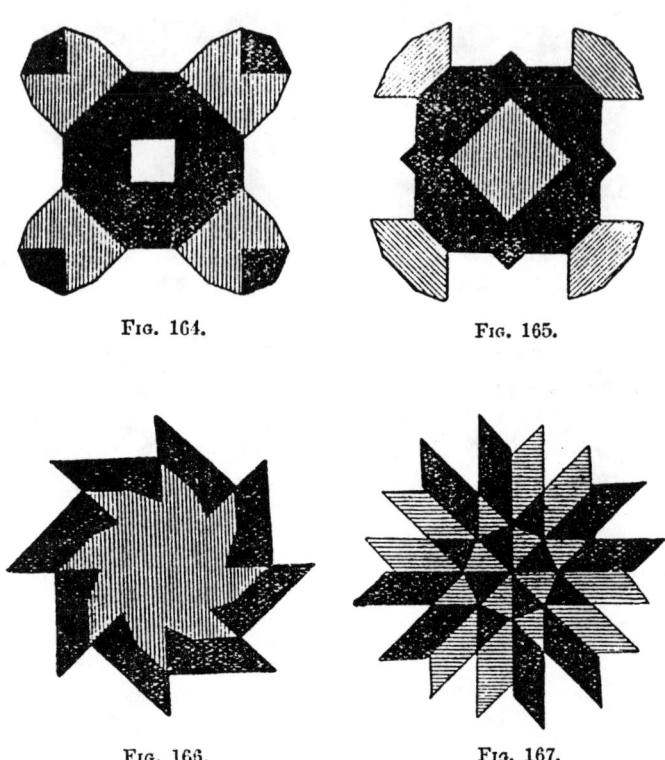

Fig. 164.   Fig. 165.

Fig. 166.   Fig. 167.

The "Star" is the last issued of the "Anchor" series.

It should be mentioned that in addition to the various figures resulting from the re-arrangement of the segments of a single puzzle of this series, there are many others which may be produced by the combination of the segments of a given pair of puzzles. For these, however, we must refer the reader to the little book which accompanies each puzzle.

No. VII.—The Zigzag Square.*

Given twelve pieces of paper or cardboard, four of each shape given in Fig. 168.

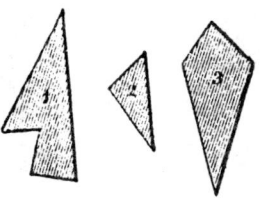

Fig. 168.

Required, so to combine these twelve pieces as to form a perfect square.

No. VIII.—The Extended Square.

Required, so to cut a cardboard square, as *a* in the diagram (Fig. 169), into two portions, in such manner that by

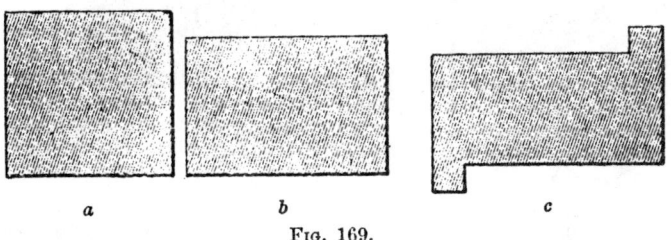

a *b* *c*
Fig. 169.

successive shiftings of their relative positions, they may form the parallelogram, *b*, and the eccentric figure, *c*, in the same diagram.

---

* There is another class of puzzle which goes by the same name—viz., a square of thin wood cu with a fretsaw into a number of segments of curved outline, after the fashion of a dissected map.

No. IX.—The Octagon Puzzle.

Given twelve pieces of paper or cardboard, five of each shape represented in Fig. 170.

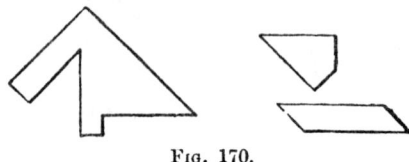

Fig. 170.

Required, so to combine them as to form an octagon.

No. X.—The Patchwork Square.

Given, eight pieces of paper or cardboard shaped as shown in Fig. 171.

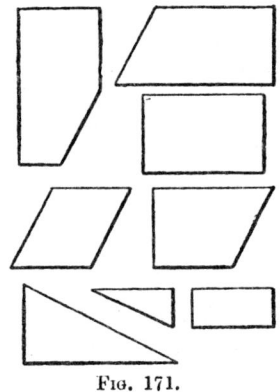

Fig. 171.

Required, by arrangement of these segments to form a perfect square.

No. XI.—**The Two Squares.**

Given, a piece of paper or cardboard of the shape depicted in Fig. 172, being that of a small square in juxtaposition with one four times its size.

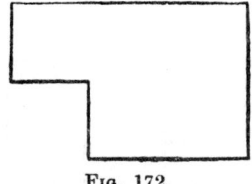

Fig. 172.

Required, by two cuts (each in a straight line) so to divide the piece of cardboard that the resulting segments shall, differently arranged, form one perfect square.

No. XII.—**The Latin Cross Puzzle.**

This has no affinity with the Cross Puzzle described at page 83.

Given, five pieces of paper or cardboard, one as *a*, one as *b*, and three as *c* (Fig. 173).

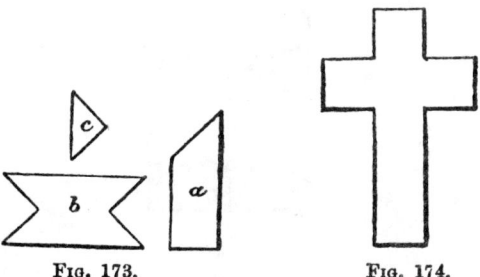

Fig. 173.   Fig. 174.

Required, of these five segments to form a Latin cross, as Fig. 174.

No. XIII.—The Greek Cross Puzzle.

Given, a piece of paper or cardboard in the form of a Greek or equal-armed cross, as Fig. 175.

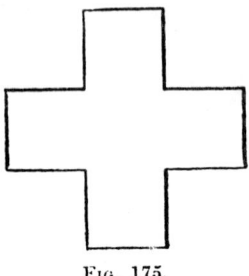

Fig. 175.

Required, by two straight cuts so to divide it that the pieces when reunited shall form a square.

No. XIV.—The Protean Puzzle.

This is a puzzle of the same class as the Anchor, Tormentor, and Pythagoras (pp. 77-83), but very much easier, from the greater number of the component parts. It consists of eleven pieces of cardboard, forming an oblong square, as

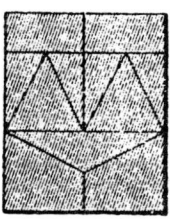

Fig. 176.

shown in Fig. 176. Figs. 177-182 illustrate a few only of the many shapes which can be constructed out of the above elements.

"Dissected" or Combination Puzzles.   95

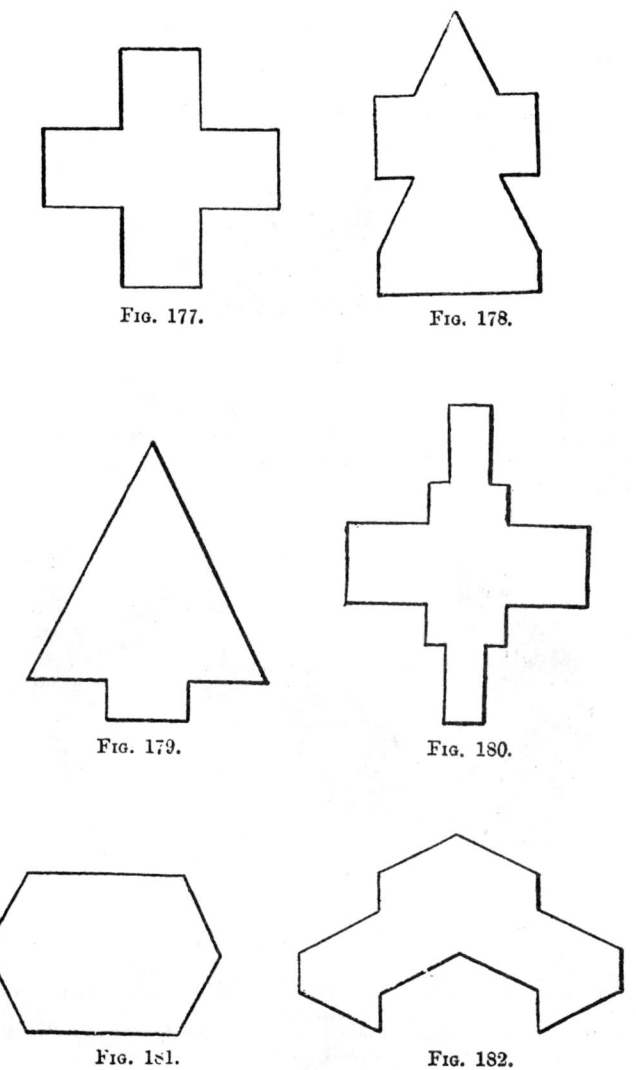

Fig. 177.

Fig. 178.

Fig. 179.

Fig. 180.

Fig. 181.

Fig. 182.

No. XV.—The Caricature Puzzle.

This puzzle consists of seven pieces of blackened cardboard; a square, five right-angled triangles, and a rhomboid, of the respective proportions shown in Fig. 183.*

With these the experimenter is required to construct

Fig. 183.

grotesque representations of the human figure, in various positions. Space only allows of our giving half a dozen examples (Figs. 184-189) but the possible number of such combinations is extraordinary, and many of them are most comical in effect.

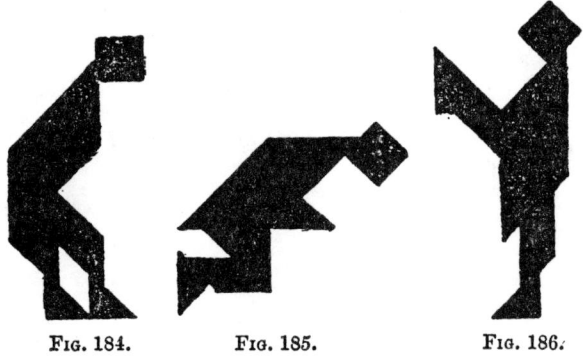

Fig. 184.   Fig. 185.   Fig. 186.

---

* It will be observed by the acute reader that these segments are identical in number and shape with those of the "Anchor" Puzzle, described at page 77. The fact that such very different results are here produced with the same elements illustrates the extraordinary fertility of this class of puzzles. New combinations are constantly offering themselves, the attempt to construct one figure suggesting some other, totally different, but equally effective.

"*Dissected*" *or Combination Puzzles.* 97

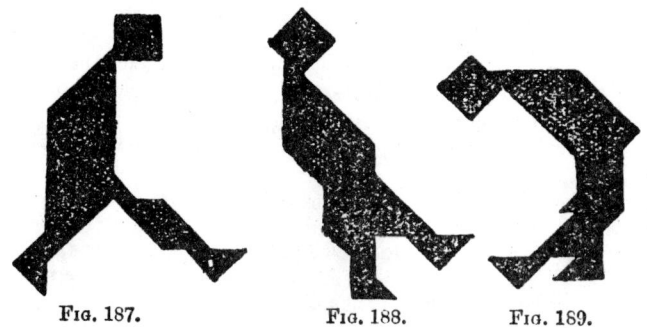

Fig. 187.   Fig. 188.   Fig. 189.

No. XVI.—The Chequers Puzzle.*

This is a dissected puzzle of a very novel kind. It consists of a miniature chessboard, five inches square, divided

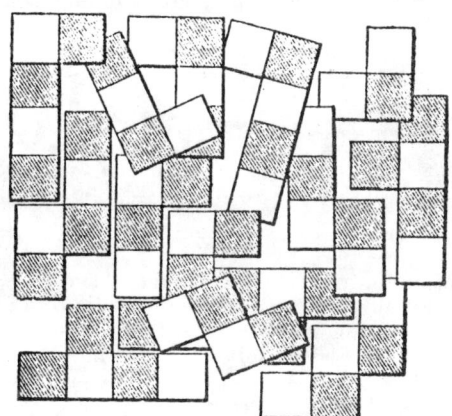

Fig. 190.

into fourteen pieces, each consisting of from three to five squares, as illustrated in Fig. 190.

The experimenter is required, out of these fourteen segments, to construct the chessboard anew. At first sight,

---

* Published by Messrs. Feltham & Co.

H

the task would seem to be one of the easiest possible, but any such idea very soon vanishes when the matter is put to the test of experiment. The pieces drop into position with enticing facility till the board is about three parts complete, but at that point the neophyte usually finds himself with half a dozen segments still in hand, which absolutely decline to accommodate themselves to the spaces left for them.

It may be mentioned, for the encouragement of the fainthearted, that there are, according to the publishers, no less than fifty ways in which the puzzle may be solved, and it should therefore be merely a matter of time and perseverance to discover one or other of them. *

No. XVII.—The "Spots" Puzzle.†

This puzzle also is very much more difficult than it looks. It consists (see Fig. 191) of a wooden cube, not quite three inches each way, cut into nine bars, of equal size. Each

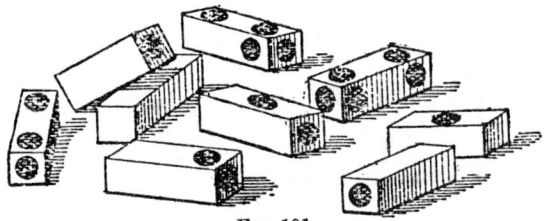

Fig. 191.

of these is decorated with one or more "spots," half an inch in diameter; and the experimenter is required to put together these bars in such manner that the resulting cube shall represent an enlarged model of the die familiar to the back-

---

* Readers who have found pleasure in the "Chequers" may be glad to know of another very pretty series of puzzles of the same kind—the "Peel" puzzles, issued by Messrs. Jaques & Son. They are three in number, each consisting of nine pieces of cardboard, bearing, some two, some three, squares of different colours. With these a larger square or other figure is to be formed, in such manner that the same colour shall not occur more than once in any row, horizontal or vertical.

We regret that it is impossible, without the aid of coloured illustrations, to give a more detailed description.

† Manufactured by Messrs. Wolff & Son.

"Dissected" or Combination Puzzles. 99

gammon player (see Fig. 192), with all its spots in proper position. These, it may be mentioned for the benefit of the uninitiated, are arranged as follows:—The "ace" point is on the opposite side to the "six"; the two on the opposite side to the "five," and the "three" on the opposite side to the "four"; the total of each pair of opposite sides being always

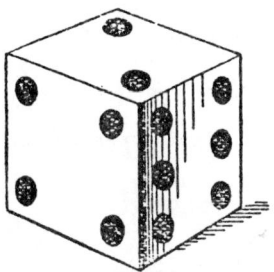

Fig. 192.

seven. A die which does not answer these conditions is regarded as fraudulent.

As an aid to the memory in this particular, the outside of the pasteboard box or case in which the segments are contained is itself an enlarged fac-simile of a die, with the spots in proper position.

No. XVIII.—The Endless Chain.

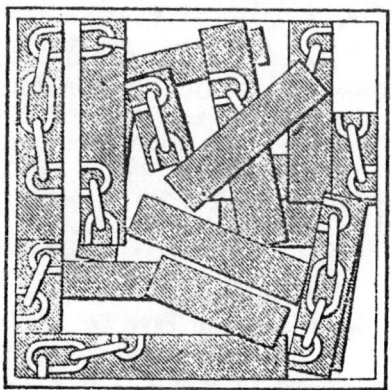

Fig. 193.

Yet another good dissected puzzle is the "Endless Chain."

A piece of cardboard, six inches square, and bearing the representation (in gold, on a blue ground) of an endless chain, is cut into eighteen pieces, of various sizes, and such pieces are placed hap-hazard, as shown in Fig. 193. The puzzle is to rearrange them, within the limits of the square box which contains them, so as to re-form the endless chain, with each link in proper connection.

No. XIX.—The Hexagon.

Given, five pieces of wood or cardboard, one of each shape depicted in Fig. 194.

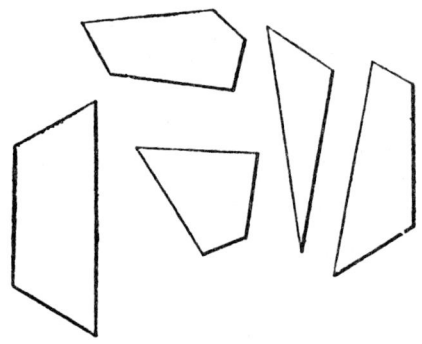

Fig. 194.

Required, with these to form a regular hexagon.

No. XX.—Eight Squares in One.

Cut out eight squares of cardboard, of equal size, and divide four of them diagonally from corner to corner. This will give you twelve pieces, four square, and eight triangular.

Required, so to arrange them as to form a single perfect square.

No. XXI.—The Five Squares.

Given, five squares of paper of cardboard, alike in size.

Required, so to cut them that by re-arrangement of the pieces you can form one large square.

No. XXII.—The Geometrical Square.

Given, six pieces of wood or cardboard, two as *a*, and four as *b* (Fig. 195).

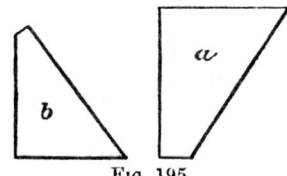

Fig. 195.

Required, so to combine them as to form one complete square, or two smaller squares.

No. XXIII.—The Dissected Square.

We have in this case nine pieces, three as *a*, three as *b*, and three as *c* (Fig. 196).

Required so to combine them as to form one perfect square, or three smaller squares.

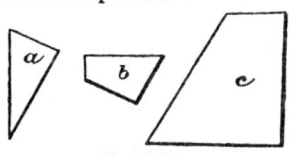

Fig. 196.

The formation of the three smaller squares will be found easy enough, but that of the single square will give more trouble, being, in fact, one of the most difficult of this class of puzzles.

No. XXIV.—The Twenty Triangles.

We have here twenty triangles, of size and shape as in

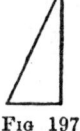

Fig. 197.

Fig. 197. The experimenter is required to form with them a perfect square.

No. XXV.—The New Triangle Puzzle.

The puzzle which goes by this name is of more than average merit. It has long ceased to be "new," though for distinction's sake it retains the qualifying adjective. It

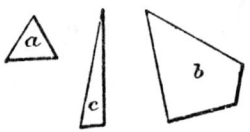

Fig. 198.

consists of seven pieces, one as *a* (Fig. 198), three as *b*, and three as *c*. With these seven segments it is required to form an equilateral triangle.

No. XXVI.—The Japanese Square.

Given, ten pieces of wood or cardboard, four as *a*, four as *b*, and two as *c* (Fig. 199).

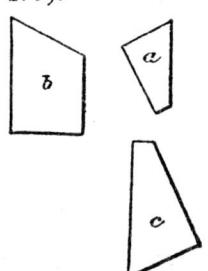

Fig. 199.

Required, to form a square with them.

No. XXVII.—The Chinese Square.

Given, sixteen pieces of wood or cardboard, four as *a*, four as *b*, and eight as *c* (Fig. 200).

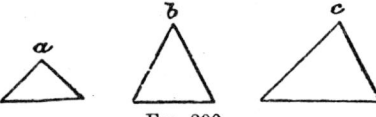

Fig. 200.

Required, to form a square with them.

No. XXVIII.—The Yankee Square.

Given, eleven pieces of wood or cardboard, two as *a*, one as *b*, three as *c*, two as *d*, two as *e*, and one as *f* (Fig. 201)

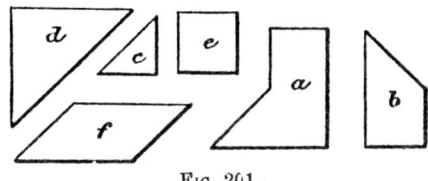

Fig. 201.

Required, to form a square with them.

No. XXIX.—Another Cross Puzzle.

Given, five pieces of wood or cardboard, three shaped as *a* (Fig. 202), and two as *b*.

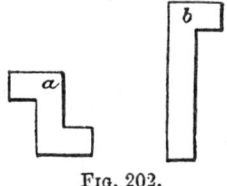

Fig. 202.

Required, so to arrange them as to form a Latin cross.

No. XXX.—The Carpenter's Puzzle. No. 1.

Given, a slip of wood, 15 inches long by 3 wide.

How is it possible to cut it so that the pieces when rearranged shall form a perfect square?

No. XXXI.—Carpenter's Puzzle. No. 2.

A carpenter's apprentice has a board 3 feet in length by 1 in width. With this he is required to fill up a space 2 feet in length by 18 inches in width, but he is not to cut the board into more than two pieces.

How can he manage it?

No. XXXII.—The Cabinet Maker's Puzzle.

A cabinet-maker has a circular piece of veneer, with which he desires to veneer the tops of two office-stools, leaving a hand-hole in the centre of each. The circular piece is exactly sufficient for the job, provided that it be cut without waste.

How can he cut it to the best advantage?

CLUSTER PUZZLES.

There is a large class of puzzles generically known as "Cluster" Puzzles. These consist of a number of pieces of wood, so interlocked together as to form some more or less fanciful shape; not flat, like the "dissected" form of puzzle, but solid. The experimenter is required to take the puzzle to pieces, and reconstruct it as at first. Many of these are extremely clever, but for our present purpose they labour under the disadvantage that it is almost impossible, even with the fullest aid from diagrams, to describe the *modus operandi* in writing. We shall, however, make the attempt with regard to a few of them; bespeaking the reader's indulgence for any unavoidable obscurity in our explanations.

No. XXXIII.—The Bonbon Nut Puzzle.

This has a very complex appearance (see Fig. 203), but it in reality consists of six pieces of wood only, generally box or willow. There is a small space in the centre, which encloses a carraway comfit, offered as prize to any one

Fig. 203.

who may succeed in extracting it. As usually happens, however, in these cases, the taking of the puzzle apart is a comparatively straightforward matter, the real difficulty being found in the endeavour to put it together again.

No. XXXIV.—The Rattle Puzzle.

This (see Fig. 204) is another puzzle of the same kind, but differing in form, being shaped like a child's rattle. It consists of twelve short pieces—fashioned exactly like those of the "Bonbon Nut"—two long flat pieces, with a square head at each end,—and a central piece forming the handle. There

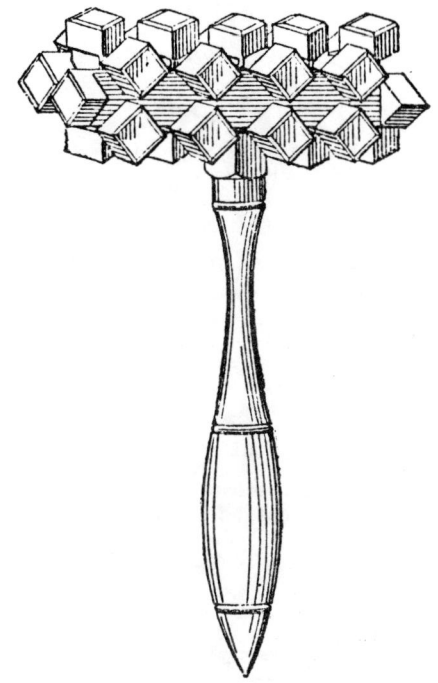

Fig. 204.

is a narrow space down the centre, in which is inserted a bonbon, or leaden pellet, the shaking about of this producing the "rattle."

The experimenter is required to take the rattle to pieces, and put it together again.

No. XXXV.—The Cross-Keys or Three-piece Puzzle.

This (see Fig. 205) is a very ingenious puzzle of its kind. It is one of the simplest, in one sense, being composed of only three pieces of wood, but they are interlocked with extreme ingenuity, and the endeavour to separate them

Fig. 205.

will give a good deal of trouble. Indeed, one's first impression, on a casual inspection, is that the whole must have been carved out of a single piece.

Contrary to the usual rule, the reconstruction of the puzzle will here be found easier than its separation.

No. XXXVI.—The Nut (or Six-piece) Puzzle.

This puzzle is (as its second name implies) composed of six pieces of wood, so cut as to fit together as shown in Fig. 206.

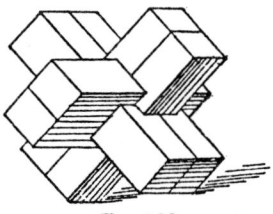

Fig. 206.

The experimenter is required to take the pieces apart, and put them together again.

No. XXXVII.—The Fairy Tea-table.

This is a pretty little table (see Fig. 207), of various coloured woods. It is composed of sixteen different pieces, even the pillar which supports it being in four different sections.

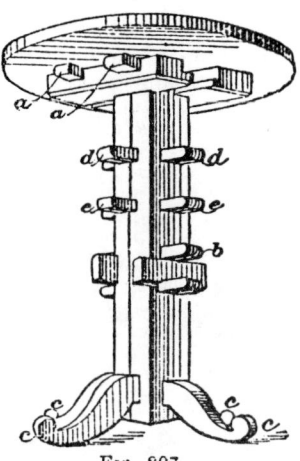

Fig. 207.

The neophyte is required to take the table to pieces, and reconstruct it, as shown in the figure. The former is a very simple operation.

No. XXXVIII.—The Mystery.

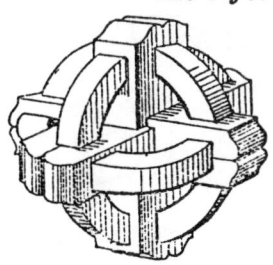

Fig. 208.

The puzzle to which this somewhat high-sounding name

is given is as depicted in Fig. 208. It is an elegant-looking affair, being made of fancy woods in three different colours. It consists of ten different sections, which the aspirant is required to take apart, and put together again.

No. XXXIX.—The Diabolical Cube.

This is a puzzle of a much simpler character, but it will, nevertheless, give some trouble to any one attempting it for the first time. It consists of six pieces, shaped as *a*, *b*, *c*, *d*, *e*, and *f*, respectively, in Fig. 209.

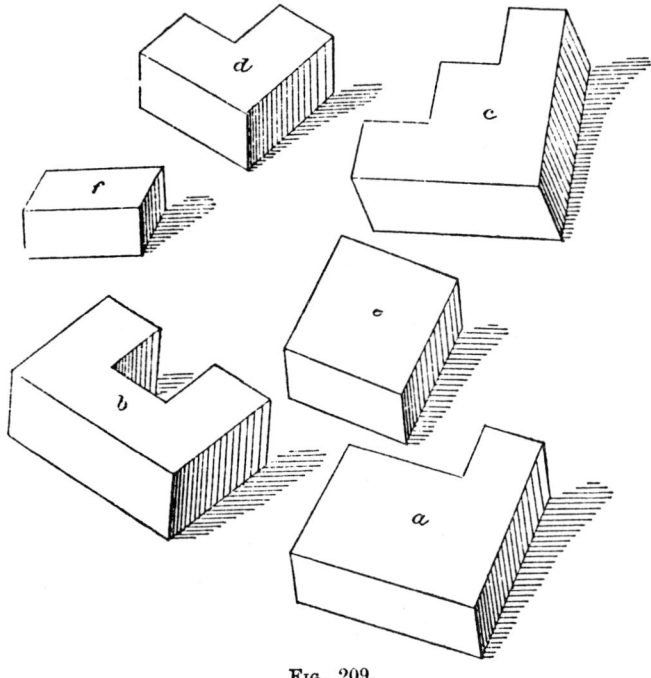

Fig. 209.

Of these six segments the experimenter is required to form a cube.

No. XL.—The Chinese Zigzag.

The reader is probably familiar with the ordinary "zigzag" puzzle, a thin, flat piece of mahogany, or other hard wood, out of which portions have been cut in wavy lines by a fretsaw, the general effect being that of a dissected map of more than ordinary complication. The piecing together of such a puzzle is, however, a mere work of patience, involving no more intellectual effort than the comparison of a given space and a given segment. The Chinese Zigzag is a much more ambitious affair, and will give some trouble even to the most experienced puzzle amateur. It

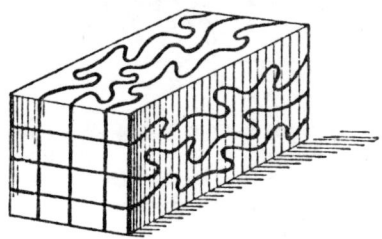

Fig. 210.

consists (see Fig. 210) of a block of mahogany, three inches in length by two in width and depth, cut into sixteen pieces, after the manner following. It is first cut vertically into four segments, after the zigzag fashion already described. The block is then laid on its side, and, without any displacement of its parts, is cut into four horizontal segments, after the same manner. From the peculiar fashion of the cutting, the sixteen pieces still remain locked together, though loosely. To take them apart, one layer (either horizontal or vertical) is removed at a time. Once removed, such layer promptly falls to pieces, the resulting segments being of the most eccentric shapes. The puzzle is to reconstruct the block as at first.

No. XLI.—The Man of Many Parts.

This is a puzzle of German origin. It consists of four slips of card about four inches in length by two in width, bearing

Fig. 211.

respectively the designs shown in Fig. 211, being of men carrying their heads and limbs in various abnormal positions.

The experimenter is required so to arrange the four cards as to produce a single perfect figure.

KEY TO CHAPTER III.

"DISSECTED" OR COMBINATION PUZZLES.

No. I.—The Anchor Puzzle. Solutions.

The first step towards the solution of puzzles of this class is to study the relative proportions of the various segments, and note what results can be obtained from the combination of a given pair. These will, of course, vary according to the particular manner in which the two parts are brought into juxtaposition, and a slight alteration in this respect will often supply the solution of an apparently hopeless puzzle.

Examining, from this point of view, the seven segments of the Anchor Puzzle, we find (see Fig. 104) that we have two

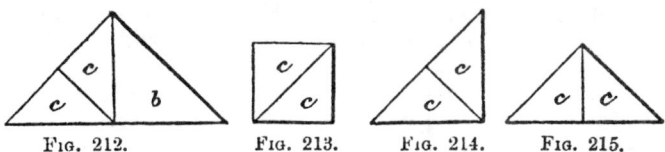

FIG. 212.   FIG. 213.   FIG. 214.   FIG. 215.

right-angled triangles, $a\ a$, each equal to one-fourth of the complete square; a third, b, equal to one-eighth, and two smaller, $c\ c$, each equal to one-sixteenth of the complete square. The three last, joined together as Fig. 212, are exactly equal to one of the larger triangles, $a\ a$. Besides these, we have a square, d; and a rhomboid, e; each exactly double the area of one of the triangles $c\ c$, and therefore also together equal to one of the larger triangles. It should also be noted that the two larger triangles, $a\ a$, together constitute one-half the square, and the remaining five segments the other half. The apprehension of these facts will often help the experimenter out of a difficulty, by enabling him to substitute segments differently shaped but geometrically equivalent, for others found unsuited to the required figure.

Further, as to the change of shape produced by change of relative position, it is to be noted that the juxtaposition of two right-angled triangles of equal size, as *c c*, *with their hypotenuses together*, produces a square (Fig. 213). With two of their shorter sides in contact, they appear as Fig. 214, or Fig. 215. Reverse one of them, and again unite, and the resulting figure is a rhomboid, as Fig. 216. Apply one of the shorter sides of each of the triangles

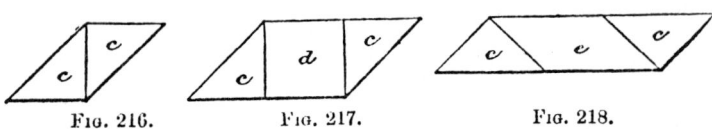

Fig. 216.   Fig. 217.   Fig. 218.

c c to the square *d*, and you have again a rhomboid, though of different proportions, as in Fig. 217. Apply one of the shorter sides of each of the triangles *c c* to one of the shorter sides of the rhomboid *e*, and you have once more a rhomboid (Fig. 218), though much narrower in proportion to its length. Apply the hypotenuse of each of the triangles *c c* to one of the *longer* sides of the rhomboid *e*, and the

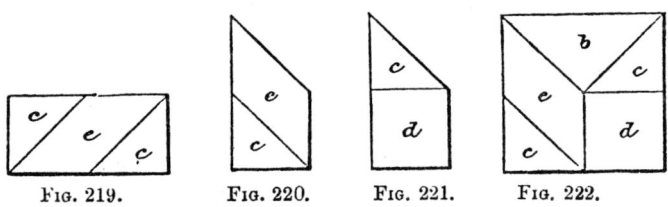

Fig. 219.   Fig. 220.   Fig. 221.   Fig. 222.

resultant figure is a rectangle, as in Fig. 219. Apply the hypotenuse of one only of the smaller triangles *c c* to one of the longer sides of *e*, and we have the trapezoid depicted in Fig. 220. Apply one of the shorter sides of the other triangle *c* to one side of the square *d*, and we have a trapezoid (Fig. 221) of the same size and shape, though produced in a different manner. Place these two trapezoids in juxta-

Key to "Dissected" or Combination Puzzles. 113

position, and insert the triangle b in the concave space between them, and we have a square (half the size of the original), as in Fig. 222.

Having thus made himself acquainted with the elementary capabilities of his materials, the neophyte will be the better prepared to attempt the formation of the more elaborate patterns depicted on pp. 78, 79.

Beginning with Fig. 105, we note in the first place that it is a rectangular parallelogram, consisting of two equal squares. We know that the two large triangles *a a* constitute one half of our available material, and that they can be made to form a square (*i.e.*, half the required figure). We have then only to form a second square, as shown in Fig. 222, side by side with this, and our rectangle is complete. (See Fig. 223.)

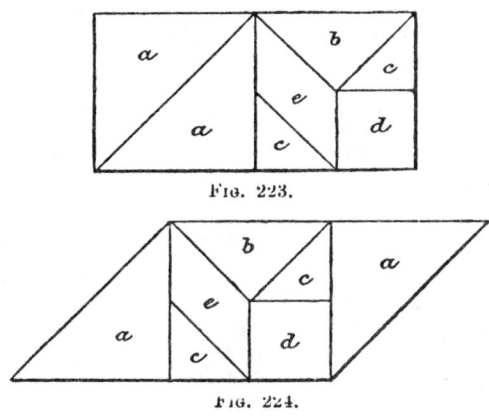

Fig. 223.

Fig. 224.

To form Fig. 106, we retain the square last formed by way of centre, remove the outer large triangle from the left-hand side, and transfer it, the reverse way up, to the opposite side. (See Fig. 224.) Again removing the triangle last placed in position, and transferring it (see Fig. 225) to the top of the square, in such manner that its hypotenuse shall be in line with the hypotenuse of the triangle on the left, we have Fig. 107.

For the composition of the remaining figures we must refer

I

114 *Puzzles Old and New.*

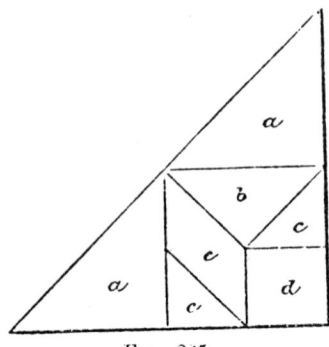

Fig. 225.

the reader to the diagrams following (Figs. 226–233.) It will be found that all the designs are constructed on the same principle, and, by means of a little intelligent analysis, can readily be resolved into their component factors.

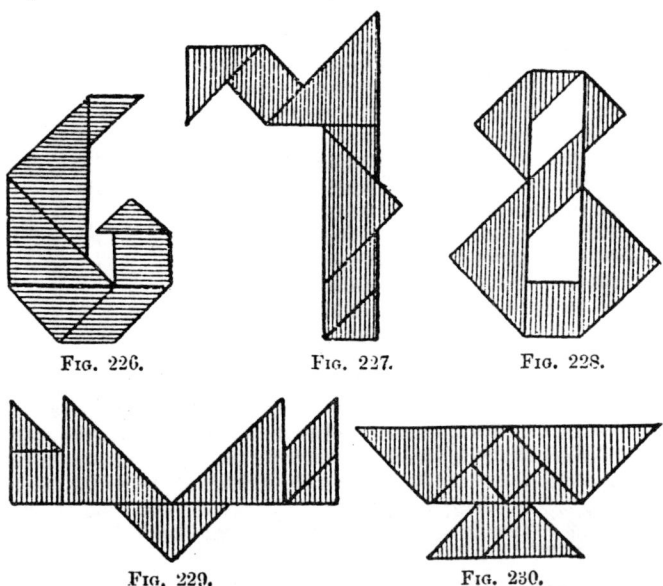

Fig. 226.   Fig. 227.   Fig. 228.

Fig. 229.   Fig. 230.

Key to "Dissected" or Combination Puzzles. 115

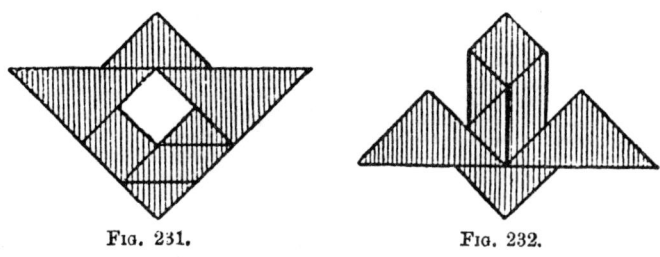

Fig. 231.   Fig. 232.

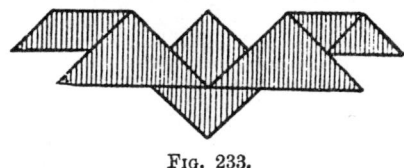

Fig. 233.

No. II.—The Tormentor Puzzle. Solutions.

See Figs. 234–241 below.

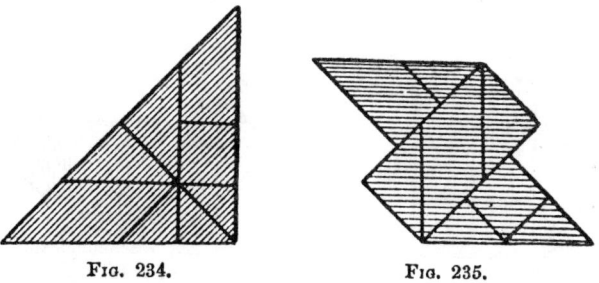

Fig. 234.   Fig. 235.

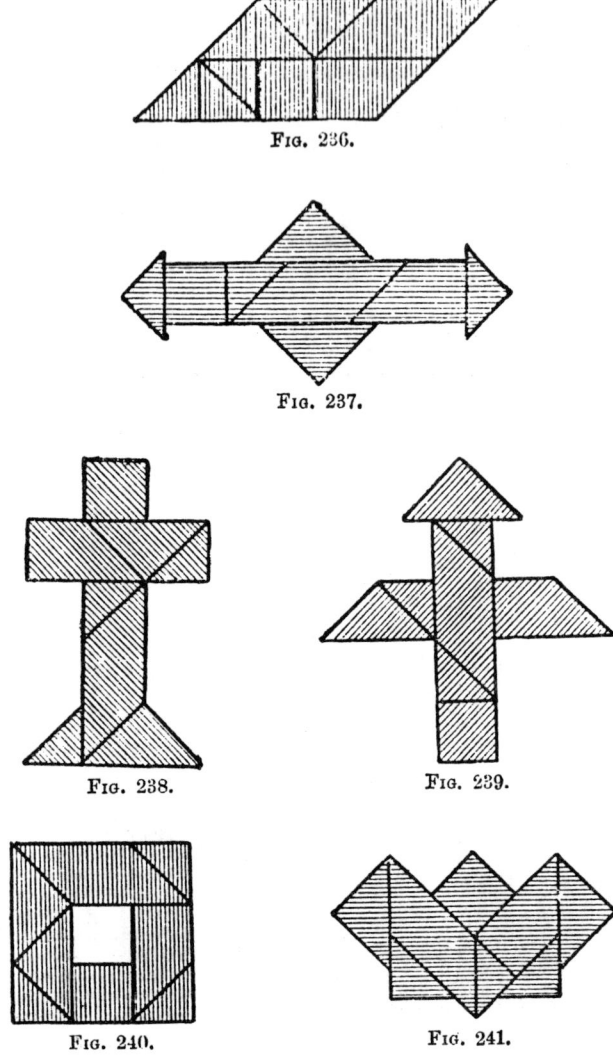

Fig. 236.

Fig. 237.

Fig. 238.

Fig. 239.

Fig. 240.

Fig. 241.

Key to "Dissected" or Combination Puzzles. 117

No. III.—The Pythagoras Puzzle. Solutions.

See Figs. 242–250 below.

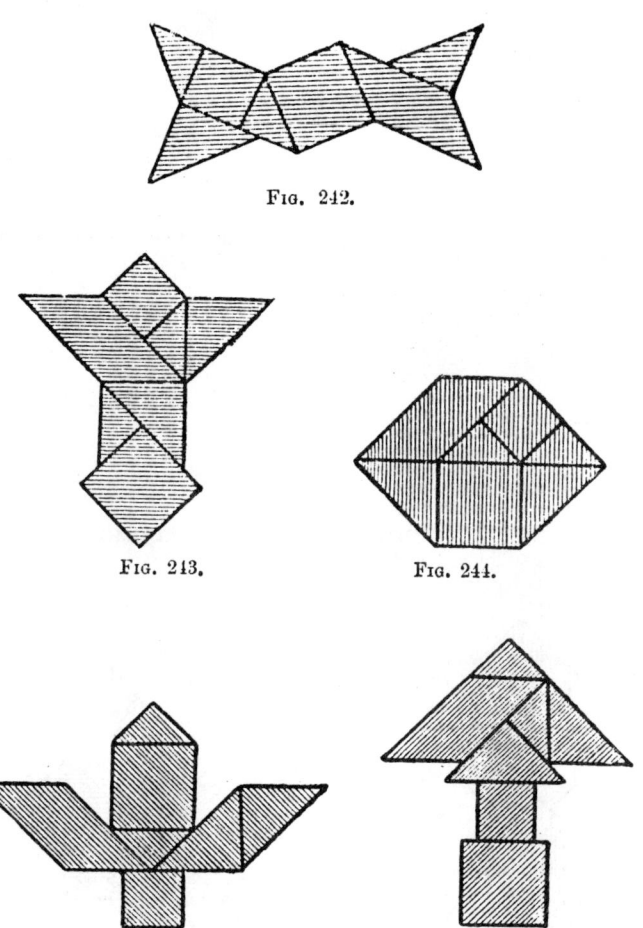

Fig. 242.

Fig. 243.

Fig. 244.

Fig. 245.

Fig. 246.

118 *Puzzles Old and New.*

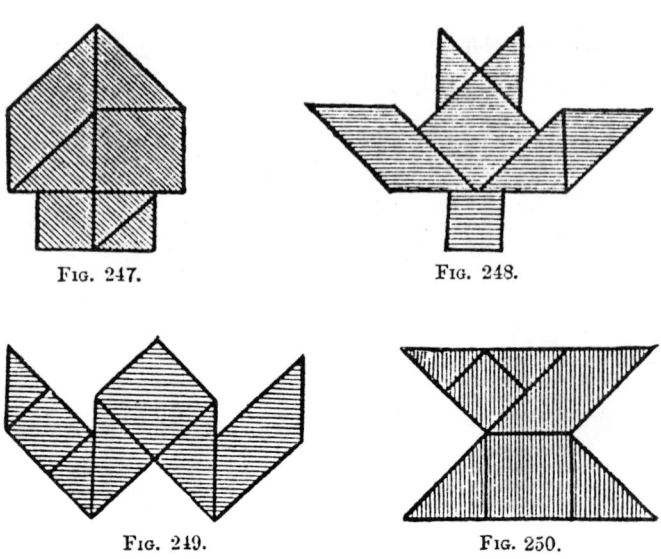

Fig. 247.   Fig. 248.

Fig. 249.   Fig. 250.

No. IV.—The Cross Puzzle. Solutions.

See Figs. 251–259 below.

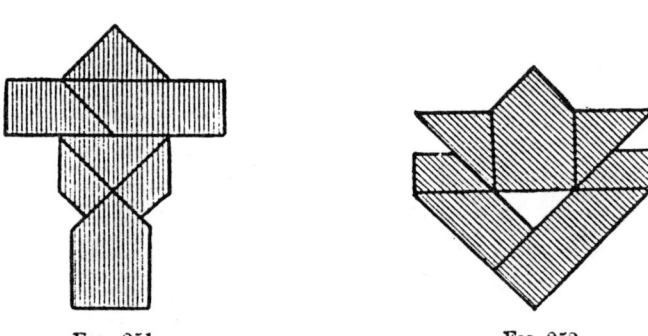

Fig. 251.   Fig. 252.

Key to "Dissected" or Combination Puzzles. 119

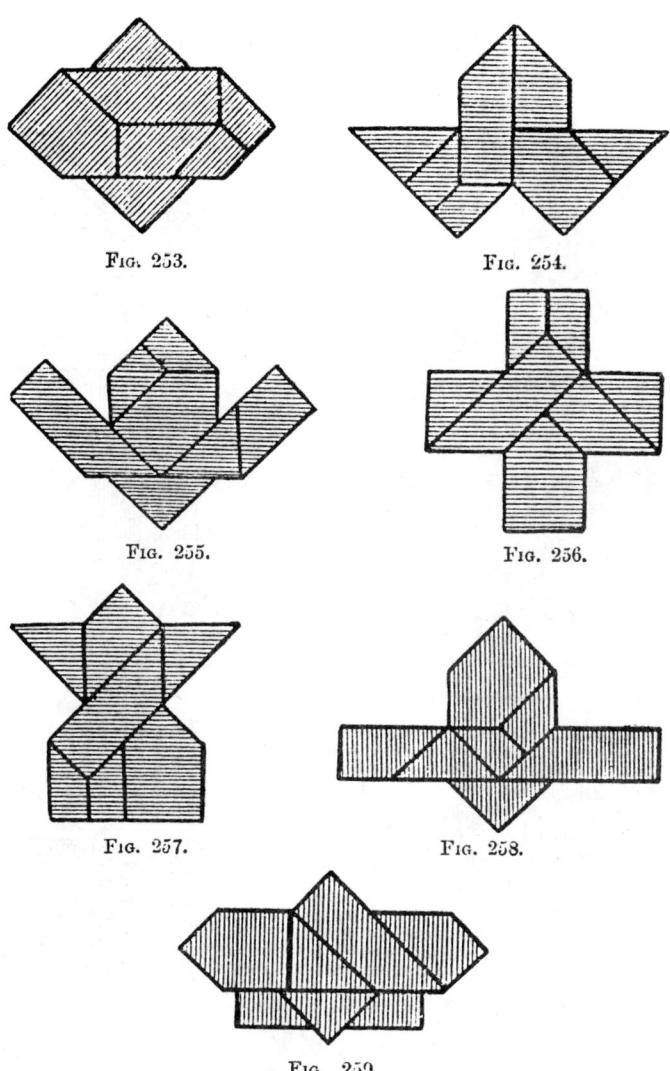

Fig. 253.

Fig. 254.

Fig. 255.

Fig. 256.

Fig. 257.

Fig. 258.

Fig. 259.

120 *Puzzles Old and New.*

No. V.—The Circular Puzzle. Solutions.

See Figs. 260–268 below.

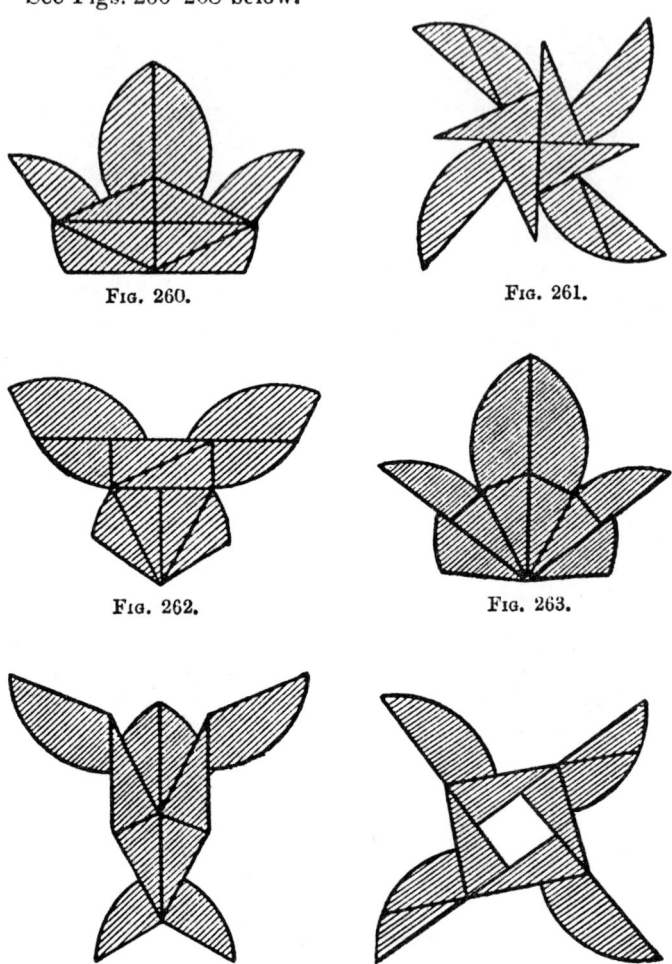

Fig. 260.

Fig. 261.

Fig. 262.

Fig. 263.

Fig. 264.

Fig. 265.

Key to "Dissected" or Combination Puzzles. 121

Fig. 266.

Fig. 267.

Fig. 268.

No. VI.—The Star Puzzle. Solutions.

See Figs. 269–280 below. Comparison with the problems will indicate which of the segments should be of the darker, and which of the lighter material.

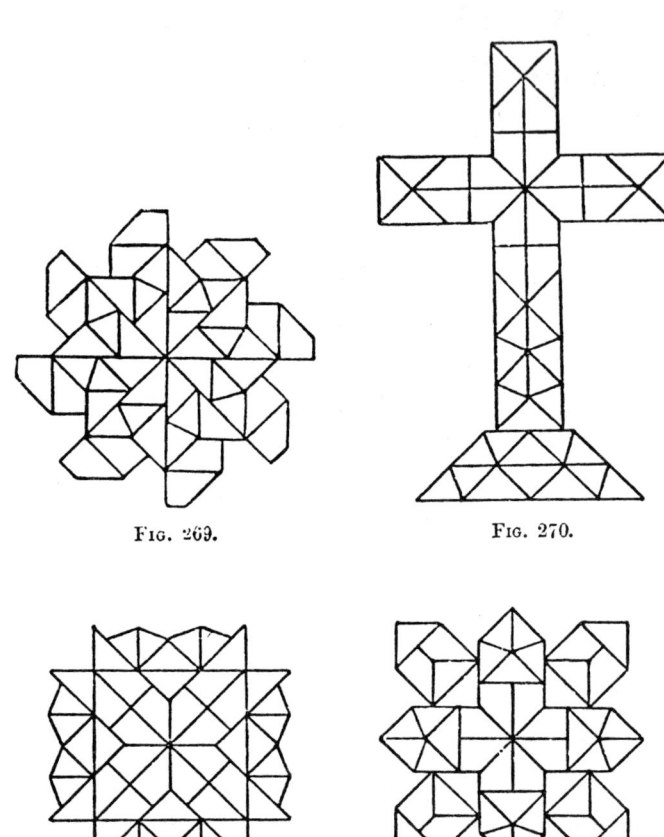

Fig. 269.

Fig. 270.

Fig. 271.

Fig. 272.

Key to "Dissected" or Combination Puzzles. 123

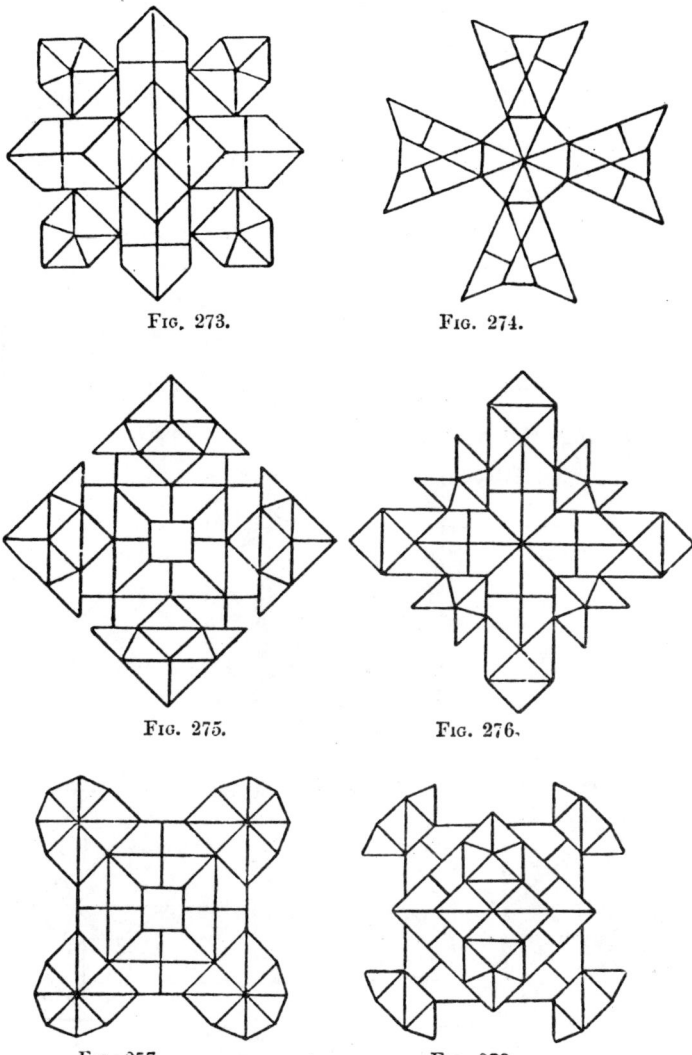

Fig. 273.   Fig. 274.

Fig. 275.   Fig. 276.

Fig. 277.   Fig. 278.

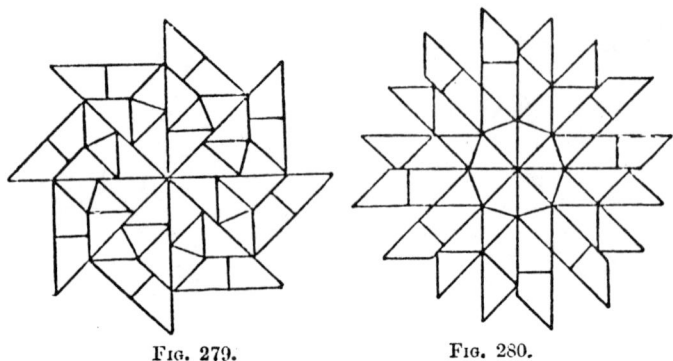

Fig. 279.   Fig. 280.

No. VII.—The Zigzag Square. Solution.

Arrange the various segments as shown in Fig. 281.

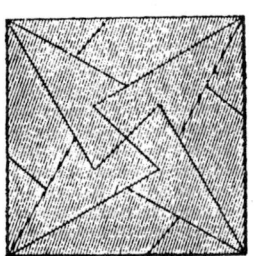

Fig. 281.

No. VIII.—The Extended Square. Solution.

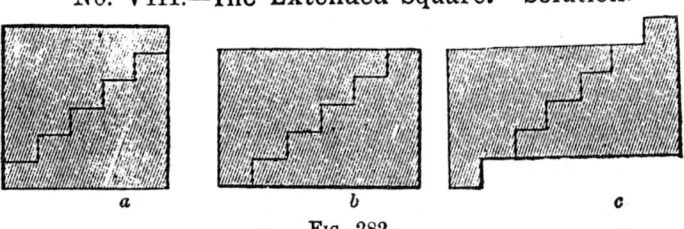

Fig. 282.

See Fig. 282. The card is cut as indicated in *a*. The

upper part is then shifted backward one step, to form the shape *b*, or two steps, to form the shape *c*.

No. IX.—The Octagon Puzzle. Solution.

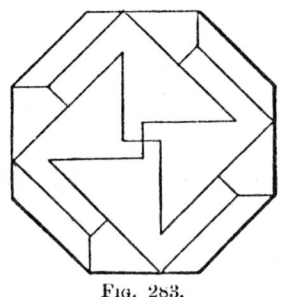

Fig. 283.

The segments are arranged as shown in Fig. 283.

No. X.—The Patchwork Square. Solution.

The segments are arranged as shown in Fig. 284.

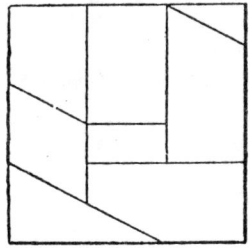

Fig. 284.

No. XI.—The Two Squares. Solution.

See Figs. 285, 286.
First divide the larger square by pencil lines from *a* to *b*, and *c* to *d*, then cut from *e* to *c*, and from *c* to *f* (Fig. 285).

The card will now be in three pieces, which, duly rearranged, will form a square, as shown in Fig. 286.

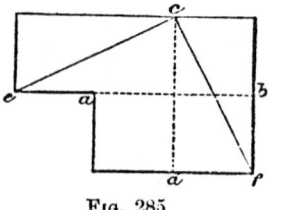
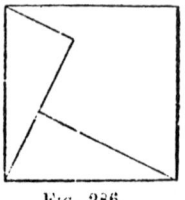

Fig. 285.   Fig. 286.

No. XII.—The Latin Cross Puzzle. Solution.

The segments are arranged as shown in Fig. 287.

Fig. 287.

No. XIII.—The Greek Cross. Solution.

Divide the cross as shown by the dotted lines in Fig. 288, and rearrange as shown in Fig 289.

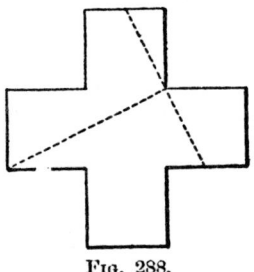
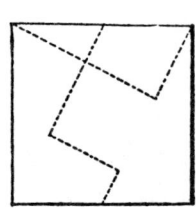

Fig. 288.   Fig. 289.

Key to "Dissected" or Combination Puzzles. 127

No. XIV.—The Protean Puzzle. Solutions.

See Figs. 290-295.

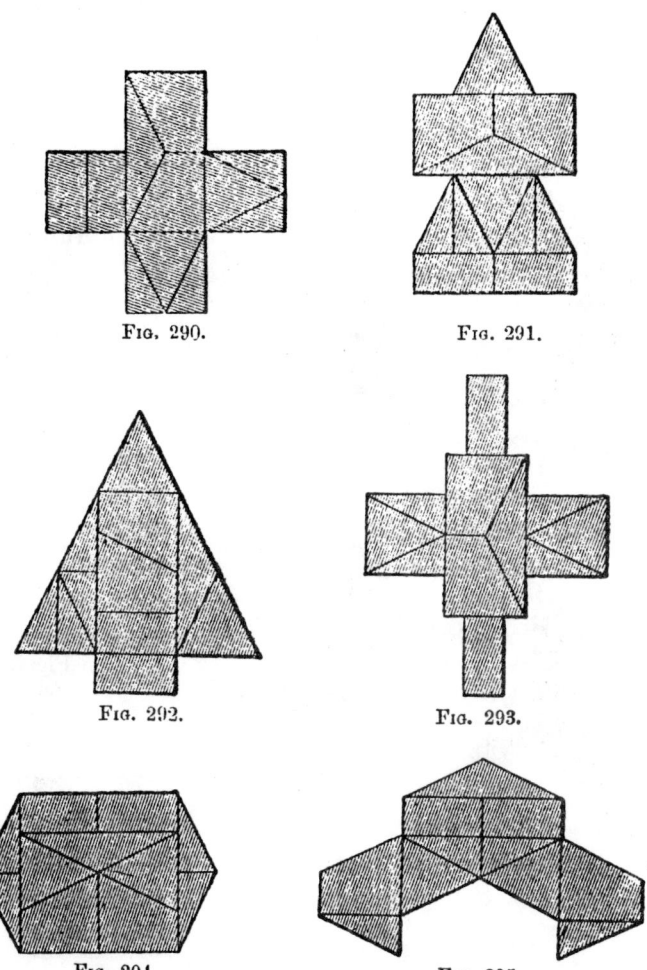

Fig. 290.

Fig. 291.

Fig. 292.

Fig. 293.

Fig. 294.

Fig. 295.

No. XV.—The Caricature Puzzle. Solutions.

See Figs. 296-301. A host of other figures, equally comical, may be formed after a similar fashion.

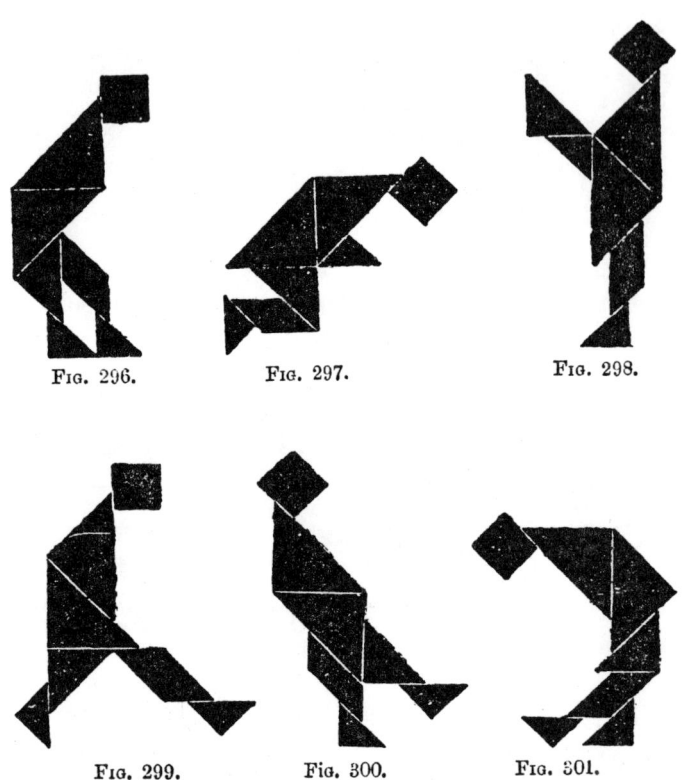

Fig. 296.   Fig. 297.   Fig. 298.

Fig. 299.   Fig. 300.   Fig. 301.

Key to "Dissected" or Combination Puzzles. 129

No. XVI.—The Chequers Puzzle. Solution.

We have not undertaken to verify the fifty ways in which it is said that this puzzle may be solved, but we append

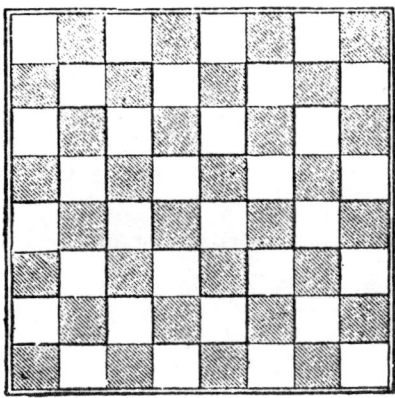

Fig. 302.

Fig. 303.

two (see Figs. 302, 303), leaving the remaining forty-eight to the ingenuity of our readers.

K

It will be seen that the two solutions given are radically different.

No. XVII.—The "Spots" Puzzle. Solution.

It will be found a great assistance towards the solution of this puzzle to close the box with the lid in the proper position (in which condition, as we have mentioned, it is an exact representation of a die), and work from it by way of model. We will assume, for the purpose of our explanation, that it is placed as shown in Fig. 192, the *six* being to the front, and, consequently, the *one* to the rear; the *two* at top, consequently the *five* at bottom; and the *four* to the left, consequently the *three* to the right, on the side concealed from view.

The lower stratum will consist of three bars as under. (See Fig. 304.)

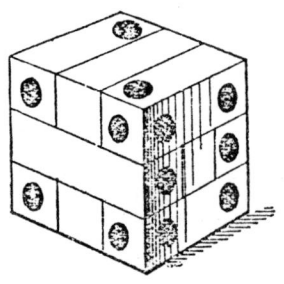

Fig. 304.

The Hinder bar.—Two spots on under side, and one on the end to the left.

Middle.—One spot in centre of under side. Otherwise blank.

Front.—Two spots on under side, two in front, and one on each end.

We next come to the middle layer; and here most people give themselves a good deal of unnecessary trouble by taking it for granted that all the nine bars must lie *in the same direction*. As a matter of fact, the three at top and three at bottom should lie parallel, but the three in the middle at

Key to "Dissected" or Combination Puzzles. 131

right angles to them. This middle layer is formed as follows:—

Left-hand.—Bar with one spot on end towards front. Otherwise blank.

Middle.—Bar with spot on hinder end. Otherwise blank.

Right-hand.—Bar with spot on forward end, and one in centre of right-hand side.

(These, as we have said, are to be laid *across* the three bars already placed.)

Upper layer.—Back. Spot on each end, and one on upper side to the right. Further side blank.

Middle.— Blank throughout.

Front.—Two spots on front, one on the end to the left, and one on the top, at the same end.

These last three bars being laid on the top, parallel to the bottom section, the die will be complete, having the appearance shown in the figure.

No. XVIII.—The Endless Chain. Solution.

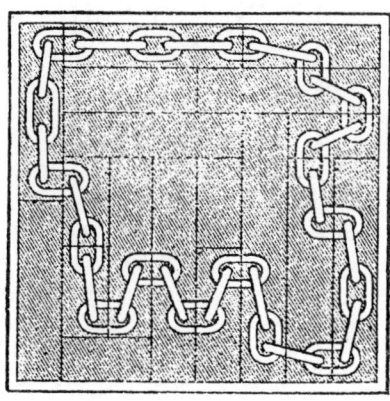

Fig. 305.

See Fig. 305, which shows the proper arrangement of the various segments.

No. XIX.—The Hexagon. Solution.

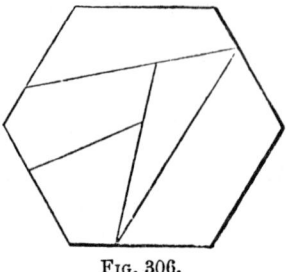

Fig. 306.

The segments are arranged as shown in Fig. 306.

No. XX.—Eight Squares in One. Solution.

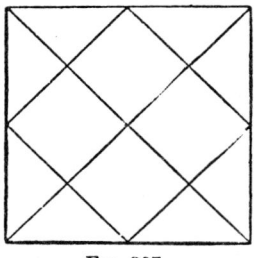

Fig. 307.

Place the four squares together to form the centre, and arrange the smaller pieces round them as shown in Fig. 307.

No. XXI.—The Five Squares. Solution.

Find the centre of either side of a given square, and cut the card in a straight line from that point to one of the opposite corners, as shown in Fig. 308. Treat four of the five squares in this manner. Re-arrange the eight segments

Key to "Dissected" or Combination Puzzles. 133

thus made with the uncut square in the centre, as shown in Fig. 309, and you will have a single perfect square.

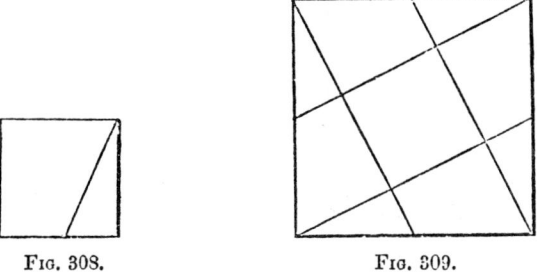

Fig. 308. Fig. 309.

No. XXII.—The Geometrical Square. Solution.

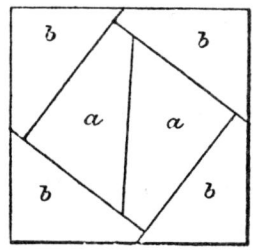

Fig. 310.

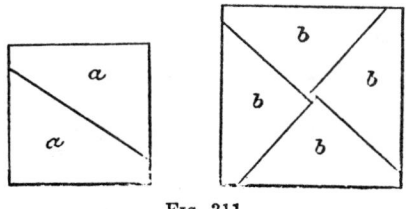

Fig. 311.

See Fig. 310, representing the larger square, and Fig. 311, showing the arrangement of the two smaller squares.

No. XXIII.—The Dissected Square. Solution.

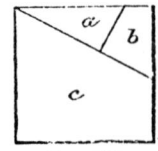

Fig. 312.

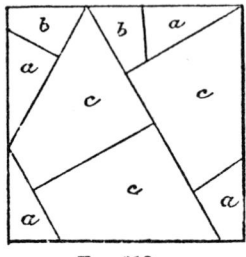

Fig. 313.

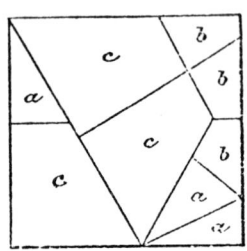

Fig. 314.

The three smaller squares are formed as shown in Fig. 312. The larger square either as Fig. 313 or Fig. 314.

No. XXIV.—The Twenty Triangles. Solution.

Place ten of the triangles alternately, so as to form a

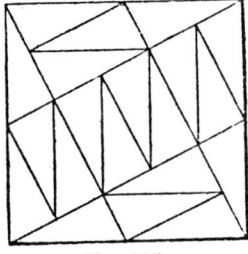

Fig. 315.

rhomboid, and complete the square with the remaining ten, as shown in Fig. 315.

Key to "Dissected" or Combination Puzzles. 135

No. XXV.—**The New Triangle Puzzle. Solution.**

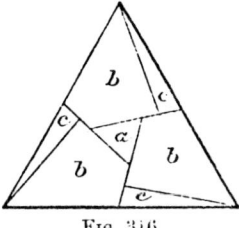

Fig. 316.

The seven segments are arranged as shown in Fig. 316.

No. XXVI.—**The Japanese Square. Solution.**

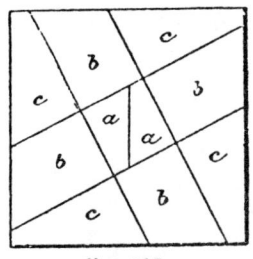

Fig. 317.

The segments are arranged as shown in Fig. 317.

No. XXVII.—**The Chinese Square. Solution.**

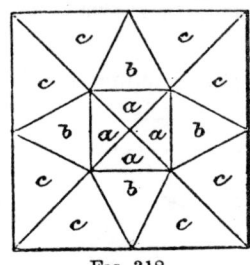

Fig. 318.

The segments are arranged as shown in Fig. 318.

No. XXVIII.—**The Yankee Square. Solution.**

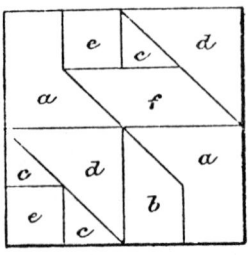

Fig. 319.

The segments are arranged as shown in Fig. 319.

No. XXIX.—**Another Cross Puzzle. Solution.**

Fig. 320.

Arrange the segments as shown in Fig. 320.

No. XXX.—**The Carpenter's Puzzle. No. 1. Solution.**

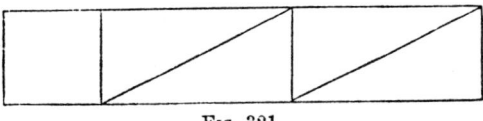

Fig. 321.

The piece of wood is cut as indicated in Fig. 321, and the

Key to "Dissected" or Combination Puzzles. 137

pieces rearranged as shown in Fig. 322.

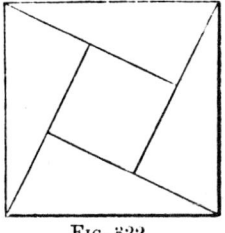

Fig. 322.

No. XXXI.—Carpenter's Puzzle. No. 2. Solution.

He cuts the board as shown in Fig. 323—viz.—from a to b (half-way across); from c to d, and then along the middle

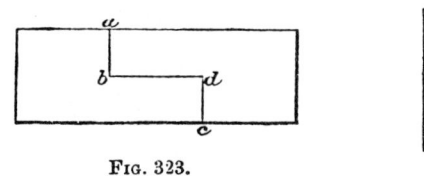
Fig. 323.

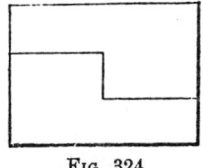
Fig. 324.

from b to d. He then reunites the two pieces as shown in Fig. 324.

No. XXXII.—The Cabinet-Maker's Puzzle. Solution.

Finding the centre of the circle,* he describes a second circle exactly half the diameter of the first, and then divides the whole into eight parts, $a, a, a, a,$ and $b, b, b, b,$ by means of two lines drawn at right angles to each other (see Fig. 325). He then cuts the veneer through the lines thus

---

* To find the centre of a given circle, draw a straight line from any one point to any other point of the circumference. Bisect this line, and draw another line at right angles to it through the point of section, terminated at each end by the circumference. Bisect this last-mentioned line, and the point of section will be the centre of the circle.

described, and re-arranges the pieces as shown in Fig. 326. The space in the centre forms the hand-hole.

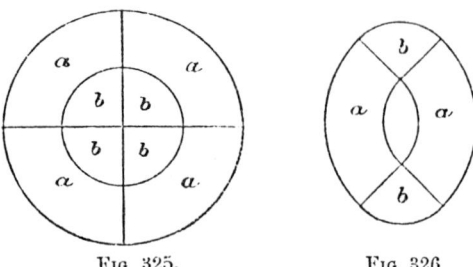

Fig. 325.   Fig. 326.

No. XXXIII.—The Bonbon Nut Puzzle. Solution.

The six pieces of which the puzzle is composed are all shaped like *a* in Fig. 327, with one exception. This has a triangular notch cut out of it, as *b* in the same figure.

The first step is to examine the puzzle carefully, in order to discover the notched piece. This, like the rest, is held between the projecting heads of two of the other pieces, but

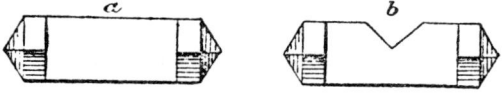

Fig. 327.

by reason of the notch may, by a little gentle pressure, be forced outwards from between them. This frees the two pieces lying at right angles to this, and these being removed, the puzzle falls to pieces.

To reconstruct the nut, you have only to replace the pieces in reverse order, the "key" or notched piece last; but considerable dexterity is needed to do this, the pieces having an aggravating knack of suddenly collapsing and falling into hopeless confusion, just as you have all but "got it right;" indeed, it seems as if four hands at least were necessary to hold the pieces in position. With perseverance, however, success should be only a question of time, and the neophyte must persevere accordingly.

No. XXXIV.—The Rattle Puzzle. Solution.

Any one who has solved the Bonbon Nut Puzzle (last described) will have little difficulty with the Rattle, the principle being identical. One of the end pieces has a notch in it, and this being removed, the remaining pieces come apart almost spontaneously.

No. XXXV.—The Cross Keys (or Three-piece) Puzzle. Solution.

The three pieces of which the puzzle is composed are shaped as *a*, *b*, and *c* (Fig. 328) respectively.

To put them together, take *a* upright between the forefinger and thumb of the left hand. Through the slot push *b*, with the cross-cut uppermost, till the farther edge of the

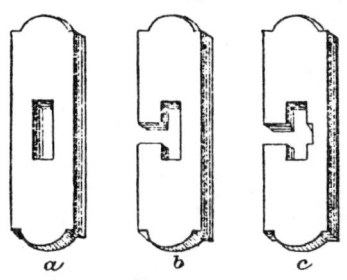

Fig. 328.

central slot comes all but flush with the outer face of *a*. Then take *c*, with the short arm of the cross towards you, and lower it gently down over the top of *a*, the uncut centre portion (next the short arm of the cross) passing through the cross-cut in *b*. You have now only to push *b* onward through *a* till the transverse cut is hidden, and the cross is complete.

To separate the parts, reverse the process.

No. XXXVI.—The Nut (or Six-piece) Puzzle. Solution.

Of the several pieces of which the puzzle is composed, one, known as the "key," is square from end to end, as *a* in Fig.

329. This key is, in all puzzles of this class, the first piece to be removed, and the last to be replaced.

The first step is to discover the key. This is done by pressing on the ends of the various pieces, the key being the only one that yields to the pressure. Having ascertained which it is, take the puzzle in the left hand, holding it in such a position that the key shall be horizontal, lying from right to left, and uppermost of its own pair. Push this out, and you will then be enabled to lift out one of the pair pointing towards you. This is shaped like *b* in the figure. Push the two uprights a little way from right to left (or

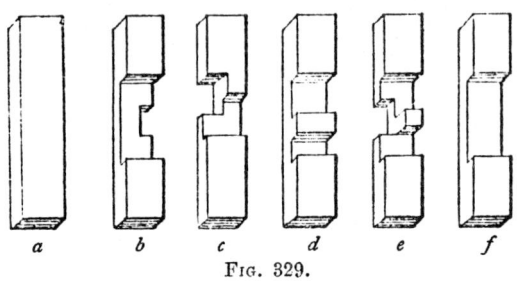

Fig. 329.

left to right, according as you may be holding the puzzle). This will release the second piece, *c*, of the pair pointing towards you. The two uprights, *d* and *e*, may now be removed, and *f* is left alone.

With a view to the subsequent putting together of the puzzle, note carefully the shape of the last three pieces. The upright pair, *d, e*, have each a projecting piece, or tongue, in the centre, one going half across, the other only half-way across. The two faces shown in our illustration are to be brought together. The third piece, *f*, has simply an oblong block cut out of its centre, half-way through, being next in simplicity to the key piece, *a*.

To reconstruct the puzzle, take this piece, *f*, with the cut part uppermost, and to it fit the pair *d, e*. From this point hold the puzzle by the lower ends of *d, e*. Next insert *c* across *f*, and push *d* and *e* to right or left (as the case may be), so as to lock it in position. Now insert *b*, with the smaller cut uppermost. Finally, insert *a*, and the deed is done.

Key to "Dissected" or Combination Puzzles. 141

No. XXXVII.—The Fairy Tea-table. Solution.

This, notwithstanding the large number of pieces of which it is composed, is by no means a difficult puzzle.

The first step, in taking it to pieces, is to draw out the two bolts a, a, which secures the top to the pillar. The next is to push or pull out the little piece b, when the three other pieces combined with it will drop out of their own accord. The pillar may then be separated into four different portions, thereby releasing the feet, c, c, c, c, and the two little crosses (each in two portions) d, d, and e, e.

To reconstruct the table, exactly reverse the process.

No. XXXVIII.—The Mystery. Solution.

This is one of the best puzzles of its kind, the clue being concealed with great ingenuity. When, however, the first step is discovered, the remaining steps of the process are by no means difficult.

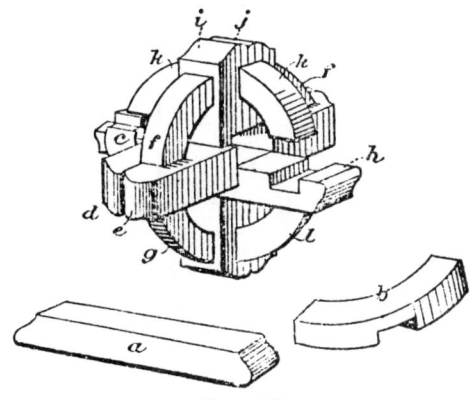

Fig. 330.

The secret lies in the fact that, as in the case of the Six-piece Puzzle (p. 139), one of the cross-pieces is simply pushed through from side to side, forming a "key." This found, hold the puzzle (as in the case of the Six-piece) in the left hand, with the key, a, horizontal from right to left, and push it out. This done (see Fig. 330), you are enabled to remove the two horizontal semi-circles, b, c. Now lift out the two pieces, *d, e*, which lie pointing towards you, and remove them (laying them side by side for greater convenience in reconstruction). Their removal in turn releases the two vertical semi-circles, *f, g*. Withdraw the remaining horizontal piece, *h*, and you have left only the two uprights, *i j*, supporting the two remaining semi-circles, *k, l*.

To reconstruct the "Mystery," insert the pieces in the reverse order, remembering to begin with *the only two straight pieces that are exactly alike* (*i, j*), holding them upright, the one behind the other. Insert a pair of the semi-circles (these are all alike) at top and bottom, then the horizontal piece, *h*, and so on.*

No. XXXIX.—The Diabolical Cube. Solution.

Stand the piece *c* (the one which looks like a flight of

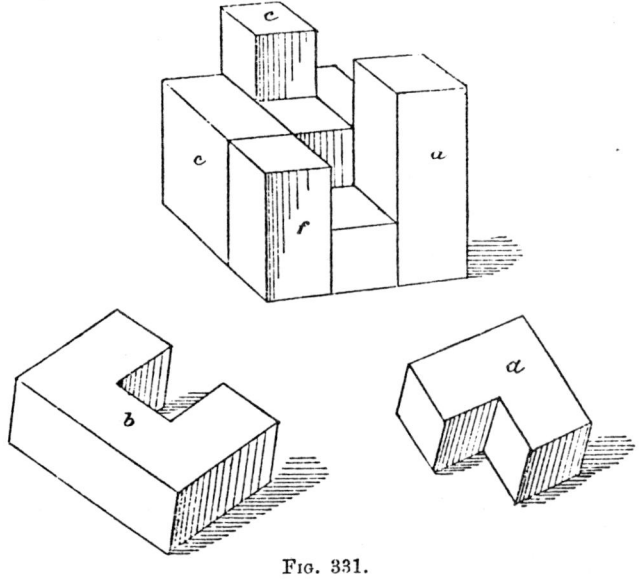

Fig. 331.

---

* It will be found a great assistance, in attempting to solve one of the more difficult puzzles of the "Cluster" class for the first time, before taking it to pieces, to make pencil marks here and there to show which

Key to "Dissected" or Combination Puzzles. 143

steps) up on end, and beside it the piece *a*, with its projecting portion uppermost, but farthest away from the highest step of *c*. Against the nearer side of *c* place the square block *e*, and stand the small block *f* on end beside it. The state of things will now be as shown in Fig. 331. Fix *d* in beside *a*, with one of its projections pointing downward and the other resting on *f*. You will find that you have now only room left for the remaining piece, *b*, whose cut-out central space just fits the projecting top of *c*. Place this in position, and the cube is complete.

No. XL.—The Chinese Zigzag. Solution.

To reconstruct the block, you must follow as closely as possible, but in reverse order, the process by which it was

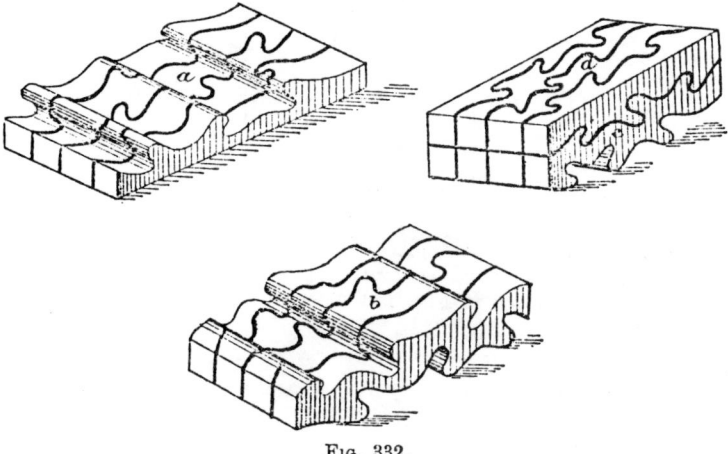

Fig. 332.

taken to pieces. First put together one of the external layers, and, having completed this, lay it, with the flat side undermost, to form the bottom of the block. Then put together the layer next in order, and slide it into position, and in like manner with the two remaining layers.

---

pair of pieces, and which faces of such pair, come together ; in one case, say, a single stroke across the line of junction ; in another, *two* strokes side by side; in another, *three* ; and so on.

A novice usually endeavours to reconstruct the block haphazard, so to speak, instead of layer by layer, under which conditions success is impossible.

Fig. 332 shows the four layers in readiness for the final reconstruction, *b* sliding (from left to right, or *vice versâ*) over *a*, and *d c* over *b* in like manner.

No. XLI.—The Man of Many Parts. Solution.

The secret lies in so arranging the cards that one half of each shall lap over half of the one next to it, thereby cover-

FIG. 333.

ing up its more eccentric features, and leaving visible only such half of the card as contributes to the desired result, which is as shown in Fig. 333.

CHAPTER IV.

ARITHMETICAL PUZZLES.

No. I.—The "Forty-five" Puzzle.

The number 45 has some curious properties. Among others, it may be divided into four parts, in such manner that if you add two to the first, subtract two from the second, multiply the third by two, and divide the fourth by two, the result will in each case be equal.

What are they?

No. II.—A Singular Subtraction.

Required, to subtract 45 from 45 in such manner that there shall be 45 left.

No. III.—A Mysterious Multiplicand.

Required, to find a number which, multiplied by 3, 6, 9, 12, 15, 18, 21, 24, or 27, shall in each case give as product the same digit, three times repeated.

No. IV.—Counting the Pigs.

A youngster asked a farmer how many pigs he had. "You shall reckon for yourself," said the farmer. "If I had as many more, and half as many more, and seven to boot, I should have 32."

How many had he?

No. V.—Another "Pig" Problem.

A farmer, being asked the same question, replied, "If I had as many more, and half as many more, and two pigs and a half, I should have just a score."

How many had he?

No. VI.—A Little Miscalculation.

A market-woman bought 120 apples at four a penny, and the same number of another sort at six a penny; but finding that they were beginning to spoil, determined to sell them off at cost-price. To save trouble, she mixed them together and sold them at ten for twopence, expecting to just get her money back again. But when all were sold, she found, to her surprise, that she had lost twopence over the transaction.

How did this happen?

No. VII.—A Simple Magic Square.

Required, to arrange the numbers 1 to 9 inclusive in the form of a square, in such manner that the total of each line, whether horizontal, vertical, or diagonal, shall be the same—viz., 15.

No. VIII.—The "Thirty-four" Puzzle.

Required, to arrange the numbers 1 to 16 inclusive in the form of a square, in such manner that the total of each line, horizontal, vertical, or diagonal, shall be the same—viz., 34.

No. IX.—The "Sixty-five" Puzzle.

Required, to arrange the numbers 1 to 25 inclusive in the form of a square, under the same conditions, the total being 65 each way.

No. X.—The "Twenty-six" Puzzle.

This is a magic square with a difference, the four corner places being omitted. The problem is to arrange the numbers 1 to 12 inclusive in the form of a cross, as shown in Fig. 334, so as to make 26 in seven different ways—viz., the two horizontal and the two vertical rows, the group of squares marked *a a a a*, the group marked *b b b b*, and

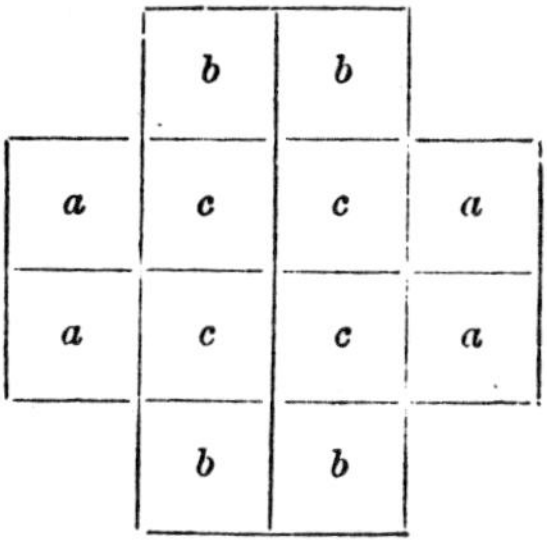

FIG. 334.

the group marked *c c c c*, each making the above-mentioned total.

No. XI.—An Unmanageable Legacy.

An old farmer left a will whereby he bequeathed his horses to his three sons, John, James, and William, in the following proportions: John, the eldest, was to have one half, James to have one-third, and William one-ninth. When he died, however, it was found that the number of horses in his stable was seventeen, a number which is divisible neither by two, by three, or by nine. In their perplexity the three brothers consulted a clever lawyer, who hit on a scheme whereby the intentions of the testator were carried out to the satisfaction of all parties.

How was it managed?

No. XII.—Many Figures, but a Small Result.

Required, of the numbers 1, 2, 3, 4, 5, 6, 7, 8, 9, 0, to compose two fractions, whose sum shall be equal to unity. Each number to be used once, and once only.

No. XIII.—Can You Name It?

Required, to find a number which is just so much short of 50 as its quadruple is above 50.

No. XIV.—Squares, Product, and Difference.

Required, to find two numbers the sum of whose squares is greater by 181 than their product, and whose product is greater by 161 than their difference.

No. XV.—A Peculiar Number.

Required, to find a number of six digits of such a nature that if you transfer the two left-hand digits (28) to the opposite end, the new number thus formed is exactly double the original number.

No. XVI.—A Novel Century.

Required, by multiplication and addition of the numbers 1 to 9 inclusive, to make 100, each number being used once, and once only.

No. XVII.—Another Century.

Required, by addition only of the numbers 1 to 9 inclusive to make 100, each number being used once, and once only.

No. XVIII.—Another Way to make a Hundred.

Required, with six nines to express the number 100.

No. XIX.—The Lucky Number.

Many persons have what they consider a "lucky" number. Show such a person the row of figures subjoined—
1, 2, 3, 4, 5, 6, 7, 9,
(consisting of the numerals from 1 to 9 inclusive, with the 8 only omitted), and inquire what is his lucky or favourite number. He names any number he pleases from 1 to 9, say 7. You reply that, as he is fond of sevens, he shall have plenty of them, and accordingly proceed to multiply the series above given by such a number that the resulting product consists of sevens only.

Required, to find (for each number that may be selected) the multiplier which will produce the above result.

No. XX.—The Two Ages.

Father and son are aged 71 and 34 respectively. At what age was the father three times the age of his son; and at what age will the latter have reached half his father's age?

No. XXI.—The Graces and the Muses.

The three Graces, each bearing a like number of roses, one day met the nine Muses. Each Grace gave to each Muse the eighteenth part of her store, when it was found that each Muse had twelve roses less than each of the three Graces.

What number of roses had each Grace originally?

No. XXII.—The Graces and the Muses Again.

Sometimes the puzzle is stated in another form. The three Graces, laden with roses as before, meet the nine Muses, and each Grace gives to each Muse such a proportion of her store that when the division is complete, each Grace and each Muse has an equal share.

How many roses had each Grace at first?

No. XXIII.—Just One Over.

A man, being asked how many sovereigns he had in his pocket, replied, "If I divide them by 2, by 3, by 4, by 5, or by 6, I shall always have one over."

What number had he?

No. XXIV.—Scarcely Explicit.

Another person, being asked a similar question, replied, "If I had half as much more, two-thirds as much more, three-fourths as much more, four-fifths as much more, five-sixths as much more, and nine sovereigns to boot, I should have exactly £100."

How much had he?

No. XXV.—Making Things Even.

Two children were discussing their pocket-money. "If you were to give me a penny," said Johnny, "I should have twice as much as you." "That would not be a fair division," said Tommy; "you had better give me a penny, and then we shall be just alike."

How much money had each?

No. XXVI.—A Rejected Proposal.

A little later Johnny and Tommy met again. "I have now just twice as much as you have," said Johnny; "but if you were to give me a penny I should have three times as much." "No, thank you," said Tommy; "but give me twopence, and we shall be equal."

How much had each?

No. XXVII.—The Market-woman and her Stock.

A woman selling apples met three boys. The first bought half her stock, and gave her back 10; the second bought a third of what she had then remaining, and gave her back 2; and the third bought half of her then remaining store, and gave her back 1; after which she found that she had 12 apples left.

How many had she at first?

No. XXVIII.—The Captives in the Tower.

An elderly queen, her daughter, and little son, weighing 195 pounds, 105 pounds, and 90 pounds respectively, were kept prisoners at the top of a high tower. The only communication with the ground below was a cord passing over a pulley, with a basket at each end, and so arranged that when one basket rested on the ground the other was opposite the window. Naturally, if the one were more heavily loaded than the other, the heavier would descend; but if the excess on either side was more than 15 pounds, the descent became so rapid as to be dangerous, and from the position of the rope the captives could not check it with their hands. The only thing available to help them in the tower was a cannon-ball, weighing 75 pounds. They, notwithstanding, contrived to escape.

How did they manage it?

No. XXIX.—Father and Son.

A father aged 45 has a son of 12.
How soon will the father be only three times the age of the son?

No. XXX.—A Complicated Transaction.

William gives Thomas as many shillings as Thomas has. Thomas then gives William as many shillings as William has left. This done, William has 36 shillings, and Thomas 42 shillings.
How much had each at first?

No. XXXI.—A Long Family.

A farmer and his wife have fifteen children, born at regular intervals, there being a difference in each case of a year and a half. The eldest is eight times the age of the youngest.
How old must the latter be?

No. XXXII.—A Curious Number.

A certain number is divisible into four parts; in such manner that the first is 500 times, the second 400 times, and the third 40 times as much as the last and smallest part.
What is the number, and what are the several parts?

No. XXXIII.—The Shepherd and his Sheep.

A shepherd was asked how many sheep he had in his flock. He replied that he could not say, but he knew if he counted them by twos, by threes, by fours, by fives, or by sixes, there was always one over; but if he counted them by sevens, there was none over.
What is the smallest number which will answer the above conditions?

No. XXXIV.—A Difficult Problem.

What is the smallest number which, divided by 2, will give a remainder of 1; divided by 3, a remainder of 2; divided by 4, a remainder of 3; divided by 5, a remainder of

4; divided by 6, a remainder of 5; divided by 7, a remainder of 6; divided by 8, a remainder of 7; divided by 9, a remainder of 8; and divided by 10, a remainder of 9.

No. XXXV.—Well Laid Out.

A lad went into a shop to buy drawing materials. He found that pencils cost twopence each, sheets of paper threepence, and drawing-pins a halfpenny, while indiarubber was fourpence. He bought a supply of each, spending two shillings, and found that he had exactly twenty-one articles.

What were they?

No. XXXVI.—The Two Travellers.

A and B are travelling the same road, A going four miles an hour, B five miles an hour. But A has two and a half hours' start.

In what length of time will B overtake A, and how far from the starting-point?

No. XXXVII.—Measuring the Garden.

A garden, oblong in shape, is three times as long as it is wide. If it were a yard more each way, its area would be increased by 149 square yards.

What are its dimensions?

No. XXXVIII.—When Will They get It?

Seven guests at a restaurant came, the first every day, the second every other day, the third every third day, and so on to the seventh, who came once a week only. The host, in a liberal mood, declared that on the first day all came together he would treat them to a dinner gratis.

How soon, according to the above order of rotation, would they be in a position to claim his promise?

No. XXXIX.—Passing the Gate.

It was the rule in a certain continental town that any one passing through either of the four city gates, whether going out or coming in, should pay a penny. A stranger arrived one day at the town, paid his penny and passed through the first gate. He spent in the town one half of the money he had left, and then went out again by the same gate, again paying a penny. The next day he did the like, entering and passing out by the second gate, and meanwhile spending half his available cash in the town. On the following two days he did the same, entering and leaving by the third and fourth gates respectively. When he left the town for the fourth time he had only one penny left.

How much had he at first?

No. XL.—A Novel Magic Square.

Required, to arrange the numbers 1 to 81 in the form of a magic square, in such manner that after removing the outermost rows you still have a magic square, and so on, removing row by row with the same result until only the number occupying the central square remains, which number shall be the greatest common divisor of the sums of the several squares.

No. XLI.—Another Magic Square.

Required, to form with the series of numbers 0, 1, 2, etc., to 63 inclusive, a magic square of 64 places, in such manner that the total of each horizontal or vertical line shall be 252; if the principal square be broken up into four smaller ones of sixteen places each, the total of each horizontal or vertical line shall be 126; and if each of these smaller squares be again broken up into four squares of four places each, the total of the numbers in each such four places shall again be 126.

No. XLII.—The Set of Weights.

With what five weights can a man weigh any quantity (proceeding by steps of half a pound) from half a pound up to 60 lbs.?

No. XLIII.—What Did He Lose?

A man goes into a shop and buys a hat, price one guinea. He offers in payment for it a £5 note. The hatter gets the note cashed by a neighbour, the purchaser pocketing his change, £3 19s., and walking off with the hat. No sooner has he left, however, than the neighbour who changed the note comes in with the news that it is a counterfeit, and the hatter has to refund the value.

How much is the hatter out of pocket by the transaction?

No. XLIV.—A Difficult Division.

A wine merchant has in his cellar 21 casks. Seven are full of wine; seven half-full, and seven empty.

How can he divide them (without transferring any portion of the liquid from cask to cask) among his three sons —Dick, Tom, and Harry—so that each shall have not only an equal quantity of wine, but an equal number of casks?

No. XLV.—The Hundred Bottles of Wine.

An innkeeper sold in eight days 100 bottles of wine, each day overpassing by three bottles the quantity sold on the previous day.

How many did he sell on the first, and on each of the succeeding days?

No. XLVI.—The Last of Her Stock.

An old market woman, finding that she had but a few apples left, divided them among her three grandchildren, as follows: to Willie she gave half her stock and one apple over; to Tommy half what she had then left and one apple over; and to Jennie half what she had still left and one apple over. This done, she had none left.

How many apples did she divide?

No. XLVII.—The Walking Match.

Three persons, A, B, C, D, start from the same point to walk round a circular piece of ground, whose circumference is one mile. A walks five miles an hour, B four miles, C three miles, and D two miles an hour.

How long will it be before all four again meet at the starting-point?

No. XLVIII.—A Feat of Divination.

A couple of dice are thrown. The thrower is invited to double the points of one of the dice (whichever he pleases), add 5 to the result, multiply by 5, and add the points of the second die. He states the total, when any one knowing the secret can instantly name the points of the two dice.

How is it done?

No. XLIX.—A Peculiar Number.

Required, a number of six digits, of such nature that if you transfer the first figure on the right hand (7) to the opposite end of the row, the number as thus altered will be five times the original number; or if you transfer the first figure on the left hand (1) to the opposite end, the resulting number shall be three times the original number. If again you transfer the three first (or three last) figures to the opposite end, the result will represent six times the original number.

No. L.—Another Peculiar Number.

What is the lowest number which, divided by 2, 3, 4, 5, or 6, leaves a remainder of 1, but divided by 11 leaves no remainder?

No. LI.—The Three Legacies.

A gentleman, making his will, left legacies to his three servants, of whom the parlourmaid had been with him three times as long as the housemaid, and the cook twice as long as the parlourmaid. He distributed his gifts in the same proportions; and the total amount given was £70.

What was the amount received by each?

No. LII.—Another Mysterious Multiplicand.

What number of two figures is that which, being multiplied by 3, 6, and 9 respectively, the three products together include every digit from 1 to 9 inclusive, each being only once employed?

No. LIII.—How to Divide Twelve among Thirteen.

A gentleman has a sum of twelve sovereigns to be distributed in charity, a sovereign to each approved candidate. On the day of distribution thirteen claimants appear. The donor has reason to believe that one of them is a less deserving object than the rest, and desires to leave him out, but without showing any apparent favouritism. He directs the claimants to stand in a circle, and announces that every ninth man, as he counts round and round, shall step out of the circle and receive his gift till the fund is exhausted, the last man receiving nothing.

Where must the distributor begin to count, in order to exclude the candidate he desires to reject?

No. LIV.—Tenth Man Out.

A somewhat more difficult puzzle of the same class runs as follows: The crew of a certain ship consisted of fifteen white men and fifteen negroes. A storm arising, it became necessary to take to the boats, but these only afforded room for half the number. It was agreed that all should stand in a circle, and that the captain should count round and round the circle by tens, each tenth man to take his place in the boat till the number of fifteen was reached, the others to take their chance with the ship.

The captain, desiring to favour his own countrymen, so placed the men that the fifteen blacks were all left behind.

How must the circle be arranged to effect this result?

No. LV.—Ninth Man Out.

Given the same conditions, save that every *ninth* man, instead of every tenth, is to go in the boat.

What will then be the arrangement of the circle?

[Puzzles of the kind next immediately following have been popular from very early times, one of the earliest known collections, that of Bachet de Mezeriac, *Recueil de Problèmes plaisants et délectables qui se font par les nombres,* bearing date as far back as 1613. Though not exactly arithmetical, in the ordinary sense, they depend upon arithmetical principles, and are therefore inserted in this chapter.]

No. LVI.—The Three Travellers.

Three travellers, accompanied by their servants, arrive at the bank of a river and desire to cross. The only means of transit is a boat which carries two persons. The travellers have reason to believe that the servants have entered into a conspiracy to rob and murder them, should they be able to get the upper hand. It is therefore essential that a single master should not be left alone with two of the servants, or two masters with all three of the servants.

How can the transit be arranged so as to avoid either of the above conditions?

No. LVII.—The Wolf, the Goat, and the Cabbages.

A boatman has to ferry across a stream a wolf, a goat, and a basket of cabbages. His boat is so small that only one of the three, besides himself, can be contained in it. How is he to manage, so that the wolf shall have no opportunity of killing the goat, or the goat of eating up the cabbages?

No. LVIII.—The Three Jealous Husbands.

Three jealous husbands, travelling with their wives, find it necessary to cross a stream in a boat which only holds two persons. Each of the husbands has a great objection to his wife crossing with either of the other male members of the party unless he himself is also present.

How is the passage to be arranged?

No. LIX.—The Captain and His Company.

The captain of a company of soldiers, in the course of his day's march, comes to a river which must be crossed. The only means of transit is a boat wherein two children are paddling about, and which is so small that it will only hold the two children or one grown person.

How is the transit to be effected?

No. LX.—The Treasure Trove.

An Irishman and a Scotchman, digging together in a field, came upon a number of gold coins. When they were about to divide them, the Scotchman, who was of an avaricious turn, conceived a plan to outwit the Irishman and secure the whole for himself. He therefore proposed to the Irishman that if, without asking any question, he could name the exact number of coins he should take the whole; if he failed, the other should take all. The Irishman readily agreed, and counted the money, taking special care that the Scotchman should not see how much it was. "Now add 666 to it," said the Scotchman. "Done," replied the Irishman. "Now, ye'll maybe subtract the whole amount from 999." "Done again," replied the Irishman; "but the divil a bit are ye nearer!" "Bide a wee," said the Scotchman. "Now jist pit down 333, and tak' awa the last figures from it, and ye'll no be far off the tottle of the bit money." "Mother o' Moses!" exclaimed the Irishman, "somebody must have tould ye;" and the Scotchman walked off with the treasure trove accordingly.

How did the Scotchman get at the right total?

No. LXI.—The Row of Counters.

This is in principle very similar to the last puzzle. In point of fact it is the same thing, though in a different form, and we therefore insert it next in order.

A spectator is invited to place upon the table two rows of counters, unequal in number. The actual numbers are immaterial, but may range, say, from ten to twenty. The person who performs the trick is, meanwhile, blindfolded, so that he can have no knowledge what the numbers are. The person who has laid out the counters is then requested—

1. To subtract the smaller number from the larger, and state the difference. (We will suppose that he states such difference to be 3.)

2. To remove a certain number (say 5) from the smaller row.

3. To subtract the number remaining in the smaller row from the larger row. The number subtracted is to be removed altogether, as also what now remain of the smaller row.

4. The operator, without asking any further question, at once names the number left in the larger row.

How does he ascertain it?

No. LXII.—A Loan and a Present.

This is another puzzle on the same principle. It is usually presented in the shape of a conjuring trick. The operator requests some one to think of a given number of shillings, large or small, as he pleases. He is then in imagination to borrow the same amount from some member of the company, and add it to the original number. "Now please suppose," says the operator, "that I make you a present of fourteen shillings, and add that also. Now give half the total amount to the poor; then return the borrowed money, and tell the company how much you have remaining. I know already what it is; in fact, I hold in my hand the precise amount." "Seven," is the reply. The operator opens his hand and shows that it contains exactly seven shillings.

How is the amount ascertained?

No. LXIII.—Eleven Guests in Ten Beds.

An innkeeper had a sudden influx of guests, eleven arriving in one party, and demanding beds. The host had only ten beds at his disposal, but he, notwithstanding, managed to accommodate them as follows: he put two in the first bed, with the understanding that the second should have a bed to himself after a brief interval; he then put the third in the second bed, the fourth in the third bed, and so on, the tenth being accommodated in the ninth bed. He had thus one bed still left, which the eleventh man, now sleeping double in the first bed, was invited to occupy.

It is clear that there must be a fallacy somewhere, but where does it lie?

No. LXIV.—A Difficult Division.

A and *B* have purchased an eight-gallon cask of wine, and desire to divide it equally; but they have only two measures wherewith to do so—one a five-gallon and the other a three-gallon.

How are they to manage?

No. LXV.—The Three Market-Women.

Three peasant-women went to market to sell apples. The first had 33, the second 29, and the third 27 only. Each of them gave the same number of apples for a penny, and yet, when they got home, they found that each had received an equal amount of money.

How could such a result come to pass?

No. LXVI.—The Farmer and His Three Daughters.

This is a puzzle of the same kind, differing only in the figures.

A farmer sent his three daughters to the market to sell apples. The elder had 50, the second daughter 30, and the younger 10. The farmer jokingly told them all to sell at the same price, and bring home the same amount of money, and, to his surprise, they actually did so.

How did they manage it?

No. LXVII.—How Many for a Penny?

A boy purchased a pennyworth of apples. He gave to a playmate one-third of his store, and one-third of an apple over, after which he had exactly one apple left.

How many did he get for his penny?

No. LXVIII.—The Magic Cards.

These are usually presented as a conjuring trick, but they also form a very effective puzzle, for it is clear that the secret must lie in the cards themselves, and, given sufficient acuteness, must be discoverable.

Prepare seven cards with numbers on them as follows:—

Arithmetical Puzzles.

I.	II.	III.	IV.
1 33 65 97	2 34 66 98	4 36 68 100	8 40 72 104
3 35 67 99	3 35 67 99	5 37 69 101	9 41 73 105
5 37 69 101	6 38 70 102	6 38 70 102	10 42 74 106
7 39 71 103	7 39 71 103	7 39 71 103	11 43 75 107
9 41 73 105	10 42 74 106	12 44 76 108	12 44 76 108
11 43 75 107	11 43 75 107	13 45 77 109	13 45 77 109
13 45 77 109	14 46 78 110	14 46 78 110	13 46 78 110
15 47 79 111	15 47 79 111	15 47 79 111	15 47 79 111
17 49 81 113	18 50 82 114	20 52 84 116	24 56 88 120
19 51 83 115	19 51 83 115	21 53 85 117	25 57 89 121
21 53 85 117	22 54 86 118	22 54 86 118	26 58 90 122
23 55 87 119	23 55 87 119	23 55 87 119	27 59 91 123
25 57 89 121	26 58 90 122	28 60 92 124	28 60 92 124
27 59 91 123	27 59 91 123	29 61 93 125	29 61 93 125
29 61 93 125	30 62 94 126	30 62 94 126	30 62 94 126
31 63 95 127	31 63 95 127	31 63 95 127	31 63 95 127

V.	VI.	VII.
16 48 80 112	32 48 96 112	64 80 96 112
17 49 81 113	33 49 97 113	65 81 97 113
18 50 82 114	34 50 98 114	66 82 98 114
19 51 83 115	35 51 99 115	67 83 99 115
20 52 84 116	36 52 100 116	68 84 100 116
21 53 85 117	37 53 101 117	69 85 101 117
22 54 86 118	38 54 102 118	70 86 102 118
23 55 87 119	39 55 103 119	71 87 103 119
24 56 88 120	40 56 104 120	72 88 104 120
25 57 89 121	41 57 105 121	73 89 105 121
26 58 90 122	42 58 106 122	74 90 106 122
27 59 91 123	43 59 107 123	75 91 107 123
28 60 92 124	44 60 108 124	76 92 108 124
29 61 93 125	45 61 109 125	77 93 109 125
30 62 94 126	46 62 110 126	78 94 110 126
31 63 95 127	47 63 111 127	79 95 111 127

A person is requested to think of any number, from 1 to 127 inclusive, and to state on which one or more of the seven cards it is to be found. Any one knowing the secret can instantly name the chosen number.

How is the number ascertained?

No. LXIX.—The "Fifteen" or "Boss" Puzzle.

This, like a good many of the best puzzles, hails from America, where, some years ago, it had an extraordinary vogue, which a little later spread to this country, the

British public growing nearly as excited over the mystic "Fifteen" as they did at a later date over the less innocent "Missing Word" competitions.

The "Fifteen" Puzzle consists of a little flat wooden or cardboard box, wherein are arranged, in four rows, fifteen little cubical blocks, each bearing a number, from 1 to 15 inclusive. The box being square, would naturally accommodate 16 such cubes,* and there is therefore one space always vacant, and by means of such vacant space, the cubes may be shifted about in the box so as to assume different relative positions.

1	2	3	4
5	6	7	8
9	10	11	12
13	15	14	

FIG. 335.

The ordinary "Fifteen" Puzzle is, having placed the cubes in the box haphazard, so to move them about (without lifting, but merely pushing one after another into the space for the time being vacant) as to bring them into regular order from 1 to 15, leaving the vacant space at the right-hand bottom corner.

In what is known as the "Boss" or Master Puzzle all the blocks are in the first instance placed in regular order, with the exception of those numbered 14 and 15, which are reversed, as in Fig. 335.

---

* As a matter of fact, 16 cubes are usually supplied, the set thereby being made available for the "Thirty-four" Puzzle (referred to at p. 146). When the "Fifteen" Puzzle is attempted, the cube bearing the number 16 is removed from the box.

No. LXX.—The Peg-away Puzzle.

The "Peg-away" Puzzle (Perry & Co.) is a variation or modification of the "Fifteen" Puzzle, the difference being that there are nine instead of sixteen cells, and that eight instead

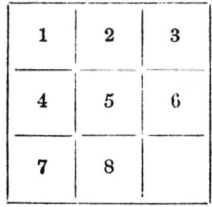

Fig. 336.

of fifteen numbered blocks or "pegs" are used. These being arranged hap-hazard in the cells, the problem is to bring them into consecutive order, as shown in Fig. 336.

No. LXXI.—The Over-Polite Guests.

Seven gentlemen met to dine at a restaurant, when a question arose as to precedence, no one desiring to take what were regarded as the more honourable seats. To settle the matter, one of them proposed that they should dine together every day until they had respectively occupied all possible positions at the table; and the suggestion was accepted.

How often must they dine together to answer the above conditions? *

---

* This problem is sometimes propounded in another shape, as follows: A party of seven students, with more wit than money, agreed with a restaurant-keeper to pay him £10 per head so soon as they should have occupied all possible positions at the table, he undertaking to entertain them daily in the meantime with a dinner costing half a crown per head.

Query, how much the host made or lost by the transaction?

No. LXXII.—The "Royal Aquarium" Thirteen Puzzle.*

This is an adaptation of the "Magic Square" idea, but modified in a very ingenious manner, the ordinary processes for forming a magic square being here quite inapplicable.

The puzzle consists of nine cards, not quite 1½ inch each way, each bearing four numbers, radiating from the centre, after the manner shown in Fig. 337.

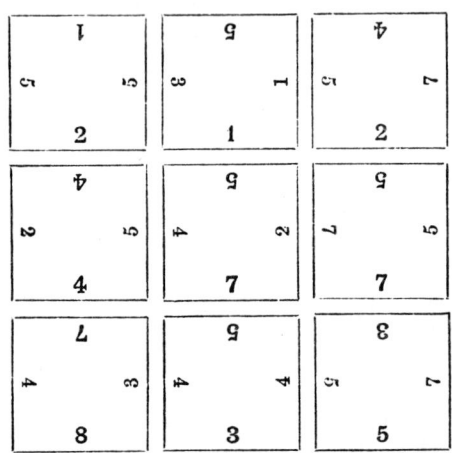

Fig. 337.

The figures shown in heavy type in the diagram are in the original printed in *red*.

The experimenter is required to arrange the nine cards in a square, the red numbers forming perpendicular lines, and the black numbers horizontal lines, the three figures in each line, whether horizontal or perpendicular, making, when added together, 13.

---

* Procurable at the Royal Aquarium, Westminster. Price 1*d*., or by post, with solution, 3*d*.

No. LXXIII.—An Easy Creditor.

A gentleman being in temporary need of money, a friend lent him £60, telling him to repay it in such sums as might suit his convenience. Shortly afterwards he made a payment on account. His second payment was half as much as the first; his third three-quarters as much; his fourth one-quarter as much, and his fifth two-fifths as much. It was then found, on striking a balance, that he still owed £2.

What was the amount of the first payment?

No. LXXIV.—The Three Arabs.

Two Bedouin Arabs halted in the desert to eat their midday meal. Their store consisted of eight small loaves, of which five belonged to the first, and three to the second. Just as they sat down, a third Arab overtook them, and asked to be permitted to share their meal, to which they agreed. Each ate an equal portion of the eight loaves, and the third Arab, at the close of the meal, handed the others eight pieces of money in payment. A dispute arose as to the division of the money, the first Arab maintaining that as he had had five loaves and the other three only, the money should be divided in the same proportion. The other maintained that as all had eaten equally, each should take half the money between them. Finally they agreed to refer the matter to the third Arab, who declared that both were in the wrong, and pointed out the proper division.

What was it?

No. LXXV.—An Eccentric Testator.

An eccentric old gentleman left a will, whereby he bequeathed to his eldest son £110, and one-ninth of what remained; to his second son £220, and one-ninth of what then remained; to his third son £330, and one-ninth of the remainder; and so on, each junior in turn taking £110 more by way of original gift, and one-ninth of the portion still remaining.

The legatees at first complained of so unequal a disposition, but on ascertaining the value of the estate and proceeding to a division, they found, to their surprise, that the division exactly exhausted the estate, and that the share of each was of exactly the same value.

How many legatees were there, and what was the total value of the estate?

No. LXXVI.—Another Eccentric Testator.

A testator, having five sons, left his property as follows: To the eldest one-sixth of the whole, and £240 in addition. To the second one-fifth of the residue, and £288. To the third one-fourth of the then residue, and £360. To the fourth one-third of the then residue and £480. And to the fifth one-half of what still remained, and £720. There was then nothing left.

What was the amount of the property, and what was the share of each son?

No. LXXVII.—An Aggravating Uncle.

An uncle with a turn for figures presented his youthful nephew with a box of soldiers, but made it a condition that he should not play with them till he could discover, on arithmetical principles, how many the box contained. He was told that if he placed them three in a row, there would be one over; if he placed them four in a row, there would be two over; if five in a row, three over; if six in a row, he would have four over. The total number was under 100.

How many soldiers did the box contain?

No. LXXVIII.—Apples and Oranges.

A paterfamilias brought home a quantity of apples and oranges, the same number of each, and distributed them among his children. After each child had received 12 apples there were 48 over, and after each child had received 15 oranges there were 15 over.

How many were there of each kind of fruit, and among how many children were they divided?

No. LXXIX.—The Two Squares.

A certain number of counters, if arranged in rows so as to form a square, leave a remainder of 146 counters unemployed. To enlarge the square by an additional row each way 31 more counters would be required.

What is the number of counters?

No. LXXX.—A Curious Division.

Required, to divide 7890 counters into three heaps, in such proportions that if the first heap be divided by three, the second by six, and the third by nine, the quotient shall in each case be the same number.

No. LXXXI.—A Curious Multiplication.

Required, to divide the same number (7890) of counters into four heaps, in such proportions that if the first be multiplied by three, the second by four, the third by six, and the fourth by twelve, the product shall in each case be the same.

No. LXXXII.—The Two Schoolmasters.

Two country schoolmasters were discussing their respective schools. The first said, "One-sixth of my pupils are away ill, eleven are haymaking, seven are gone to the fair, and I have thirty-seven here at work." The other replied, "You have a pretty large school, but mine is larger than yours, for I have seventy-two pupils."

What was the difference of their numbers?

No. LXXXIII.—Nothing Left.

There is a certain number from which, if you subtract ten, multiply the remainder by three, find the square root of the product, and from such square root subtract eighteen, nothing is left.

What is the number?

No. LXXXIV.—The Three Generations.

An old man was asked how old he was. He replied, "The united ages of my son and myself are 109 years; those of my son and my grandson are 56 years; and my grandson and myself together number 85 years."

How old was each?

No. LXXXV.—The Two Brothers.

"How old is your brother?" a man was asked. "Two-thirds of his age," he replied, "is just five-twelfths of mine, and I am nine years older than he."

What was the age of each?

No. LXXXVI.—The Two Sons.

An elderly mathematician was asked what were the ages of his two sons. He replied, "The one is five and a quarter years older than the other, and six times the age of the elder, added to five times the age of the younger, would be 301."

What was the age of each?

No. LXXXVII.—The Two Nephews.

The same man was asked the ages of his two nephews. "The elder," he replied, "is just three times as old as the younger, and if you add together the squares of their ages, the total will be 360."

What was the age of each?

No. LXXXVIII.—The Reversed Number.

There is a number consisting of two digits; the number itself is equal to five times the sum of its digits, and if nine be added to the number, the position of its digits is reversed.

What is the number?

No. LXXXIX.—Another Reversed Number.

There is another number of two digits, which itself is equal to seven times the sum of its digits. If 18 be subtracted from it, the position of its digits is reversed.

What is the number?

No. XC.—The Shepherd and his Sheep.

A shepherd was asked how many sheep he had. He replied, "I have 100, in five sheep-folds. In the first and second there are altogether 52 sheep; in the second and third, 43; in the third and fourth, 34; and in the fourth and fifth, 30."

How many sheep had he in each fold?

No. XCI.—The Shepherdess and her Sheep.

A shepherdess had the care of a number of sheep, in four different folds. In the second were twice as many as the first, in the third twice as many as the second, and in the fourth twice as many as the third. The total number was 105.

How many sheep were there in each fold?

No. XCII.—A Weighty Matter.

With how many weights, and of what denominations respectively, can you weigh any number of pounds from 1 to 127 inclusive?

No. XCIII.—The Three Topers.

Three topers were discussing how long it would take each of them to drink forty quarts of lager beer. Peter undertook to do it between four in the morning and twelve at night; Paul between ten in the morning and twelve at night; and Roger between two in the afternoon and twelve at night.

Assuming that they could do as they boasted, how long would it take them to get through the same quantity, all drinking simultaneously?

No. XCIV.—The False Scales.

A cheese put into one of the scales of a false balance was found to weigh 16 lbs. When placed in the opposite scale it weighed 9 lbs. only.

What was its actual weight?

No. XCV.—An Arithmetical Policeman.

A belated reveller, hearing the clock strike, but being too obfuscated to be quite sure as to the number of strokes, proceeded to "ask a policeman" what time it was. The policeman replied, "Take half, a third, and a fourth of the hour that has just struck, and the total will be one larger."

What was the hour?

No. XCVI.—The Flock of Geese.

Two friends, passing a woman with a flock of geese, made a wager as to who should guess nearest at their number, without actually counting, one maintaining that there were not more than thirty, the other that there were over forty of them. On asking the market-woman which was right, she replied, "If I had as many more, and one-half as many more, and one-fourth as many more, I should have one short of a hundred. Now puzzle it out for yourselves."

What was the number of the flock?

No. XCVII.—The Divided Cord.

A piece of cord is thirty-six inches in length. Required, so to divide it into two parts that one of them shall be exactly four-fifths the length of the other.

No. XCVIII.—The Divided Number.

Divide the number 46 into two parts in such manner that if the one be divided by 7 and the other by 3, the sum of the quotients shall be 10.

No. XCIX.—The Two Numbers.

There are two numbers, such that twice the first *plus* the second = 17, and twice the second *plus* the first = 19.

Find the numbers.

No. C.—The Horse and Trap.

A man purchased a horse and trap. Five times the price of the horse was just equal to twelve times the price of the trap, and the two together cost £85.

What was the price of each?

No. CI.—The Two Workmen.

A, working 7 hours a day, can do a piece of work in 10 days, and *B*, working 8 hours a day, can do it in 7 days. Supposing both employed together, how many hours a day must they work in order to complete it in 5 days?

No. CII.—Another Divided Number.

Required, to divide the number 237 into three parts, in such manner that 3 times the first shall be equal to 5 times the second and 8 times the third.

No. CIII.—The Three Reapers.

A, *B*, and *C*, working together, can reap a certain field in 5 days. *B*, working alone, would take twice as long as *A* and *C* together; and *C*, working alone, would take three times as long as *A* and *B* together.

How long would each take to do the work separately?

No. CIV.—The Bag of Marbles.

Three boys have a bag of marbles given to them, and it is agreed that they shall be divided in proportion to their ages, which together amount to $17\frac{1}{2}$ years. The bag contains 770 marbles, and as often as Tom takes 4 Jack takes 3, and as often as Tom takes 6 Dick takes 7.

How many marbles will each get, and what are their respective ages?

No. CV.—The Expunged Numerals. A.

Given, the following sum in addition:—

111
777
999
———

Required, to strike out six of these numbers, so that the total of the remaining numbers shall be 20 only.

No. CVI.—The Expunged Numerals.

Given, the sum following:—

111
333
555
777
999
———

Required, to strike out nine of the above figures, so that the total of the remaining figures shall be 1111.

No. CVII.—A Tradesman in a Difficulty.

A man went into a shop in New York and purchased goods to the amount of 34 cents. When he came to pay, he found that he had only a dollar, a three-cent piece, and a two-cent piece. The tradesman had only a half- and a quarter-dollar. A third man, who chanced to be in the shop, was asked if he could assist, but he proved to have only two dimes, a five-cent piece, a two-cent piece, and a one-cent piece.* With this assistance, however, the shopkeeper managed to give change.

How did he do it?

No. CVIII.—Profit and Loss.

A tradesman sells a parcel of soiled goods at a loss for £2 16s. The market price was £3 5s., at which price he would have made three times as much by them as he actually lost.

What did they cost him originally?

No. CIX.—A Curious Fraction.

What like fractions of a pound, of a shilling, and of a penny will, when added together, make exactly a pound?

No. CX.—The Menagerie.

The proprietor of a menagerie was asked how many birds and how many beasts it included. He replied, "Well, the lot have 36 heads and 100 feet."

How many of each were there?

---

* For the assistance of readers who may not be familiar with the American coinage, we may mention that the cent is equivalent to our halfpenny. Of these 100 go to the dollar, which is therefore worth 4s. 2d., while the half and quarter are equivalent to 2s. 1d. and 1s. 0½d. (50 cents and 25 cents) respectively. The dime is the tenth part of a dollar, and is therefore worth 10 cents, or 5d.

No. CXI.—The Market-woman and her Eggs.

A market-woman, selling eggs, sold to her first customer the half of her stock and half an egg over. To her second customer she sold one-half of the remainder and half an egg over. To a third customer she sold half her yet remaining stock and half an egg over, when she found that she had none left.

How many eggs had she originally?

No. CXII.—The Cook and his Assistants.

This is a problem of the same kind, differing only in the figures. A cook distributes eggs to his three assistants, to the first one-half and half an egg over, to the second one-half of the remainder and half an egg over, and to the third one-half of what still remains and half an egg over. He has still four eggs left.

How many had he at first?

KEY TO CHAPTER IV.

ARITHMETICAL PUZZLES.

The solution of problems of this class is greatly facilitated by an elementary knowledge of the Properties of Numbers. We append, therefore, a statement of some of such properties, not limited to the particular examples we have given (the majority of which depend upon much simpler considerations), but of general utility in relation to such problems. We offer in each case a brief demonstration of the fact stated, though for the purpose of the present work it will be quite sufficient if the reader is content to accept the propositions laid down without demanding mathematical proof of their accuracy.

Elementary Properties of Numbers.

Proposition 1.—*The sum or difference of two even numbers is always an even number.*

> Proof.—This becomes self-evident if the proposition be expressed in algebraic form. Thus—
> Let $2x =$ the larger number,
> and $2y =$ the smaller number.
> Then their sum will be $2x + 2y$,
> and their difference will be $2x - 2y$;
> each of which is obviously divisible by 2, without fraction or remainder—*i.e.*, an even number.

Prop. 2.—*The sum or difference of two odd numbers is always an even number.*

> Proof.—Let $2x + 1 =$ the larger number,
> and $2y + 1 =$ the smaller number.
> Then their sum will be $2x + 2y + 2$;
> and their difference $2x - 2y$;
> each of which is obviously divisible by 2: *i.e.*, an even number.

PROP. 3.—*The sum of an even and an odd number is always an odd number.*

PROOF.—Let $2x$ = the even number,
and $2y + 1$ = the odd number.
Then their sum will be $2x + 2y + 1$, which is obviously *not* divisible by 2 without a fraction or remainder—*i.e.*, is an odd number.

PROP. 4.—*The difference of an even and an odd number is always an odd number.*

PROOF.—Here there are two possible cases to be considered, as the odd or the even number may be the larger. In the first case—
Let $2x + 1$ = the larger number,
and $2y$ = the smaller number.
Here their difference will be represented by $2x + 1 - 2y$, which is obviously an odd number.

In the second case—
Let $2x$ = the larger number,
and $2y + 1$ = the smaller number.
Then their difference will be represented by $2x - 2y - 1$, which is obviously an odd number.

PROP. 5.—*If the sum of two numbers be an even number, then their difference is also an even number.*

PROOF.—This follows from preceding propositions. The sum of the two numbers being, *ex hypothesi*, even, the numbers themselves must either (by Props. 1, 2, 3) be both even or both odd; and if so, their difference (by Props. 1, 2) must be even.

PROP. 6.—*If the sum of two numbers be an odd number, then their difference is also an odd number.*

PROOF.—This follows from Props. 3 and 4. The sum of the two numbers being odd, the numbers themselves must (by Prop. 3) be one odd, and one even, in which case their difference (by Prop. 4) will be odd.

PROP. 7.—*For a number to be divisible by 2, its last digit must be* EVEN.

PROOF.—(Self-evident. *All odd numbers divided by 2 leave a remainder of 1.*)

Prop. 8.—*If a number to be divisible by 3, the sum of its digits will also be divisible by 3.*

Proof.—Let a represent the units, b the tens, c the hundreds, d the thousands, and so on. Then the whole number may be expressed in the form of a sum in addition, as follows:

```
         a
        b 0
       c 0 0
      d 0 0 0
      ─────────
.....  d c b a
```

Now $b\,0\ =b\,10\ =b\,(9\ +1)=b\,9\ +b$
and $c\,00\ =c\,100\ =c\,(99\ +1)=c\,99\ +c$
and $d\,000=d\,1000=d\,(999+1)=d\,999+d$.

The whole number is therefore equal to

$$a$$
$$b\,9+b$$
$$c\,99+c$$
$$d\,999+d$$

And as $b9+c99+d999$ is obviously divisible by 3, it follows that, to make the whole number exactly divisible by 3, $a+b+c+d$ (the sum of its digits), must be divisible by 3 in like manner.

Prop. 9.—*Any number, less the sum of its digits, is divisible by 3.*

Proof. — This is incidentally proved in the course of the demonstration of Prop. 8, where we have seen that any number may be thrown into the form $b\,9+c\,99+d\,999+a+b+c+d$. Deducting from this $a+b+c+d$, representing the sum of the digits of the original number, it is clear that the remainder is a multiple of, and therefore divisible by, 3.

Prop. 10.—*Any number, to be exactly divisible by 4, must have the number formed by its last two digits divisible by 4.*

Proof.—Any number of more than two digits consists of so many hundreds as may be expressed by the preceding digits, *plus* the number expressed by the last two digits. (Thus 532 is equivalent to 500+32; 1429 to 1400+29, and so on). Each hundred, being a multiple of 4, is necessarily divisible by that number. If, therefore, the remaining digits (the last two) are divisible by 4, the whole number must be so divisible.

PROP. 11.—*For a number to be divisible by 5, it must have either 5 or 0 for its units digit.*

PROOF.—When any given number is divided by 5, the only possible remainder is 0, 1, 2, 3, or 4. Whichever of such remainders be left over from the division up to the *tens* place, it is clear that there must be a 0 or a 5 in the units place to enable the division to be completed without remainder.

PROP. 12.—*For a number to be divisible by 6, it must be an even number, and the sum of its digits must be divisible by 3.*

PROOF.—As $6 = 2 \times 3$, the divisibility of a given number by 6 depends upon its divisibility by 2 and 3; for the tests of which divisibility see Props. 7 and 8.

PROP. 13.—(There is no general criterion as to divisibility by 7.*)

PROP. 14.—*For a number to be evenly divisible by 8, its last three digits must be divisible by 8.*

PROOF.—The proof here follows the same line of argument as that of Prop. 10. Any number of more than three digits consists of a given number of *thousands*, *plus* the number expressed by the last three digits. Each thousand, being a multiple of 8, is necessarily divisible by 8, and if therefore the number represented by the remaining three digits is divisible by 8, the whole number will be so divisible.

---

* It should, however, be noted that *every cube number* is either exactly divisible by 7, or may be made so by adding or subtracting 1 to or from it.

Prop. 15.—*For a number to be evenly divisible by 9, the sum of its digits must be evenly divisible by 9.*

Proof.— See the proof of Prop. 8, where it is shown that any given number can be expressed in the form $d\ 999 + c\ 99 + b\ 9 + a + b + c + d$. The portion $d\ 999 + c\ 99 + b\ 9$ being obviously divisible by 9, it follows that to make the whole sum divisible by 9, the remaining portion of the number, $a + b + c + d$ (representing the sum of its digits), must also be divisible by 9.

Prop. 16.—*For a number to be divisible by 10, its last digit must be 0.*

Proof.— This proposition is practically self-evident. Any given number represents so many tens *plus* the number of units expressed by the last digit. If such last digit be 1, 2, 3, 4, 5, 6, 7, 8, or 9 (*i.e.*, any number save 0), it will represent a remainder of that amount, and the whole number cannot be divided evenly by 10.

Prop. 17.—*The product of any two consecutive numbers (as 4 and 5, 14 and 15, or 26 and 27) is always divisible by 2.*

Proof.—Of any two consecutive numbers one must be an even number, and therefore a multiple of 2. By whatever other number it may be multiplied, the product will therefore also be divisible by 2.

Prop. 18.—*The product of any three consecutive numbers is always divisible by 6.*

Proof.—This is demonstrable in like manner, for of three consecutive numbers one must be a multiple of 3, and one of 2*; and if a number is divisible by 3 and by 2, it is also divisible by 6.

Prop. 19.—*The product of any four consecutive numbers is always divisible by 24; of any five, by 120, and so on (the new divisor in each case being obtained by multiplying the last divisor by the number of consecutive figures).*

Proof.—The proof is a mere extension of that of Prop. 18.

---

* Both characters may be united in the intermediate number, as in the case of 11, 12, 13; 23, 24, 25.

Prop. 20.—*The difference between the squares of two numbers is equal to the product of their sum and difference.*

$$e.g., \; 5^2 - 3^2 = 25 - 9 = 16$$
$$(5+3) \times (5-3) = 8 \times 2 = 16.$$

Proof.—This is but a re-statement of the well-known algebraical formula—
$$x^2 - y^2 = (x+y)(x-y).$$

But it may be made equally clear without recourse to algebra, thus:—

Take any two numbers—say 5 and 3.

$(5-3)$ multiplied by $(5+3)$ means $(5-3)$ multiplied by 5 and (added on to this) $(5-3)$ multiplied by 3.

Now $(5-3)$ multiplied by 5 gives $5^2 - (5 \times 3)$
and $(5-3)$,, ,, 3 ,, $(5 \times 3) - 3^2$.

Adding the two results together,
$$(5-3) \text{ multiplied by } (5+3) = 5^2 - 3^2.$$

And this holds with any numbers, so that generally $n^2 - m^2 = (n+m) \times (n-m)$.

Prop. 21.—*The difference between the squares of any two numbers is always divisible by the difference of the two numbers. It is also divisible by the sum of the two numbers.*

Proof.—This is a necessary consequence of the preceding proposition.

Prop. 22.—*The difference of the squares of any two odd numbers is always divisible by 8.*

Proof.—Suppose $(2x+1)$ and $(2y+1)$ to be the two odd numbers.

Then (by Prop. 20) the difference of their squares equals the product of their sum and difference: *i.e.* $(2x+1)^2 - (2y+1)^2 = \{(2x+1) + (2y+1)\} \times \{(2x+1) - (2y+1)\}$
$$= \{2x+2y+2\}\{2x-2y\}$$
$$= 4\{x+y+1\}\{x-y\}$$

Now if x and y are both odd or both even, then (by Prop. 1) $(x-y)$ is even, in which case $4(x+y+1)(x-y)$ is divisible by 4 and further by 2; that is to say, by 8.

But if x and y are unlike,—that is to say one odd and the other even,—then $x+y$ is odd, and

180 *Puzzles Old and New.*

therefore $(x+y+1)$ is even; in which case $4(x+y+1)(x-y)$ is again divisible by 4 and further by 2; that is to say, by 8.

Wherefore $(2x+1)^2 - (2y+1)^2$ is divisible by 8.

PROP. 23.—*The difference between a number and its cube is the product of three consecutive numbers, and is consequently divisible by 6.*

Suppose n^3 and n to be the cube and the number; then difference between them is $n^3 - n$. This evidently $= n(n^2 - 1)$.

But looking upon 1 as a square number (the square of unity) we have $(n^2 - 1) = (n - 1) \times (n + 1)$, as in Prop. 20.

So that $n^3 - n = n(n-1)(n+1)$.

But $(n-1)$, n, and $(n+1)$ are obviously three consecutive numbers, and therefore (by Prop. 18) divisible by 6.

PROP. 24.—*Any prime number which, divided by 4, leaves a remainder 1 is the sum of two square numbers.*

The mathematical proof of the universal truth of this proposition is very complicated, and would be beyond the scope of a work like the present. We subjoin a list of all such numbers below 400, and from the evident truth of the theorem in this large number of cases the reader may be content to infer its general accuracy.

LIST OF ALL PRIME NUMBERS BELOW 400 WHICH, BEING DIVIDED BY 4, LEAVE A REMAINDER OF 1.

$5 = 4 + 1 = 2^2 + 1^2$
$13 = 9 + 4 = 3^2 + 2^2$
$17 = 16 + 1 = 4^2 + 1^2$
$29 = 25 + 4 = 5^2 + 2^2$
$37 = 36 + 1 = 6^2 + 1^2$
$41 = 25 + 16 = 5^2 + 4^2$
$53 = 49 + 4 = 7^2 + 2^2$
$61 = 36 + 25 = 6^2 + 5^2$
$73 = 64 + 9 = 8^2 + 3^2$
$89 = 64 + 25 = 8^2 + 5^2$
$97 = 81 + 16 = 9^2 + 4^2$
$101 = 100 + 1 = 10^2 + 1^2$
$109 = 100 + 9 = 10^2 + 3^2$
$113 = 64 + 49 = 8^2 + 7^2$
$137 = 121 + 16 = 11^2 + 4^2$
$149 = 100 + 49 = 10^2 + 7^2$
$157 = 121 + 36 = 11^2 + 6^2$
$173 = 169 + 4 = 13^2 + 2^2$
$181 = 100 + 81 = 10^2 + 9^2$
$193 = 144 + 49 = 12^2 + 7^2$
$197 = 196 + 1 = 14^2 + 1^2$
$229 = 225 + 4 = 15^2 + 2^2$
$233 = 169 + 64 = 13^2 + 8^2$
$241 = 225 + 16 = 15^2 + 4^2$
$257 = 256 + 1 = 16^2 + 1^2$
$269 = 169 + 100 = 13^2 + 10^2$

Key to Arithmetical Puzzles.   181

$$277 = 196 + 81 = 14^2 + 9^2$$
$$281 = 256 + 25 = 16^2 + 5^2$$
$$293 = 289 + 4 = 17^2 + 2^2$$
$$313 = 169 + 144 = 13^2 + 12^2$$
$$317 = 196 + 121 = 14^2 + 11^2$$
$$337 = 256 + 81 = 16^2 + 9^2$$

$$349 = 324 + 25 = 18^2 + 5^2$$
$$353 = 289 + 64 = 17^2 + 8^2$$
$$373 = 324 + 49 = 18^2 + 7^2$$
$$389 = 289 + 100 = 17^2 + 10^2$$
$$397 = 361 + 36 = 19^2 + 6^2$$

With this brief introduction we proceed to give the solutions of the various puzzles propounded in the preceding pages.

It is generally very much more easy to solve puzzles of this class by the aid of algebra, and in some instances we have exhibited the solution in this form. But this is scarcely regarded as a legitimate method of solving an arithmetical puzzle, and where the reader can solve such a puzzle by step-by-step argument, without the use of algebraic symbols, he may consider that he has attained a considerably higher measure of success. Even if algebra be used in the first place, the problem should, if possible, be worked out arithmetically afterwards.

No. I.—The Forty-five Puzzle. Solution.

The first of the required numbers is 8.
$$8 + 2 = 10$$
The second is 12.
$$12 - 2 = 10$$
The third is 5.
$$5 \times 2 = 10$$
The fourth is 20.
$$20 \div 2 = 10$$

$$8 + 12 + 5 + 20 = 45.$$

No. II.—A Singular Subtraction. Solution.

This is somewhat of a quibble. The number 45 is the sum of the digits 1, 2, 3, 4, 5, 6, 7, 8, 9. The puzzle is solved by arranging these in reverse order, and subtracting the original series from them, when the remainder will be found to consist of the same digits in a different order, and therefore making the same total—viz., 45.

$$987654321 = 45$$
$$123456789 = 45$$
$$\overline{864197532} = 45$$

No. III.—A Mysterious Multiplicand. Solution.

The number 37 will be found to answer the conditions of the problem. Multiplied by 3, it is 111; by 6, 222; by 9, 333; by 12, 444; by 15, 555; by 18, 666; by 21, 777; by 24, 888; and by 27, 999.

No. IV.—Counting the Pigs. Solution.

Answer.—He had ten.

PROOF: $10 + 10 + 5 + 7 = 32$.

No. V.—Another Pig Problem. Solution.

He had seven.

PROOF: $7 + 7 + 3\frac{1}{2} + 2\frac{1}{2} = 20$.

No. VI.—A Little Miscalculation. Solution.

By the time she has sold 20 lots at 10 for twopence (four of the one kind and six of the other), the 120 cheaper apples are exhausted, while she has only sold 80 of the dearer. So far, she has neither gained nor lost, but she has still on hand 40 of the dearer apples, worth, at cost price, tenpence. By selling these at 10 for twopence she only gets eightpence, leaving a deficit of twopence.

No. VII.—A Simple Magic Square. Solution.

The arrangement depicted in Fig. 328 answers the conditions of the problem, the total being 15 in each direction.

Key to Arithmetical Puzzles. 183

No. VIII.—The Thirty-four Puzzle. Solution.

It is computed that no less than 3456 arrangements of the sixteen figures will answer the required conditions. Whether this total be exact we will not undertake to decide,

2	9	4
7	5	3
6	1	8

Fig. 338.

but it is certain that such arrangements may be numbered by some hundreds. The fact that, with so many possible solutions, they were not oftener hit upon by the hundreds of thousands who, during its temporary "boom," racked their brains over the "Thirty-four" Puzzle arises from the fact that, numerous as they are, they are but as a drop in the ocean compared with the number of combinations (amounting to over twenty billions) of which sixteen given articles are capable.

We append, by way of specimens, a few of the possible solutions (Figs. 339-344).

1	15	14	4
12	6	7	9
8	10	11	5
13	3	2	16

Fig. 339.

1	14	15	4
8	11	10	5
12	7	6	9
13	2	3	16

Fig. 340.

1	12	6	15
13	8	10	3
16	5	11	2
4	9	7	14

Fig. 341.

1	8	15	10
14	11	4	5
12	13	6	3
7	2	9	16

Fig. 342.

1	7	16	10
12	14	5	3
6	4	11	13
15	9	2	8

Fig. 343.

1	11	6	16
8	14	3	9
15	5	12	2
10	4	13	7

Fig. 344.

In each of these cases the number 34 can be counted in ten different directions—viz., four horizontal, four perpendicular, and two diagonal. The simplest method of constructing such squares is as follows:—First arrange the figures (which may be any series in arithmetical progression) in the form of a square in their natural order, as, for example, the series shown in Fig. 345. Regard this as *two* squares, one within the other, as indicated by the heavy black lines. Now re-arrange the series, reversing the diagonals of each such square, when the figures will be as in Fig. 346, counting 46 in each of the directions above-mentioned.

By marshalling, in the first instance, the figures in vertical instead of horizontal rows, the resulting arrangement will be slightly different, but yet producing the same totals (see Figs. 347 and 348).

Key to Arithmetical Puzzles.

4	5	6	7
8	9	10	11
12	13	14	15
16	17	18	19

FIG. 345.

19	5	6	16
8	14	13	11
12	10	9	15
7	17	18	4

FIG. 346.

4	8	12	16
5	9	13	17
6	10	14	18
7	11	15	19

FIG. 347.

19	8	12	7
5	14	10	17
6	13	9	18
16	11	15	4

FIG. 348.

Magic squares may, however, be so arranged as to produce the same total in a far greater number of ways. The

1	15	10	8
12	6	3	13
7	9	16	2
14	4	5	11

FIG. 349.

American "34" Puzzle required that the total in question (34) should be produced in twenty different directions.

The problem in such a shape is beyond the scope of any but skilled mathematicians; but our readers may be interested to know that such a result has not only been achieved, but even surpassed, as in the arrangement given in Fig. 349, where 34 is obtained in no less than 24 different ways.

34 may here be counted—

Horizontally	4 ways.
Perpendicularly	4 ,,
Diagonally	2 ,,
The four corner squares (1, 8, 14, 11)	1 ,,
The four centre squares (6, 3, 9, 16)	1 ,,
The four corner groups of 4 squares, each 1, 15, 12, 6; 10, 8, 3, 13; 7, 9, 14, 4; and 16, 2, 5, 11	4 ,,
The four groups of 4 forming the centre of each side—15. 10, 6, 3; 12, 6, 7, 9; 3, 13, 16, 2; and 9, 16, 4, 5	4 ,,
TOTAL	20 ways.

These are the twenty totals required by the conditions of the American puzzle. But there are yet four other ways in which 34 can be made—viz., by means of adding together the groups on opposite sides of the "octagon"—15, 10, 4, 5; 10, 13, 7, 4; 13, 2, 12, 7; and 12, 15, 5, 2, making in all twenty-four.

Any reader caring to follow the subject further will find much interesting matter in relation to it in a little penny pamphlet published by Heywood of Manchester, entitled *The Curiosities of the Thirty-four Puzzle*, and giving no less than 150 solutions of the problem, with instructions for obtaining the whole number of which it is capable.

No. IX.—The Sixty-Five Puzzle. Solution.

The arrangement shown in Fig. 350 answers the conditions of the problem, the total being 65 in each direction.

We have given in the last answer the method of forming the simpler magic squares where they consist of an even number of cells. Where the square consists of an odd number of cells, another method is employed. We will take,

Key to Arithmetical Puzzles.

in the first place, the simplest possible example: a square of nine cells, and an arithmetical series * rising by 1 only, say the numbers 3 to 11 inclusive.

3	20	7	24	11
16	8	25	12	4
9	21	13	5	17
22	14	1	18	10
15	2	19	6	23

Fig. 350.

Having drawn a square of the required number of cells, add an additional cell on either side, contiguous to the centre square on that side. It will be seen that this gives three parallel diagonals, of three squares each, in four different directions. Arrange your series of numbers in

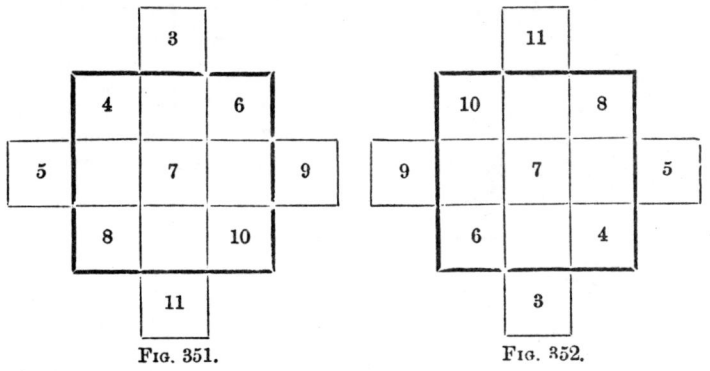

Fig. 351.   Fig. 352.

---

* It was formerly believed that *only* series of figures in arithmetical progression were capable of being formed into magic squares; but this belief has long since been shown to be unfounded.

Fig. 353.

Fig. 354.

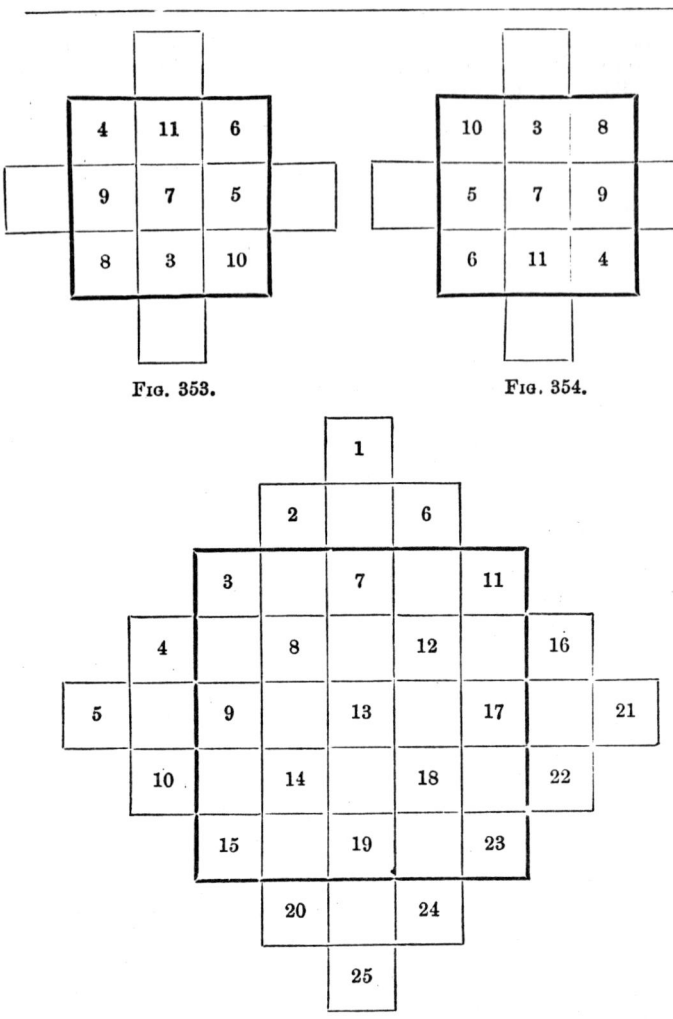

Fig. 355.

consecutive order in either set of parallels, say as in Fig. 351 or as in Fig. 352. Then transfer the number in each external cell to the vacant cell on the opposite side of the square. The respective results will be as shown in Figs. 353 and 354 respectively, either of which will answer the required conditions, giving a total of 21 each way.

With a larger number of cells the process is a little more elaborate, but the principle is the same. Thus, suppose it be required to form a magic square of 25 cells with the numbers 1 to 25 inclusive. We now add extra cells so as to

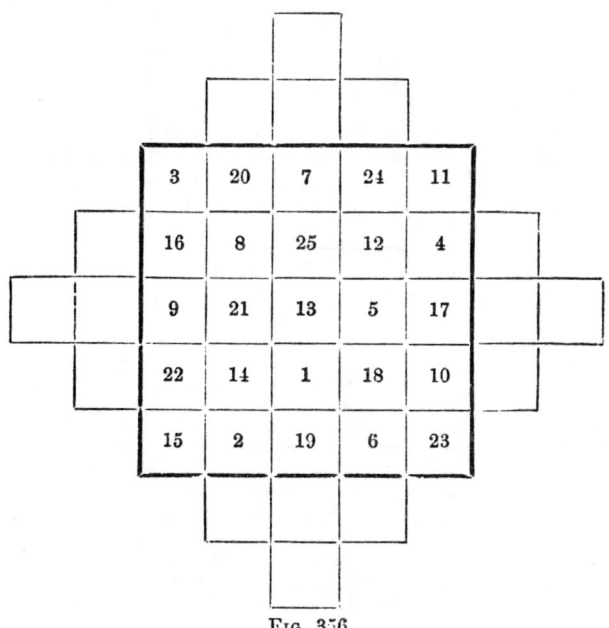

Fig. 356.

form *five* parallel diagonals, as in Fig. 355. Proceeding as before, we arrange the series as shown in the same figure, and then transposing each of the outlying numbers to the vacant square on the opposite side, we have the result shown in Fig. 356, giving a total of 65 each way.

It is to be observed that we have in each case moved the outlying number *five* places onwards, *i.e.* the exact length of one side of the square. Bearing this fact in mind, it becomes

Puzzles Old and New.

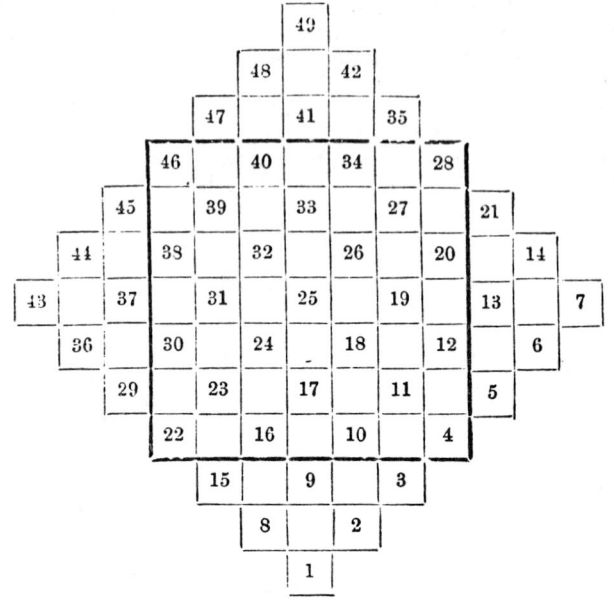

Fig. 357.

Fig. 358.

equally easy to deal with squares of a still larger number of cells (provided always that they consist of an odd

number). Nos. 357 and 358 illustrate the same process as applied to the numbers 1 to 49, arranged to form a magic square of 49 cells, with a total in each direction of 175. (We have in this case started from the bottom, and worked upwards from left to right.) The square in this case having seven cells on a side, each of the outlying figures is moved forward *seven* places, with the result shown in Fig. 358.*

No. X.—The Twenty-Six Puzzle. Solution.

We append, in Figs. 359, 360, two solutions, or varia-

	1	4	
11	6	7	2
8	10	3	5
	9	12	

Fig. 359.

	12	9	
2	7	6	11
5	3	10	8
	4	1	

Fig. 360.

tions of the same solution. It is not impossible that there are many others which would equally answer the conditions of the problem.

No. XI.—An Unmanageable Legacy. Solution.

The lawyer had a horse of his own, which he drove into the stable with the rest. "Now," he said to John, "take your half." John took nine horses accordingly. James and William were then invited to take their shares, which they did, receiving six and two horses respectively. This division exactly disposed of the seventeen horses of the testator; and the lawyer, pocketing his fee, drove his own steed home again.

N.B.—The above solution rests on the fact that the sum of

---

* Further information on the subject of Magic Squares will be found in *Hutton's Mathematical Recreations*, and in the *Encyclopédie des Jeux* of M. de Moulidars, p. 430.

the three fractions named, $\frac{1}{2}$, $\frac{1}{3}$, and $\frac{1}{9}$, when reduced to a common denominator, will be found not to amount to unity, but only to $\frac{17}{18}$. The addition of another horse ($=\frac{1}{18}$) bringing the total number up to eighteen, renders it divisible by such common denominator, and enables each to get his proper share, the lawyer then resuming his own $\frac{1}{18}$, which he had lent for the purpose of the division.

In the administration of the Mahomedan Law of Inheritance, which involves numerous and complicated fractions, this expedient is frequently employed.

No. XII.—Many Figures, but a Small Result. Solution.

$\frac{35}{70} + \frac{148}{296}$.

(Reducing each fraction to its lowest denominator, it will be found to be equal to $\frac{1}{2}$, and $\frac{1}{2} + \frac{1}{2} = 1$.)

No. XIII.—Can You Name it? Solution.

Answer, 20.
$50 - 20 = 30$. $80 - 50 = 30$.

No. XIV.—Squares, Product, and Difference. Solution.

Answer, 11 and 15.

Their product is 165, and their difference 4. The former exceeds the latter by 161. The sum of their squares is 346, and $346 - 165 = 181$.

No. XV.—A Peculiar Number. Solution.

The required number is 285714, which, multiplied by 2, becomes 571428.

From the conditions of the question, it is clear that the required number must begin with 28, and end with 14 (one half of 28). As it has six digits, it must therefore take the form 28 . . 14, the two intermediate digits being unknown. It is equally clear that the double number must end with 1428, the last two figures being affixed to the final 14 of the original number. Again, it must begin with either 56 or 57, for any higher number divided by 2 would have a larger quotient than 28, and therefore is by the terms of the problem inadmissible. This gives us as the double number either 561428 or 571428.

Key to Arithmetical Puzzles.

Dividing each by 2, we have 280714 and 285714, the second of which is found to answer the required conditions.*

No. XVI.—A Novel Century. Solution.

$9 \times 8 + 7 + 6 + 5 + 4 + 3 + 2 + 1 = 100.$

No. XVII.—Another Century. Solution.

There are several ways of fulfilling the conditions of the puzzle. The first takes the form of a sum in addition:

```
   15
   36
   47
  ---
   98
    2
  ---
  100
```

Other solutions are as follow:

$1\frac{3}{6} + 98\frac{27}{54} + 0 = 100.$ $\qquad 80\frac{27}{54} + 19\frac{3}{6} = 100.$

$70 + 24\frac{9}{18} + 5\frac{3}{6} = 100.$ $\qquad 87 + 9\frac{4}{5} + 3\frac{12}{60} = 100.$

No. XVIII.—Another Way to Make 100. Solution.

$99\frac{99}{99}.$

No. XIX.—The Lucky Number. Solution.

Multiply the selected number by *nine*, and use the product as the multiplier for the larger number. It will be found that the results will be respectively as under:—

```
12345679 ×  9 = 111 111 111
    ,,   × 18 = 222 222 222
    ,,   × 27 = 333 333 333
    ,,   × 36 = 444 444 444
    ,,   × 45 = 555 555 555
    ,,   × 54 = 666 666 666
    ,,   × 63 = 777 777 777
    ,,   × 72 = 888 888 888
    ,,   × 81 = 999 999 999
```

It will be observed that the result is in each case the "lucky" number, nine times repeated.

---

* See also Puzzle No. XLV.

No. XX.—The Two Ages. Solution.

The father was three times the age of his son $15\frac{1}{2}$ years earlier, being then fifty-five and a half, while his son was eighteen and a half. The son will have reached half his father's age in three years' time, being then thirty-seven, while his father will be seventy-four.

No. XXI.—The Graces and the Muses. Solution.

The number each Grace had originally was 36, for—

She gave to each Muse $\frac{1}{18}$ of her store: *i.e.*, to the nine $\frac{9}{18} = \frac{1}{2}$, leaving $\frac{1}{2}$ still in her own possession; and each Muse receiving $\frac{1}{18}$ from each Grace, had in all $\frac{3}{18} = \frac{1}{6}$.

But the $\frac{1}{2}$ left to each Grace exceeded the $\frac{1}{6}$ held by each Muse by 12, and if $\frac{1}{2} - \frac{1}{6} (= \frac{1}{3})$ be 12, the whole number must have been 36.

No. XXII.—The Graces and the Muses again. Solution.

Twelve, or any multiple of twelve, will answer the conditions of the puzzle. Assuming the number to be twelve, each Grace gives one rose to each Muse. Each Muse will thus have three (one received from each Grace), while the Graces have each three roses left.

No. XXIII.—Just One Over. Solution.

61, being the least common multiple of 2, 3, 4, 5, and 6 (60) + 1.

No. XXIV.—Scarcely Explicit. Solution.

He had £20, as may be seen by the following demonstration:—

Let x be the number of pounds in his pocket. Then, according to the conditions of the puzzle,

$$x + \tfrac{1}{2}x + \tfrac{2}{3}x + \tfrac{3}{4}x + \tfrac{4}{5}x + \tfrac{5}{6}x + 9 = 100$$

Reducing the fractions to a common denominator:

$$x + \left(\frac{30 + 40 + 45 + 48 + 50}{60}\right)x = 100 - 9$$

i.e.
$$x + \frac{213x}{60}\left(= x + \frac{71}{20}x\right) = 91$$

$$\frac{20x + 71x}{20} = 91$$

$$\frac{91x}{20} = 91$$

$$\frac{x}{20} = 1$$

$$x = 20$$

No. XXV.—Making Things Even. Solution.

Johnny had sevenpence, and Tommy fivepence.

No. XXVI.—A Rejected Proposal. Solution.

Johnny had eightpence, and Tommy fourpence.

No. XXVII.—The Market Woman and her Stock. Solution.

Her original stock was 40 apples. Her first customer, buying half her stock, and giving back 10, left her with 30; the second, buying one-third of 30, and giving her back 2, left her with 22; and the third, buying half of these, and giving her back 1, left her with 12.

To solve the problem, however, it is necessary (unless algebra be used) to work the process backwards. Take away 1 (given back by the last boy) from her ultimate remainder, 12, thus leaving 11. It is clear that as he purchased half her stock, she must before he did so have had 22 apples. Of these, 2 had been given back to her by the second boy, so that prior to his so doing she must have had 20. As he bought one-third of her stock, the number previous to his purchase must have been 30. Of these 30, 10 were given back to her by the first boy, prior to which she must have had 20; and as this 20 represents half her original stock (for the first boy bought the other half), she must at the outset have had 40.

No. XXVIII.—The Captives in the Tower. Solution.

The boy descended first, using the cannon-ball as a counterpoise. The queen and her daughter then took the cannon-ball out of the upper basket, and the daughter descended, the boy acting as counterpoise. The cannon-ball was then allowed to run down alone. When it reached the ground, the daughter got into the basket along with the cannon-ball, and their joint weight acted as counterpoise while the queen descended. The princess got out, and the cannon-ball was sent down alone. The boy then went down, the cannon-ball ascending. The daughter removed the cannon-ball and went down alone, her brother ascending. The latter then put the cannon-ball in the opposite basket, and lowered himself to the ground.

No. XXIX.—Father and Son. Solution.

In four years and a half, when the son will be sixteen and a half, the father forty-nine and a half. When the son reaches 16, the father will be 49—*i.e.*, still a little more than three times the son's age. But when the son reaches 17, his father will be 50, which is not quite three times 17. It is, therefore, clear that the required age is between those two points, and a little reflection will show that only the ages stated exactly answer the conditions of the problem.

No. XXX.—A Complicated Transaction. Solution.

William had 48 shillings, and Thomas 30.

The arithmetical solution of this question is somewhat intricate, but by the algebraic method it is simple enough.

Thus: Let w = William's number,
and t = Thomas' number.

Then the state of William's finances at the close of the transaction will be represented by $w - t + (w - t)$, and by the terms of the question this $= 36$. We also have it stated in the question that the joint finances $w + t = 36 + 42 = 78$, so that $w = 78 - t$.

Reducing the first equation to simpler form, we have
$$2w - 2t = 36$$
$$\text{or } w - t = 18$$
$$\text{and } w = 18 + t$$

Comparing the values of w thus ascertained, we have
$$18 + t = 78 - t$$
$$2t = 78 - 18 = 60$$
$$\therefore t = 30$$
and w being $= 18 + t = 18 + 30 = 48$.

No. XXXI.—A Long Family. Solution.

Their respective ages are as follows: the youngest 3, and the eldest 24.

Here again the assistance of algebra is needed for a ready solution.

Let $x =$ the age of the youngest (fifteenth). Then $8x =$ the age of the eldest.

And by the terms of the question—
$8x = (x + 1\frac{1}{2} + 1\frac{1}{2} + 1\frac{1}{2} + 1\frac{1}{2} + 1\frac{1}{2} + 1\frac{1}{2} + 1\frac{1}{2} + 1\frac{1}{2} + 1\frac{1}{2} + 1\frac{1}{2} + 1\frac{1}{2} + 1\frac{1}{2} + 1\frac{1}{2} + 1\frac{1}{2} = x + 21$.
i.e. $7x = 21$.
$\therefore x = 3$: the age of the youngest,
and $8x = 24$: the age of the eldest.

No. XXXII.—A Curious Number. Solution.

This problem seems at first sight somewhat formidable, but it is in reality very easy.

It is susceptible of various answers, equally correct, according to the value assigned to the smallest part, or unit of measurement. Thus, if such smallest part be 1, the number will be
$$1 + 40 + 400 + 500 = 941$$

If such unit be 2, the number will be
$$2 + 80 + 800 + 1000 = 1882$$
and so on, *ad infinitum*.

No. XXXIII.—The Shepherd and his Sheep.

To ascertain the number of the flock, find in the first place the least common multiple of 2, 3, 4, 5, and 6—*i.e.*, 60. Then take the lowest multiple of this, which, with 1 added, will be divisible by 7. This will be found to be 301, which is the required answer.*

---

* See also answer to No. L.

No. XXXIV.—A Difficult Problem. Solution.

The solution of this problem depends upon certain of the Properties of Numbers referred to at the commencement of this section (see pp. 174-181), where we find it stated that the condition that a number shall be evenly divisible by—

(I.) 2, is that its last digit shall be an even number. (Prop. 7.)

(II.) 3, is that the sum of its digits shall be divisible by 3. (Prop. 8.)

(III.) 4, is that its last two digits shall be divisible by 4. (Prop. 10.)

(IV.) 5, is that it shall end with 5 or 0. (Prop. 11.)

(V.) 6, is that the sum of its digits shall be divisible by 3, and its last digit be an even number. (Prop. 12.)

(VI.) 8, is that its last three digits shall be divisible by 8. (Prop. 14.)

(VII.) 9, is that the sum of its digits shall be divisible by 9. (Prop. 15.)

(VIII.) 10, is that its last digit shall be 0.* (Prop. 16.)

To find the required number, let a be the digit occupying the "units" place, b the digit occupying the "tens" place, c that occupying the "hundreds" place, d the "thousands," and so on, as far as may be necessary.

Now, bearing in mind the conditions of the problem, we are enabled at once to fix the value of a. As the required number when divided by 2 is to leave a remainder of 1, we know (by I.) that a must be an even number $+ 1$—*i.e.*, an *odd* number. As the required number is to be divisible by 5, with a remainder of 4, a must (by IV.) be $5 + 4$ *or* $0 + 4$—*i.e.*, 9 or 4. But as it is to be divisible by 10, with remainder 9, it can only (by VIII.) be $0 + 9 = 9$.

From III. we gather that the required number being divisible by 4, with remainder 3, ba must be a multiple

---

* Some of these conditions might in the actual working out of the problem be disregarded—*e.g.*, if a number be divisible by 8, with remainder 7, it will, as a matter of course, be divisible by 4, with remainder 3, or by 2, with remainder 1. If divisible by 6, with remainder 5, it will necessarily be divisible by 3, with remainder 2; and if divisible by 10, with remainder 9, it will in like manner be divisible by 5, with remainder 4.

of 4, + 3. As $a = 9$, $a - 3$ must $= 6$, and such multiple of 4 must therefore be one ending with 6. Now of such multiples (consisting of two digits only) there are but five—viz., 16, 36, 56, 76, and 96. $b\,a$ must therefore be one or other of these $+ 3$: i.e., either 19, 39, 59, 79, or 99. But neither of these standing alone answers the remaining conditions of the problem. The required number must therefore be one of more than two digits, terminating with one or other of the double numbers above-mentioned.

As the required number is divisible by 9, with remainder 8, we know (by VII.) that the sum of its digits, *less* 8, must be exactly divisible by 9. Deducting 8 from each of the five possible values of $b\,a$, we have as remainders 11, 31, 51, 71, and 91; the sum of whose digits is 2, 4, 6, 8, and 10 respectively. If, therefore, the required number be one of three figures, c must be either $9 - 2 = 7$; $9 - 4 = 5$; $9 - 6 = 3$; $9 - 8 = 1$; *or* $18 - 10 = 8$; and $c\,b\,a$ must be either 719, 539, 359, 179, or 899.

Neither of these, however, is divisible by 7, with remainder 6; and it is therefore clear that no number of three digits only will answer the required conditions.

Proceeding to the consideration of numbers of four digits, we naturally begin with such as have 1 as the value of d. Now (by VII.) we know that, to answer the required conditions, $(1 + c + b + a)$ must be a multiple of 9, with 8 over; or, substituting the known value of a, we have
$$1 + c + b + 9 = (9 \text{ or } 18)^* + 8$$
$$= 17 \text{ or } 26$$
$$\therefore c + b = 7 \text{ or } 16$$
And as we already know that b is either 1, 3, 5, 7, or 9, c must be either 6, 4, 2, 0, or 7. The only possible solutions commencing with 1 are therefore 1619, 1439, 1259, 1079, or 1799. Of these, however, none save 1259 is divisible by 7, with 6 over, and this number is not divisible by 8, with 7 over.

We proceed to try 2 as the value of d. Then, as before:
$$2 + c + b + a = (9 \text{ or } 18) + 8$$
$$2 + c + b + 9 = 17 \text{ or } 26$$
$$c + b = 6 \text{ or } 15$$

---

* 18 is the highest possible multiple of 9 that will suit the equation. For, even supposing the unknown values of c and b to be each 9, $1 + 9 + 9 + 9$ would obviously not $= 27$ (the next highest multiple) $+ 8$.

in which case, b being known to be either 1, 3, 5, 7, or 9, c must be either 5, 3, 1, 8, or 6, and the only possible solutions commencing with 2 are—

2519, 2339, 2159, 2879, and 2699.

Of these, 2519 is the only one which answers all the conditions of the problem, and 2519 is therefore the required number.

No. XXXV.—Well Laid Out. Solution.

Either of the solutions following will answer the conditions of the problem :—

		s.	d.
2 pieces indiarubber	@ 4d. =		8
2 sheets of paper	@ 3d. =		6
1 pencil	@ 2d. =		2
16 drawing-pins	@ $\frac{1}{2}d$. =		8
21 articles.	Cost	2.	0

		s.	d.
or, 5 pencils	@ 2d. =		10
1 sheet of paper	@ 3d. =		3
1 piece indiarubber	@ 4d. =		4
14 drawing-pins	@ $\frac{1}{2}d$. =		7
21 articles.	Cost	2.	0

To arrive at the result we, in the first place, consider what one article of each kind would together amount to. The result is as under :—

1 piece indiarubber	@ 4d.
1 sheet of paper	@ 3d.
1 pencil	@ 2d.
1 drawing-pin	@ $\frac{1}{2}d$.
4	9$\frac{1}{2}$

We have thus only *four* articles (less than one-fifth of the required number), for 9$\frac{1}{2}d$., which is more than one-third of the total sum to be expended. It is therefore clear that to make up the total of 21 articles a considerable proportion, numerically, must be pins; and it is further clear that, to avoid an odd halfpenny in the total, the number of pins must of necessity be *even*.

We proceed to try one of each of the three more costly articles (value 4d. + 3d. + 2d. = 9d.), with such a number of pins as will bring the total number nearer to the required 21. 18 would bring it to exactly that number, but the cost would be only 9d. + 9d. = 1s. 6d.; so that the quantity of the cheaper items (the pins) is obviously now in excess. With 16 pins we have 3 + 16 = 19 articles, value 1s. 5d. This is 2 articles and 7 pence short of the limit. We have therefore to consider what 2 additional articles would together represent 7d. in value, and we find that a second piece of rubber, value 4d., and a second sheet of paper, value 3d., just answer the required conditions. This leads us to the first of the solutions above given.

But we have further to consider whether this is the *only* solution—and we accordingly proceed to try 14 drawing-pins (value 7d.), with one of each of the other articles. This gives us a total of 17 articles, value 1s. 4d. This is 8d. short in value, and 4 short in number of the required result. The only 4 articles that would make up the required value are 4 additional pencils. Adding these, and their value, we have the second solution.

We proceed to try whether the required conditions can be answered with *twelve* pins, and one of each of the more costly articles. This gives us 15 articles, value 1s. 3d., being 6 short in number, and 9d. short in value. Now, 6 pencils (the cheapest of the more costly articles) would cost 1s., being 3d. in excess of our limit in price; and any further diminution of the number of drawing-pins would bring us still more in excess of such limit. It follows that the above-mentioned are the only possible solutions.

No. XXXVI.—The Two Travellers. Solution.

A, in his 2$\frac{1}{2}$ hours' start, has travelled 10 miles. As B gains on him at the rate of a mile an hour, it will take him ten hours to recover this distance, by which time A will have been travelling 12$\frac{1}{2}$ hours, and will be 50 miles from the point whence he started.

No. XXXVII.—Measuring the Garden. Solution.

The garden is 111 yards long by 37 wide, and contains, therefore, 4107 square yards. If it were a yard more each way (112 yards by 38) its area would be 4256 square yards. $4256 - 4107 = 149$.

The problem may be solved algebraically as follows:—

Let x = breadth in yards
Then $3x$ = length ,,
And $3x^2$ = area.

And $(x+1)(3x+1) = (3x^2 + 4x + 1)$ = area if length and breadth increased by one yard each way.

By the terms of the question, such last-mentioned area—

$$3x^2 + 4x + 1 = 3x^2 + 149$$
$$4x + 1 = 149$$
$$i.e., 4x = 148$$
$$\therefore x = 37 \text{ the required breadth.}$$
$$\text{and } 3x = 141 \quad ,, \quad \text{length.}$$

No. XXXVIII.—When Will They Get It? Solution.

In 420 days; 420 being the least common multiple of 1, 2, 3, 4, 5, 6, and 7.

No. XXXIX.—Passing the Gate. Solution.

He had at the outset five shillings and one penny.

On the first day he pays one penny at the gate, spends half a crown, and pays a penny on going out, leaving him with two and fivepence.

The second day he pays a penny on entering, spends fourteen-pence, and after paying a penny on going out is left with thirteenpence.

The third day he brings in one shilling, spends sixpence, and is left, on going out, with fivepence.

The fourth day he brings in fourpence, spends twopence, and after paying the toll to go out, is left with one penny only.

To solve the problem, the calculation must be worked backwards. Thus, on the fourth day he pays a penny on coming out, and has still one left, together making twopence. He had spent *half* his available money in the town. The total must therefore on that day have been fourpence, exclusive of the penny he paid to come in. This gives us fivepence as the amount with which he came out the previous evening. The penny he paid to get out brings this amount to sixpence, and as he had first spent a like amount, he must previously have had a shilling, exclusive of the penny to come in.

By continuing the same process, it is easy to arrive at his original capital.

No XL.—A Novel Magic Square. Solution.

(See Fig. 361.) This is an interesting example of what is called the "bordered" magic square, the repeated removal of the border not affecting its magic quality. The sums of the various rows are 369, 287, 205, and 123, of which the central number, 41, is the greatest common divisor. As to the

5	80	59	73	61	3	63	12	13
1	20	55	30	57	29	71	26	81
4	14	31	50	29	60	35	68	78
76	58	46	38	45	40	36	24	6
7	63	33	43	41	39	49	17	75
74	64	48	42	37	44	34	18	8
67	10	47	32	53	22	51	72	15
66	56	27	52	25	54	11	62	16
69	2	23	9	21	79	19	70	77

Fig. 361.

mode of constructing such squares, see *Hutton's Mathematical Recreations*, and other works of the same kind.

We append, for the purpose of comparison (Fig. 362), the ordinary magic square of the numbers 1 to 81, constructed according to the rule given on pp. 187-189. It will be seen that this, though perfect as an ordinary magic square, wholly fails to meet the special conditions of the problem. The total of each row is in this case 369.

5	54	13	62	21	70	29	78	37
46	14	63	22	71	30	79	38	6
15	55	23	72	31	80	39	7	47
56	24	64	32	81	40	8	48	16
25	65	33	73	41	9	49	17	57
66	34	74	42	1	50	18	58	26
35	75	43	2	51	10	59	27	67
76	44	3	52	11	60	19	68	36
45	4	53	12	61	20	69	28	77

FIG. 362.

No. XLI.—Another Magic Square. Solution.

45	17	58	6	55	11	32	28
10	54	29	33	16	44	7	59
23	43	0	60	13	49	26	38
48	12	39	27	42	22	61	1
62	2	41	21	36	24	51	15
25	37	14	50	3	63	20	40
4	56	19	47	30	34	9	53
35	31	52	8	57	5	46	18

FIG. 363.

Key to Arithmetical Puzzles.

The solution is as shown in Fig. 363. This is a very pretty example of what is known to mathematicians as the Tesselated Magic Square.*

No. XLII.—The Set of Weights. Solution.

The five weights are as under:—

½ lb., 1½ lb., 4½ lbs., 13½ lbs., and 40½ lbs.

To weigh the intermediate quantities from 1 lb. upwards, the weights are distributed between the two scales as follows:—

	In Weight Scale.	In Goods Scale.
To weigh 1 lb.	1½ lb. weight	The goods to be weighed plus ½ lb. weight.
,, 2 lbs.	1½ and ½ lb. weight.	Goods only.
,, 2½ ,,	4½ lb. weight.	Goods + 1½ and ½ lbs.
,, 3 ,,	4½ ,,	Goods + 1½ lb.
,, 5 ,,	4½ and ½ lb ,,	Goods only.
,, 5½ ,,	4½ and 1½ lb. ,,	Goods + ½ lb.
,, 6 ,,	4½ and 1½ lb. ,,	Goods only.
,, 6½ ,,	4½, 1½, and ½ ,,	,,
,, 7 ,,	13½ lb. ,,	Goods, 4½, 1½, and ½ lbs.
,, 7½ ,,	13½ lb. ,,	,, 4½ and 1½ lbs.
,, 8 ,,	13½ and ½ lb. ,,	,, 4½ and 1½ lbs.
,, 8½ ,,	13½ lb. ,,	,, 4½ and ½ lbs.
,, 9 ,,	13½ lb. ,,	,, 4½ lbs.

And so on; to weigh 60 lbs., all of the weights, with the exception of the ½ lb., being placed in the weight scale.

N.B.—If preferred, the weighing of any given quantity up to 60 lbs. with the weights named may be propounded as an independent puzzle.

No. XLIII.—What Did He Lose? Solution.

The reply of most people is, almost invariably, that the hatter lost £3 19s. 0d. and the value of the hat, but a little consideration will show that this is incorrect. His actual

---

* We are indebted for this particular Magic Square to a recent issue (May 13th, 1893) of the *Queen*, where it appears in connection with a more than ordinarily complex example of the Knight's Tour Puzzle.

loss was £3 19s. 0d., *less* his trade profit on the hat; the nett value of the hat, *plus* such trade profit, being balanced by the difference, 21s., which he retained out of the proceeds of the note.

No. XLIV.—A Difficult Division. Solution.

According to the conditions of the problem, each son's share will be seven casks (irrespective of contents), and of wine, $3\frac{1}{2}$ casks.

The division can be made in either of two ways, as under :—

Dick and Tom each take 2 full, 2 empty, and 3 half-full casks; and

Harry, 3 full, 3 empty, and 1 half-full;

or

Dick and Tom each take 3 full, 3 empty, and 1 half-full cask; and Harry 1 full, 1 empty, and 5 half-filled casks.

No. XLV.—The Hundred Bottles of Wine. Solution.

He sold on the first day 2 bottles only; on the second, 5; on the third, 8; on the fourth, 11; on the fifth, 14; on the sixth, 17; on the seventh, 20; and on the eighth day, 23.

$$2 + 5 + 8 + 11 + 14 + 17 + 20 + 23 = 100$$

To ascertain the first day's sale, or first term of the series, take the ordinary formula for ascertaining the sum of an arithmetical progression.

$$S = \frac{n}{2}(2a + \overline{n-1b})$$

Now S (the sum of the series), n (the number of terms), and b (the daily rate of increase), are known, being 100, 8, and 3 respectively. Substituting these known values in the formula, that of the first term, a, is readily ascertained. Thus :—

$$\begin{aligned} 100 &= \tfrac{8}{2}(2a+21) \\ &= 4(2a+21) \\ &= 8a + 84 \\ 100 - 84 &= 8a \\ 16 &= 8a \\ a &= 2 \end{aligned}$$

No. XLVI.—The Last of her Stock. Solution.

She had 14, of which Willie got 8 (7+1); Tommy, 4 (3+1); and Jennie, 2 (1+1).

No. XLVII.—The Walking Match. Solution.

They will meet in an hour, by which time A will have gone round the circle exactly five times, B four times, C three times, and D twice.

No. XLVIII.—A Feat of Divination. Solution.

All that is necessary is to deduct 25 from the final sum named. This will give a remainder of two figures, representing the points of the two dice.

Thus, suppose that the points thrown are 6 and 1, and that the thrower selects the former to be multiplied. The figures will then be as follows:—

$$(6 \times 2 + 5) \times 5 + 1 = 86$$
$$86 - 25 = 61$$

which, as will be seen, corresponds with the points of the two dice.

If the thrower had selected the 1 as the starting-point of the process, the only difference in the result would be that the two digits would come out in reverse order. Thus:—

$$(1 \times 2 + 5) \times 5 + 6 = 41$$
$$41 - 25 = 16$$

The same process, in a slightly modified form, is equally applicable to three dice. In this case the steps are as under:—

Multiply the points of the first die by 2;
Add 5;
Multiply the result by 5;
Add the points of the second die.
Multiply the total by 10;
Add the points of the third die;

On the final result being announced, the operator subtracts from it 250, when the remainder will give the points of the three dice.

Thus, suppose the points of the three dice to be 5, 4, and 2. Then—

$$5 \times 2 + 5 = 15$$
$$15 \times 5 = 75$$
$$75 + 4 = 79$$
$$79 \times 10 = 790$$
$$790 + 2 = 792$$

And $792 - 250 = 542$, giving the three numbers required.

No. XLIX.—A Peculiar Number. Solution.

The required number is 142,857, which, if multiplied by 5, is 714,285; if multiplied by 3, is 428,571; or, if multiplied by 6, is 857,142.*

Formidable as the problem may appear, the result is readily obtained by means of a simple equation, as follows:—

The figure which occupies the units place in the original number being 7, let $x =$ the remaining part of the number (the other five digits). Then $10x + 7$ will be the required number. When the 7 is transposed to the left-hand end of the row, the new number will be represented by $700,000 + x$, and by the terms of the problem this latter number is five times the former, $i.e.$—

$$700,000 + x = 5(10x + 7)$$
$$= 50x + 35$$
$$\text{Or } 49x = 700,000 - 35 = 699,965$$
$$\text{Then } x = 14,285$$
$$\text{And } 10x + 7 = 142,857\text{—the required number.}$$

Multiplication by 3 and by 6 proves that this number also answers the remaining conditions.

No. L.—Another Peculiar Number. Solution.

Answer, 121.

To discover the required number in questions of this class, find the least common multiple of all but the number which divides without remainder. Add 1 to such L.C.M., and see whether the result answers the further condition of the problem—$i.e.$, equal division by the remaining number.

If not, multiply the L.C.M. by 2, 3, 4, and so on in succession, each time adding 1, till you obtain a result which is evenly divisible by such number.

---

* For other peculiarities of this number, *see* Puzzle XV.

Applying this rule to the question under consideration, we find that the L.C.M. of 2, 3, 4, 5 and 6 is 60; but 60 + 1 (= 61) is not evenly divisible by 11. We proceed to try 60 × 2 + 1 (= 121), which is found to be so divisible, and is therefore the number required.

No. LI.—The Three Legacies. Solution.

As the amount of each share is to correspond with length of service, it is plain that the housemaid will receive one share, the parlourmaid three, and the cook six—in all, ten shares. The value of a single share is therefore one-tenth of £70, or £7, which is the portion of the housemaid, the parlourmaid receiving £21, and the cook £42.

No. LII.—Another Mysterious Multiplicand. Solution.

The conditions of the problem are answered by the number 73, which, being multiplied by 3, 6, and 9, the products are 219, 438, and 657 respectively. The correctness of the solution is obvious. The rationale of the fact and the process whereby the required number is ascertained, we must confess ourselves unable to explain.

No. LIII.—How to Divide Twelve among Thirteen.

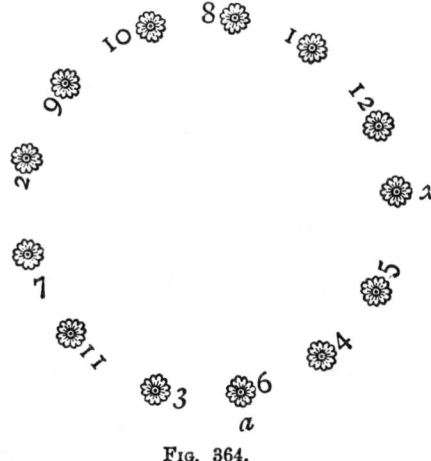

Fig. 364.

It will be found that, counting as described in the problem, the person standing *eleventh* from the point at which you begin will be excluded. The distributor will therefore begin ten places farther back, or (which is the same thing) three places farther forward, in the circle. Thus, if *x* (see Fig. 364) be the person to be excluded, the distributor will begin to count at the point *a*. The numbers placed against the various places show the order in which the gifts will be distributed and the men drop out of the circle.

No. LIV.—Tenth Man Out. Solution.

The arrangement was as shown in Fig. 365, the white

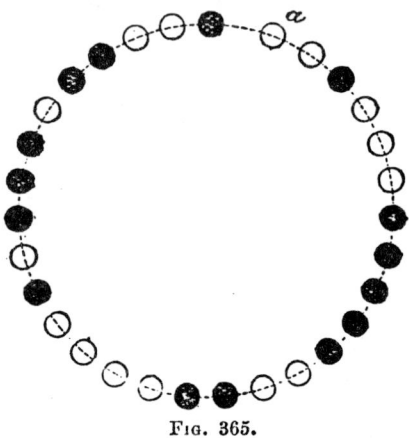

Fig. 365.

spots representing the white men, and the black spots the black men. The counting begins with the man marked *a*.

No. LV.—Ninth Man Out. Solution.

In this case the arrangement will be as shown in Fig. 366.

The proper order may be readily remembered by the aid of the Latin line—

Populeam Virgam Mater Regina Ferebat,

signifying, "The Mother Queen carried a poplar switch."

Key to Arithmetical Puzzles.

The interpretation has, however, nothing to do with the matter. The significance of the formula lies in the *vowels*

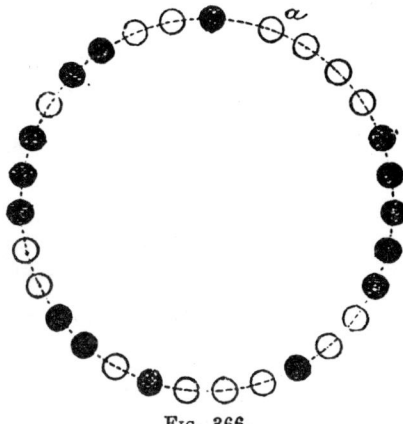

Fig. 366.

which occur in it, and which are taken to mean—*a*, 1; *e*, 2; *i*, 3; *o*, 4; and *u*, 5, respectively. The line, therefore, to the initiated, reads as under:—

Po-pu-le-am Vir-gam Ma-ter Re-gi-na Fe-re-bat;
4 5 2 1 3 1 1 2 2 3 1 2 2 1

which will be found to correspond with the grouping of whites and blacks around the circle. Thus, the *o* in *Po* indicates that the first group is to consist of 4 whites, the *u* in *pu* that the next group is to consist of 5 blacks, and so on, black and white alternately throughout.

No. LVI.—The Three Travellers. Solution.

The plan adopted is as follows:—

1. Two of the servants are sent over.
2. One of the servants brings back the boat, and takes over the third servant.
3. One of the servants brings the boat back, lands, and two of the masters go over.
4. One of the masters and one of the servants return. The servant lands, and the third master crosses with the second.

The position of matters is now as follows: The three

masters are on the farther side, and one of the servants, who is sent back with the boat, and fetches, one at a time, the other two servants.*

No. LVII.—The Wolf, the Goat, and the Cabbages. Solution.

This is a very simple problem. It is solved as under:—

1. He first takes across the goat, and leaves him on the opposite side.
2. He returns and fetches the wolf, leaves him on the opposite side, and takes back the goat with him.
3. He leaves the goat at the starting-point, and takes over the basket of cabbages.
4. He leaves the cabbages with the wolf, and returning, fetches the goat.

Or,

1. He takes over the goat.
2. He returns and fetches the cabbages.
3. He takes back the goat, leaves him at the starting-point, and fetches the wolf.
4. He leaves the wolf on the opposite side with the basket of cabbages, and goes back to fetch the goat.

No. LVIII.—The Three Jealous Husbands. Solution.

For the sake of clearness, we will designate the three husbands A, B, and C, and their wives, a, b, and c, respectively. The passage may then be made to the satisfaction of the husbands in the following order:—

1. a and b cross over, and b brings back the boat.
2. b and c cross over, c returning alone.

---

* It will be found a great advantage in this class of puzzles to have some material representative of each character. This requirement is met by Messrs. Jaques & Son in the present case by a little mechanical arrangement, under the name of "The Boat Puzzle." A little boat is mounted on a grooved board, representing the stream, while the masters and servants are represented by six movable figures, three white and three black.

For lack of such an appliance, counters or cardboard discs, with the names of the various persons or objects written upon them, will be found useful.

3. *c* lands, and remains with her husband, while *A* and *B* cross over. *A* lands, *B* and *b* return to the starting-point.

4. *B* and *C* cross over, leaving *b* and *c* at the starting-point.

5. *a* takes back the boat, and *b* crosses with her.

6. *a* lands, and *b* goes back for *c*.

Arithmeticians have racked their brains to devise a means of transit for four husbands and four wives under like conditions, but, with a boat holding two persons only, the problem is insoluble. If we suppose, however, that the boat contains three persons, it may be solved as follows:—

(Distinguishing the four husbands as *A*, *B*, *C*, and *D*, and the four wives as *a*, *b*, *c*, and *d*, respectively.)

1. *a*, *b*, and *c* cross over; *c* brings back the boat.
2. *c* and *d* cross over, and *d* brings back the boat.
3. *A*, *B*, and *C* cross over; *C* and *c* bring back the boat.
4. *C*, *D*, and *c* cross over.
5. *c* takes back the boat and fetches *d*.

No. LIX.—The Captain and his Company. Solution.

The captain orders the two children to pass to the farther side. One of them then brings back the boat, lands, and a soldier crosses alone to the farther side. The second child then brings back the boat.

The state of things (save that one man has crossed) is now just as at first, the boat and the two children being on the hither side of the stream. The process is repeated until the whole of the company have passed over.

No. LX.—The Treasure Trove. Solution.

The secret lies in the fact that the process indicated by the Scotchman simply brings back the number with which it started; *i.e.*, the number of coins in the "find," as will be seen by the following demonstration. Let us suppose x to be the unknown number. Then $x + 666$ will represent the result of the first step; $999 - (x + 666)$ or $333 - x$ that of the second step; and $333 - (333 - x) = x$ that of the third step.

The real value of x is, throughout, unknown to the Scotchman; but the Irishman, finding that the suggested process has brought out the required amount, rashly assumes that his antagonist must be acquainted with it.

No. LXI.—The Row of Counters. Solution.

The required number will be the original difference *plus* the number removed, at the second stage of the puzzle, from the smaller row; in this case, therefore, $3 + 5 (= 8)$. This result will be correct whatever were the actual numbers of the two rows originally. This may be illustrated algebraically as follows:—

Let x = number in larger row,
y = ,, ,, smaller row,
and R = ultimate remainder of larger row.

As the difference of the two rows is stated to be 3, it follows that $x = y + 3$.

And the smaller row, after deduction of the special number indicated, which we will call z, will be $y - z$, and R, the ultimate remainder of the larger row, after deduction of $y - z$, will be $x - (y - z)$, or $x + z - y$.

Substituting for x the value above found, we have

$$R = (y + 3) + z - y$$
$$= 3 + z$$

And z being a known number (in this case 5); $R = 8$; or, in other words, the original difference *plus* the number removed from the smaller row prior to the second deduction.

An example may render the process clearer. Thus, suppose that the first row consists of eighteen, and the second of thirteen counters. The difference is in such case 5. Subtract what number you please, say 7, from the smaller row. This leaves 6. 6 being subtracted from 18, the number of the larger row, the remainder will be 12. (5 + 7).

No. LXII.—A Loan and a Present. Solution.

The remainder in this case will be one half of the amount added by way of "present." This is very easily demonstrated.

Let x equal the number thought of; then $2x + 14$ will equal that number *plus* the imaginary loan and present. Half that amount being professedly given to the poor, will leave a remainder of $x + 7$, and on the repayment of the imaginary loan the figures will stand as $x + 7 - x$ $(= 7)$, the value of x having no bearing whatever on the result.

No. LXIII.—Eleven Guests in Ten Beds. Solution.

The fallacy lies in the fact that the real eleventh man remains unprovided with a resting-place. The tenth man having taken possession of the ninth bed, the eleventh man should in due course occupy the tenth bed, but he does not do so. The man who is called from sleeping double in the first bed to occupy this is not the eleventh, but the second man, and the real eleventh man goes bedless.

No. LXIV.—A Difficult Division. Solution.

	8 gal.	5 gal.	3 gal.
1. They begin by filling the five-gallon from the eight-gallon measure. The contents of the three vessels are then—	3 ,,	5 ,,	0 ,,
2. They fill the three gallons from the five gallons, making—	3 ,,	2 ,,	3 ,,
3. They empty the three gallons into the eight-gallon measure	6 ,,	2 ,,	0 ,,
4. They empty the two gallons from the five-gallon into the three-gallon measure	6 ,,	0 ,,	2 ,,
5. They fill the five-gallon from the eight-gallon measure	1 ,,	5 ,,	2 ,,
6. They fill up the three-gallon from the five-gallon measure	1 ,,	4 ,,	3 ,,
7. They empty the three gallons into the eight-gallon measure	4 ,,	4 ,,	0 ,,

Making the required equal division.

No. LXV.—The Three Market-Women. Solution.

They began by selling at the rate of three apples for a penny. The first sold ten pennyworth, the second eight pennyworth, and the third seven pennyworth. The first had then left three apples, the second five, and the third six. These they sold at one penny each, receiving, therefore, in the whole—

$$\begin{aligned}\text{The first,} \quad & 10d. + 3d. = 13d. \\ \text{The second,} \quad & 8d. + 5d. = 13d. \\ \text{The third,} \quad & 7d. + 6d. = 13d.\end{aligned}$$

No. LXVII.—The Farmer and his Three Daughters. Solution.

They began by selling at the rate of seven a penny, the first selling seven pennyworth, the second four, and the youngest one pennyworth. But they had saved the choicest of the fruit, the first having one apple left, the second two, and the youngest three. Meeting a liberal customer, they sold these at threepence each, and the respective amounts received by them were therefore as under—

The first, $7d. + 3d. = 10d.$
The second, $4d. + 6d. = 10d.$
The third, $1d. + 9d. = 10d.$

No. LXVII.—How Many for a Penny. Solution.

He bought two apples for his penny.

To arrive at the result, let $x =$ the whole number of apples. He gives away $\frac{x}{3} + \frac{1}{3}$, and has still one apple left. Then—

$$\frac{x}{3} + \frac{1}{3} + 1 = x$$
$$\text{or } x + 1 + 3 \, (= x + 4) = 3x$$
$$\therefore 2x = 4$$
$$x = 2$$

No. LXVIII —The Magic Cards. Solution.

The seven cards are drawn up on a mathematical principle, in such manner that *the first numbers of those in which a given number appears*, when added together, indicate that number.

Suppose, for instance, that the chosen number is 63. This appears in cards I., II., III., IV., V., and VI. The key numbers of these are 1, 2, 4, 8, 16, and 32; and $1+2+4+8+16+32=63$.

If the number 7 were selected, this appears only in cards I, II, and III, whose key numbers are 1, 2, and $4=7$.

The principle of construction seems at first sight rather mysterious, but it is simple enough when explained. The reader will note, in the first place, that the first or "key" numbers of each card form a geometrical progression, being 1, 2, 4, 8, 16, 32, 64. The total of these is 127, which is accordingly the highest number included.*

It is further to be noted that by appropriate combinations of the above figures *any* total, from 1 up to 127, can be produced.

The first card consists of the alternate numbers from 1 to 127 inclusive. The second, commencing with 2 (the second term of the geometrical series), consists of alternate groups of two consecutive figures—2, 3; 6, 7; 10, 11, and so on. The third, beginning with 4, the third term of the series, consists of alternate groups of *four* figures—4, 5, 6, 7; 12, 13, 14, 15; 20, 21, 22, 23; and so on. The fourth, commencing with 8, consists in like manner of alternate groups of *eight* figures. The fifth, commencing with 16, of alternate groups of *sixteen* figures. The sixth, commencing with 32, of alternate groups of *thirty-two* figures; and the last, commencing with 64, of a single group, being those from 64 to 127 inclusive.

It will be found that any given number of cards arranged on this principle will produce the desired result, limited by the extent of the geometrical series constituting the first numbers.

No. LXIX.—The "Fifteen" or "Boss" Puzzle. Solution.

Notwithstanding the enormous amount of energy that has been expended over the "Fifteen" Puzzle, no absolute rule for its solution has yet been discovered, and it appears to be now generally agreed by mathematicians that out of the vast number of hap-hazard positions in which the fifteen cubes may at the outset be placed,† about half admit of the blocks being so moved as to finally assume their proper order.

To test whether a given arrangement admits of such a possibility, the following rule has been suggested. Reckon how many transpositions of given pairs are necessary to

---

* If there had been six cards only, the series would have terminated with 32, and the highest number would have been 63. If eight cards were used, the final term of the series would have been 128, and its total 255, which would accordingly have been the maximum number.

† The possible number of such positions is *only* 1,307,674,368,000.

bring the blocks into the required order. If the total number of such transpositions be even, the desired re-arrangement is possible. If the number be odd, such re-arrangement is impossible.

Applying this rule to the "Boss" Puzzle (see Fig. 335), it will be seen that only *one* transposition (that of blocks 14 and 15) is here needed, and one being an *odd* number, the problem is insoluble; as, in fact, the "Fifteen" Puzzle in this form has been found by all who have hitherto tried it.

No. LXX.—The Peg-away Puzzle. Solution.

The possibility of success in solving this puzzle appears to be governed by precisely the same rule as the "Fifteen" Puzzle—viz., that if the number of needful transpositions is

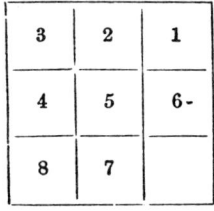
Fig. 367.

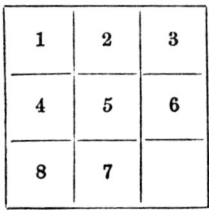
Fig. 368.

even, the puzzle can be solved; if *odd*, it is insoluble. Thus, if the "pegs" be arranged at starting as in Fig. 367. the aspirant will probably succeed; if as shown in Fig. 368, he will fail.

No. LXXI.—The Over-Polite Guests. Solution.

To obtain the answer, all that is needed is to find the number of permutations of seven objects—viz., 5040. It would take, therefore, 5040 days, or nearly fourteen years, to exhaust the possible positions.

In the alternative form of the problem, the host would supply 5 040 dinners at half a crown (value £630) for a payment of £70.

Key to Arithmetical Puzzles. 219

No. LXXII. — **The " Royal Aquarium Thirteen."
Solution.**

When the puzzle is solved the arrangement of the cards will be found to be as shown in Fig. 369.

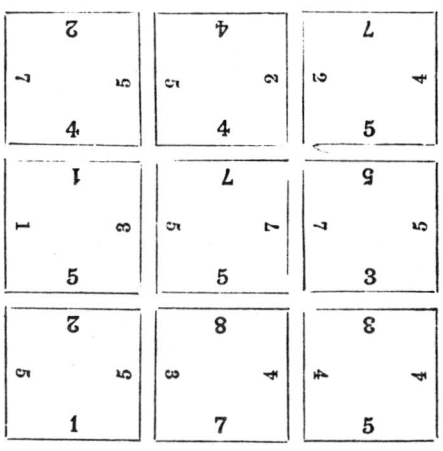

Fig. 369.

There is no royal road to the solution. The proper order must be arrived at by successive transpositions until the conditions are fulfilled.

No. LXXIII.—**An Easy Creditor. Solution.**

The amount of the first payment was £20.

To ascertain such amount, let $x =$ the first payment. Then, according to the conditions of the puzzle—

$$x + \frac{x}{2} + \frac{3x}{4} + \frac{x}{4} + \frac{2x}{5} + 2 = 60$$

Multiplying by 20, the least common multiple of the various denominators,

$$20x + 10x + 15x + 5x + 8x + 40 = 1200$$
$$58x = 1200 - 40 = 1160$$
$$\therefore\ x = 20$$

No. LXXIV.—The Three Arabs. Solution.

The first Arab was entitled to seven, and the second to one only of the eight coins. For, the consumption being equal, each person ate $\frac{8}{3} = 2\frac{2}{3}$ loaves. Of the portion eaten by the stranger the first Arab contributed $2\frac{1}{3}$ loaves, while the second contributed $\frac{1}{3}$ loaf. The former therefore contributed seven parts, while the second contributed one only, and the proper division of the money was seven coins to the first, and one to the second.

No. LXXV.—The Eccentric Testator. Solution.

As the division left nothing over, it is clear that the share of the younger son consisted solely of the fixed sum bequeathed to him, and that there was in his case no residue on which the bequest of a ninth part could operate. Further, as the "fixed sum" gift advanced by degrees of £110, the share of such youngest son must have been £110 multiplied by the total number of inheritors. As each was to take one-ninth of a certain amount, and there was in the last case no ninth to be taken, it follows that the number of legatees was the denominator of the fraction $\frac{1}{9}$, less 1; in other words, 8.

The share of the youngest son was therefore £110 × 8 = £880; and as each of the eight took a like amount, the total value of the estate must have been £7040. Testing this sum by the conditions of the problem, the share of the eldest son is found to be

$$110 + \frac{7040 - 110}{9} = 110 + \frac{6930}{9} = 110 + 770 = 880$$

leaving a remainder of £6160.

The share of the second son will therefore be

$$220 + \frac{6160 - 220}{9} = 220 + \frac{5940}{9} = 220 + 660 = 880$$

and that of the third son

$$330 + \frac{5280 - 330}{9} = 330 + \frac{4950}{9} = 330 + 550 = 880$$

and so on throughout, the increasing value of the fixed amount exactly compensating for the diminished value of the fraction.

Key to Arithmetical Puzzles. 221

No. LXXVI.—Another Eccentric Testator. Solution.

The estate amounted to the sum of £7200, and each son took an equal share—*i.e.*, £1440.

For convenience of reference, we will call what remained after the eldest son had taken his share the *first* residue; what remained after the second had taken his share, the *second* residue; what remained after the third had taken his share, the *third* residue; and what remained after the fourth had taken his share, the *fourth* residue.

Now, according to the conditions of the problem, the fifth son took one half of the fourth residue, *plus* £720. As the fourth residue was thereby exhausted, with no remainder, it is clear that the £720 constituted the remaining half of such residue, and that the fourth residue therefore consisted of twice £720, or £1440.

The fourth son took $\frac{1}{3}$ of the third residue, *plus* £480, and what remained after these two deductions constituted the fourth residue, whose value we have found to be £1440. In other words, $\frac{2}{3}$ of the third residue, *less* £480 = £1440, and $\frac{2}{3}$ of the third residue = £1440 + £480, or £1920. Two-thirds of the third residue being £1920, the whole, or $\frac{3}{3}$, of such residue, must be £2880.

As the third son took $\frac{1}{4}$ of the second residue, *plus* £360, and there then remained £2880, $\frac{3}{4}$ of the second residue must in like manner = £2880 + £360, or £3240, and the whole of such second residue must be £3240 + £1080 = £4320.

As the second son took $\frac{1}{5}$ of the first residue, *plus* £288, and there was then left £4320, we deduce, by a like process of reasoning, that the amount of the first residue was £5760.

As the eldest son took $\frac{1}{6}$ of the whole property, *plus* £240, and there was then left £5760, it is clear, in like manner, that $\frac{5}{6}$ of the whole inheritance was £5760 + 240, or £6000; and if £6000 represent $\frac{5}{6}$, the whole will necessarily be £7,200.

Testing the correctness of our demonstration by the conditions of the puzzle, we find that—

The eldest son takes $\dfrac{7200}{6}$ + 240 = 1200 + 240 = £1440.

First residue 7200 − 1440 = 5760.

The second son takes $\dfrac{5760}{5}$ + 288 = 1152 + 288 = 1440.

Second residue 5760 − 1440 = 4320.

The third son takes $\frac{4320}{4}$ + 360 = 1080 + 360 = 1440.

Third residue 4320 − 1440 = 2880.

The fourth son takes $\frac{2880}{3}$ + 480 = 960 + 480 = 1440.

Fourth residue 2880 − 1440 = 1440.

The fifth son takes $\frac{1440}{2}$ + 720 = 720 + 720 = 1400.

Total £7200.

No. LXXVII.—An Aggravating Uncle. Solution.

The number of soldiers was 58.

On examination of the conditions of the puzzle, it will be found that in each case, whether divided by 3, 4, 5, or 6, there are always *two* short of an even division. All that is needed, therefore, is to find the least common multiple of 3, 4, 5, and 6, and deduct 2 from it. The L.C.M. of 3, 4, 5, and 6 is 60, and 60 − 2 = 58, the required number.

No. LXXVIII.—The Apples and Oranges. Solution.

As each child had 3 more oranges than apples, and this caused a difference of 33 (48 − 15) in the number left over, it follows that the number of children must have been 11. As each child received 12 apples, and there were 48 over, the total number of apples must have been (11 × 12) + 48 = 132 + 48 = 180. As each child received 15 oranges, and there were 15 over, the total number of oranges must have been (11 × 15) + 15 = 165 + 15 = 180.

No. LXXIX.—The Two Squares. Solution.

As the 146 counters remaining from the first arrangement were insufficient by 31 to make the two additional rows desired, the actual number needed for such two rows must have been 146 + 31 = 177. Of these, one (the counter at the corner) would be common to both rows, and the number in one row would therefore be $\frac{176}{2} + 1 = 89$.

A square of 89 counters each way would be 89 × 89 = 7921. But according to the terms of the problem the actual number of counters was 31 short of this—*i.e.*, 7890.

The correctness of this conclusion may be tested by calculating the number in the original square, which was one counter less (viz., 88) each way. The square of 88 is 7744. But in this case there were 146 counters left over. 7744 + 146 = 7890, the same number arrived at by the first process.

No. LXXX.—A Curious Division. Solution.

To ascertain the common quotient, add together the three divisors, 3, 6, and 9, and divide 7890 by their total, 18. The quotient is $438\frac{1}{3}$. Multiply the number thus obtained by 3, 6, and 9 respectively, and the three products will give the numbers contained in the three heaps.

Thus—
$$438\frac{1}{3} \times 3 = 1315$$
$$438\frac{1}{3} \times 6 = 2630$$
$$438\frac{1}{3} \times 9 = 3945$$
$$\overline{7890}$$

No. LXXXI.—A Curious Multiplication. Solution.

This is a very much easier problem, as the proportions of the four heaps are almost self-evident. Taking the fourth, or smallest heap, as the unit of measurement, and calling it 1 accordingly, the third, which is of obviously double the size (as requiring to be multiplied by 6 only, instead of 12, to raise it to the same amount), will = 2. The second heap will in like manner = 3, and the first = 4, and their collective values will be 1 + 2 + 3 + 4 = 10. Divide the whole number by this amount; the quotient is 789. This gives us the value of our unit of measurement, and from it we may deduce the value of all four heaps, thus :—

The fourth heap contains ... ... 789 counters.
The third ,, ,, 789 × 2 = 1578 ,,
The second ,, ,, 789 × 3 = 2367 ,,
The first ,, ,, 789 × 4 = 3156 ,,

Total 7890

No. LXXXII.—The Two Schoolmasters. Solution.

The difference was 6, the smaller school having 66 pupils only.

For, inasmuch as one-sixth of the pupils were away ill, the remainder, viz.—

11 haymaking,
7 at the fair,
and 37 at school,

together making 55—must have been five-sixths of the whole number, and $55 \div 5 (= 11)$, one-sixth. The whole number of the smaller school was therefore $11 \times 6 = 66$.

No. LXXXIII.—Nothing Left. Solution.

The required number is 118.

To obtain it, work the process indicated in reverse order, as follows:—

$$0 + 18 = 18$$
$$18^2 = 324$$
$$324 \div 3 = 108$$
$$108 + 10 = 118$$

No. LXXXIV.—The Three Generations. Solution.

The old man was 69, his son 40, and his grandson 16.

As the old man and his son were together 109 years old, and the old man and his grandson only 85 years old, it follows that the age of the son was $109 - 85 (= 24)$ years greater than that of the grandson. As the son and grandson were together 56 years old, and the former was 24 years older than the latter, it follows that the grandson's age was

$$\frac{56 - 24}{2} = \frac{32}{2} = 16 \text{ years.}$$

The son's age was therefore $16 + 24 = 40$ years.

As the united ages of the old man and his son were together 109, the age of the former must have been $109 - 40 = 69$ years.

No. LXXXV.—The Two Brothers. Solution.

As $\frac{2}{3}$ of the age of the younger is $\frac{5}{12}$ that of the elder, the actual age of the younger must be $\dfrac{5 + 2\frac{1}{2}}{12} = \dfrac{7\frac{1}{2}}{12} = \dfrac{15}{24} = \dfrac{5}{8}$

that of the elder, and the difference between them $\frac{3}{8}$ that of the elder. By the terms of the question, we know that this $\frac{3}{8}$ = 9 years, in which case $\frac{1}{8}$ must = 3 years, and the whole age of the elder 3 × 8 (= 24) years. The age of the younger will consequently be 24 − 9 = 15 years.

No. LXXXVI.—The Two Sons. Solution.

The younger son is $24\frac{1}{2}$; the elder, $29\frac{3}{4}$ years old.

The solution is most easily got at by means of a simple equation, thus:—

Let y = age of younger.

Then $y + 5\frac{1}{4}$ = age of elder.

By the terms of the question—

$5y + 6(y + 5\frac{1}{4}) = 301$

$5y + 6y + 31\frac{1}{2} = 301$

$11y = 301 - 31\frac{1}{2} = 269\frac{1}{2}$

$y = 24\frac{1}{2}$

The younger son is therefore $24\frac{1}{2}$ years old, and the elder $24\frac{1}{2} + 5\frac{1}{4} = 29\frac{3}{4}$.

No. LXXXVII.—The Two Nephews. Solution.

The one was 18, the other 6 years old.

It is clear that as the larger number is three times the smaller, it must be a multiple of 3. It cannot be a larger number than 18, because the square of the next multiple of 3—viz., 21—would alone exceed 360. We proceed to try 18 accordingly as the larger number, and $\frac{18}{3}$ (=6) as the smaller number, when we find that $18^2 + 6^2$ = 324 + 36 = 360, the total required. 18 and 6 years are therefore the respective ages.

No. LXXXVIII.—The Reversed Number. Solution.

The required number is 45. It may be got at either algebraically or arithmetically. In the first case—

Let $x =$ the first, or left-hand, digit,
and $y =$ the second, or right-hand, digit.

Then (as x represents *tens*) $10x + y$ will be the total number, and $10y + x$ the number produced by reversing its digits, while $x + y$ will be the sum of such digits. Now, by the terms of the question,

$$10x + y = 5(x + y)$$
$$= 5x + 5y$$
$$\therefore 5x = 4y$$
$$\text{And } x = \frac{4y}{5}$$

Further, by the terms of the question—

$$10x + y + 9 = 10y + x.$$

Substituting the value above obtained for x—

we have $\quad \dfrac{40y}{5} + y + 9 = 10y + \dfrac{4y}{5}$

or, $40y + 5y + 45 = 50y + 4y$
$$45y + 45 = 54y$$
$$9y = 45$$
$$y = 5$$

Then $\quad x \left(= \dfrac{4y}{5}\right) = 4$

and $10x + y$ (the whole number) $= 45$.

The arithmetical process is, however, in this case the simpler, thus—

As the required number is equal to five times the sum of its digits (*i.e.*, a multiple of 5), its final digit must be 5 or 0[*]. But such final digit is also the first digit of the reversed number. 0 would not answer this condition, and the final digit must therefore be 5. Nine added to any number ending in 5 makes the final digit 4. This gives us the reversed number as 54, and the actual number consequently as 45, which is found to fully answer the required conditions.

---

[*] See *Properties of Numbers*, p. 177.

No. LXXXIX.—Another Reversed Number. Solution.

The required number is 42.

Here again either the algebraical method or the arithmetical method may be used. Let x = the first digit, and y the second digit. Then $10x + y$ = the required number, and $10y + x$ = the reversed number.

By the terms of the problem—

(1) $\quad 10x + y = 7(x + y)$
(2) $\quad 10x + y - 18 = 10y + a$
$$10x + y = 7x + 7y$$
$$3x = 6y$$
$$x = 2y$$

Substituting this value in equation (2), we have

$$20y + y - 18 = 10y + 2y$$
$$21y - 18 = 12y$$
$$9y = 18$$
$$y = 2$$

and as $x = 2y$ the number must be 42.

The arithmetical or logical process is as follows:—

By the terms of the question, the required number is a multiple of 7. As it has only two digits, and its remainder *less* 18 is also a number of two digits, this limits the selection to 35, 42, 49, 56, 63, 72, 77, 84, 91, or 98. Among these the only number which answers the remaining conditions is 42, which is accordingly the answer.

No. XC.—The Shepherd and his Sheep. Solution.

There were in the first fold				27
,,	,,	,,	second	25
,,	,,	,,	third	18
,,	,,	,,	fourth	16
,,	,,	,,	fifth	14
			Total	100

For as there were—

In the first and second folds		52
,, second and third		43
,, third and fourth		34
,, fourth and fifth		30

The number in the first and fifth, with double the respective numbers in the second, third and fourth, will be   159

As the actual number is 100, it follows that the number in the second, third and fourth folds = 159 − 100 = 59.

And as there were in the second and third 43, the number in the fourth fold must have been 59 − 43 = 16.

As there were in the fourth and fifth 30, the number in the fifth fold must have been 30 − 16 = 14.

As in the third and fourth there were 34, the number in the third fold must have been 34 − 16 = 18.

In like manner, the number in the second fold was 43 − 18 = 25.

And the number in the first fold was 52 − 25 = 27.

$$27 + 25 + 18 + 16 + 14 = 100.$$

No. XCI.—The Shepherdess and her Sheep. Solution.

The numbers are 7, 14, 28, and 56 respectively.

By the terms of the question, it appears that the numbers in the four folds are in geometrical progression, with a common ratio of 2. Taking experimentally the smallest possible such progression, we find it to be $1 + 2 + 4 = 8 = 15$. But the total of the actual progression is stated to be 105. Dividing this by 15, we have as quotient 7, which we use as a common multiplier to bring the series up to the required total. Thus:—

$$7 \times 1 = 7$$
$$7 \times 2 = 14$$
$$7 \times 4 = 28$$
$$7 \times 8 = 56$$

Total   105

No. XCII.—A Weighty Matter. Solution.

Seven weights are required, of 1, 2, 4, 8, 16, 32, and 64 lbs. respectively, together making 127 lbs. It will be found that, by using one, two, or more of these, any weight from 1 to 127 lbs. can be weighed.*

No. XCIII.—The Three Topers. Solution.

The quantity would be consumed in $4\frac{16}{31}$ hours.

For—as Peter can drink 40 quarts in 20 hours, he would drink in 1 hour $\frac{40}{20} = 2$ quarts.

As Paul can drink 40 quarts in 14 hours, he would drink in 1 hour $\frac{40}{14} = 2\frac{6}{7}$ quarts.

As Roger can drink 40 quarts in 10 hours: he would drink in 1 hour $\frac{40}{10} = 4$ quarts.

And they would together drink in 1 hour $2 + 2\frac{6}{7} + 4$ ($= 8\frac{6}{7}$) quarts, and 40 quarts in $(40 \div 8\frac{6}{7}) = 4\frac{16}{31}$ hours.

No. XCIV.—The False Scales. Solution.

Answer, 12 lbs.

Problems of this class are solved by ascertaining the square root of the product of the two weights.

In this case $9 \times 16 = 144$, and $\sqrt{144} = 12$, the required answer.

No. XCV.—An Arithmetical Policeman. Solution.

The hour struck was twelve.

The fractions mentioned, $\frac{1}{2}$, $\frac{1}{3}$, and $\frac{1}{4}$, if regarded as fractions of a single hour, will be found, when added together, to amount to $1\frac{1}{12}$ of an hour. To raise the surplus $\frac{1}{12}$ to the value of a complete hour, it must be multiplied by 12, and 12 is therefore the hour that was struck.

---

* The numbers, it will be observed, are in geometrical progression. For another illustration of the fact here stated, see The Magic Cards, p. 161.

No. XCVI.—The Flock of Geese. Solution.

The number of the flock was 36.

For, taking the lowest number (4), which is divisible by 2 and by 4 (as, from the conditions of the problem, it is clear that the required number must be), and going through the process suggested with such number, we have the following result:—

4 + 4 (as many more) + 2 (half as many more) + 1 (one-fourth as many more) = 11.

Dividing 99 (the total to be obtained after going through the same process with the actual number in the flock) by the number thus obtained, we find the quotient to be 9. 4, therefore, multiplied by 9 (= 36) should be the required number. Putting it to the test, we find that 36 + 36 + 18 + 9 = 99, exactly answering the conditions.

No. XCVII.—The Divided Cord. Solution.

The one portion is 16, and the other 20 inches.

As the one segment is to be $\frac{4}{5}$ of the other, their respective proportions will be 4 to 5, or in all 9 parts. One ninth part of 36 inches is 4 inches. Taking this as the unit of measurement, we find that—

the longer segment is $5'' \times 4'' = 20$ inches,
and the shorter ,, ,, $4'' \times 4'' = 16$,,

Together, 36 ,,

No. XCVIII.—The Divided Number. Solution.

The parts are 28 and 18 respectively.

It is clear from the conditions of the problem that the first part is a multiple of 7, and the second a multiple of 3. Now there are in the number 46 six multiples of 7—viz., 7, 14, 21, 28, 35, and 42. In like manner there are in the same number fifteen multiples of 3—viz., 3, 6, 9, 12, 15, 18, 21, 24, 27, 30, 33, 36, 39, 42, and 45. Of these, the only pairs which together make 46 are 7 and 39, and 28 and 18. The first pair clearly does not answer the conditions of the question, for $\frac{7}{7} + \frac{39}{3} = 1 + 13 = 14$. We proceed to try the second pair, and find that $\frac{28}{7} + \frac{18}{3} = 4 + 6 = 10$. 28 and 18 are therefore the required numbers.

By the aid of algebra the problem may be solved much more neatly. Thus—
Let $x =$ the portion to be divided by 7, and y the portion to be divided by 3.
Then, by the terms of the question—
$$x + y = 46$$
$$i.e. \quad x = 46 - y.$$
Further, $\quad \dfrac{x}{7} + \dfrac{y}{3} = 10$

or, substituting the value above found for x—
$$\frac{46 - y}{7} + \frac{y}{3} = 10$$
$$3(46 - y) + 7y = 210$$
$$138 - 3y + 7y = 210$$
$$4y = 210 - 138 = 72$$
$$y = 18$$
$$\text{And as } x = 46 - y$$
$$x = 46 - 18$$
$$= 28.$$

No. XCIX.—The Two Numbers. Solution.

The required numbers are 5 and 7. For if twice the first + the second = 17, and twice the second + the first = 19, then the above added together—*i.e.*, three times the first + three times the second must be $17 + 19 = 36$, and the sum of the numbers themselves must be $\frac{36}{3} = 12$.

And since twice the first + the second is an odd number, the second is also an odd number, and the first, being an even number (12) *less* an odd number, must also be an odd number.*

---

* Because twice any whole number is always an even number; and an even number *plus* an even number is always an even number. See p. 174.

Now the only pairs of odd numbers which together make 12 are 1 and 11, 3 and 9, and 5 and 7. Of these, we find by experiment that 5 and 7 are the only two that answer the conditions; $5 \times 2 + 7 = 17$, and $7 \times 2 + 5 = 19$.

Here again the problem is much more readily solved by algebra. Thus—

Let x = first number,

And y = second number.

We have then the equations

$$2x + y = 17$$
$$2y + x = 19.$$

From the latter equation we deduce that

$$x = 19 - 2y.$$

Substituting this value in the first equation, we get

$$2(19 - 2y) + y = 17$$
$$38 - 4y + y = 17$$

or $\quad -3y = 38 - 17 = 21$

$$y = 7.$$

Substituting this value in the second equation—

$$2y + x = 19$$

we have $14 + x = 19$

$$x = 19 - 14$$
$$= 5$$

No. C.—The Horse and Trap. Solution.

The horse cost £60, and the trap £25.

As five times the value of the horse = twelve times the value of the trap, it is clear that the latter was worth $\frac{5}{12}$ as much as the former. The value of the two together may, therefore, be expressed as $1 + \frac{5}{12}$ (or $\frac{17}{12}$), and this by the conditions of the problem = £85. If $\frac{17}{12}$ of the value of the horse be £85, $\frac{1}{12}$ of such value will be $\frac{1}{17}$ of that amount—*i.e.*, £5. The total value of the horse is therefore £5 × 12 = £60. The value of the trap, being $\frac{5}{12}$ of £60, is £25.

No. CI.—The Two Workmen. Solution.

They must work $6\frac{2}{9}$ hours per day.

For A, doing the whole in 70 hours, does $\frac{1}{70}$ in 1 hour.

And B, doing the whole in 56 hours, does $\frac{1}{56}$ in 1 hour.

Or, together, in 1 hour $\frac{1}{70} + \frac{1}{56} = \frac{4}{280} + \frac{5}{280} = \frac{9}{280}$.

They would, therefore, do the whole in $\frac{280}{9} = 31\frac{1}{9}$ hours.

And to complete it in 5 days, they must work $\frac{31\frac{1}{9}}{5} = 6\frac{2}{9}$ hours per day.

No. CII.—The Divided Number. Solution.

The required numbers are 120, 72, and 45.

For since 3 times the first = 5 times the second, the second must be $\frac{3}{5}$ of the first.

And since 3 times the first = 8 times the third, the third must be $\frac{3}{8}$ of the first.

The three parts are therefore as 1, $\frac{3}{5}$, and $\frac{3}{8}$, or as 40, 24, and 15.

Now, $40 + 24 + 15 = 79$, and $237 \div 79 = 3$.

Using this as a common multiplier, we have

$$\therefore \begin{array}{rcl} 40 \times 3 &=& 120 = \text{first part.} \\ 24 \times 3 &=& 72 = \text{second part.} \\ 15 \times 3 &=& 45 = \text{third part.} \\ \hline & & 237 \end{array}$$

No. CIII.—The Three Reapers. Solution.

As A, B, and C, working simultaneously, reap the field in 5 days, it is obvious that they together reap in one day $\frac{1}{5}$ of it. Now A's and C's day's work are together equal to twice B's. Therefore B's *plus* twice B's (or three times B's) also $= \frac{1}{5}$; and B's day's work = one-third of $\frac{1}{5} = \frac{1}{15}$.

Further, as A's and B's day's work together = three times C's, then C's plus three times C's (= four times C's) also = $\frac{1}{5}$, and C's day's work = $\frac{1}{4}$ of $\frac{1}{5} = \frac{1}{20}$.

Again, as all three together in one day do $\frac{1}{5}$, A must in one day do $\frac{1}{5} - (\frac{1}{15} + \frac{1}{20})$.

$$= \frac{12-(4+3)}{60} = \frac{12-7}{60} = \frac{5}{60} = \frac{1}{12}.$$

A would therefore take 12 days, B 15 days, and C 20 days to do the work singly.

No. CIV.—The Bag of Marbles. Solution.

If when Tom takes 4, Jack takes 3, and if when Tom takes 6, Dick takes 7, then when Tom takes 12 (the least common multiple of 4 and 6), Jack and Dick will take 9 and 14 respectively, and they will together have taken $12 + 9 + 14 = 35$ marbles. Now 35 is contained in 770 22 times, and therefore :—

$$\begin{array}{rl} \text{Tom's share will be } 12 \times 22 &= 264 \\ \text{Jack's } \quad,, \quad\quad 9 \times 22 &= 198 \\ \text{Dick's } \quad,, \quad\quad 14 \times 22 &= 308 \\ \hline & 770 \end{array}$$

Again, their respective ages will be as 12, 9, and 14; but 12, 9, and 14 together make 35, and the total of their ages is only $17\frac{1}{2}$ years, or one-half of 35. Their ages are therefore one-half the above figures, or 6, $4\frac{1}{2}$, and 7 respectively.

No. CV.—The Expunged Numerals. A. Solution.

The puzzle is solved by striking out the first figure of the top row, the whole of the second row, and the two first figures of the last row. The sum will then stand as under :—

```
        . 11
        . . .
        . . 9
        ----
          20
```

No. CVI.—The Expunged Numerals. B. Solution.

The dots indicate the figures to be expunged.

```
        . 11
        33 .
        . . .
        77 .
        . . .
        ----
        1111
```

No. CVII.—A Tradesman in a Difficulty. Solution.

1. The purchaser gives his one-dollar and his two-cent piece to the tradesman, and his three-cent piece to the stranger.
2. The tradesman gives his half-dollar to the purchaser, and his quarter-dollar to the stranger.
3. The stranger gives his two dimes and his one-cent piece to the purchaser, and his five-cent piece and his two-cent piece to the tradesman, when each has his right amount.

The correctness of the arrangement is not at once obvious, but it is easily proved. For the sake of brevity, we will call the purchaser P, the tradesman T, and the stranger S.

P has at the outset 1 dollar, 3 cents, and 2 cents, together = 105 cents. He should, therefore, have left, after paying for his goods, $105 - 34 = 71$ cents.

T has at the outset a half-dollar and a quarter-dollar, together = 75 cents. After receiving payment for his goods he should, therefore, have $75 + 34 = 109$ cents.

S has 2 dimes, 5 cents, 2 cents, and 1 cent, in all 28 cents. He has neither to gain nor lose by the transaction, so should be left at the close with the same amount. Let us now see how these figures correspond with the result of the transaction.

P parts with 1 dollar and 2 cents to T, and 3 cents to S, in all 105 cents. He has therefore no cash of his own left; but he receives from T 50 cents and from S 21 cents. He has, therefore, at the close of the transaction $50 + 21 = 71$ cents. T hands to P half a dollar, and to S a quarter-dollar; but, on the other hand, he receives from P 1 dollar and 2 cents, and from S 7 cents—in all, 109 cents.

S has given 2 dimes and 1 cent to P, and 7 cents to the tradesman. This ($= 28$ cents in all) clears him out. On the other hand, he receives from S a quarter-dollar, and from P 3 cents, which also together amount to 28 cents.

Each has therefore received the precise amount to which he was entitled.

No. CVIII.—Profit and Loss. Solution.

The original cost was £2 18s. 3d.

The difference between the marked price (65 shillings) and

the price obtained (56 shillings) is 9 shillings. This sum represents the amount of the actual loss, *plus* three times the amount of such loss (which latter item would have been the profit)—in all, four times the amount of the loss. The loss was, therefore, $\frac{9}{4}$ shillings, or 2s. 3d. Add this amount to the price obtained, £2 16s., and we have £2 18s. 3d., the cost price.

No. CIX.—A Curious Fraction. Solution.

The fraction in question is $\frac{240}{253}$.

To obtain the result, take the three denominations named, £1, 1s., and 1d: reduce all to pence, and add them together. The total $(240+12+1=253)$ will give us the denominator of the required fraction, while the value of £1 in pence (240) will be the numerator. The process is perhaps clearer in algebra. Thus:—

Let $\frac{x}{y}$ be the required fraction.

Then $\frac{x}{y}$ pounds $+\frac{x}{y}$ shillings $+\frac{x}{y}$ pence $=1$ pound.

Or, reducing all to the "pence" denomination—

$$\frac{240x + 12x + x}{y} = 240$$

$$\frac{253x}{y} = 240$$

$$\frac{x}{y} = \frac{240}{253}$$

Examining the correctness of the above result, we find that

$\frac{240}{253}$ of £1 $=$ 18s. $11\frac{169}{253}d.$

$\frac{240}{253}$ of 1s. $=$ $\quad 11\frac{97}{253}d.$

$\frac{240}{253}$ of 1d. $=$ $\quad \frac{240}{253}d.$

$\overline{\quad £1 \quad 0 \quad 0 \quad}$

No. CX.—The Menagerie. Solution.

There being 36 heads (*i.e.*, 36 creatures in all), if all had been birds they would have had 72 feet. If all had been beasts, they would have had 144 feet. It is clear, therefore, that there were some of each. Suppose the numbers equal, the feet would then count as under:—

    18 birds: 36 feet.
    18 beasts: 72 feet.

    36   108 feet (being an excess of 8 over the stated number.)

Each bird added to the "bird" half (involving at the same time the deduction therefrom of one beast) produces a diminution of 2 in the number of feet. As the equal division gives an excess of 8 feet, we must therefore deduct 4 beasts and add 4 birds.

    This gives us $18+4=22$ birds, having 44 feet.
                  $18-4=14$ beasts ,, 56 ,,

                        36   100

No. CXI.—The Market Woman and her Eggs. Solution.

Her original stock was seven.

To discover it, it is sufficient to note that she gave her last customer half her remaining stock, *plus* half an egg. As this left her with none, the half egg must have been equal to the half of her then stock, which must, therefore, have been 1 egg only. She gave the second customer *half* her then stock, *plus* half an egg; and as this left her with one egg only, it is obvious that the half in question must have been $1\frac{1}{2}$ egg. She had, therefore, prior to this second transaction 3 eggs left. At the first sale she gave half her original stock, *plus* half an egg, and as this left her with 3 eggs, it follows that her original stock must have been 7.

No CXII.—The Cook and his Assistants. Solution.

His original stock was 39. He gave half *plus* half an egg (*i.e.*, 20) to the first assistant. This left him with 19. He gave half of these *plus* half an egg ($9\frac{1}{2} + \frac{1}{2} = 10$) to the second assistant, and had then 9 left. He gave half of these *plus* half an egg ($4\frac{1}{2} + \frac{1}{2} = 5$) to the third assistant, and had 4 left.

The method of obtaining the solution is the same as in the last case.

The reader may be interested to know how problems of this class are constructed. As the division is by moieties, 2 is taken as the basis number, and this is raised to the power corresponding to the number of divisions. Thus in the two cases supposed, of *three* divisions, we take $2^3=8$. Multiply this by any number you please; subtract 1 from the result. The ultimate remainder, when the original number has been three times diminished as described, will be less by 1 than the number you multiplied by. Thus if we take as the starting-point,—

$(8 \times 1) - 1 = 7$, the ultimate remainder will be *nil*.
$(8 \times 2) - 1 = 15$,   ,,   ,,   ,, 1.
$(8 \times 3) - 1 = 23$,   ,,   ,,   ,, 2.
$(8 \times 4) - 1 = 31$,   ,,   ,,   ,, 3.
$(8 \times 5) - 1 = 39$,   ,,   ,,   ,, 4.

and so on.

Why the process indicated should have this peculiar result is a further puzzle, which we will leave to the ingenuity of our mathematical readers.

CHAPTER V.

WORD AND LETTER PUZZLES.

No. I.—A Puzzling Inscription.

The following queer inscription is said to be found in the chancel of a small church in Wales, just over the Ten Commandments. The addition of a single letter, repeated at various intervals, renders it not only intelligible, but appropriate to the situation:

P R S V R Y P R F C T M N

V R K P T H S P R C P T S T N.

What is the missing letter?

No. II.—An Easy One.

E D O R N O W.

Make one word of the above letters.

No. III.—Pied Proverbs.

Each of the following series of letters, duly arranged, will be found to form a popular proverb.

A. aeegghillmnnnoooorrsssstt.

B. aaceeeffhhiiiiimnoooprrssttttt.

C. aaaddeefiiimmunnoorttw.

D. aabbddeehhhhhiiiinnnoorrssttttuww.

E. aadegghiillllnoorsssttttt.

F. abdeefiinnnoopprrrssssttuw.

G. aabdeeeeefffhiiikmnnnrrsst.

H. aadeeehlllllllnssttww.

No. IV.—Scattered Sentiment.

Daruno em hslal verho,
Ni dasesns ro lege,
Lilt silfe rdaems eb vero,
Twees riemem's fo ethe.

The above, duly re-arranged, will be found to form a couplet suitable for a valentine.

No. V.—Dropped-Letter Proverbs.

Supply the missing letters, and each of the series following will be found to represent a popular proverb.*

a. A-t-t-h-n-t-m-s-v-s-n-n.

b. F-i-t-h-a-t-e-e-w-n-a-r-a-y.

c. S-r-k-w-i-e-h-i-o-s-h-t.

d. H-l-g-s-b-s-w-o-a-g-s-l-t.

e. B-r-s-f-f-t-r-f-c-t-g-t-r.

f. H-w-o-g-s-b-r-w-g-g-s-s-r-w-g.

g. C-l-r-n-d-f-o-s-p-k-h-t-t-h.

h. W-e-t-e-w-n-s-n-h-w-t-s-t.

---

* Each dash represents either a dropped letter or the space between two words. In some of the later examples one dash stands for two dropped letters.

i. S-r-r-k-n-n-s-m-k-l-n-f-n-s.

k. H-n-s-y-s-t-b-s-p-l-c-.

l. A-p-n-d-y-s-g-t-y-r.

m. T-k-c-r-f-h-p-n-n-t-e-p-n-s-w-l-t-k-c-r-f-t-e-s-l-s.

No. VI.—Dropped-Letter Nursery Rhymes.

The following, the missing letters being duly supplied, will be found to represent familar quotations of the juvenile order:—

(1.)   H-w-o-h-h-l-t-l-b-s-b-e
           I-p-o-e-a-h-h-n-n-h-u-;
           H-g-t-e-s-o-e-a-l-h-d-y
           F-o-e-e-y-p-n-n-f-o-e-.

(2.)   J-c-a-d-i-l-e-t-p-h-h-l-
           T-f-t-h-p-i-o-w-t-r :
           J-c-f-l-d-w-a-d-r-k-h-s-r-w-
           A-d-i-l-a-e-u-b-i-g-f-e-.

(3.)   H-y-i-d-e-i-d-c-h-c-t-n-t-e-i-d-l-
           T-e-o-j-m-e-o-e-t-e-o-n
           T-e-i-t-e-o-l-u-h-d-o-e-s-c-f-n-s-o-t
           A-d-h-d-s-r-n-w-y-i-h-h-s-o-n.

No. VII.—Transformations.

This is a form of word-puzzle that deserves to be better known, as it may be made productive of considerable amusement. It consists in taking a word of a given number of letters, and trying in how many "moves" or transpositions, altering only one letter each time, you can transform it into some other pre-arranged word of the like number of letters, but of different or opposite meaning; as Light into Heavy, Rose into Lily, Hard into Easy, or the like. Each step of the process must be a known word. We will take the last-named pair as an example. Five "moves" will in this case suffice, as under :—

R

Hard—(1) card, (2) cart, (3) cast, (4), east, (5) Easy.

This, however, is a more than usually favourable specimen, one of the letters, *a*, being common to both words, and, therefore, requiring no change. A considerably larger number of moves will usually be found necessary.*

The reader is invited to transform :—

> Hand into Foot—in six moves.
> Sin into Woe—in three moves.
> Hate into Love—in three moves.
> Black into White—in eight moves.
> Wood into Coal—in three moves.
> Blue into Pink—in four moves.
> Cat into Dog—in three moves.
> More into Less—in four moves.
> Rose into Lily—in five moves.
> Shoe into Boot—in three moves.†

No. VIII.—Beheaded Words.

1. Behead a tree, and leave the roof of a vault.
2. Behead "on high," and leave the topmost story.
3. Behead "thrown violently," and leave an organ of the body.
4. Behead a preposition, and leave a contest.
5. Behead your own property, and leave ours.
6. Behead to delete, and leave to destroy.
7. Behead a reproach, and leave a relative.
8. Behead to annoy, and leave comfort.
9. Behead an occurrence, and leave an airhole.

The deleted initials, taken in the above order, will give the name of an American general, after whom a well-known street in Paris is named.

---

* Unless one or more letters are common to both words, the number of moves cannot possibly be *less* than the number of letters in each word.

† Where several persons take part, this may be made a very amusing game. Certain pairs of words having been agreed upon, each takes the list, and tries in how few moves he can effect the required transformations, the player with the smallest total winning the game.

No. IX.—Anagrams.

An anagram is defined by Ogilvie as "the transposition of the letters of a name, by which a new word is formed." This definition hardly goes far enough, inasmuch as it ignores the far more interesting class of anagrams, in which the letters of a whole sentence are re-arranged so as to assume a different sense. To be worthy of serious consideration, however, the anagram must have a further quality—viz., that the new rendering must have some sort of relation to the original. In some cases a new rendering of this kind has happened to be singularly appropriate; so much so, indeed, that in less enlightened times people have claimed for anagrams a sort of inspiration, or magical significance. There is a historic instance in the case of James I., of England, whose name, *James Stuart*, was transposed by his courtiers, to his great delight, into *A just master*, and who was more than half persuaded of his descent from the mythical King Arthur, on the ground that his full name, *Charles James Stuart*, was capable of transposition into *Claims Arthur's Seat*. Another well-known instance is that of Lady Eleanor Davies, wife of the poet, Sir John Davies (*temp.*, Charles I.), who claimed to be a prophetess, on the somewhat unsubstantial ground that the letters of her name, *Dame Eleanor Davies*, duly shuffled, form the sentence *Reveal, O Daniel.* Her pretensions ultimately caused her to be arraigned before the Court of High Commission, when the Dean of Arches pointed out that the same letters might also read *Never so mad a ladie.* The public preferred the latter rendering, and no more was heard of the *soi-disant* prophetess.

A recent prize competition among readers of *Tit-Bits*, for the best anagrammatic rendering of the title of either of the articles in a given number, produced the following, "Dangers of amateur physicking," "The sick men pay for drugs again." This is a model of what an anagram should be, and we can well understand a credulous person believing that there must be something more than mere chance in so pregnant a warning.

The following are instances of specially meritorious anagrams, in various languages:—

Ie charme tout, an anagrammatic rendering, attributed to

Henri IV., of the name of *Marie Touchet*, the mistress of Charles IX.

Honor est a Nilo—Horatio Nelson.

Quid est veritas? (the Latin rendering of Pilate's question, "What is truth?"). *Est vir qui adest*—"It is the man who is before you."

Flit on, cheering angel.—Florence Nightingale.

The Tichborne trial gave rise to a somewhat complicated anagram. *Sir Roger Charles Doughty Tichborne, Baronet—You horrid butcher, Orton, biggest rascal here.*

We append a brief selection for our readers to exercise their ingenuity upon.

a. *Rare mad frolic.* Transposed, represents—a political cry.

b. *Got a scant religion :*—the name of a prominent division of Nonconformists.

c. *Best in prayer :*—ditto, ditto.

d. *Lady mine :*—what every unmarried lady should be.

e. *City life :*—happiness.

f. *Tournament :*—a description of tilting.

g. *Melodrama :*—what melodrama ought to be.

h. *Misanthrope :*—what he deserves.

i. *Old England :*—the same country poetically described.

j. *Telegraphs :*—what they are to commerce.

k. *Lawyers :*—a satirical description of themselves.

l. *Astronomers :*—ditto.

m. *Astronomers :*—their occupation gone.

No. X.—Word Squares.

The problem in this case is to arrange a series of words, having the like number of letters each, one above the other, in such manner that they shall read alike, whether in a horizontal or vertical direction. The following are examples of sixteen letter squares.

Take the equivalent (a word in four letters) of—

Word and Letter Puzzles.

a.
1. A narrow road.
2. A plane surface.
3. A preposition signifying propinquity.
4. Two parts of the body.

b.
1. Not any.
2. Across.
3. Not far.
4. Does wrong.

c.
1. Halting.
2. Dry.
3. A possessive pronoun.
4. Paradise.

d.
1. A burden.
2. A river.
3. Begs.
4. A piece of writing-furniture.

e.
1. A puppet.
2. A river.
3. A wild beast.
4. Solitary.

f.
1. A noted city.
2. A stone, reputed unlucky.
3. To knock about.
4. A girl's name.

The next two examples are of words of *five* and *six* letters:—

g.
1. To squander.
2. A stage player.
3. A mineral concretion.
4. A pick-me-up.
5. Upright.

h.
1. A shepherd.
2. Dress.
3. Thick-headed.
4. Walking on the toes.
5. A bird.
6. To ransom.

No. XI.—Word Diamonds.

Sometimes, instead of a square, the letters are required to be arranged in the form of a diamond, say, one letter in the top line, three in the second, five in the third, three in the fourth, and one in the last line, subject to the same condition—that, horizontally or vertically, they shall read alike. The following are examples:—

a.
1. A single letter.
2. The juice of the olive.
3. Fir trees.
4. A meadow.
5. A single letter.

b.
1. A single letter.
2. A garden tool.
3. Substantives.
4. An extremity.
5. A single letter.

c.
1. A single letter.
2. The cry of a sheep.
3. A sweetmeat.
4. A girl's name.
5. A single letter.

d.
1. A vowel.
2. An animal.
3. Eve's bane.
4. A tree.
5. A vowel.

e.
1. A consonant.
2. The ocean.
3. Arab dwellings.
4. Consumed.
5. A consonant.

f.
1. A single letter.
2. Smoked pig-meat.
3. A male Christian name.
4. The title of a married lady.
5. A single letter.

g.
1. A consonant.
2. To place.
3. A fruit.
4. An adverb denoting excess.
5. A consonant.

h.
1. A consonant.
2. A feature.
3. A boundary.
4. A deep hole.
5. A consonant.

The next pair are a trifle more elaborate, the longest word having seven, instead of five, letters.

i.
1. A consonant.
2. A point.
3. The Papal crown.
4. A precious stone.
5. Haughty.
6. A conjunction.
7. A consonant.

j.
1. A consonant.
2. Phœbus.
3. Tasty.
4. Jove.
5. Saltpetre.
6. A river.
7. A consonant.

In the next pair the longest word is of *nine* letters.

k.
1. A consonant.
2. A precious stone.
3. Danger.
4. A military officer.
5. A performer of nocturnal music.
6. A marvel.
7. A long spoon.
8. Sheltered from the wind.
9. A consonant.

l.
1. A consonant.
2. Instead of.
3. Apple centres.
4. Pincers.
5. Chinaware.
6. To choose again.
7. Vacancy.
8. To occupy a seat.
9. A consonant.

No. XII.—A Cross of Diamonds.

This is an extremely ingenious puzzle. Required, to form a cross consisting of four diamonds of five words each, united in the centre by five additional letters, forming a smaller diamond, after the fashion shown in Fig. 370:—

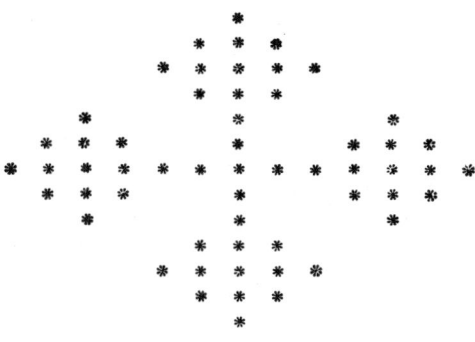

Fig. 370.

The diamond at top is to be made up as follows: 1, a single letter; 2, the queen of the fairies; 3, a title of courtesy applied to ladies; 4, wicked; 5, a single letter.

The right-hand diamond as follows: 1, a single letter; 2, past tense of a verb meaning to possess; 3, a colourless fluid; 4, the abode of a wild animal; 5, a single letter.

The left-hand diamond: 1, a single letter; 2, a fruit; 3, a flower; 4, a metal; 5, a single letter.

The bottom diamond: 1, a single letter; 2, to strike; 3, close; 4, an article; 5, a single letter.

The central diamond, read in conjunction with the bottom letter of the top diamond, the top letter of the bottom diamond, the left-hand letter of the right-hand diamond, and the right-hand letter of the left-hand diamond, will form as follows:—From centre to top, a male sheep; from centre to bottom, a small animal; from centre to right, crude; from centre to left, a quick blow; from top to centre, to deface; from bottom to centre, a resinous substance; from right to centre, open hostility; from left to centre, equal value.

Each diamond (other than that in the centre) must be perfect in itself, forming the same words both horizontally and vertically.

No. XIII.—Knight's Tour Letter Puzzles.

The principle of the "Knight's Tour" on the chessboard has been made the foundation of another and different class of puzzles. The squares of the chessboard are here occupied by letters or words (one in each square), which, if read

R	L	T	E	Y	L	R	O
Y	H	L	T	O	B	T	A
T	A	A	A		H	T	I
E	L		E	I	N	E	O
D	H	W		Y	E	S	Y
R	T	E	S	D		B	W
Y	N	E	S	N	D	A	E
H	A	A	A	W	I	D	E

A. Fig. 371.

in due sequence, according to Knight's Tour rules, form a proverb, a verse of poetry, or a well-known quotation. A (Fig. 371) is an example of this class. The letters, read aright, will be found to form a popular proverb.

B (Fig. 372), furnishes another example, and C (Fig. 373), a third.

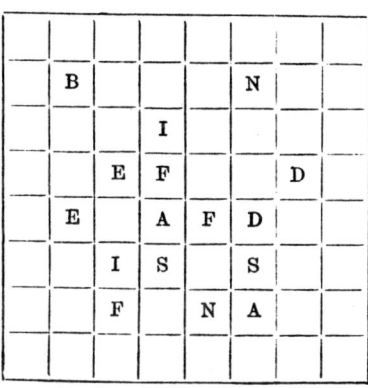

B. Fig. 372.

C. Fig. 373.

No. XIV.—Knight's Tour Word Puzzle.

The words of the following puzzle (Fig. 374), duly read

sym-pathy	man	the	link	in	granted	body	it
is	the	the	in	be-neath	liveth	fierce	soon as
to	secret	alone	not	silver	and	fly;	in
silken,	it.	given	the	soul	mind,	wishes	desire,
has	heaven	it	to	the	fan-tasy's	can	to
die;	tie	gift	not	desire	heart,	with	whose
it	God	heart	doth	hot	love's	mind	bind.
which	not	is	which	and,	dead	fire,	true

Fig. 374.

according to Knight's Tour rules, will be found to form a well-known passage from the "Lay of the Last Minstrel."

No. XV.—Hidden Proverbs.

```
R E N O W N E D T H A N W
S Y O U R C A K E A N D A
S T E T O B E F E A R H R
E A R K S S P O I L E A F
L E O O H E R S N T D V O
O T M O T L I N O H T E U
N O S C A L A G M E H I R
S N I Y G O R S O B A T S
E N G N E N O T S R N P A
I A O A M O O T S O A E W
R C D E V I L A H T D A S
O U O Y N O I L D A E C A
T C I V R E H H T A H E Z
```

The above apparent jumble contains five well-known proverbs, arranged in a systematic order. When the clue is once discovered, the proverbs can be read without difficulty.

PUZZLE: *To find it.*

No. XVI.—The Five Arab Maxims.

The subjoined table (Fig. 375), to any one who can read

never	all	for he who	all	often	more than
tell	you may know	tells	he knows	tells	he knows
attempt	you can do	attempts	he can do	attempts	he can do
believe	you hear	believes	he hears	believes	he hears
spend	you can afford	spends	he can afford	spends	he can afford
decide upon	you may see	decides upon	he sees	decides upon	he sees

Fig. 375.

it rightly, contains five maxims, said to be held in great esteem by the Bedouin Arabs.

KEY TO CHAPTER V.

WORD AND LETTER PUZZLES.

No. I.—A Puzzling Inscription. Solution.

The letter E, which, inserted at the proper intervals, makes the inscription read as under:—

PERSEVERE YE PERFECT MEN,
EVER KEEP THESE PRECEPTS TEN.

No. II.—An Easy One.

This is a problem of the "quibble" order. The seven letters duly arranged form ONE WORD.

No. III.—Pied Proverbs. Solutions.

A. Rolling stones gather no moss.
B. Procrastination is the thief of time.
C. Time and tide wait for no man.
D. A bird in the hand is worth two in the bush.
E. All is not gold that glitters.
F. Fine words butter no parsnips.
G. Fine feathers make fine birds.
H. All's well that ends well.

No. IV.—Scattered Sentiment. Solution.

The lines should read as follows:—

Around me shall hover,
In sadness or glee,
Till life's dreams be over,
Sweet mem'ries of thee.

No. V.—Dropped-Letter Proverbs.

a. A stitch in time saves nine.
b. Faint heart never won fair lady.
c. Strike while the iron's hot.
d. He laughs best who laughs last.
e. Birds of a feather flock together.
f. He who goes a borrowing goes a sorrowing.
g. Children and fools speak the truth.
h. When the wine is in, the wit is out.
i. Short reckonings make long friends.
k. Honesty is the best policy.
l. A pin a day is a groat a year.
m. Take care of the pence, and the pounds will take care of themselves.

No. VI.—Dropped-Letter Nursery Rhymes.

(1) How doth the little busy bee
Improve each shining hour;
He gathers honey all the day
From every opening flower.

(2) Jack and Jill went up the hill
To fetch a pail of water;
Jack fell down and broke his crown,
And Jill came tumbling after.

(3) Hey diddle diddle, the cat and the fiddle,
The cow jumped over the moon,
The little dog laughed to see such fine sport,
And the dish ran away with the spoon.

No. VII.—Transformations. Solutions.

Hand; hard; lard;* lord; ford; fort; Foot.
Sin; son; won; Woe.
Hate; have; lave; Love.
Black; slack; stack; stalk;* stale; shale; whale; while; White.

---

* These are examples of a necessity, which frequently arises, of inter-

Wood; wool; cool; Coal.
Blue; bile; pile; pine; Pink.
Cat; cot; cog; Dog.
More; lore; lose; loss; Less.
Rose; lose; lost; list; lilt; Lily.
Shoe; shot; soot; Boot.

No. VIII.—Beheaded Words.

1. L-arch.
2. A-loft.
3. F-lung.
4. A-bout.
5. Y-ours.
6. E-rase.
7. T-aunt.
8. T-ease.
9. E-vent.

The initials, as will be seen, give the word LAFAYETTE.

No. IX.—Anagrams.

a. Radical reform.
b. Congregationalist.
c. Presbyterian.
d. Maidenly.
e. Felicity.
f. To run at men.
g. Made moral.
h. Spare him not.
i. Golden Land.
j. Great helps.
k. Sly ware.
l. Moon-starers.
m. No more stars.

---

posing a move which does not directly aid the transformation, but indirectly as a link with some more desirable word.

In the first example, the word "food" might (in place of "fort") form the intermediate step between "ford" and "foot."

No. X.—Word Squares.

a. L A N E
    A R E A
    N E A R
    E A R S

b. N O N E
    O V E R
    N E A R
    E R R S

c. L A M E
    A R I D
    M I N E
    E D E N

d. L O A D
    O U S E
    A S K S
    D E S K

e. D O L L
    O H I O
    L I O N
    L O N E

f. R O M E
    O P A L
    M A U L
    E L L A

g. W A S T E
    A C T O R
    S T O N E
    T O N I C
    E R E C T

h. P A S T O R
    A T T I R E
    S T U P I D
    T I P T O E
    O R I O L E
    R E D E E M

No. XI.—Word Diamonds. Solutions.

In solving puzzles of this class, endeavour, if the indications be sufficient, to guess the centre or key word. Arrange this word in the form of a cross, thus—

         P
         I
P I N E S.
         E
         S

If you have guessed rightly so far, the discovery of the remaining words is a comparatively easy matter.

If the indication given as to the key word is too vague to guide you, endeavour to discover one or both of the next

Key to Word and Letter Puzzles.

longest words, which will frequently give a clue to the principal word.

```
a.      P                    b.      N
      O I L                        H O E
    P I N E S                    N O U N S
      L E A                        E N D
        S                            S


c.      C                    d.      A
      B A A                        A P E
    C A N D Y                    A P P L E
      A D A                        E L M
        Y                            E


e.      T                    f.      H
      S E A                        H A M
    T E N T S                    H A R R Y
      A T E                        M R S
        S                            Y


g.      M                    h.      L
      S E T                        L I P
    M E L O N                    L I M I T
      T O O                        P I T
        N                            T


i.        D                  j.        J
        T I P                        S U N
      T I A R A                    S A P I D
    D I A M O N D              J U P I T E R
      P R O U D                    N I T R E
        A N D                        D E E
          D                            R
```

k.
```
           S                  l.            P
         G E M                            F O R
       P E R I L                        C O R E S
     G E N E R A L                    F O R C E P S
   S E R E N A D E R              P O R C E L A I N
     M I R A C L E                    R E E L E C T
       L A D L E                        S P A C E
         L E E                            S I T
           R                                N
```

No. XII.—A Cross of Diamonds. Solution.

```
              M
            M A B
          M A D A M
            B A D
      T       M       W
    N U T     A     H A D
  T U L I P A R A W A T E R
    T I N     A     D E N
      P       T       R
            H I T
          T I G H T
            T H E
              T
```

No. XIII.—Knight's Tour Letter Puzzles.
Solution.

A. Fig. 376 indicates the order in which the letters are to be taken, when they will be found to read as follows:—

"Early to bed and early to rise
Is the way to be healthy, and wealthy, and wise."

3	40	19	36	5	50	21	34
18	37	4	51	20	35	6	49
41	2	39	54		52	33	22
38	17		1	58	55	48	7
13	42	57		53	60	23	32
16	27	14	59	56		8	47
43	12	29	26	45	10	31	24
28	15	44	11	30	25	46	9

Fig. 376.

In B the order of the letters is as shown in Fig. 377, the hidden proverb being, "Safe bind, safe find."

	5				7		
			6				
		4	13			8	
	12		10	3	16		
		14	1		9		
		11		15	2		

FIG. 377.

In C the order is as shown in Fig. 378, and the proverb, "More haste, less speed."

				9			
		4				8	
			10	5			
	17		3		7		
		11	6	13			
18		16		2		14	
			12	15		1	

Fig. 378.

No. XIV.—The Knight's Tour Word Puzzle. Solution.

43	10	41	46	29	24	59	26
40	47	44	61	12	27	30	23
9	42	11	28	45	60	25	58
48	39	8	13	62	57	22	31
7	14	35	52	3	18	63	56
38	49	4	17	34	53	32	21
15	6	51	36	19	2	55	64
50	37	16	5	54	33	20	1

FIG. 379.

The key to this puzzle will be found in Fig. 379. Read according to the order here indicated, it will be found that the words make the following stanza:—

> "True love's the gift which God has given
> To man alone beneath the heaven:
> It is not fantasy's hot fire,
> Whose wishes, soon as granted, fly;
> It liveth not in fierce desire,
> With dead desire it doth not die:
> It is the secret sympathy,
> The silver link, the silken tie,
> Which heart to heart, and mind to mind,
> In body and in soul can bind."
>
> *Lay of the Last Minstrel.   Canto V.*

Key to Word and Letter Puzzles.

The construction of other problems on the same model will be found very interesting. Should the passage used be less than the full number of sixty-four words, a word may here and there be cut in two, so as to occupy two squares, or the superfluous squares may be left unoccupied. If the quotation be too long, two words may be made to occupy a single square, like "soon as" in the example given.

No. XV.—Hidden Proverbs. Solution.

The five proverbs are as follows:—
  A rolling stone gathers no moss.
  Too many cooks spoil the broth.
  A live dog is more to be feared than a dead lion.
  You cannot eat your cake and have it.
  Peace hath her victories, no less renowned than war.

To read them, first find the central letter, which is A. This begins the first proverb. Immediately below this will be found R, to the left of this O, and above the O two L's. To the right of the last L are the letters I N. The G, completing the word "rolling," comes next below the N, and below this, S, the initial of the next word, "stone." From the S, moving to the left, we have the remaining letters, T O N E, and so we read on, following the course of the sun, round each square of letters in succession.

For greater clearness we exhibit separately the central square and a few letters of the next square, showing the commencement of the process.

```
      L I N
      L A G
      O R S
    E N O T
```

No. XVI.—The Five Arab Maxims. Solution.

The key to this puzzle consists in reading first the words in the first and second lines alternately. Then those in the first and third alternately. Then in the first and fourth, the first and fifth, and first and sixth in succession. The maxims will then be found to run as follows:—

"Never tell all you know; for he who tells all he knows, often tells more than he knows."

"Never attempt all you can do; for he who attempts all he can do often attempts more than he can do."

"Never believe all you hear, for he who believes," etc., etc.

And so on, the words in the first line being common to each maxim.

CHAPTER VI.

PUZZLES WITH COUNTERS.

Puzzles of this class are frequently propounded in more or less fanciful forms,—*e.g.*, a gardener is required to plant trees, or an officer to place his men, in such manner as to answer the conditions of the problem. From considerations of space, we have thought it best to leave such fanciful elaborations for the most part to the imagination of the reader. Should he prefer to put the question in such a shape, he will have little difficulty in inventing an appropriate legend.

No. I.

Required, to arrange eleven counters in such manner that they shall form twelve rows, with three counters in each row.

No. II.

Required, to arrange nine counters in such manner that they shall form ten rows, with three counters in each row.

No. III.

Required, to arrange twenty-seven counters in such manner as to form nine rows, with six counters in each row.

No. IV.

Required, to arrange ten counters in such manner that they shall form five rows, with four counters in each row.

No. V.

Required, to arrange twelve counters in such manner that they shall make six rows of four counters each.

No. VI.

Required, to arrange nineteen counters in such manner that they shall form nine rows of five counters each.

No. VII.

Required, to arrange sixteen counters so as to form ten rows, with four counters in each row.

No. VIII.

Required, to arrange twelve counters in such manner that they shall count four in a straight line in seven different directions.

No. IX.

Required, to arrange nine white and nine red counters in such manner that there shall be ten rows, of three counters each, *white*, and eight rows of three each *red*.

No. X.

Given, a square, divided into nine smaller squares. Required, to arrange counters in the eight outer squares in such manner that there shall always be nine on each side of the square, though the total be repeatedly varied, being 24, 20, 28, 32, and 36 in succession.

This is a very ancient problem. It is usually propounded after the fashion following: A blind abbot was at the head

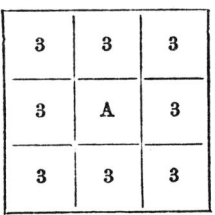

FIG. 380.

of a monastery of twenty-four monks, who were domiciled three in a cell in eight cells, occupying the four sides of a square, while the abbot himself occupied a cell in the centre. To assure himself that all were duly housed for the night, he was in the habit of visiting the cells at frequent intervals, and counting the occupants, reckoning that if he found nine monks in each row of three cells (see Fig. 380), the tale was complete.

But the brethren succeeded in eluding his vigilance. First

four of them absented themselves (reducing the number to twenty), but still the abbot counted and found nine in a row. Then these four returned, bringing four friends with them, thus making twenty-eight persons, and yet the normal nine in a row was not increased. Presently four more outsiders came in, making thirty-two. The result was the same. Again, four more visitors arrived, making a total of thirty-six, but the abbot, going his rounds, found nine persons in each row as before.

How was this managed?

No. XI.

Required, so to place ten counters that they shall count four in a row in eight different directions.

No. XII.

Required, so to place thirteen counters that they shall count five in a straight line in twelve different directions.

No. XIII.

This is a puzzle of a different character.

Given, an eight-pointed star, as shown in Fig. 381, and seven counters. You are required to place the counters on

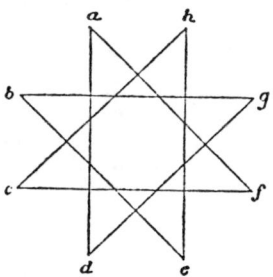

Fig. 381.

seven of the points of the star, in so doing strictly following the rule following—viz., Each counter is to be drawn from a vacant point along the corresponding line to another vacant point, and there left. You then start from another vacant point, and proceed in like manner till the seven points are covered.

No. XIV.—The "Okto" Puzzle.

The puzzle brought out under this name is a variation on the foregoing. Each point of the star terminates in a small circle, on which is printed the name of a given colour—black, yellow, carmine, and so on. The counters, eight in number, are of corresponding colours. The aspirant is required to cover seven of the circles, according to the rule laid down for the last puzzle, each with the counter of its proper colour.

No. XV.

Given, the figure described in Fig. 382.

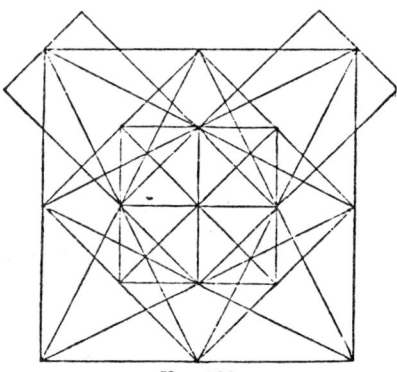

Fig. 382.

Required, to place at the intersections of its various lines twenty-one counters, in such manner as to form thirty rows of three counters each, each group of three being united by one of the lines.

No. XVI.

This is sometimes known as the "crowning" puzzle. The reader will remember that at the game of draughts a man reaching the opposite side of the board becomes a king, and is "crowned" by having a second man placed on the top of it. In the case of the puzzle we are about to describe ten counters, or men, are placed in a row, and the player is required to "crown" five of them after the following fashion. He is to take up one counter, pass it to right or left *over two others*, and crown the one next in order, proceeding in like manner till the whole are crowned.

A king, it should be stated, is still regarded as being *two* counters.

No. XVII.—The "Right and Left" Puzzle.

This is a very excellent puzzle, and has the special recommendation of being very little known. Rule on cardboard a rectangular figure consisting of seven equal spaces, each one inch square (see Fig. 383). In the three spaces to the left place three red, and in the three spaces to the right three white counters, the space in the middle being left unoccupied.

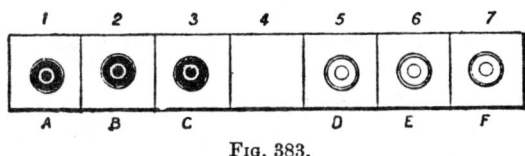

Fig. 383.

The puzzle is to transpose the red and white counters, so that the three white shall be in the left hand, and the three red in the right hand spaces. This is to be done in accordance with the following conditions, viz.:—

1. Each counter can only be moved one space at a time.

2. If a counter is divided from a vacant space by a single counter only, it may pass over it into such vacant space.

3. Counters may only be moved in a *forward* direction— *i.e.*, red to the right, and white to the left. A move once made cannot be retracted.

No. XVIII.

This is a further development of the same problem. Rule a sheet of paper into squares so that each horizontal row shall contain seven, and each vertical row five, and upon them place red and white counters (17 of each colour), as shown in the diagram* (Fig. 384), the central space (No. 18) being left vacant.

---

* If preferred, one corner of a draught- or gobang-board may be used, in place of the ruled paper.

270   *Puzzles Old and New.*

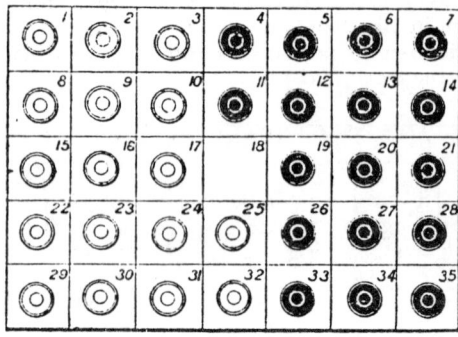

Fig. 384.

You are required, under the same conditions as in the last case, to transpose the red and white counters.

No. XIX.—The "Four and Four" Puzzle.

This is in general idea very similar to the two puzzles last described, but it is wholly different in working.

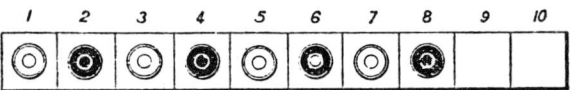

Fig. 385.

Rule on cardboard a rectangular figure, divided into ten squares, as Fig. 385, and in the first eight spaces, beginning from the left hand, dispose eight counters, red and black alternately.

The puzzle is, moving them *two at a time*, to get the four

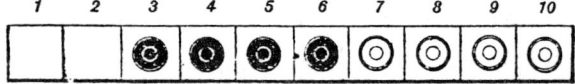

Fig. 386.

red and the four black counters grouped each colour **together** without any interval, and this must be done *in four moves* *only*. At the close of the operation the eight counters should be as shown in Fig. 386.

They are then to be worked back again, after the same fashion, to their original positions.

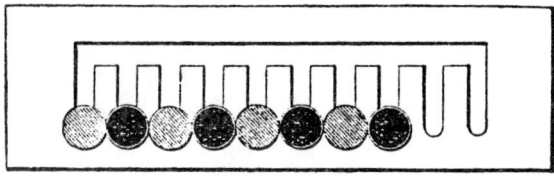

Fig. 387.

This puzzle is sometimes arranged in the form of a slip of wood, seven inches by two, with its central portion cut out with a fret-saw, as shown in Fig. 387. The counters are here replaced by little blocks of wood, each in the shape of a collar-stud. They may be shifted backwards and forwards from gap to gap with great ease, but cannot be detached from the board, and are therefore always available for use.

No. XX.—The "Five and Five" Puzzle.

This is the same as that last described, save that *ten* counters, five of each colour, are used, and that the desired transposition is to be effected in *five* moves.

No. XXI.—The "Six and Six" Puzzle.

This is again the same problem, but with *twelve* counters, six of each colour, the transposition to be effected in *six* moves.

No. XXII.—The Thirty-six Puzzle.

Thirty-six counters are arranged in the form of a square, six rows of six each.

Required, to remove six counters in such manner that the remaining counters shall still have an even number in each row, horizontal and vertical.

No. XXIII.—The "Five to Four" Puzzle.

Twenty-five counters are arranged in the form of a square, five rows of five each.

Required, to remove five counters in such manner that the remainder shall be four in a row, horizontally and vertically.

No. XXIV.—No Two in a Row.

With an ordinary draught-board, and eight draughtsmen or counters.

Required, so to dispose the eight men upon various squares of the board that no two shall be in the same line, either vertically, horizontally, or diagonally.

No. XXV.—The "Simple" Puzzle.

A further and very interesting development of the last-mentioned "poser" has been brought out, under the name

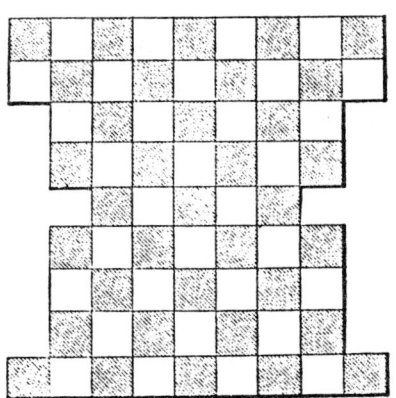

Fig. 388.

of the "Simple" Puzzle, by Messrs. Feltham. Simple as it may be, in a sense, we have known much keen thought expended upon it before the coveted solution was obtained.

A special board of 67 squares is used, arranged as shown in
Fig. 388, and the problem is to place *nine* counters upon it,
in accordance with the conditions of the last puzzle.

N.B.—It should be stated that the indentations on either
side of the board do not affect the conditions. Thus, two
counters placed respectively in the left hand top and bottom
corner squares would be regarded as being in the same
line, notwithstanding that there is a break of continuity
between them.

No. XXVI.—The "English Sixteen" Puzzle.

A clever puzzle, under the above title, is issued by
Messrs. Heywood, of Manchester. In the result to be attained it is almost identical with No. XVIII. (p. 269), but
the conditions are in this case somewhat different, and the
puzzle considerably more difficult.

A board, as illustrated in Fig. 389, is used, with eight

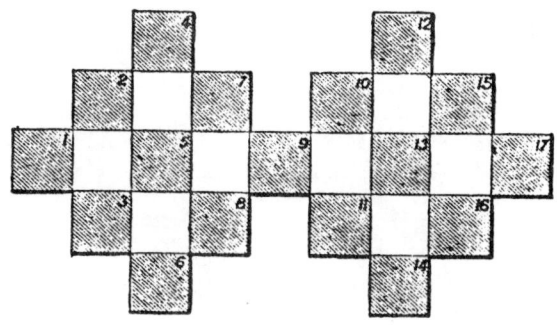

Fig. 389.

white and eight red counters. These are arranged on the
black squares, the red to the right, the white to the left, the
central square, No. 9 in the figure, being left vacant. The
problem, as in the puzzle above-mentioned, is to transpose
the red and white counters, the men to be moved according to "draughts" rules—*i.e.*, forward only; the whites
towards the spaces occupied by the reds, and the reds
towards the spaces occupied by the whites. The men move
only on the black squares, and therefore diagonally. A

white man can pass over a black man, or a black man over a white man, provided that the space next beyond is vacant.

No. XXVII.—The Twenty Counters.

Required, (*a*) so to arrange twenty counters as to form therewith thirteen different squares.

(*b*) To remove six counters only from the figure formed as above, so that no single square shall remain.

KEY TO CHAPTER VI.

PUZZLES WITH COUNTERS.

N.B.—It must not be taken for granted, in the case of puzzles which demand a particular arrangement of counters, that the solution given is the only one possible, as there may frequently be two or more modes of arrangement which will equally answer the conditions of the problem.

No. I.—Solution.

The eleven counters are arranged as shown in Fig. 390.

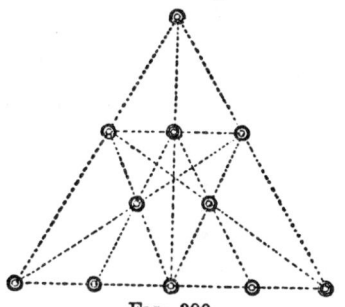

Fig. 390.

The five at bottom count as two rows of three, the counter in the middle being common to both.

No. II.—Solution.

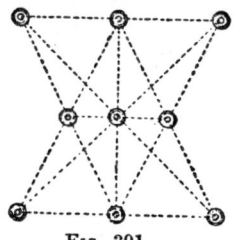

Fig. 391.

Arrange the nine counters as shown in Fig. 391.

No. III.—Solution.

There are several different arrangements which will

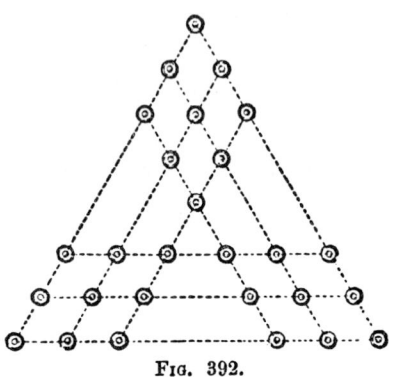

Fig. 392.

answer the conditions of this problem. Figs. 392 and 393 represent two of such arrangements.

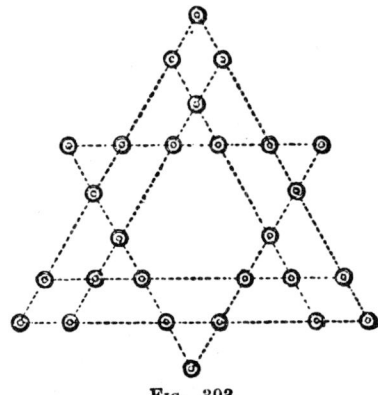

Fig. 393.

Key to Puzzles with Counters.

No. IV.—Solution.

This again may be solved in various ways. Either of

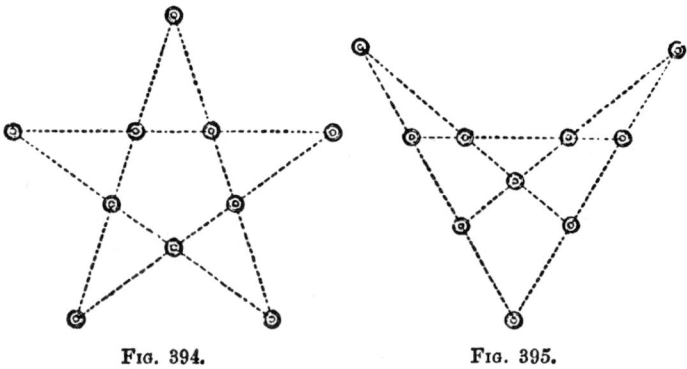

FIG. 394.   FIG. 395.

the subjoined arrangements (Figs. 394 and 395) will answer the required conditions.

No. V.—Solution.

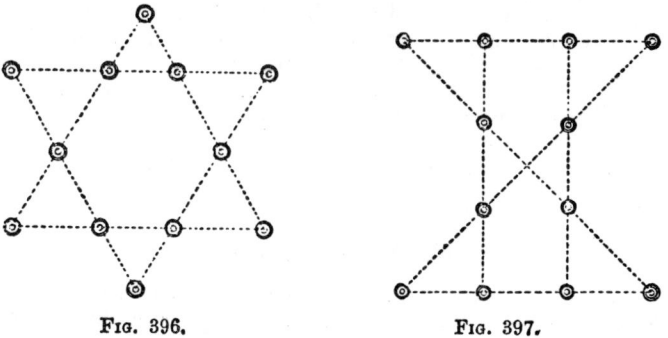

FIG. 396.   FIG. 397.

The counters may be arranged as shown in Fig. 396 or Fig. 397.

No. VI.—Solution.

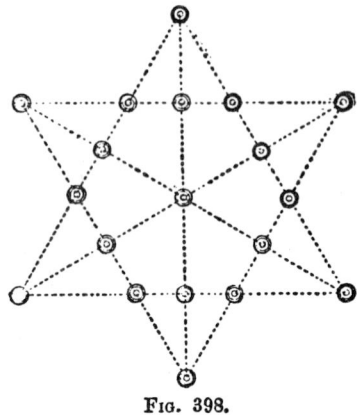

Fig. 398.

The nineteen counters should be arranged as shown in Fig. 398.

No. VII.—Solution.

This is a puzzle of a class that sometimes perplexes by reason of its very simplicity, the experimenter seeking for some abstruse method of solution, while the real mode lies close to his hand. All that is needed in this case is to arrange the sixteen counters in four rows of four each, forming a square. There are thus four vertical and four horizontal rows, while the diagonals from corner to corner supply the two additional rows required by the problem.

No. VIII.—Solution.

Lay out nine counters in three rows of three each, so as to form a square. This done, distribute the remaining three as follows:—place one counter on the first of the first row, another on the second of the second row, and the third on the last of the third row.

No. IX.—Solution.

The counters must be arranged as in the subjoined dia-

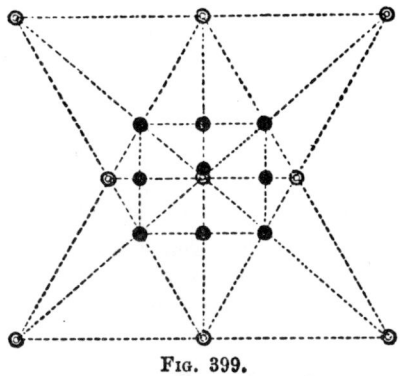

Fig. 399.

gram (Fig. 399). Note that the centre counter is duplicated, a red counter lying half over a white counter, or *vice versâ*, so as to do double duty.

No. X.—Solution.

The secret lies in increasing or diminishing, as the case may require, the number of persons in the corner cells,

4	1	4
1		1
4	1	4

Fig. 400.

2	5	2
5		5
2	5	2

Fig. 401.

each of which counts twice over, and so, to a person as doddering as the abbot must be assumed to have been, seems at first sight to increase the general total. Thus when the four monks absented themselves, the remaining twenty were re-arranged as in Fig. 400; and when they returned with four other persons, the twenty-eight were dis-

1	7	1
7		7
1	7	1

Fig. 402.

0	9	0
9		9
0	9	0

Fig. 403.

posed as in Fig. 401. When four more visitors arrived, the thirty-two were distributed as in Fig. 402; and when the final four arrived, the party, now numbering thirty-six, were arranged as in Fig. 403.

No. XI.—Solution.

This is a quibble dependent on the special wording of the problem. You begin by distributing the counters in three rows of three each, forming a square, and then place the remaining counter on the centre one. You have now four rows of four each; but as each row can be counted in two different directions—*i.e.*, from right to left or left to right, and vertical rows upwards or downwards—you are enabled to count four in eight different directions, as required by the problem.

No. XII.—Solution.

This is effected on a similar principle. You arrange nine of the counters in three rows of three each, forming a square as above described, and place the remaining four one on each of the four "corner" counters. This gives you six rows of five each, enabling you to count five in twelve different directions.

No. XIII.—Solution.

The secret lies in working backwards throughout, each time covering the point from which you last started. Thus, placing a counter on *a*, draw it along the line *a d*, and leave

Key to Puzzles with Counters. 281

it on *d*. *a* is now the next point to be covered, and there is only one vacant line, *f a*, which leads to it. Place, therefore, your second counter on *f*, draw it along *f a*, and leave it on *a*. The third counter must be placed on *c*, drawn along *c f*, and left on *f*. The next placed on *h*, and left on *c*. The fifth is placed on *e*, and left on *h*. The sixth is placed on *b*, and left on *e*; and the seventh placed on *g*, and left on *b*.

You now have the whole seven counters duly placed, and only one point, *g*, left uncovered.

No. XIV.—The "Okto" Puzzle. Solution.

The requirement in this case that each circle shall be covered with a counter of a given colour does not in reality add anything to the difficulty of the puzzle, though it appears to do so to any one attempting it for the first time. The experimenter has only to proceed as indicated in the last solution, taking care in each case to use the counter corresponding in colour with the circle on which he proposes to leave it.

No. XV.—Solution.

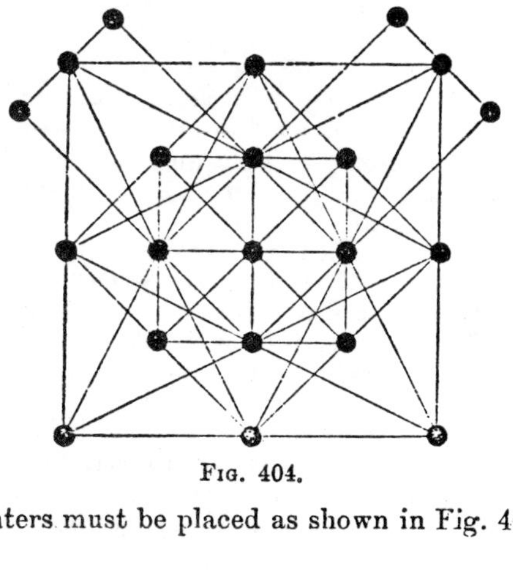

Fig. 404.

The counters must be placed as shown in Fig. 404.

No. XVI.—Solution.

Supposing the row of counters to be indicated from left to right by numbers as under—

1, 2, 3, 4, 5, 6, 7, 8, 9, 10.

Proceed as follows:—

Place 4 on 1, 6 on 9, 8 on 3, 2 on 5, and 10 on 7.

or

Place 4 on 1, 7 on 3, 5 on 9, 2 on 6, and 10 on 8.

There are several formulas which will answer the problem, but a person trying the puzzle for the first time will find some difficulty in hitting upon one of them.

No. XVII.—The "Right and Left" Puzzle. Solution.

The key to this puzzle lies in the observance of the following rules:—

1. After having moved a counter, one *of the opposite colour* must invariably be passed over it.

2. After having passed one counter over another, the next advance will be *with the same colour* as such first-mentioned counter. The position will guide you whether to move or to pass over, only one of such alternatives being usually open to you.

The above rules, however, only apply up to a certain point. After the ninth move you will find that the next should be with a counter of the same colour; but none such is available. By this time, however, the puzzle is practically solved. The counters are white and red alternately, with the space to the extreme left vacant, and two or three obvious moves place the counters so as to answer the conditions of the problem.

Thus, if we begin with the white counters, the moves will be as under (see Fig. 383), the spaces being designated by the numbers, and the counters by the letters:—

1. *D* moves into space 4.
2. *C* passes over *D* into space 5.
3. *B* moves into space 3.
4. *D* passes over *B* into space 2.
5. *E* passes over *C* into space 4.
6. *F* moves into space 6.
7. *C* passes over *F* into space 7.

Key to Puzzles with Counters.

8. *B* passes over *E* into space 5.
9. *A* passes over *D* into space 3.

Here occurs the state of things to which we have referred the position being as in Fig. 405.

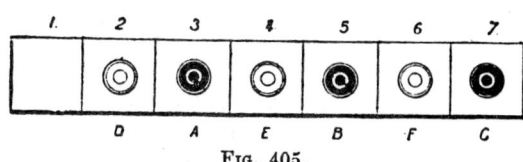

Fig. 405.

The next move should, according to the rule, be with a red counter; but there is only one counter, and that a white one, *D*, which is capable of being moved in a forward direction, and that *only* into 1. This move is made accordingly, and the solution proceeds as follows, the remaining moves being almost a matter of course:—

10. *D* moves into space 1.
11. *E* passes over *A* into space 2.
12. *F* passes over *B* into space 4.
13. *B* moves into space 6.
14. *A* passes over *F* into space 5.
15. *F* moves into space 3, and the trick is done.

If the operator prefers to begin with the *red* counters, the moves will be as follows:—

1. *C* moves into 4.
2. *D* passes over into 3.
3. *E* moves into 5.
4. *C* passes over into 6.
5. *B* passes over into 4.
6. *A* moves into 2.
7. *D* passes over into 1.
8. *E* passes over into 3.
9. *F* passes over into 5.

(From this point, as before, the rule ceases to apply.)

10. *C* moves into 7.
11. *B* passes over into 6.
12. *A* passes over into 4.
13. *E* moves into 2.
14. *F* passes over into 3.
15. *A* moves into 5.

When the principle is once fairly mastered, the movements can be executed with great rapidity, and with little fear of any onlooker being able to repeat them from recollection.

The solution we have given is equally applicable to any larger (even) number of counters, so long as the number of spaces be one greater, and a vacant space be left in the middle.

No. XVIII.—Solution.

You first deal with the middle row (15 to 21) after the manner described in the last solution. You then move the white counter now occupying space 25 into the central space (18), and deal in like manner with the fourth row (22 to 28), leaving space 25 vacant. Pass the counter occupying 11 into this space, and you are then in a position to deal with the second row (8 to 14). When space 11 is again vacant, move the counter occupying space 4 into it, and you are then enabled to deal with the uppermost line (1 to 7).

Pass the counter occupying space 18 into space 4, and that occupying space 32 into space 18. You are now in a position to rearrange the last row (29 to 35). You have then a vacant space (32) in the centre of the bottom row. Move the counter occupying space 25 into this space, then pass that occupying 11 into 25, and finally move the counter now in 18 into 11.

No. XIX.—The "Four and Four" Puzzle. Solution.

The necessary transpositions are as follows:—

Shift the counters occupying spaces 2 and 3 to 9 and 10;
,, ,, ,, ,, 5 and 6 ,, 2 and 3;
,, ,, ,, ,, 8 and 9 ,, 5 and 6;
,, ,, ,, ,, 1 and 2 ,, 8 and 9.

To work the counters back again, you have merely to reverse the process, but to do this from memory is rather more difficult than the original puzzle, and some amount of practice is necessary before it can be done with facility.

No. XX.—The "Five and Five" Puzzle. Solution.

For the sake of brevity, we will distinguish the red and black counters by the letters r and b respectively. They will then stand at the outset as under:—

Key to Puzzles with Counters.

```
                         b r b r b r b r b r . .
Position after 1st move: b . . r b r b r b r r b
    ,,      ,, 2nd  ,,   b b r r b r . . b r r b
    ,,      ,, 3rd  ,,   b b r . . r r b b r r b
    ,,      ,, 4th  ,,   b b r r r r r b b . . b
    ,,      ,, 5th  ,,   . . r r r r r b b b b b
```

N.B.—Where the number of pairs is *odd*, the second move should be with the pair next following that in the centre.

No. XXI.—The "Six and Six" Puzzle. Solution.

Distinguishing the counters as before, we have at the outset:—

```
                         b r b r b r b r b r b r . .
Position after 1st move: b . . r b r b r b r b r r b
    ,,      ,, 2nd  ,,   b b r r . . b r b r b r r b
    ,,      ,, 3rd  ,,   b b r r r b b r b . . r r b
    ,,      ,, 4th  ,,   b b r r r . . r b b b r r b
    ,,      ,, 5th  ,,   b b r r r r r r b b b . . b
    ,,      ,, 6th  ,,   . . r r r r r r b b b b b b
```

No. XXII.—The Thirty-Six Puzzle. Solution.

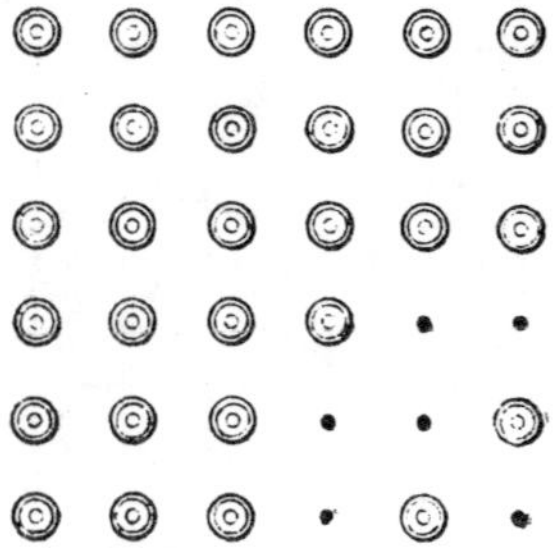

Fig. 406.

The six counters are so removed as to leave the remainder as under (Fig. 406).

No. XXIII.—The "Five to Four" Puzzle. Solution.

Remove the five counters of either diagonal, when those remaining will be found to answer the conditions of the problem.

No. XXIV.—No Two in a Row. Solution.

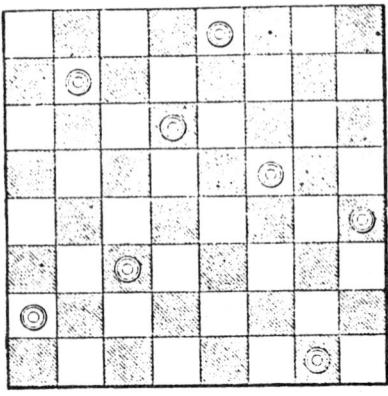

Fig. 407.

Arrange the eight draughtsmen, or counters, as shown in Fig. 407.

No. XXV.—The "Simple" Puzzle. Solution.

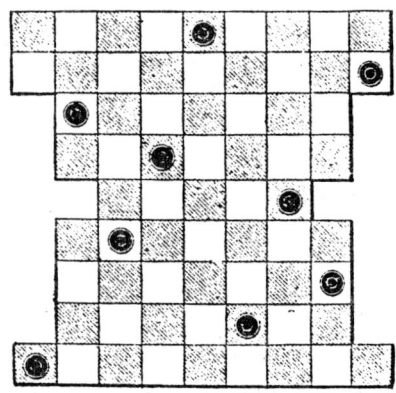

Fig. 408.

The arrangement of the nine counters is as shown in Fig. 408.

No. XXVI.—The "English Sixteen" Puzzle. Solution.

We know of no rule for working this puzzle. There are several possible solutions. Among others, moving the men in the following order will be found to answer the conditions of the problem. The man to be moved is in each case indicated by the number of the square (see Fig. 389). It is not necessary to specify the square to which it is to be moved. As there is never more than one square vacant, the experimenter cannot well go wrong in this particular.

It will be observed that the number of moves is 52, which we believe to be the smallest which will suffice to transfer the whole of the men.

11, 7, 9, 8, 10, 13, 11, 14, 9, 6, 8, 5, 7,
11, 9, 10, 8, 2, 1, 6, 3, 5, 7, 4, 9, 12,
15, 17, 14, 16, 13, 15, 11, 7, 9, 14, 11, 13, 10,
8, 9, 6, 8, 2, 5, 7, 11, 9, 12, 10, 8, 9.

No. XXVII.—"The Twenty Counters." Solution.

(*a*) If the counters be arranged as shown in Fig. 409, it will be found that they form seventeen perfect squares.

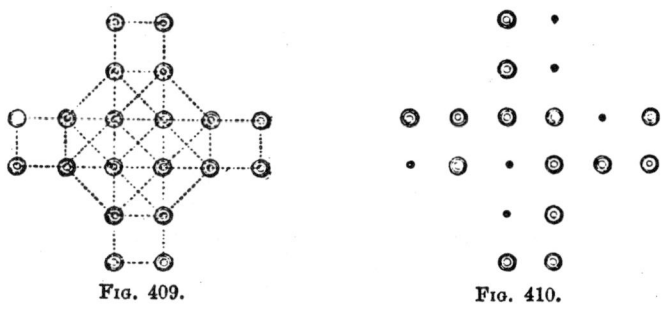

Fig. 409. Fig. 410.

(*b*) Fig. 410 shows the same arrangement of counters, less six removed. Not a single square now remains.

CHAPTER VII.

PUZZLES WITH LUCIFER MATCHES.

There are many puzzles, of various degrees of merit, performed with the aid of lucifer matches. We append a brief selection:—

No. I.

With eleven matches. Required, so to place them as to make nine of them.

No. II.

With nine matches. Required, so to place them as to make three dozen of them.

No. III.

With nine matches. Required, so to place them as to make three and a half dozen of them.

No. IV.

With three matches. Required, so to lay them on the table as to make four of them.

No. V.

With three matches. Required, so to lay them on the table as to make six of them.

No. VI.

With three wine-glasses and three matches. Required, with the three matches to form a bridge between the three wine-glasses, strong enough to support a fourth wine-glass.

N.B.—Each match must rest on one glass only, and touch such glass only at a single point.

No. VII.

With four wine-glasses and four lucifer matches. Required, so to place them as to form a bridge to support a fourth wine-glass, under the same conditions as in the last puzzle.

No. VIII.

Four and twenty matches being arranged on the table so

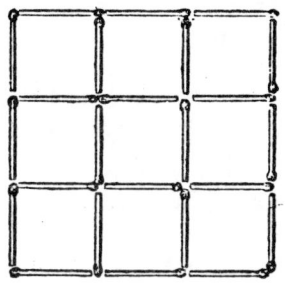

Fig. 411.

as to form nine squares as in Fig. 411, required, to take away eight matches and leave two squares only.

No. IX.

Having formed the two squares, as required by Puzzle No. VIII., to form, with two matches only, a bridge from the one to the other.

No. X.

Seventeen matches being laid on the table so as to form

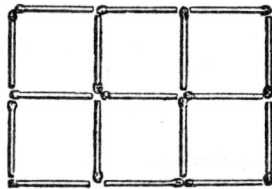

Fig. 412.

six equal squares as in Fig. 412, required, by taking away five matches, to leave three squares only.

No. XI.

Seventeen matches being laid on the table so as to form six equal squares (see last figure), required, by taking away six matches to leave two squares only.

No. XII.

Twelve matches being laid on the table so as to form four equal squares (see Fig. 413), required, to remove and

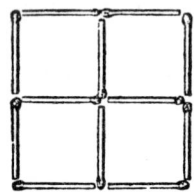

Fig. 413.

replace four matches so as to form three squares only, of the same size as at first.

No. XIII.

Fifteen matches being laid on the table so as to form five

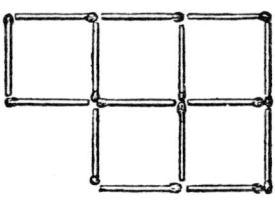

Fig. 414.

equal squares, as in Fig. 414, required, to remove three matches so as to leave three such squares only.

No. XIV.

With five matches, to form two equilateral triangles.

No. XV.

With six matches, to form four triangles of equal size.

No. XVI.

Four matches are here used. With a sharp penknife split the upper end of one of them so as to form a notch, and pare the end of another to a wedge shape. Insert the wedge into the notch, so that the two matches shall form an angle

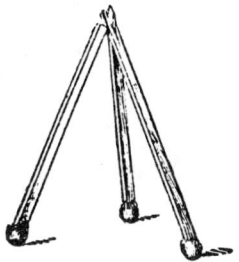

Fig. 415.

of about 60°. With these two and a third match, placed so as to lean against the point of juncture, form a tripod on the table, as shown in Fig. 415.

The puzzle is to lift these three simultaneously with the end of the fourth match. One hand only must be used.

No. XVII.

Ten matches are here used. You are required so to arrange them as to lift nine of them with the tenth, using one hand only.

No. XVIII.—The Magnetised Matches.

Break eight or ten matches in half. Fill a saucer with water, and when the liquid has had time to become quite still, lay the non-phosphoric ends on its surface in a circle, like the spokes of a wheel, with a vacant space of about an inch diameter in the centre.

Required: to compel the pieces of wood, without touching them, to move towards the common centre, and when they have done so, to make them again separate, and move outwards towards the edges of the saucer.

No. XIX.—The Fifteen Matches Puzzle.

This is in form a game, but it may also be presented as a puzzle.

Fifteen lucifer matches (or counters) are laid side by side on the table. One player takes one end of the row, the other player the other. Each takes it in turn to remove as many as he pleases, not exceeding three.

The object of each player is to avoid being the one to remove the last match. To all appearance it is an equal chance which shall do so, but a player who knows the secret, if opposed to a novice, can always compel his adversary to take it.

How is it done?

KEY TO CHAPTER VII.

PUZZLES WITH LUCIFER MATCHES.

No. I.—Solution.

The matches are placed so as to form the word **NINE**.

No. II.—Solution.

The matches are placed so as to form the number **XXXVI**, the Roman equivalent for 36.

No. III.—Solution.

This puzzle is solved by placing three matches in one heap, and six in another. Total, three and a half-dozen.

No. IV.—Solution.

The matches are so placed as to form the number **IV**.

No. V.—Solution.

This is the same as the last, save that the **V** is in this case placed first, making the number **VI** (six).

Two matches may be made five (**V**) in like manner.

No. VI.—Solution.

The three matches are interlaced as shown in Fig. 416, one resting on the brim of each wine-glass. The superincumbent weight binds them together, so that they will sustain a fourth wine-glass without difficulty.

Tobacco pipes (long clays) are sometimes used instead of

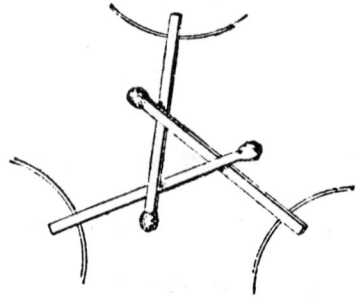

Fig. 416.

lucifer matches, and made to support a tankard, with even better effect.

No. VII.—Solution.

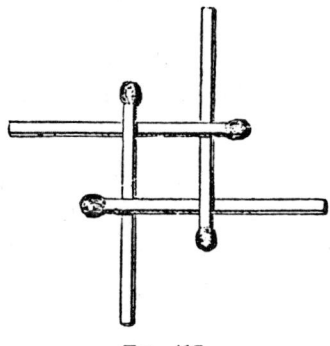

Fig. 417.

This is on the same principle as No. VI., the arrangement being as shown in Fig. 417.

No. VIII.—Solution.

Take away the matches forming the inner sides of the

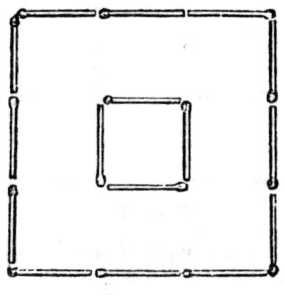

Fig. 418.

four corner squares, when you will have left two squares only, the one in the centre of the other, as in Fig. 418.

No. IX.—Solution.

It will be found that the distance between the external and inner squares is too great to be bridged by the length of

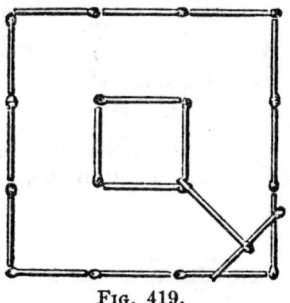

Fig. 419.

a single match. To construct the bridge, place one match across one of the corners of the larger square, and a second at right angles to it, resting on the corresponding corner of the smaller square, as in Fig. 419.

No. X.—Solution.

Take away the two matches forming each of the upper

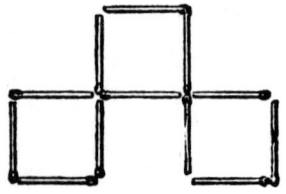

FIG. 420.

corners, and the centre match of the lower side. This will leave three squares only, as in Fig. 420.

No. XI.—Solution.

Take away the four-matches forming the inner sides of the four squares to the left, and the two matches forming

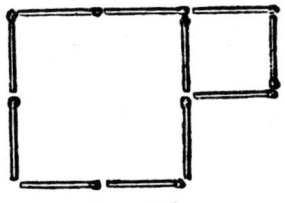

FIG. 421.

the outer sides of the lower square to the right. You will then have only two squares left, a larger and a smaller, as in Fig. 421.

No. XII.—Solution.

Take away the two matches forming the outer sides of the upper right hand square, and the two forming the outer sides of the lower left hand square. You have then left two squares, lying diagonally. With the four matches you have removed, form a third square in continuation of the

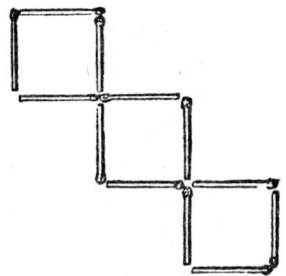

FIG. 422.

diagonal line, when you will have three squares, as shown in Fig. 422.

No. XIII.—Solution.

You remove the centre match of the upper side of the

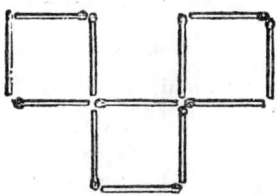

FIG. 423.

figure, and the two matches forming the outer sides of the lower square to the right, as in Fig. 423.

No. XIV.—Solution.

Arrange the five matches as shown in Fig. 424.*

---

* This is all but self-evident, and the puzzle would not have been worth insertion but for the fact that it forms an appropriate "lead" to the really clever puzzle which next follows.
The illustration is not quite exact. The ends of the two matches on either side should be in contact with those of the one laid transversely.

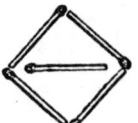

Fig. 424.

No. XV.—Solution.

Place three of the matches on the table in the form of a triangle, and hold the remaining three above them so as to

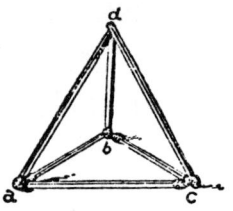

Fig. 425.

form a triangular pyramid, as shown in Fig. 425, *a b c* representing the base, and *d* the apex.

No. XVI.—Solution.

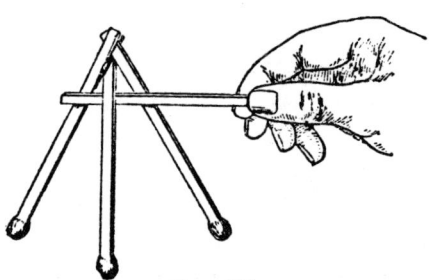

Fig. 426.

Take the fourth match in your hand, and with its point gently raise the two joined matches to a slightly more vertical position, so that the upper end of the third match shall fall forward into the angle of the other two, as shown in Fig. 426. By slightly raising the fourth match you lock all three together, and they may be lifted without difficulty.

No. XVII.—Solution.

Lay one match, which we will call *a*, on the table, and eight others across it, on alternate sides, with the heads inwards, as shown in Fig. 427. Lay the last match, *b*, in the furrow formed by the intersection of the eight crossed matches. Now take hold of the end of *a*, and you may lift the whole, as shown in Fig. 428, the one last placed form-

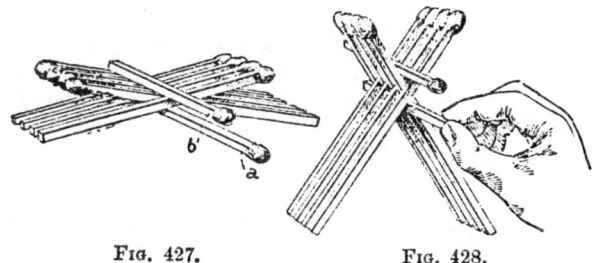

FIG. 427.   FIG. 428.

ing a wedge between the upper ends of the eight suspended matches, and so holding them together.

The matches used should be of wood, not wax, and fairly large. It will be found a good plan to break off the head of *b*, which otherwise projects inconveniently to the one side or the other, and is now and then found to tip up, and disturb the operation.

No. XVIII.—The Magnetised Matches. Solution.

This is a puzzle of a scientific character. To make the matches gather in the centre, take a slip of blotting-paper, three inches wide by twelve or fifteen long, and roll it loosely into a solid cylinder, in diameter about as large as a sixpence. Hold this vertically above the saucer, letting its lower end just touch the surface of the water. As the water rises by capillary attraction in the roll of blotting-paper, a minute current is created moving from the centre towards it, and the little pieces of lucifer match consequently begin also to move in that direction. A good-sized lump of sugar may be substituted for the roll of blotting-paper.

To cause the matches to move *away* from the centre, you have only to proceed in the same way with a piece of soap cut into a cylindrical shape, letting one end touch the water in the centre of the group of matches, when they will forthwith scatter in all directions.

This new phenomenon, which has quite a magical appearance, depends upon what is known as the "surface tension" of the water, which is disturbed by the introduction of the soap.

We have not space to go more minutely into the *rationale* of this very curious experiment, but any reader who is interested in the subject will find full information in the new edition of *Chambers' Encyclopædia*. Titles—*Capillarity* and *Surface Tension*.

No. XIX.—The Fifteen Matches Puzzle. Solution.

Victory will always lie with the player who removes the tenth match, leaving five on the table. Thus suppose A and B to be the players, and B to have the move, five matches being left. If B now removes

              1, A removes 3;
              2, A „   2;
              3, A „   1;

in each case leaving the last to be removed by B.

After one or two trials, the novice will probably perceive that five is the critical remainder, and will endeavour to leave that number. To prevent his doing so, his adversary must so play in the earlier stages of the game as to leave *nine* matches, when it will be equally impossible for the novice to leave five, for, again

              if B play 1, A will play 3;
              if B play 2, A will play 2;
              if B play 3, A will play 1;

and five will be left, with B to play.

In like manner, to make sure of leaving *nine*, the adept plays in the first instance so as to leave *thirteen*—*i.e.*, if he is the first to play, he removes *two*.

As between two players both of whom know the secret, the first must necessarily win.

CHAPTER VIII.

WIRE PUZZLES.

One of the simplest of these is:—

No. I.—The United Hearts.

We have here (see Fig. 429) the representation, in

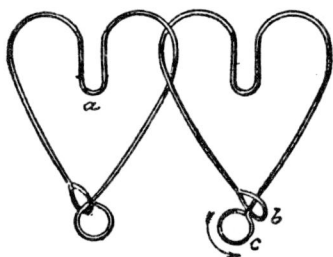

Fig. 429.

copper wire, of a couple of hearts, the one interlaced within the other. The problem is to separate them.

No. II.—The Triangle.

The wire is here bent into a triangle, or rather succession of triangles, the one within the other, and terminates on the outside in a ring passing round the next adjacent portion of the wire (see Fig. 430). From the triangle hangs a long wire loop, like a lady's hairpin, save that it is secured by a sort of cross-bar at the opposite end.

The puzzle is to detach the loop from the triangle.

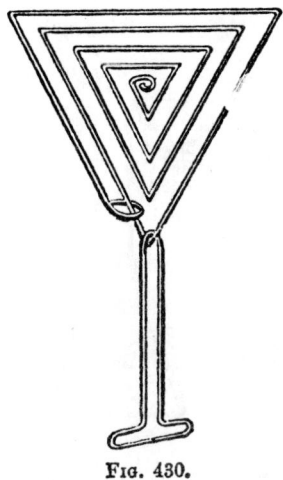

Fig. 430.

No. III.—The Snake and Ring.

The puzzle to which this name is given consists of a spiral coil of wire securely fastened off at the two ends. Threaded on the wire is a brass ring (see Fig. 431), and the problem is to disengage the ring from the spiral.

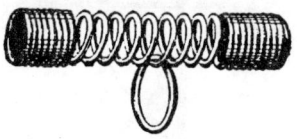

Fig. 431.

This is one of the simplest, and at the same time cleverest puzzles of the wire series. To any one taking up the puzzle for the first time its solution seems an impossibility, and yet any one in the secret can disengage the ring in a single second.

No. IV.—The Hieroglyph.

The puzzle to which, on account of its quaint shape, we

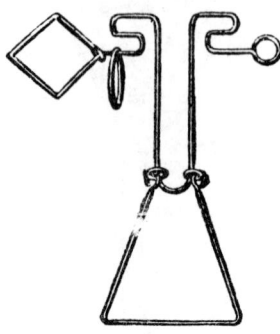

Fig. 432.

have given the above name is as depicted in Fig. 432. The problem is to disengage the ring.

No. V.—The Interlaced Triangles.

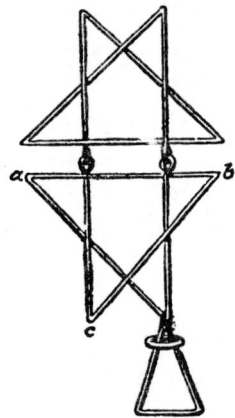

Fig. 433.

The wire is in this case so manipulated as to form five

triangles, four of them in pairs, lying one above the other; the fifth of smaller size, connected with the larger triangles by a tiny ring, and forming a "stop" to a larger ring, which it is the "crux" of the puzzle to disengage (see Fig. 433).

No. VI.—The Double Bow and Ring.

This is a puzzle of especially simple appearance, consisting merely of two bows of wire united in such manner as to form the shape of an hour-glass, with a ring encircling its narrower portion. (See Fig. 434.)

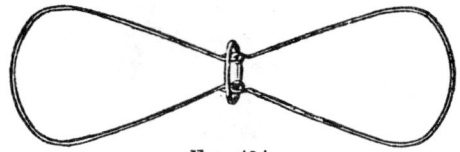

Fig. 434.

Although so simple in its elements, the usual problem (the removal of the ring) will be found by no means easy of solution until the secret is known.

No. VII.—The Egyptian Mystery.

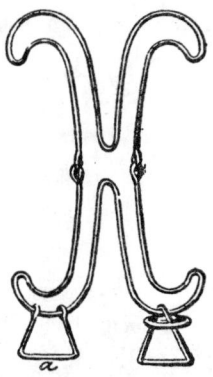

Fig. 435.

The puzzle to which this high-sounding title is given is of

the same class, and a very good one of its kind. In appearance it is as depicted in Fig. 435.

The problem is to disengage the ring.

No. VIII.—The Ball and Spiral.

This, shown in Fig. 436, is another very clever puzzle

Fig. 436.

The ball is permanently attached to the ring, and the latter threaded on the spiral. The experimenter is required to detach the ring from the spiral.

No. IX.—The Unionist Puzzle.

The puzzle to which this name is given consists of two pieces of stout iron or brass wire, about three inches in length and $\frac{1}{8}$ of an inch in diameter, bent into horse-shoe

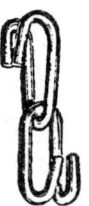

Fig. 437.

shape, the ends being bent back on themselves with the points slightly converging. These are interlaced as shown in Fig. 437, and the puzzle is to disengage them. To do so looks as it were the simplest thing in the world, but the experimenter moves the two horse-shoes this way and that way to no purpose, till suddenly, just as he is about to "give it up," he hits by a happy accident on the right position, and they come apart in his hands. He unites them again readily enough, for it is a peculiarity of this class of puzzles that their parts unite with delusive ease, their proper position for this purpose being generally obvious. Again he tries to separate them, flattering himself that this time he will have little trouble in doing so, but, to his disgust, he finds himself as far off as ever; one position being, to the uninstructed eye, pretty much the same as another, while one only, of a score of possible positions, will admit of the desired release.

It is, of course, an understood thing that no force is to be used.

No. X.—The Eastern Question.

Two pieces of stout wire are bent as shown in Fig. 438, each forming an open ring, or segment of a spiral, with a

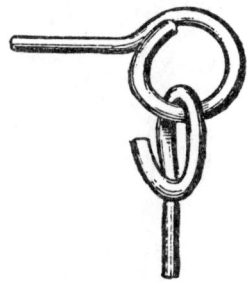

Fig. 438.

short straight piece by way of handle. They are interlaced like the horse-shoes, and the puzzle is to separate them.

No. XI.—The Handcuff Puzzle.

We have here (see Fig. 439) four rings, each forming a circular segment of a close-coiled spiral, interlaced the one with another.

To solve the puzzle, all four must be disconnected.

Fig. 439.

No. XII.—The Stanley Puzzle.

The Stanley Puzzle (Perry & Co.), though not consisting entirely of wire, belongs to this class. We have, in the first place, a little medallion of stamped brass, bearing the pre-

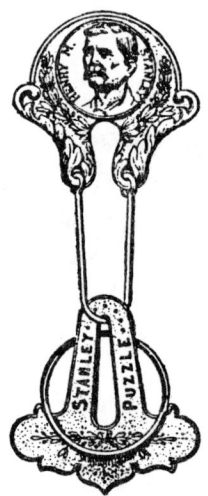

Fig. 440.

sentment of the celebrated explorer. From this (see Fig. 440) depends a wire loop, and from this again another piece of stamped brass, narrow at the top, but widening towards its lower end. Over this hangs a ring, which it is the problem of the puzzle to remove.

KEY TO CHAPTER VIII.

WIRE PUZZLES.

No. I.—The United Hearts. Solution.

Pass the loop *a* of the left-hand heart (see Fig. 429) through the ring *b* of the right-hand heart, and over the ring *c*, in the direction shown by the arrow, when the two will come apart. They may be joined again by reversing the process.

No. II.—The Triangle. Solution.

Push the point of the long loop through the ring *a* (see Fig.

Fig. 441.

441), then pass it over the angles *b*, *c*, and *d*, in succession; this done, it may be drawn out clear through *a*. To reengage it, reverse the process.

No. III.—The Snake and Ring. Solution.

Give the ring a quarter-turn from left to right (it will be found that it will only twist in one direction); and though its relation to the spiral is apparently unaltered, it will be found that it is now quite free, the condition of things being as if the spiral had been simply passed through the ring, and the latter then allowed to drop into its folds.

To again secure it, give it a turn in the opposite direction.

Why so simple a movement should produce so curious a result is, we confess, a mystery to ourselves. Perhaps some of our readers will be more successful in finding a scientific reason for it.

No. IV.—The Hieroglyph. Solution.

Hold the puzzle by the diamond-shaped handle, and with the opposite hand raise what, for want of a better name, we may call the "triangle" up the perpendicular loop, as shown in Fig. 442. It will be found that the triangle does not work rigidly on the loop, but that either side of it may in turn be brought close to the loop. Avail-

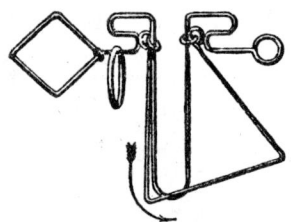

Fig. 442.

ing yourself of this fact, work the ring down the left-hand sides of the triangle and loop simultaneously in the direction shown by the arrow. When it reaches the bottom of the loop, push the triangle over to the left, and thence work the ring in like manner up their *right* sides. When it reaches the top of the loop on the right-hand side it will be free.

No. V.—The Interlaced Triangles. Solution.

Hold the puzzle by the corner *a* (Fig. 433), and fold back the upper part behind the lower. Push the movable triangle (with the ring upon it) to the top of the upright from which it hangs, and then pass the ring along down the

Key to Wire Puzzles. 311

two uprights now folded together, and up the two slanting portions to *a*. Again open the puzzle, and push the ring along the two horizontal wires to *b.* Fold the puzzle again, and slide the ring down along the double wires to *c*, then upwards in a perpendicular direction, and it will be free.

To put it on again, repeat the process in the opposite direction.

No. VI.—The Double Bow and Ring. Solution.

Bend the two bows together, so that the one shall partially cross the other, as shown in Fig. 443. Get the ring be-

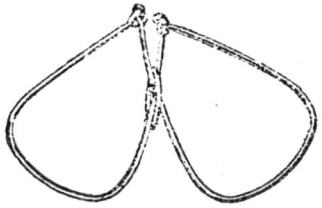

Fig. 443.

tween the two joints, pull it downwards over the two inner wires, and the trick is done.

No. VII.—The Egyptian Mystery. Solution.

The secret here lies in the proper manipulation of the move-

Fig. 444.

able loop *a* (see Fig. 435). Get this into the position shown in Fig. 444. Then fold the puzzle in half; lift the ring so as to bring it over the two curved ends on the opposite side; work it up to the centre, down the opposite curve and up again to the top, *a* in its present position offering no obstacle to your doing so. When the ring reaches the top at the left-hand side, it is free.

No. VIII.—The Ball and Spiral. Solution.

Twist the ball up to the top of the spiral. When it reaches this point, turn it over, so that the ring is no longer engaged in the turns of the spiral, but lies between them, encircling the upright wire in the centre. Now work it downwards round and round in the opposite direction to that by which you brought it up. When you reach the bottom, pass the ring over the loop of the upright wire, and the ball will be free.

No. IX.—The Two Horse-shoes. Solution.

To separate the horse-shoes, hold them between the finger and thumb of the right hand in manner shown in Fig. 445. To get the right positions, note that both horse-shoes have the loop end downwards, but that the hook ends of the upper one are turned towards the experimenter, while those

Fig. 445.

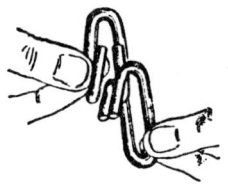
Fig. 446.

of the lower are turned away from him, and that the disengaged arm of the lower horse-shoe is to the left. With the forefinger and thumb of the left hand take hold of the loop of the lower horse-shoe, slide it up the arm of the upper horse-shoe, at the same time turning it over till it assumes the position shown in Fig. 446. Now move it vertically downward, and the two horse-shoes are free.

To reunite them, you have only to pass the points of the one horse-shoe between the points of the other, give them a shake, so as to make them assume a casual position, and the difficulty of separation is as great as ever.

No. X.—The Eastern Question Puzzle. Solution.

To separate the rings, get them into the position depicted in Fig. 447, when they can be drawn apart with the

Fig. 447.

greatest ease, the one curved end sliding smoothly past the other. To reunite them, hold them in the same position and reverse the movement.

No. XI.—The Handcuff Puzzle. Solution.

To separate the first or outer pair, get them with the cut ends *in the same straight line*, when they may be drawn apart with ease. The other links are united on the same principle as those of the Eastern Question Puzzle, last described. By studying the instructions given in that case, and adapting them to the present, success should be merely a question of a little perseverance.

No. XII.—The Stanley Puzzle. Solution.

To get the ring off, fold the loop backwards against the Stanley medallion, as shown in Fig. 448. Then push the ring upward into the horse-shoe-shaped space, and then work the outer portion of its circumference round the medallion from left to right, till it reaches the position shown in the diagram. When it reaches this point, it is free.

Fig. 448.

The solution seems almost childishly simple when known, but the puzzle will, notwithstanding, give a good deal of trouble to any one trying it for the first time.

CHAPTER IX.

"QUIBBLE" OR "CATCH" PUZZLES.

The present Chapter will be devoted to puzzles which depend upon some double meaning or non-natural interpretation of the question, whereby it assumes a second and less obvious signification.

No. I.—A Remarkable Division.

A gentleman divided seven and sixpence between two fathers and two sons, each father and each son receiving half a crown. How did he manage it?

No. II.—Subtraction Extraordinary.

Required, to take one from nineteen and leave twenty. How is it to be done?

No. III.—Two Halves Greater than the Whole.

Prove that seven is the half of twelve.

No. IV.—A Distinction and a Difference.

What is the difference between twice twenty-five and twice five and twenty?

No. V.—The Family Party.

A family gathering included 1 grandfather, 1 grandmother, 2 fathers, 2 mothers, 4 children, 3 grandchildren, 1 brother, 2 sisters, 2 sons, 2 daughters, 1 father-in-law, 1 mother-in-law, and 1 daughter-in-law, and yet there were only seven persons present.

How can the two statements be reconciled?

No. VI.—A Sum in Subtraction.

What is the difference between six dozen dozen and half a dozen dozen?

No. VII.—Another Sum in Subtraction.

What is the difference in capacity between twenty four quart bottles and four-and-twenty quart bottles?

No. VIII.—Three Times Six.

Place three sixes together so as to make seven.

No. IX.—A New Way of Writing 100.

Required, to express 100 by repetition of the same figure six times over.

No. X.—A Seeming Impossibility.

Required, to find six times thirteen in twelve.

No. XI.—Multiplication Extraordinary.

What three figures, multiplied by five, will make six?

No. XII.—A Question in Notation.

How would you write in figures twelve thousand twelve hundred and twelve?

No. XIII.—The Miraculous Herrings.

Five herrings were divided among five persons. Each had a herring, and yet one remained in the dish.
How was this managed?

No. XIV.—Two Evens make an Odd.

Prove that two sixes make eleven.

No. XV.—Six made Three.

Out of six chalk or pencil strokes—thus, | | | | | |
to make three, without striking out or rubbing out any.

No. XVI.—A Singular Subtraction.

Required, to take ten from ten so that ten shall remain.

No. XVII.—A Sum in Addition.

Required, to add 2 to 191 and make the total less than 20.

No. XVIII.—The Flying Sixpence.

A sixpence being placed in each hand, and the arms extended shoulder high, required, to bring both coins into one hand without allowing the arms to approach each other.

No. XIX.—The Last Thing Out.

You undertake to show another person something which you never saw before, which he never saw before, and which, after you both have seen it, no one else will ever see again.

How is it to be done?

No. XX.—The Three Gingerbread Nuts.

This is propounded in the shape of a conjuring-trick, usually after two or three *bonâ-fide* tricks have been performed. You place three gingerbread nuts* on the table, and cover each with a borrowed hat. You make a great point of having nothing concealed in your hands, and profess your willingness to allow the audience, if they please, to mark the three articles, so that there can be no question of substitution.

You then take up each hat in succession, pick up the nut beneath it, and gravely eat it, replacing the hat mouth downward on the table. Any one is at liberty to see that there is nothing left under either hat. You then undertake to

---

* In default of gingerbread nuts, three almonds, raisins, or any other small eatable articles may be substituted.

bring the three nuts under whichever of the three hats the company may select; and the choice being made, you at once do so.

How is it to be done?

No. XXI.—The Mysterious Obstacle.

You undertake to clasp a person's hands in such manner that he cannot leave the room without unclasping them.

How is it to be done?

No. XXII.—The Bewitched Right Hand.

You undertake to put something into a person's left hand which he cannot possibly take in his right.

How is it to be done?

No. XXIII.—The Invisible Candle.

You undertake to place a lighted candle in such a position that it shall be visible to every person save one; such person not to be blindfolded, or prevented from turning about in any manner he pleases.

How is it to be done?

No. XXIV.—The Draper's Puzzle.

A draper, dividing a piece of cloth into yard lengths, found that he cut off one yard per second. The piece of cloth was 60 yards in length.

How long did it take him to cut up the whole?

No. XXV.—The Portrait.

A portrait hung in a gentleman's library. He was asked whom it represented. He replied,—

"Uncles and brothers have I none,
But that man's father is my father's son."

What relation was the subject of the portrait to the speaker?

No. XXVI.—The Charmed Circle.

You invite a gentleman to stand in the middle of the room. Taking a piece of chalk, you undertake to draw round him a circle which he cannot jump out of.
How is it to be done?

No. XXVII.—The Egg and the Cannon-ball.

Exhibiting an egg and a cannon-ball, you hold forth learnedly on the extraordinary strength of a perfect arch, and, still more, of a perfect dome, remarking that few people know how strong even the shell of an egg is, if it is placed in a proper position. In proof of your assertion, you undertake to place the egg, without covering it in any way, in such a position that no one present can break it with the cannon-ball.
How is it to be done?

No. XXVIII.—A Curious Window.

A window in a certain house has recently been made twice its original size, but without increasing either its height or width.
How can that be?

No. XXIX.—A Queer Calculation.

A hundred and one by fifty divide,
And next let a cipher be duly applied;
Then, if the result you should rightly divine,
You'll find that the whole makes but one out of nine.

No. XXX.—Arithmetical Enigma.

Write down a cipher, prefix fifty, to the right place five, and to the whole add one-fifth of eight. The result will give you the most important factor in human happiness.

No. XXXI.—A Short Year.

The year 1892 was one of the shortest on record.
How do you prove it?

No. XXXII.—The Mysterious Addition.

1. I add one to five, and make it four.
How can that be?
2. What must I add to nine to make it six?

No. XXXIII.—Arithmetical Enigma.

From a number that's odd cut off its head,
   It then will even be;
Its tail, I pray, next take away,
   Your mother then you'll see.

No. XXXIV.—A New Valuation.

If five times four are thirty-three,
What will the fourth of twenty be?

No. XXXV.—Easy, when You Know It.

What two numbers multiplied together will produce seven?

No. XXXVI.—Necessity the Mother of Invention.

I have a bottle of wine, corked in the ordinary way. Unfortunately, I have no corkscrew.

How can I get the wine out, without breaking the glass, or making a hole in the cork?

No. XXXVII.—A Singular Subtraction.

From six take nine, from nine take ten, from forty take fifty, and yet have six left.

How is it to be done?

No. XXXVIII.—A Vanishing Number.

There is a number of three figures, in value not very far short of a thousand, but when halved its value is nothing.

What is it?

"Quibble" or "Catch" Puzzles.

No. XXXIX.—A Queer Query.

Twice ten are six of us,
Six are but three of us,
Nine are but four of us;
  What can we possibly be?
Would you know more of us,
Twelve are but six of us,
  Five are but four, do you see?

No. XL.—The Mouse.

A mouse found in a box a number of ears of corn, and set to work to carry them off to his hole. He brought out with him three ears at each journey, and it took him nine journeys to remove the whole.

How many ears of corn were there in the box?

No. XLI.—The Fasting Man.

How many hard-boiled eggs can a hungry man eat on an empty stomach?

No. XLII.—The Family Party.

An old gentleman was asked who dined with him on Christmas Day. "Well, we were quite a family party," he replied; "there was my father's brother-in-law, my brother's father-in-law, my father-in-law's brother-in-law, and my brother-in-law's father-in-law."

It afterwards transpired that he had dined alone, and yet his statement was correct.

How could that be?

No. XLIII.—A Reversible Fraction.

Required, to find a fraction whose numerator is less than its denominator, but which, reversed, shall remain of the same value.

Y

No. XLIV.—The Three Counters.

Three counters are laid in a row on the table.

Required, to take the middle one away from the middle without touching it.

No. XLV.—Magic Made Easy.

Borrow a half-crown and a penny, and hold them one in each hand, with the hands open, in front of you, the hands being about two feet apart. Now close the hands, and announce that you will make the coins change places without again opening your hands, which you proceed to do accordingly.

How is it done?

KEY TO CHAPTER IX.

"QUIBBLE" OR "CATCH" PUZZLES.

No. I.—A Remarkable Division. Solution.

There were only three persons who shared in the gift, related to each other as son, father, and grandfather. Each is necessarily a son (of somebody), while the two elder are fathers also.

No. II.—Subtraction Extraordinary. Solution.

Write nineteen in Roman numerals—XIX. Remove the I., and you have XX.

No. III.—Two Halves Greater than the Whole. Solution.

Write twelve in Roman numerals—XII. Halve the number by drawing a line horizontally across its centre, and the upper half is VII.

No. IV.—A Distinction and a Difference. Solution.

There is a difference of twenty; twice twenty-five being fifty, while twice five, and twenty, make thirty only.

No. V.—The Family Party. Solution.

The party consisted of three children (two girls and a boy), their father and mother, and their father's father and mother. It will be found that these, in their various relations to each other, fill all the characters named. Thus the father, in relation to his own father, is also a son, and so on.

No. VI.—A Sum in Subtraction. Solution.

The former are six gross, the latter six dozen only. The difference is therefore $864 - 72 = 792$.

No. VII.—Another Sum in Subtraction. Solution.

56 quarts: twenty four-quart bottles holding 80 quarts, while four-and-twenty quart bottles hold 24 quarts only.

No. VIII.—Three times Six. Solution.

$6\frac{6}{6}$.

No. IX.—A New Way of Writing 100. Solution.

$99\frac{99}{99}$ ($=100$).

No. X.—A Seeming Impossibility. Solution.

If you write down the numbers 1 to 12 inclusive, taking in pairs the first and last, the second and last but one, and so on, you have—

        1 and 12 make 13
        2 and 11 ,,   13
        3 and 10 ,,   13
        4 and 9 ,,   13
        5 and 8 ,,   13
        6 and 7 ,,   13

Your six thirteens are thus accounted for.

No. XI.—Multiplication Extraordinary. Solution.

Answer, $1\frac{1}{5}$. $1\frac{1}{5} \times 5 = 6$.

No. XII.—A Question in Notation. Solution.

Answer, 13212.

No. XIII.—The Miraculous Herrings. Solution.

The last of the five received his herring in the dish.

Key to "Quibble" or "Catch" Puzzles. 325

No. XIV.—Two Evens make an Odd. Solution.

This is another of the "catches" dependent upon the use of Roman numerals. One six (VI.) is placed above another six, but the latter in an inverted position (ΛI), the combination making XI.

No. XV.—Six made Three. Solution.

Add the necessary lines to complete the word "three," thus
T H R E E.

No. XVI.—A Sum in Subtraction. Solution.

The propounder of this puzzle should be wearing gloves, and the problem is solved by taking them off. The ten fingers of the gloves are taken from the ten fingers of the hand, and the latter still remain.

No. XVII.—A Sum in Addition. Solution.

Draw a line under the final 1, and place the 2 under it, when the result will be $19\frac{1}{2}$.

No. XVIII.—The Flying Sixpence. Solution.

Place yourself so as to bring one hand just over the mantelpiece, and drop the coin contained in such hand upon the latter. Then, keeping the arms still extended, turn the body round till the other hand comes over the coin. Pick it up, and you have solved the puzzle, both coins being now in one hand.

No. XIX.—The Last Thing Out. Solution.

The puzzle is solved by cracking a nut, showing your interlocutor the kernel, and then eating it.

No. XX.—The Three Gingerbread Nuts. Solution.

This is a very ancient "sell," but it still finds victims. The performer's undertaking is performed by simply putting on the hat selected. No one can deny that the three nuts are thereby brought under the hat.

No. XXI.—The Mysterious Obstacle. Solution.

You perform your undertaking by clasping the person's hands round the leg of a loo table, a piano, or other object too bulky to be dragged through the doorway.

No. XXII.—The Bewitched Right Hand. Solution.

You place in the person's left hand *his own right elbow*, which, obviously, he cannot take in his right hand.

No. XXIII.—The Invisible Candle. Solution.

You place the candlestick *upon the head* of the person who is not to see it.

No. XXIV.—The Draper's Puzzle. Solution.

It took him 59 seconds. Most people are apt to say 60, forgetting that the 59th cut separates the last two lengths, and that, therefore, a 60th is unnecessary.

No. XXV.—The Portrait. Solution.

The portrait represented the speaker's son, as will be seen after a moment's consideration. The speaker says in effect, "The father of that man is my father's son"; in which case the father of the subject must be either a brother of the speaker, or himself. He has already told us that he has no brother. He himself must therefore be the father, and the portrait represents his son.*

No. XXVI.—The Charmed Circle. Solution.

The circle is drawn on the clothes of the victim, round the waist.

---

* This venerable puzzle forms the subject of a humorous article, entitled "Prove It," in a recent number of the *Idler*. Its most amusing feature is that the writer has himself gone astray, the story proceeding on the assumption that *the speaker himself* is the subject of the portrait, and being based on the (by no means imaginary) difficulty of demonstrating that fact to other people.

No. XXVII.—The Egg and the Cannon Ball. Solution.

You place the egg on the floor, in one corner of the room, in which position the walls on either side make it impossible to touch it with the cannon ball.

No. XXVIII.—A Curious Window. Solution.

The window was diamond-shaped. By enlarging it to a square its area is exactly doubled, without increasing either its height or width.

A window shaped as an isosceles or right-angled triangle will equally answer the conditions of the puzzle.

No. XXIX.—Queer Calculations. Solution.

Take the Roman equivalent for 101 (CI), and divide the two letters by inserting between them the equivalent for 50 (L). Add O, and you have CLIO, one of the nine Muses.

No. XXX.—An Arithmetical Enigma. Solution.

This is on the same principle. L stands for 50, the cipher for the letter O, and V for 5, while E is one-fifth of eight (e i g h t), the whole forming the word LOVE.

No. XXXI.—A Short Year. Solution.

It began on a Friday, and ended on Saturday.

No. XXXII.—The Mysterious Addition. Solution.

1. Write five in Roman characters (V); add I, and it becomes IV.
2. The letter S, which makes IX SIX.

No. XXXIII.—An Arithmetical Enigma. Solution.

Seven—Even—Eve.

No. XXXIV.—A New Valuation. Solution.

$8\frac{1}{4}$.

No. XXXV.—Easy, when You Know It. Solution.

Seven and one.

No. XXXVI.—Necessity the Mother of Invention. Solution.

Push the cork in.

No. XXXVII.—A Singular Subtraction. Solution.

| SIX | IX | XL |
IX	X	L
S	I	X

No. XXXVIII.—The Vanishing Number. Solution.

The number is 888. When halved it becomes $\frac{000}{000} = 0$.

No. XXXIX.—A Queer Query. Solution.

This is a mere "sell." The answer is "Letters." In the word "twenty" there are six letters, in the word "six" three, and so on.

No. XL.—The Mouse. Solution.

There were *nine* ears of corn in the box. The mouse brought out three *ears* at each journey, but two of them were his own.

No. XLI.—The Fasting Man. Solution.

One only; for after eating one his stomach would no longer be empty.

No. XLII.—The Family Party. Solution.

The very peculiar state of things described is accounted for as follows. The old gentleman was a widower, with a daughter and sister. The old gentleman and his father (who was also a widower) married two sisters (the wife of the old gentleman having a daughter by a former husband);

Key to "Quibble" or "Catch" Puzzles.

the old gentleman thus became his father's brother-in-law. The old gentleman's brother married the old gentleman's step-daughter; thus the old gentleman became his brother's father-in-law. The old gentleman's father-in-law married the old gentleman's sister, and the old gentleman thus became his father-in-law's brother-in-law. The old gentleman's brother-in-law married the old gentleman's daughter, whereby the old gentleman became his brother-in-law's father-in-law. He therefore himself filled all the four characters mentioned.

No. XLIII.—A Reversible Fraction. Solution.

$\frac{6}{9}$. Turn the paper upside down, so as to bring the denominator into the place of the numerator, and *vice versâ*. The fraction will still be $\frac{6}{9}$.

No. XLIV.—The Three Counters. Solution.

Remove one of the end counters and transfer it to the opposite end. You have not touched the middle counter, but it is no longer in the middle.

No. XLV.—Magic Made Easy.

This puzzle, like that last described, depends on a double meaning. The spectators naturally prepare themselves for some more or less adroit feat of jugglery, but you perform your undertaking by simply crossing the closed hands. The right hand (and the coin in it) is now where the left was previously, and *vice versâ*.

CHAPTER X.

MISCELLANEOUS PUZZLES.

No. I.—The John Bull Political Puzzle.

The appliances for this puzzle, brought out by Messrs. Jaques & Son, consist of a cardboard box, on the bottom of which are described three strongly-marked concentric circles, with other fainter lines connecting them (see Figs. 449, 450), and nine small counters, three white, three red, and three blue. Each group of three bears the letters, *C*, *U*,

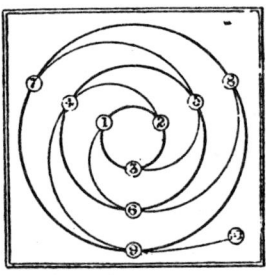
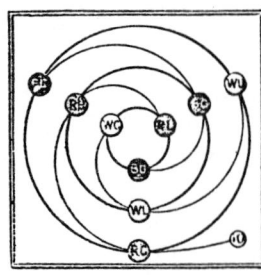

FIG. 449.   FIG. 450.

and *L*, standing for Conservative, Unionist, and Liberal, respectively. Wherever on the board a thin line intersects a thick one, the point of juncture is marked by a circular "spot," a quarter of an inch in diameter. These are nine in number, forming straight radial lines of three each. At one corner of the board is a tenth spot (marked 10 in the figure), connected with the main diagram by a faint curved line.

The nine counters are to be placed at the outset promiscuously upon the nine spots, the outer one, 10, being at starting unoccupied. The counters are then to be moved, one at a time, along the thick or thin lines, into the spot which happens for the time being to be vacant, until all three colours and all three letters are found in each circle and in each row of spots.

The first move is, as a matter of course, to shift the nearest counter into the 10 spot, thereby giving room to manipulate the others. The last move will be to replace this counter in its original position, leaving the 10 vacant as at first.

No. II.—The Pig in Sty.

This is a small board, 4½ inches square, and marked as shown in Fig. 451, each of the twenty-five circles representing an opening a quarter of an inch deep. Of these, all save the centre square are at the outset occupied by cylindrical wooden pegs, of which the eight occupying the middle of the

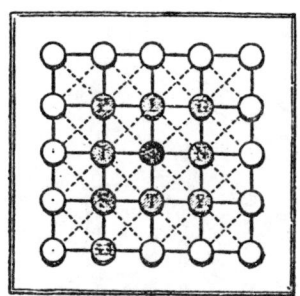

Fig. 451.

board are lettered as shown, the various letters forming, as will be observed, the words PIG IN STY. The peg occupying the second hole in the bottom row bears the effigy of a pig, the others being left blank.

The object to be achieved is to get the "Pig" into the middle hole, representing the "Sty," and this is to be done according to the rules following: A peg can only be moved into the hole for the time being vacant. If moved along the solid black lines, it must overleap two other pegs. If moved along the dotted diagonals, it can only be moved into an adjoining space, without overleaping. Subject to these two rules, a peg may be moved in any direction.

When the puzzle is solved, the lettered pegs must again

332 *Puzzles Old and New.*

occupy their original positions. The pig must be in the sty, and the hole he previously occupied must be vacant.

The necessary moves should not exceed twelve in number.

No. III.—Hide and Seek.*

This is a puzzle of a very novel and ingenious kind; indeed, we believe it to be unique. At any rate, we have come across no other upon precisely the same principle.

It consists of a cardboard box, four inches square, with the top and bottom of glass. The intermediate space is occupied by a metal plate, divided by upright partitions (just high enough to touch the glass) into a number of different compartments, somewhat after the fashion of a maze (see Fig. 452). On turning the box over, we find that the under

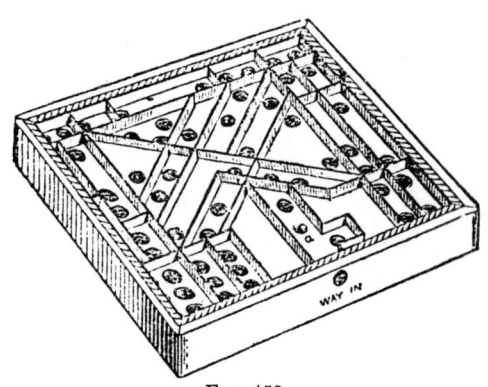

Fig. 452.

side of the plate is divided after a similar fashion, but that the shape of the compartments is in this case different, the partitions on this side running in different directions. There is no direct communication between the compartments of the top, or between those of the bottom, each being fully enclosed on all sides; but the intermediate "floor" is perforated with a number of holes, (in most cases two to each com-

---

* Perry & Co., Limited.

partment), which form a means of communication between the upper and the lower compartments, and therefore indirectly between compartments on the same side.

In the front of the box (see the diagram) will be seen a small round hole. A little leaden ball, *a*, is introduced at this point, and allowed to drop through the hole immediately in front of the opening. It is then to be made to travel, up one hole and down another, from compartment to compartment, till it comes out again at the hole to the right of the opening, the box being turned over at each stage so as to enable it to fall in the desired direction.

No. IV.—The Brahmin's Puzzle.*

This very clever puzzle is professedly based on a Hindu legend, to the following effect:—

At the beginning of the world, Brahma set up in the great Temple of Benares three diamond pyramids. Round the first of them he hung sixty-four rings, made of purest gold, and arranged in regular order, the largest ring en-

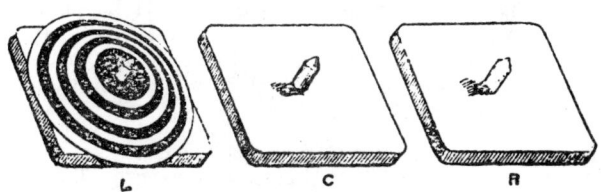

Fig. 453.

circling the foot of the pyramid and the smallest its top. And Brahma said unto the priests, "Transfer these sixty-four rings from the first pyramid to the third, transposing one ring at a time only, and putting it either on a vacant pyramid or on a larger ring. By the time you have executed this task the end of the world will be near."

As few persons would care to attempt a puzzle which professedly takes some thousands of years to solve, it has been found necessary to modify the conditions of the problem, the number of rings to be transposed being reduced from 64 to

---

* This puzzle also is published by Messrs. Perry & Co., Limited.

8. Instead of gold, they are in this case discs of cardboard, coloured alternately orange and black. The three diamond cones are represented by three little wooden slabs (see Fig. 453), each with a cylindrical peg standing up in its centre. The method of transposition is the same as laid down in the legend.

No. V.— Cardan's Rings.

We take this puzzle next in order, as having a close affinity in principle with the problem of Brahma, which precedes it. It is one of the oldest of known puzzles, having been learnedly discussed by the mathematician, Jerome Cardan, as early as the sixteenth century. Whether it was his own invention is doubtful, but it was for many generations associated with his name. At the present day people have forgotten all about Cardan, and the problem is now more frequently referred to by the less distinctive title of "The Puzzling Rings." In French it is known as *La Baguenaudier*, and it is said to be now and then found on an enlarged scale in English rural districts, forged in iron, and appropriately called "The Tiring Irons." It has more than once been deemed worthy of notice by mathematicians, the learned Savilian professor, Dr. Wallis, devoting to it a special section of his treatise on Algebra (1685), under the title *De Complicatis Annulis*.

The apparatus consists of four parts :—

(1) A wire bow or shuttle (sometimes provided with a handle at one end).

(2) A flat bar of wood, metal, or bone, a trifle larger than the bow, with holes through it at regular intervals, corresponding in number with the rings.

(3) A number (six to twelve, as the case may be), of rings, which should in internal diameter be just double the external width, and in thickness one-third of the internal width of the bow.

(4) A series of short wires, corresponding in number with that of the rings.

One end of each wire passes through one of the holes in the bar, and is rivetted on the opposite side, though the hole is of such a size as to allow it free play. It thence passes through the bow, and through one of the rings, and its opposite end is then bent round another ring, the result being as shown in Fig. 454 (representing the 10-ring form of the puzzle). The rings are all threaded on the bow, each (with one exception) passing around the wire of its right-hand

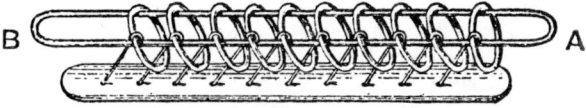

Fig. 454.

neighbour. The exception is the ring to the extreme right, which, having no neighbour on its outer side, enjoys a degree of liberty not shared by the remaining rings. The puzzle is to get the rings off the bow.

It should be mentioned that, as in the case of the Brahmin Puzzle, each additional ring doubles the time occupied in the solution. With seven rings, the puzzle requires 85 moves to solve it; with eight rings, 170; with nine, 341; and with ten, 682. With eleven it would require 1,365 movements, and with twelve, 2,730. Ten rings are the popular limit, and we have therefore selected the puzzle in this form for illustration.*

No. VI.—The Knight's Tour.

Chess problems, in the ordinary sense, are interesting only to the chess-player, and would, therefore, be out of place in the present pages, which are designed for all and sundry. But there is one particular chess-puzzle, the so-called Knight's Tour, which requires no knowledge of chess, and may be attempted with success even by a person quite unacquainted with the game.

We may take it for granted that every reader knows that the chess-board consists of 64 squares (eight rows of eight squares each, black and white alternately). Some readers may, however, not be aware of the nature of the knight's move. The knight at chess moves in a rather peculiar way

---

* The solution given in the Key will equally apply to the case of any smaller number of rings, the only difference being that the process will be cut short at an earlier stage.

—viz., one square straight (either forward, backward, or sideways), and one square diagonally (to right or left) from the square thus reached, forming a sort of zigzag. Thus, assuming the knight to be placed on the square marked *K* in Fig. 455, he might be moved to either of those indicated by an asterisk.

The problem known by the name of The Knight's Tour is to move the knight from square to square of the board in such manner that he shall, in the course of 64 moves, have rested (once and once only) on *every* square.

The experimenter is sometimes permitted to choose for himself from which square he will start. Under stricter conditions, he is required to start from a given square.

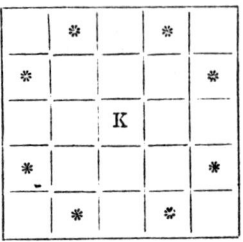

Fig. 455.

It is sometimes also made a condition that he should finish within a single move of the square from which he started. Indeed, no solution is now regarded as "perfect" which does not fulfil this requirement.

Before attempting to solve the puzzle, the reader is recommended, if using the actual chess-board, to provide himself with a supply of small counters, and to place one by way of "mark" on each square to which he moves the knight, so that there may be no doubt as to which squares have or have not been visited.

Another method, preferred by some, is to use, instead of the actual board, a piece of paper ruled in sixty-four squares, to represent a chess-board. Each move may then be noted by simply drawing with a pencil a straight line from the one square to the other.

No. VII.—The Knotted Handkerchief.

Required, to take a handkerchief, twisted ropewise, by its opposite ends, and, *without letting go of either end*, to tie a knot in the middle.

No. VIII.—Crossette.

Arrange in the form of a circle ten smaller circles (say coins or counters), as shown in Fig. 456.

Starting from any circle you please, and calling such circle 1, the next 2, and so on, strike out the fourth. Then start

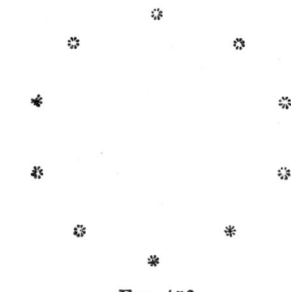

Fig. 456.

again from any circle you please, count 1, 2, 3, 4, and strike out the fourth. Proceed as above until all but one have been struck out.

You may count either backwards or forwards. Circles already struck out are to be reckoned in counting, but the count of "four" must in each case fall upon a circle not already struck out.

This puzzle may be most conveniently worked with the aid of "*reversi*" counters, which, as the reader is probably aware, are red on the one side and black on the other. Ten of these are arranged in a circle, with the *red* side uppermost, and as each is "struck out" it is turned over, so as to bring the *black* side uppermost.

z

No. IX.—Single-Stroke Figures.

A good deal of ingenuity may be exercised in the attempt to describe geometrical figures without taking off the pencil, or passing over any line for the second time.

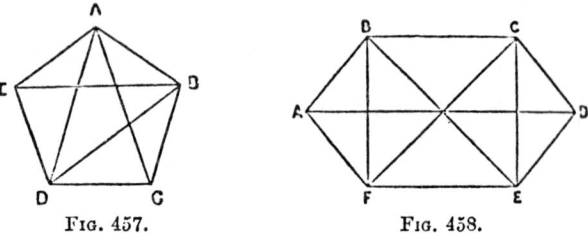

Fig. 457.   Fig. 458.

Figs. 457 and 458 may be tried by way of examples. From these other figures may be constructed, and tested in like manner.

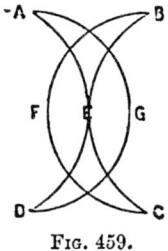

Fig. 459.

Fig. 459, the double crescent, or so-called Seal of Mahomet, is another pretty example, the legend being that the prophet was accustomed to describe it with one stroke of his scimitar, by no means a difficult feat, notwithstanding its apparent complexity.

No. X.—The Balanced Egg. Another Method.

We have already (p. 72) described a method of performing this feat with a mechanical egg, constructed for the purpose; but it is also quite possible to perform it with an ordinary

Miscellaneous Puzzles.

egg, and without having recourse to the somewhat heroic expedient of the great navigator.

How is it to be done?

No. XI.—Solitaire Problems.

Solitaire, though commonly referred to as a "game," belongs rather to the category of puzzles, the problems which it affords being numerous and interesting. It is played with a circular board, as shown in Figs. 460, 461, with thirty-seven hemispherical depressions,* in each of which rests a small marble, or glass ball. One of these being removed from the board, another is moved into the vacant space thus created, but in so doing it must pass over one intervening ball, lying

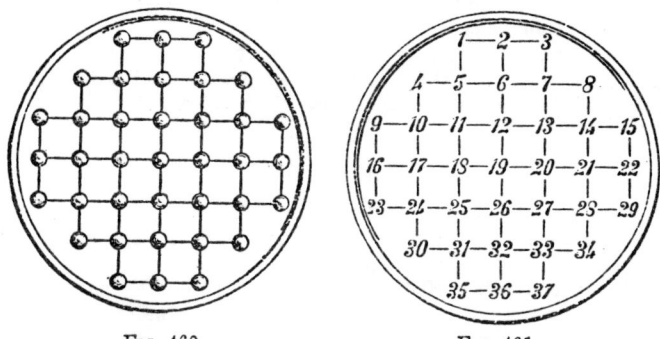

Fig. 460.   Fig. 461.

in a straight line (not diagonally) between it and the hole. This intervening ball is removed from the board (just as a man is "taken" at draughts), and another move is then made, after the same fashion, into one or other of the two holes now left vacant, a fresh man being removed from the board at each move.

For the third move there will be *three* holes vacant, for the next *four*, and so on, one ball being removed from the board at each move. The puzzle, in its simplest form, is to remove all the balls save one, which last cannot be removed, inasmuch as it has no second ball to pass over.

---

* Some Solitaire boards are made without the four corner holes, Nos. 4, 8, 30, and 34 in the diagram. In this case 33 balls only are used.

Sometimes it is left optional in what part of the board such last ball shall remain. In more elaborate forms of the puzzle the player is required to leave one or more balls in a particular hole or holes, previously determined.

Each alteration of the starting-point makes a fresh problem. We have selected three examples, viz :—

1. Starting with No. 1 as the vacant hole, to leave the last ball in No. 37.

2. Starting with No. 19 (the centre hole) vacant, to leave all the outer holes (1, 2, 3, 8, 15, 22, and so on) occupied, and the last ball in the centre hole. (This is sometimes known as "The Curate and his Flock.") To be done in 19 moves.

3. (The Triplets.) Starting with the centre hole vacant, to leave holes 1, 3, 6, 9, 12, 15, 17, 18, 20, 21, 23, 26, 29, 32, 35, and 37 occupied, forming a geometrical figure. (To be done in 20 moves).

By devising other geometrical figures, and endeavouring to produce them according to the conditions laid down, a very interesting series of puzzles may be produced.

No. XII.—Skihi.

This also is sold as a game, but comes more properly within the category of puzzles. It is a patent, and the property of the Skihi Novelty Company, London, W.C.

The set consists of 48 square cards, 2 inches each way, and of various colours. Each card has four slots cut in it,

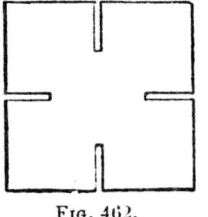
Fig. 462.

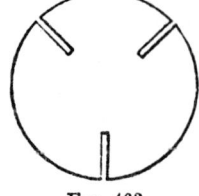
Fig. 463.

as shown in Fig. 462. There are also 10 circular cards, each with three slots, as shown in Fig. 463.

These cards may be utilized to form an almost unlimited number of fanciful designs. We subjoin a few examples (see Figs. 464–467), which will give some idea of the very

Miscellaneous Puzzles. 341

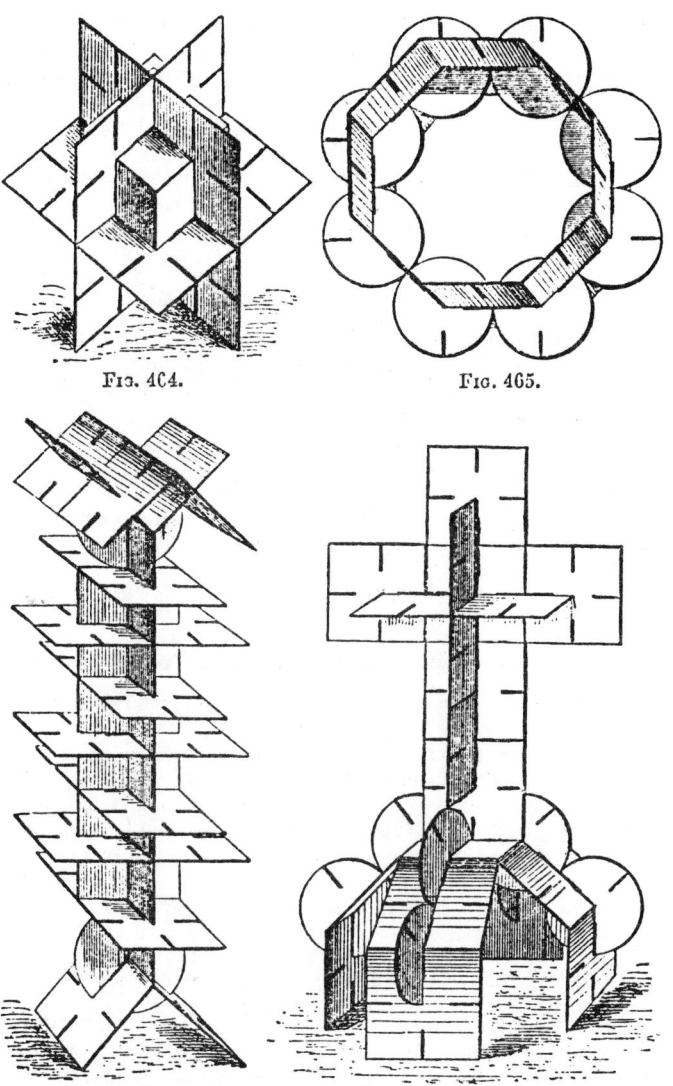

Fig. 464.

Fig. 465.

Fig. 466.

Fig. 467.

wide capabilities of this clever toy. All of these may be constructed with a single set. By using three or four sets in conjunction, very much more ambitious designs may be executed.

No. XIII.—A Card Puzzle.

Taking the four "fives" from a pack of cards, you are required to arrange them, face upwards, in such manner that only four pips of each shall be visible.

No. XIV.—Another Card Puzzle.

The aces and court cards being removed from the pack, required to arrange them in four rows, in such manner that neither horizontally nor perpendicularly shall there be two of same rank or same suit in any one row.

No. XV.—The Floating Corks.

The requirements for this puzzle are seven wine-corks (not tapering but of cylindrical form) and a basin of water.

The experimenter is required, without weighting them in any way, to make the seven corks float *upright* in the water.

No. XVI.—The Obstinate Cork.

For this puzzle a wine-bottle is required, and a cork a size or two too small for the neck, so that if inserted in the ordinary way it would fall into the bottle.

The bottle being held horizontally, with the cork resting just within the neck, the experimenter is invited to try whether he can, by blowing, force it into the bottle. If he does not know the secret, he will pretty certainly fail.

No. XVII.—Fixing the Ring.

This is described, with a touch of poetry, as a "matrimonial" puzzle. It is, in fact, a puzzle for two persons, who, to give it the proper touch of sentiment, should be a lady and a gentleman.

The appliances consist of a silken cord and a plain gold ring. The lady holds the cord, and the gentleman the ring, and they are required, by their joint efforts, to tie the cord in a knot round the ring, each using *one hand only*.

No. XVIII.—The Treasure at Medinet.

This puzzle comes from Germany, but is said to be of Oriental origin. The legend accompanying it is to the effect that an Eastern prince, Haroun al Elim, in far back times, ruled over a range of country with eight sugar-loaf hills, on each of which was erected a fortress. Each fortress, with the surrounding district, was under the command of a

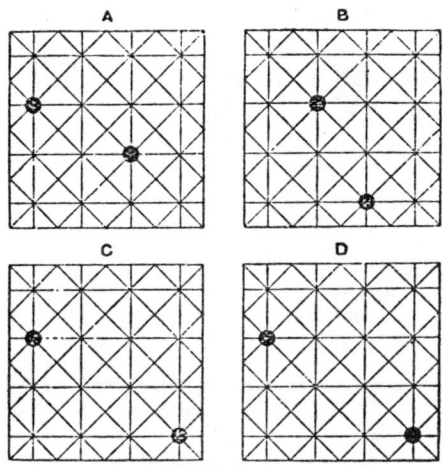

Fig. 468.

governor, but the jealousies of the eight governors and their respective under lings led to affrays and bloodshed whenever they chanced to meet. To lessen the chance of such meetings, Haroun made a number of roads, eight crossing his kingdom in one direction, eight more at right angles to them, and others crossing diagonally. These were so arranged with reference to the castles that the occupants of each castle had a clear road in each direction through and out of the prince's territory without passing any other castle.

The castles, says the legend, are now in ruins, and the roads no longer traceable; but a plan of them is still preserved among the archives of the Mosque Al Redin, at Medinet, on the coast of the Red Sea. Unfortunately, the plan, which was folded in four, has been worn by age into four separate fragments, and the utmost skill of the Cadi of the mosque has failed to discover their proper relative positions. He has therefore offered a reward—a treasure of ancient jewellery, preserved at Medinet—to any one who may succeed in placing the four fragments in their original positions—viz., with no two castles on either road, either horizontal, perpendicular, or diagonal.

For the use of the Infidel, the severed map has been reproduced on four separate cards, as *A*, *B*, *C*, and *D*, in Fig. 468.

No. XIX.—The Four Wine-Glasses.

Given, four wine-glasses, of same shape and size.

Required, so to arrange them that the centre of the foot of any one of them shall be equi-distant from all the rest.

No. XX.—One-Peg to Fit Three Holes.

A brass plate (Fig. 469) has three openings, one circular, one square, and one triangular. The experimenter is handed a knife, and a cork which just passes through the circular

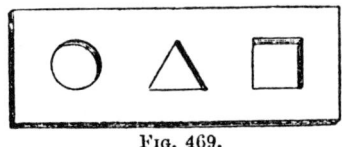

Fig. 469.

hole. He is required so to cut the cork that it shall exactly fill any one of the three openings.

For lack of the brass plate, a piece of stiff cardboard may be cut so as to answer the same purpose.

No. XXI.—The Balanced Pencil.

Given, a lead pencil, and a penknife, with which you sharpen the pencil to the finest possible point.

Required, to balance the pencil in an upright, or nearly upright, position on the tip of the forefinger.

No. XXII.—To Balance an Egg on the Point of a Walking-Stick.

We have already described a puzzle (No. X) in which an ordinary egg is made to stand upright, but in this case the difficulty of the feat is enhanced by the fact that the egg is to be balanced on the end of a walking-stick.

The articles employed are an egg, a cork, and a couple of dinner forks.

Required, to balance the egg, by the aid of the other three articles, on the smaller end of the stick.

No. XXIII.—The Ashantee Horseshoe.

The requirements for this puzzle are a miniature horseshoe of wood or cardboard, and a couple of pieces of stout brass wire, of the same length as the horseshoe. By the aid of one of these the horseshoe is propped up in a slanting position,* as shown in Fig. 470.

Fig. 470.

The experimenter is required (without touching either with the hands) to lift both wire and horseshoe simultaneously with the second piece of wire.

No. XXIV.—A Feat of Dexterity.

Fill a wine-glass to the brim with water, and place it on the corner of a table-napkin or pocket-handkerchief spread

---

* The horseshoe should have a minute notch or depression on its hinder side, to receive the upper end of the wire, and so prevent slipping.

over the edge of a table,* the remaining part hanging down, and being kept from falling by the weight of the glass.

Puzzle: to remove the handkerchief without touching the glass or spilling any of the water.

No. XXV.—The Divided Square.

Given, a square of cardboard of, say, two inches each way. Required, to divide it into five equal squares.

No. XXVI.—The "Oval" Problem.

Given, a sheet of drawing-paper and a pair of ordinary drawing-compasses.

Required, without any other aid, to describe an oval on the paper.

No. XXVII.—The Floating Ball.

This is more of a game than a puzzle, though it partakes of the nature of the latter.

A hollow rubber-ball, two inches in diameter, is set afloat in a tub or basin of water, and the players are challenged to take it out, using *the mouth only*.

Any one not acquainted with the secret will make a great many attempts before he finally succeeds.

No. XXVIII.—The Cut Playing-Card.

Given, a playing-card or an oblong piece of cardboard of corresponding size.

Required, so to cut it, still keeping it in one piece, that a person of ordinary stature may be able to pass through it.

N.B.—A bit of roan or morocco leather makes a very good substitute for the cardboard.

---

* The napkin or handkerchief should be in direct contact with the polished surface of the table, no second cloth intervening.

No. XXIX.—The Mitre Puzzle.

Given, a piece of paper or cardboard shaped as Fig. 471 (a distant likeness of a bishop's mitre).

Fig. 471.

Required, to divide it into four parts, all of the same shape and size.

No. XXX.—The Five Straws.

Given, five straws, each three to four inches in length, and a shilling.

Required, by holding the end of one straw only, to lift all the remainder.

No. XXXI.—The Three Fountains.

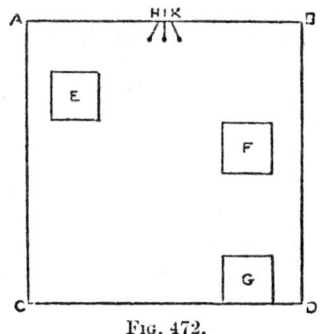

Fig. 472.

A, B, C, D (Fig. 472) represents a walled space; $E, F,$ and

G, three houses, and H, I, K, three fountains. It is required to lay pipes in such manner as to bring water from I to G, from H to F, and from K to E; but the pipes must not cross each other, nor must they pass outside the enclosure.

How is it to be done?

No. XXXII.—The Two Dogs.

The two dogs depicted in Fig. 473 are obviously dead.

Fig. 473.

Required, by the addition of four more lines, to restore them to life again.

How is it to be done?

No. XXXIII.—Water Bewitched.

Required, to place a glass of water in such a position that the glass cannot be lifted without spilling the whole of the water.

No. XXXIV.—The Balanced Halfpenny.

The requirements for this puzzle are an ordinary hairpin, a long steel pin, such as ladies use to keep their bonnets in position, a halfpenny, and a finger-ring, about equal to it in weight.

You are required, by the aid of the other two articles, to balance the halfpenny on the point of the bonnet-pin.

No. XXXV.—The Balanced Sixpence.

It would stagger most people to be invited to balance a sixpence on edge on the point of a needle, and yet, if you know how to do it, the feat is not only possible, but easy.

The requirements for the trick are to be found in any household. They are a corked wine-bottle, a second cork, of somewhat smaller size, a needle, and a couple of dessert-forks of equal size and weight. Last, but not least in importance, the sixpence.*

Having provided himself with these aids, the reader is invited to try whether he can solve the puzzle.

No. XXXVI.—Silken Fetters.

This is a puzzle for two persons, preferably a lady and gentleman. Two pieces of ribbon, each, say, a yard and a half in length, are required. One end of the first ribbon is

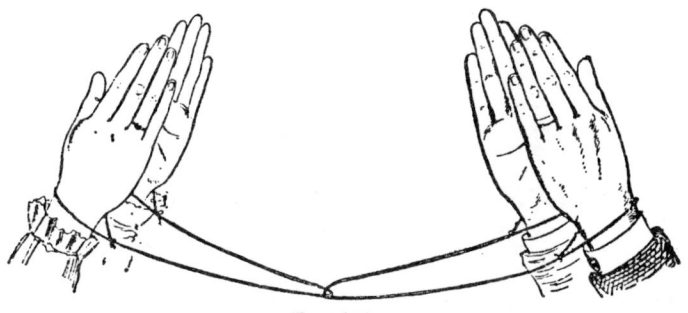

Fig. 474.

to be tied round each of the lady's wrists, and the second ribbon is then in like manner secured to the gentleman's wrists, one end of it, however, being first passed inside the lady's ribbon, so that the pair are held captive, after the manner illustrated in Fig. 474.

---

* Should there be any difficulty in procuring a sixpence, a half-sovereign will do equally well. Two penknives, of equal size and weight, may be substituted for the forks.

350   *Puzzles Old and New.*

The puzzle is to disconnect them, but without untying either of the knots.

How is it to be done?

No. XXXVII.—The Orchard Puzzle.

A farmer had an orchard, wherein were twelve fruit-trees, in the positions shown in Fig. 475. On his decease he directed that the orchard should be equally divided between

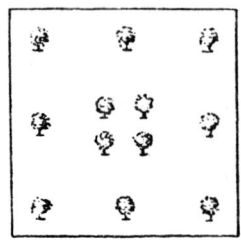

Fig. 475.

his four sons, with the proviso that the portion taken by each was to be of the same size and shape, and to contain three of the twelve fruit-trees.

How was it done?

No. XXXVIII.—The Cook in a Difficulty (*La Question de la Marmite*).

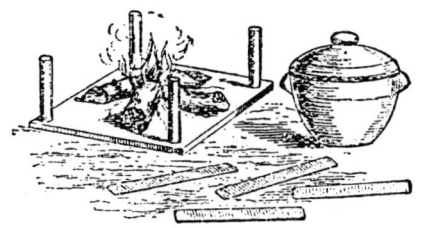

Fig. 476.

This is a puzzle of French origin. Our illustration (Fig. 476) represents a fire in the open, and a stewpan, which is

Miscellaneous Puzzles.

to be suspended over it. As will be seen, the four uprights are too far apart to support it, and, being of wood, the cook dares not drive them in any nearer to the fire. The only appliances at his command are four pieces of hoop-iron, as shown, in length a little less than the distance from upright to upright. With these he is required to form a support for his stewpan.

How does he manage it?

No. XXXIX.—The Devil's Bridge (*Le Pont du Diable*).

This is a puzzle on the same principle.

Given, three uprights (see Fig. 477), representing three hills, or towers, and three flat pieces, representing three

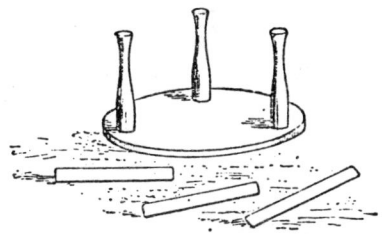

Fig. 477.

planks or girders, not long enough to reach from upright to upright.*

Required, with these materials to construct a bridge from point to point.

No. XL.—The Two Corks.

Take two wine-bottle corks, and hold them as shown in Fig. 478—viz., each laid transversely across the fork of the thumb. Now with the thumb and second finger of the *right* hand (one on each end) take hold of the cork in the *left* hand, and, at the same time, with the thumb and second

---

* If the specially manufactured form of the puzzle is not available three wine-glasses may supply the place of the three uprights, and three table-knives that of the cross pieces.

finger of the *left* hand take hold of the cork in the *right* hand, and draw them apart.

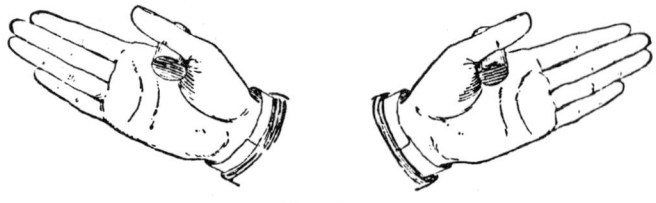

Fig. 478.

The above sounds simple enough, but the neophyte will find that the corks are brought crosswise, as shown in Fig.

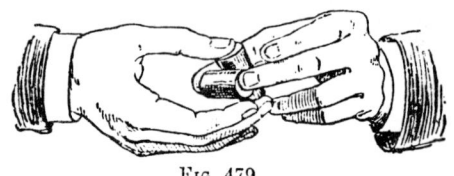

Fig. 479.

479. The puzzle is to avoid this, and enable them to part freely.

No. XLI.—The Divided Farm.

This is a puzzle of the same class as No. XXXVII. (see p. 350). A house, *H*, (see Fig. 480) stands in a square enclosure.

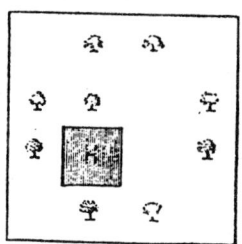

Fig. 480.

Within the same enclosure are ten trees, placed as shown in the figure. The owner (one of those eccentric persons whom we only hear of in connection with puzzles) made a will whereby he directed that the house should be occupied by his five sons jointly, but that the land was to be divided between them, each to have a piece of the same size and shape, and each piece to enclose two of the ten trees.

How must the land be divided, in order to carry out the testator's intentions?

No. XLII.—The Conjurer's Medal.

This is as represented in Fig. 481. The medal has five holes in it, and the puzzle is to work the ring (which, as will

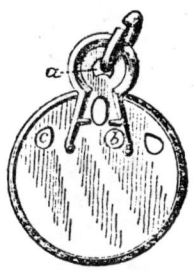

Fig. 481.

be observed, has a gap in it) from hole to hole until it is finally detached from the medal.

No. XLIII.—The Maze Medal.

This (see Fig. 482) is a puzzle of the same kind, but somewhat more complicated, and different as regards the object aimed at, the experimenter in this case being required to start with the ring detached from the medal, and to work it into the hole marked *Home*.

A A

Fig. 482.

No. XLIV.—The Puzzle Key-Ring.

We have here a key-ring in the form of a horseshoe, with the space between its arms closed by a smaller horseshoe (see

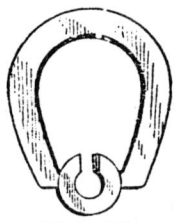

Fig. 483.

Fig. 483). The ring is not "split," but the keys are put on and taken off by a little secret process, the nature of which the experimenter is invited to discover.

No. XLV.—The Singular Shilling.

A handkerchief being spread out squarely upon the table, and a shilling laid on its centre, required, so to pick up the handkerchief as to bring it into a vertical position, the shilling still remaining in the centre, supported by the handkerchief only.

No. XLVI.—The Entangled Scissors.

Pass the loop end of a piece of doubled string through one of the bows of a pair of scissors, then pass the opposite ends through the loop, thence through the second bow, and finally tie them round a walking-stick or ruler, as shown in Fig. 484.

Fig. 484.

The puzzle is to disengage the scissors without untying the cord, or slipping the string off the stick.

If preferred, the ends of the cord may be held by a second person, in which case the use of the stick will be unnecessary.

No. XLVII.—The Penetrative Penny.

In a piece of stout paper cut a circular hole the size of a shilling—*i.e.*, about $\frac{1}{16}$ less than an inch. Invite any one to pass a penny through the hole without touching the coin or tearing the paper. He will naturally tell you that it can't be done, the diameter of a penny being $1\frac{1}{4}$ inch, or $\frac{5}{16}$ inch larger than the hole. And yet the thing *can* be done—easily done; and the reader is invited to find out how to do it.

No. XLVIII.—The Packer's Secret.

This is a very ingenious little puzzle, of French origin. It consists of a shallow cardboard box, $3\frac{1}{2}$ inches in diameter, containing twelve boxwood discs, each three quarters of an inch in diameter and rather more than an eighth of an inch in thickness. The puzzle is so to arrange these in the box (whose area they only about three parts cover) that it may be turned upside down without their falling out.

KEY TO CHAPTER X.

MISCELLANEOUS PUZZLES.

No. I.—The John Bull Political Puzzle. Solution.

No absolute rule can be given for the solution of this puzzle, as the number and direction of the moves will necessarily vary according to the position in which the nine counters happen to be placed at the outset. We propose to take a couple of specimen positions, and if the reader duly studies the *modus operandi* in these two cases, he should have little difficulty in finding appropriate solutions for other positions.

Distinguishing the counters for facility of reference as follows:—

Red Conservative	as R.	C.
White ,,	,, W.	C.
Blue ,,	,, B.	C.
Red Liberal	,, R.	L.
White ,,	,, W.	L.
Blue ,,	,, B.	L.
Red Unionist	,, R.	U.
White ,,	,, W.	U.
Blue ,,	,, B.	U.

we will suppose that the original (haphazard) position is as follows:—

On spot 1 (see Fig. 449)	B. C.
,, ,, 2	B. U.
,, ,, 3	W. C.
,, ,, 4	R. L.
,, ,, 5	W. L.
,, ,, 6	W. U.
,, ,, 7	B. L.
,, ,, 8	R. U.
,, ,, 9	R. C.

The puzzle may then be solved as follows:—

Move R. C. from 9 to 10.
" R. U. " 8 " 9.
" W. U. " 6 " 8.
" B. C. " 1 " 6.
" W. C. " 3 " 1.
" B. U. " 2 " 3.
" R. L. " 4 " 2.
" B. C. " 6 " 4.
" W. L. " 5 " 6.
" B. C. " 4 " 5.
" R. U. " 9 " 4.
" R. C. " 10 " 9.

leaving the counters in this case as shown in Fig. 450; though, of course, many other final arrangements would equally answer the conditions of the puzzle.

Again, suppose the original position to be as follows:—

R. L on 7.
W. C. " 4.
B. U. " 1.
B. C. " 8.
R. U. " 5.
W. L. " 2.
R. C. " 3.
B. L. " 6.
W. U. " 9.

The puzzle may then be solved as follows:—

Move W. U. from 9 to 10.
" R. L. " 4 " 9.
" W. C. " 6 " 4.
" B. L. " 5 " 6.
" R. U. " 7 " 5.
" R. L. " 9 " 7.
" W. U. " 10 " 9.

No. II.—The Pig in Sty. Solution.

For convenience of reference, it will be desirable to distinguish the various holes by numbers, as under (Fig. 485), each square representing a hole.

Key to Miscellaneous Puzzles.

The "pig" at the outset is placed in No. 22, and No. 13 (the centre hole) is vacant.

1	2	3	4	5
6	7	8	9	10
11	12	13	14	15
16	17	18	19	20
21	22	23	24	25

Fig. 485.

First Solution. In Twelve Moves.

Move 9 to 13; 3 to 9; 7 to 3; 22 to 7; 18 to 22; 24 to 18; 9 to 24; 13 to 9; 7 to 13; 3 to 7; 18 to 3; 22 to 18.

Second Solution. In Eleven Moves.

Move 19 to 13; 4 to 19; 10 to 4; 7 to 10; 22 to 7; 25 to 22; 19 to 25; 13 to 19; 7 to 13; 10 to 7; 22 to 10.

No. III.—Hide and Seek. Solution.

Figs. 486 and 487, the first representing the upper, and the second the under side of the puzzle, show the course which the ball must travel in order to fulfil the conditions. The letter *A* indicates the point of entrance and exit, and the numbers show the order in which the various holes are to be passed.

A *dot* beneath a number indicates that the ball (relatively to the side represented by the diagram) passes *downwards* through the hole in question. A *cross*, that the ball is to be brought *through that hole from the opposite side*.

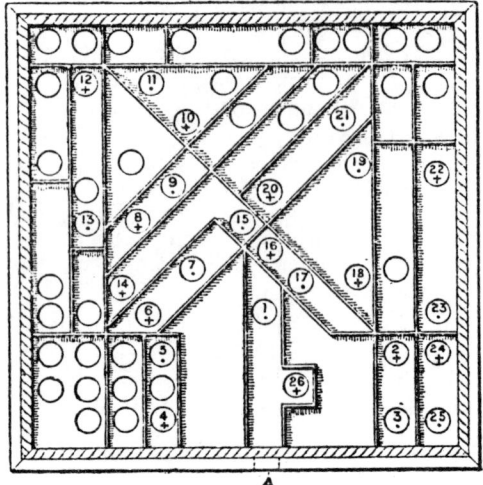

Fig. 486.—Upper Side.

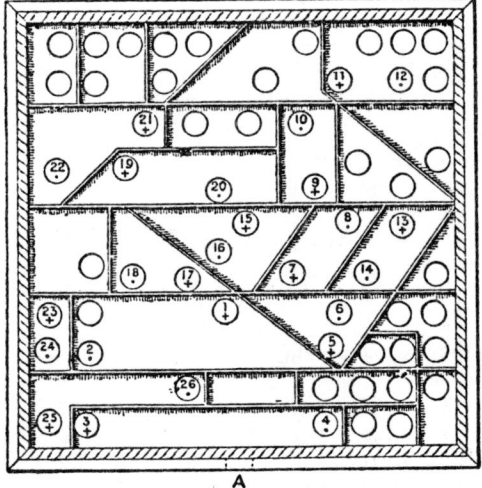

Fig. 487.—Under Side.

No. IV.—The Brahmin's Rings. Solution.

For facility of reference it will be desirable to distinguish the rings or discs by numbers, calling the smallest No. 1, the next larger No. 2, and so on up to the largest, which will be No. 8. The three "cones," which we will assume to be placed in a row before us, we will distinguish (see Fig. 453) by the letters L, C, and R, respectively equivalent to Left, Centre, and Right; and we will suppose that the rings are arranged at the outset in proper order (No. 1 uppermost, and so on) upon the left-hand cone, L. We then proceed to move as follows:—

(1) 1 on C : (2) 2 on R : (3) 1 on R.

We have now transferred two of the rings, and it will be observed that it has taken *three* moves to do it. A rash experimenter might hence conclude that it would only require eight times three moves to transfer all eight rings, but he would be vastly mistaken, for before each following ring can be brought to the base of the new heap a constantly increasing number of transpositions is necessary.

We proceed:—

(4) 3 on C : (5) 1 on L : (6) 2 on C : (7) 1 on C.

We have now transferred *three* of the rings.

(8) 4 on R :	(9) 1 on R :	(10) 2 on L :
(11) 1 on L :	(12) 3 on R :	(13) 1 on C :
(14) 2 on R :	(15) 1 on R.	

Four rings are now transferred. Continuing:—

(16) 5 on C :	(17) 1 on L :	(18) 2 on C :
(19) 1 on C :	(20) 3 on L :	(21) 1 on R :
(22) 2 on L :	(23) 1 on L :	(24) 4 on C :
(25) 1 on C :	(26) 2 on R :	(27) 1 on R :
(28) 3 on C :	(29) 1 on L :	(30) 2 on C :
(31) 1 on C.		

Five rings are now transferred, and it has taken 31 moves to transfer them.

(32) 6 on R :	(33) 1 on R :	(34) 2 on L :
(35) 1 on L :	(36) 3 on R :	(37) 1 on C :
(38) 2 on R :	(39) 1 on R :	(40) 4 on L :
(41) 1 on L :	(42) 2 on C :	(43) 1 on C :
(44) 3 on L :	(45) 1 on R :	(46) 2 on L :

362   *Puzzles Old and New.*

(47) 1 on L :   (48) 5 on R :   (49) 1 on C :
(50) 2 on R :   (51) 1 on R :   (52) 3 on C :
(53) 1 on L :   (54) 2 on C :   (55) 1 on C :
(56) 4 on R :   (57) 1 on R :   (58) 2 on L :
(59) 1 on L :   (60) 3 on R :   (61) 1 on C :
(62) 2 on R :   (63) 1 on R.

Six rings have now been transferred.

(64) 7 on C :   (65) 1 on L :   (66) 2 on C :
(67) 1 on C :   (68) 3 on L :   (69) 1 on R :
(70) 2 on L :   (71) 1 on L :   (72) 4 on C :
(73) 1 on C :   (74) 2 on R :   (75) 1 on R :
(76) 3 on C :   (77) 1 on L :   (78) 2 on C :
(79) 1 on C :   (80) 5 on L :   (81) 1 on R :
(82) 2 on L :   (83) 1 on L :   (84) 3 on R :
(85) 1 on C :   (86) 2 on R :   (87) 1 on R :
(88) 4 on L :   (89) 1 on L :   (90) 2 on C :
(91) 1 on C :   (92) 3 on L :   (93) 1 on R :
(94) 2 on L :   (95) 1 on L :   (96) 6 on C :
(97) 1 on C :   (98) 2 on R :   (99) 1 on R :
(100) 3 on C :   (101) 1 on L :   (102) 2 on C :
(103) 1 on C :   (104) 4 on R :   (105) 1 on R :
(106) 2 on R :   (107) 1 on L :   (108) 3 on R :
(109) 1 on C :   (110) 2 on R :   (111) 1 on R :
(112) 5 on C :   (113) 1 on L :   (114) 2 on C :
(115) 1 on C :   (116) 3 on L :   (117) 1 on R :
(118) 2 on L :   (119) 1 on L :   (120) 4 on C :
(121) 1 on C :   (122) 2 on R :   (123) 1 on R :
(124) 3 on C :   (125) 1 on L :   (126) 2 on C :
(127) 1 on C.

We have now transferred *seven* of the eight rings. We have made no less than 127 moves, and have, as a matter of fact, completed just *half* our task. We proceed :—

(128) 8 on R :   (129) 1 on R :   (130) 2 on L :
(131) 1 on L :   (132) 3 on R :   (133) 1 on C :
(134) 2 on R :   (135) 1 on R :   (136) 4 on L :
(137) 1 on L :   (138) 2 on C :   (139) 1 on C :
(140) 3 on L :   (141) 1 on R :   (142) 2 on L :
(143) 1 on L :   (144) 5 on R :   (145) 1 on C :
(146) 2 on R :   (147) 1 on R :   (148) 3 on C :
(149) 1 on L :   (150) 2 on C :   (151) 1 on C :
(152) 4 on R :   (153) 1 on R :   (154) 2 on L :
(155) 1 on L :   (156) 3 on R :   (157) 1 on C :

Key to Miscellaneous Puzzles. 363

(158) 2 on R :   (159) 1 on R :   (160) 6 on L :
(161) 1 on L :   (162) 2 on C :   (163) 1 on C :
(164) 3 on L :   (165) 1 on R :   (166) 2 on L :
(167) 1 on L :   (168) 4 on C :   (169) 1 on C :
(170) 2 on R :   (171) 1 on R :   (172) 3 on C :
(173) 1 on L :   (174) 2 on C :   (175) 1 on C :
(176) 5 on L :   (177) 1 on R :   (178) 2 on L :
(179) 1 on L :   (180) 3 on R :   (181) 1 on C :
(182) 2 on R :   (183) 1 on R :   (184) 4 on L :
(185) 1 on L :   (186) 2 on C :   (187) 1 on C :
(188) 3 on L :   (189) 1 on R :   (190) 2 on L :
(191) 1 on L :   (192) 7 on R :   (193) 1 on C :
(194) 2 on R :   (195) 1 on R :   (196) 3 on C :
(197) 1 on L :   (198) 2 on C :   (199) 1 on C :
(200) 4 on R :   (201) 1 on R :   (202) 2 on L :
(203) 1 on L :   (204) 3 on R :   (205) 1 on C :
(206) 2 on R :   (207) 1 on R :   (208) 5 on C :
(209) 1 on L :   (210) 2 on C :   (211) 1 on C :
(212) 3 on L :   (213) 1 on R :   (214) 2 on L :
(215) 1 on L :   (216) 4 on C :   (217) 6 on C :
(218) 2 on R :   (219) 1 on R :   (220) 3 on C :
(221) 1 on L :   (222) 2 on C :   (223) 1 on C :
(224) 6 on R :   (225) 1 on R :   (226) 2 on L :
(227) 1 on L :   (228) 3 on R :   (229) 1 on C :
(230) 2 on R :   (231) 1 on R :   (232) 4 on L :
(233) 1 on L :   (234) 2 on C :   (235) 1 on C :
(236) 3 on L :   (237) 1 on R :   (238) 2 on L :
(239) 1 on L :   (240) 5 on R :   (241) 1 on C :
(242) 2 on R :   (243) 1 on R :   (244) 3 on C :
(245) 1 on L :   (246) 2 on C :   (247) 1 on C :
(248) 4 on R :   (249) 1 on R :   (250) 2 on L :
(251) 1 on L :   (252) 3 on R :   (253) 1 on C :
(254) 2 on R :   (255) 1 on R.

The whole of the eight rings are now transferred. It will be observed, on studying the steps of the process, that each additional ring doubles the number of moves necessary to the transposition, with one move in addition. The number of moves, therefore, which would be needed to transfer 64 rings, according to the legendary shape of the original problem, would be considerably *higher* (by reason of the unit added at each stage of the progression) than the number of grains of corn in the familiar "Chess-board" problem (1 for the first square, 2 for the second, 4 for the third, and so on throughout the sixty-four squares of the board). As the total number of grains in the last-mentioned case is 18,446,774,073,709,551,615: and as it is computed that the counting of a single billion (1,000,000,000,000), at the rate of 100 a minute, would occupy 19,024 years, it may well be imagined that the assurance of Brahma, that the end of the world would arrive before the priests' task was complete, was really a mild way of putting the matter.*

No. V.—Cardan's Rings.

We quote the following instructions, the clearest and most practical that we have yet seen for the solution for this puzzle, from an anonymous American writer.†

"Take the bow in your left hand, holding it at the end, B, and consider the rings as being numbered 1 to 10. The first will be the extreme ring to the right, and the tenth the nearest to your left hand. (See Fig. 454.)

"It will be seen that the difficulty arises from each ring passing round the wire of its right-hand neighbour. The extreme ring at the right hand, of course, being unconnected with any other wire than its own, may at any time be drawn off the end of the bow at A, raised up, dropped through the bow, and finally released. After you have done this, try to pass the second ring in the same way, and you will not succeed, as it is obstructed by the wire of the first ring; but if you bring the first ring on again, by reversing the process by which you took it off,—viz., by putting it up through the bow and on to the end of it,—you will then find that by taking the first and second rings together they will both draw off, lift up, and drop through the bow. Having done this, try to pass the third ring off, and you will not be able, because it is fastened on one side to its own wire, which is within

---

* As a somewhat similar example of an impossible task, a person may be invited to try in how many ways he can arrange the 28 "cards" of a set of dominoes according to domino rules—*i.e.*, 1 against 1, 2 against 2, and so on. A German mathematician, Dr. Reiss, has computed that the possible number of such combinations is 15,918,459,863,040; and that supposing two minutes to be occupied in making each combination, the time occupied for the whole would be something over 60,000 years.

† For another very clever explanation of this puzzle see the *Encyclopédie Méthodique des Jeux*, pp. 424 *et seq.*

the bow, and on the other side to the second ring, which is without the bow.

"Therefore, leaving the third ring for the present, try the fourth ring, which is now at the end all but one, and both of the wires which affect it being within the bow, you will draw it off without obstruction. In doing this, you will have to slip the third ring off, which will not drop through for the reasons before given; so, having dropped the fourth ring through, you can only slip the third ring on again. You will now comprehend that (with the exception of the first ring) the only ring which can at any time be released is that which happens to be *second on the bow, at the right-hand end*; because both the wires which affect it being within the bow, there will be no impediment to its dropping through.

"You have now the first and second rings released, and the fourth also, the third still fixed, to release which we must make it last but one on the bow. To effect this, pass the first and second rings together through the bow, and on to it; then release the first ring again by slipping it off and dropping it through, and the third ring will stand as second on the bow, in its proper position for releasing, by drawing the second and third off altogether, dropping the third through, and slipping the second on again. Now, to release the second, put the first up, through and on the bow, then slip the two together off, raise them up, and drop them through.

"The sixth will now stand second, consequently in its proper position for releasing, therefore draw it towards the end, *A*; slip the fifth off, then the sixth, and drop it through; after which, replace the fifth, as you cannot release it until it stands in the position of a second ring. In order to effect this, you must bring the first and second rings together, through and on to the bow; then, in order to get the third on, slip the first off, and down through the bow; then bring the third up, through and on to the bow, then bring the first ring up and on again, and releasing the first and second together, bring the fourth through and on to the bow, replacing the third. Then bring the first and second together on, drop the first off and through, then the third the same; replace the first on the bow, take off the first and second together, and the fifth will then stand second, as you desired; draw it towards the end, slip it off and through, replace the fourth, bring the first and second together up and on again;

release the first, bring on the third, passing the second ring on to the bow again; replace the first, in order to release the first and second together, then bring the fourth toward the end, slipping it off and through; replace the third, bring the first and second together up and on again, release the first, then the third, replacing the second, bring the first up and on, in order to release the first and second together, which having done, your eighth ring will then stand second; consequently you can release it, slipping the seventh on again.

"To release the seventh, you must begin by putting the first and second up and on together, and going through the movements in the same succession as before, until you find you have only the tenth and ninth on the bow; then slip the tenth off and through the bow, and replace the ninth. This dropping of the tenth ring is the first effectual movement toward getting the rings off, as all the changes you have gone through were only to enable you to get at the tenth ring.

"You will now find that you have only the ninth left on the bow, and you must not be discouraged on learning that in order to get that ring off, all the others to the right hand must be put on again, beginning by putting the first and second together, and working as before, until you find that the ninth stands as second on the bow, at which time you can release it. You will then have only the eighth left on the bow; you must again put on all the rings to the right hand, beginning by putting up the first and second together, till you find the eighth standing as second on the bow, or in its proper position for releasing, and so you proceed until you find all the rings finally released.

"As you commence your operations with all the rings ready fixed on the bow, you will release the tenth ring in 170 moves; but as you then have only the ninth on, and as it is necessary to bring on again all the rings up to the ninth, in order to release the ninth (which requires sixteen moves more), you will, consequently, release the ninth ring in 256 moves. For your encouragement, your labour will diminish by one half with each following ring which is finally released. The eighth comes off in 128 moves. The seventh in 64 moves, and so on, until you arrive at the second and first rings, which come off together, making 681 moves, which are necessary to take off all the rings.

"With the experience you will by this time have acquired, it is only necessary to say that, to replace the rings, you begin by putting up the first and second together, and follow precisely the same system as before, in reverse order."

No. VI.—The Knight's Tour. Solutions.

This puzzle, like the foregoing, has repeatedly engaged the attention of mathematicians, and a great many solutions have been placed on record. Of these we select a few, of various character, by way of specimens. Figs. 488 and 489

42	59	44	9	40	21	46	7
61	10	41	58	45	8	39	20
12	43	60	55	22	57	6	47
53	62	11	30	25	23	19	38
32	13	54	27	56	23	48	5
63	52	31	24	29	26	37	18
14	33	2	51	16	35	4	49
1	64	15	34	3	50	17	36

Fig. 488. (Euler).

represent the solution of the celebrated mathematician Euler, the first indicating by *numbers* the order of the squares visited, and the second showing the geometrical effect, by straight lines drawn from square to square, after the manner mentioned on p. 336. Fig. 490 gives the solution of Du Malabare, and Fig. 491 that of Monneron. The reader will observe that, of these three, only the last fulfils what (as we have elsewhere stated) is now regarded as an indispensable condition of a "perfect" solution—viz, that the knight should

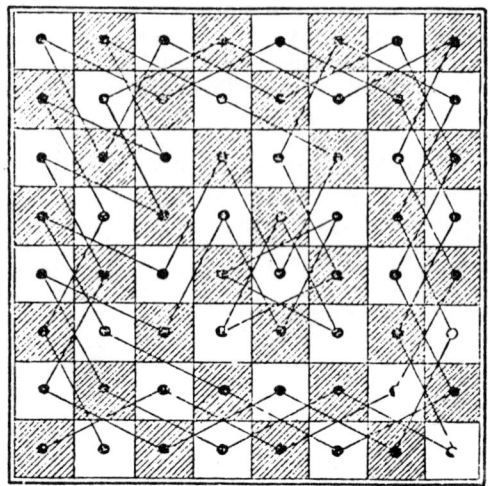

Fig. 489. (Euler).

17	20	39	4	37	22	49	6
40	53	18	21	8	5	36	23
19	16	3	38	61	50	7	48
54	41	52	1	64	9	24	35
15	2	13	60	51	62	47	10
42	55	30	63	12	59	34	25
29	14	57	44	27	32	11	46
56	43	28	31	58	45	26	33

Fig. 490. (Du Malabare.)

Key to Miscellaneous Puzzles.

finish within one move of the square from which he started. If this condition be fulfilled, it is clear that the beginning may be made from *any* square, the series of moves forming an endless chain, which may be broken at any point without otherwise interfering with its regular sequence. Euler begins at the left-hand bottom corner square, and finishes on the square next adjoining. Du Malabare begins nearly in the centre of the board, and also finishes on the square next adjoining.

1	6	51	8	11	60	57	54
50	13	2	61	52	55	10	59
5	64	7	12	9	58	53	56
14	49	62	3	16	47	36	31
63	4	15	48	35	30	17	46
24	21	26	41	44	39	32	37
27	42	23	20	29	34	45	18
22	25	28	43	40	19	38	33

Fig. 491. (Monneron.)

Figs. 492, 493, and 494 represent other "perfect" solutions. It will be observed that the diagram formed by the indicating lines now and then falls into the shape of a more or less symmetrical figure, and the reader will find it an entertaining exercise to describe either the centre or marginal portion, or both, of such a figure on his paper chess-board, and then try whether he can complete the "tour," taking the lines already laid down as part of the route to be travelled. The feasibility of such an attempt will, of course, depend upon the figure selected, but can only be determined by actual experiment.

Meanwhile, the less ambitious reader, who does not aim at

370   *Puzzles Old and New.*

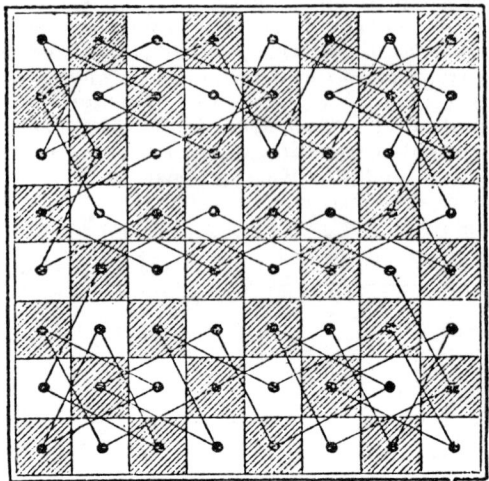

Fig. 492.

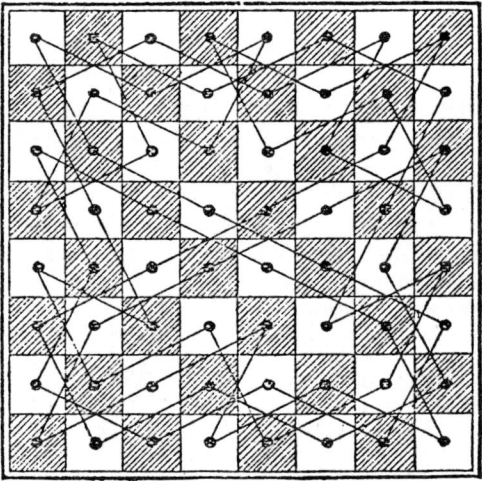

Fig. 493.

Key to Miscellaneous Puzzles.

these higher flights, but merely desires to perform the feat in the easiest and simplest way, may do so by adopting the following method, the invention of a scientific German writer, named Warnsdorf: "Place the knight on any square you like, and begin by moving him to that square from which he would command *the fewest points of attack*; observing that if his power would be equal on any two squares, you may play him to either; and that when a square is once covered, it is not to be reckoned among those which he commands. Continue moving him on this principle, and he will traverse the 64 squares in as many moves."*

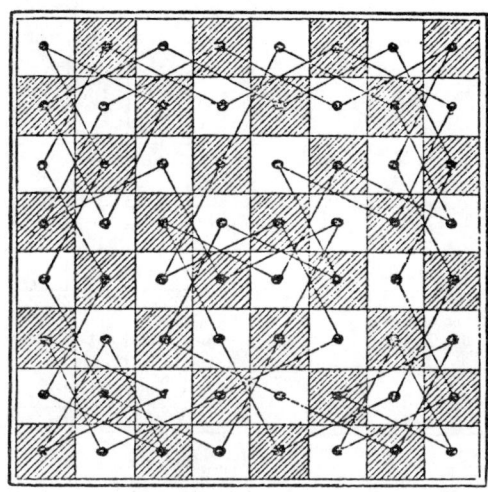

Fig. 494.

As an aid to the observance of this rule, it should be noted that the knight, from either of the corner squares, commands two squares only. If placed on an outer row of the board next to a corner square, he commands three squares. From any other square of an outer row he commands four squares. From the square next diagonally adjoining a corner square he commands four squares. From any other point in a second row he commands six squares, and from either of the

---

* George Walker: *A New Treatise on Chess*, 1832.

sixteen squares in the centre he commands eight squares, assuming, of course, that they have not been already visited. It follows that the squares in the outer rows, and particularly the corner squares, should be first disposed of, thence gradually working round and round to the centre. We append (Fig. 495) an example of the Knight's Tour worked on this principle. We have selected as starting-point the same square as in Du Malabare's solution. In accordance with the rule given,

3	40	19	36	5	50	21	34
18	37	4	51	20	35	6	49
41	2	39	54	61	52	33	22
38	17	62	1	58	55	48	7
13	42	57	60	53	64	23	32
16	27	14	63	56	59	8	47
43	12	29	26	45	10	31	24
28	15	44	11	30	25	46	9

Fig. 495.

we first make for the nearest corner. From this point up to the thirteenth the moves are a matter of course. At the fourteenth move we have a choice of two squares, one next the starting-point, the other diagonally adjoining the square to which a twelfth move was made. But we find on comparison, that at the former the knight would command seven vacant squares, while from the latter he commands six only, and we therefore give the preference to this square. From this point we work outwards again. We cannot move to a corner square, but we can secure one next to a corner, and commanding only two vacant squares. We now run on, skirting the board as before, to the twenty-seventh move, inclusive; and then back again, still on the two outer rows, and securing another corner on our way, to the thirty-eighth move, inclusive. For the thirty-ninth we are compelled to move into the third row, but immediately get back into the outer rows, and again run on, in these same rows, to number fifty-one, inclusive At fifty-two we are compelled to move into the centre. We have at this point the choice of three squares, but two of these command three squares each, while the other commands one only. We therefore decide for this one. Fifty-three is a forced move. For fifty-four we have a choice of two moves, both equally eligible, and a like alternative for fifty-five. Fifty-six demands more caution. One possible square commands two others, another one only. We therefore choose the latter. Fifty-seven and fifty-eight are forced moves. For fifty-nine there are again two squares available, one commanding two, the other one square only. If we were to move to the former, we should fail, even though on the very point of success; but, avoiding this pitfall, the remaining moves are found to be compulsory, and to bring the problem to a successful issue.

It will be observed that the final move, 64, has brought the knight to within one move of the point from which he started, according to the condition of the perfect tour.

When the starting-point is a corner square, a little extra precaution will be needed to fulfil this condition; for, inasmuch as a corner square commands two squares only, and the second move occupies one of such two squares, the other must be kept vacant to receive the knight at the sixty-fourth move.*

---

* The Knight's Tour is frequently performed as a show feat, by means of a mnemonic formula. The squares of the board are in this case regarded as being numbered consecutively, 1 to 8 in the top row, 9 to 16 in the second row, and so on. The proper sequence of the squares for the purpose of the "tour" is then committed to memory by means of a doggrel verse, or prose sentence, each syllable of which is so arranged as to recall a corresponding number. The performance of the feat in this shape involves no intellectual process beyond a very trifling effort of memory.

No. VII.—The Knotted Handkerchief. Solution.

The secret lies in the manner of taking hold of the handkerchief. This is laid, twisted ropewise, in a straight line upon the table. The performer then folds his arms, the fingers of the right hand coming out *above* the biceps of the *left* arm, and the fingers of the left hand being passed *below* the biceps of the *right* arm. With the arms still in this position, he bends forward and picks up the handkerchief, the right hand seizing the end lying to the left, and the left hand that which lies to the right. On drawing the arms apart, it will be found that a knot is formed upon the centre of the handkerchief.

No. VIII.—Crossette. Solution.

It will be found that unless the experimenter proceeds in accordance with a regular system he will fail, the count of four beginning very soon to fall upon circles already crossed out, and so failing to meet the conditions.

To solve the puzzle, after striking out a given circle, *miss three before starting again*. Thus, suppose the start to be made from No. 1 (Fig. 496):—

```
              1
       10           2

    9                   3

    8                   4

       7            5
              6
```
Fig. 496.

No. 4 will in such case be the first to be struck out. Miss three, and start again at 8; No. 1 will then be the one to be struck out. Begin again at 5, and strike out 8.

Again at 2, and strike out 5.
Again at 9, and strike out 2.
Again at 6, and strike out 9.
Again at 3, and strike out 6.
Again at 10, and strike out 3.
Again at 7, and strike out 10.

You have thus struck out nine of the ten circles.

It will be observed that you strike out at each round the number with which you started at the previous round.

No. IX.—Single Stroke Figures. Solution.

Fig. 457 may be described, according to the conditions of the puzzle, by starting at the point E, thence carrying the pencil from E to A, from A to B, from B to C, from C to D, and from D to E; then from E to B, B to D, D to A, and A to C.

Fig. 458 may be described by tracing the lines from A to B, B to C, C to D, D to A, A to F, F to C, C to E, E to F, F to B, B to E, and E to D.

Fig. 459 may be described by starting at A, then passing along the curve AGD, from D along DEB, from B along BFC, and from C along CEA.

The solubility of a puzzle of this kind by no means depends upon the intricacy of the figure. A square with diagonals united, for instance (see Fig. 497), cannot possibly be de-

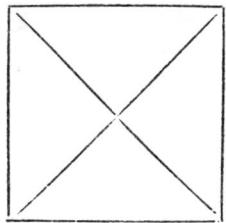

FIG. 497.

scribed without taking off the hand. The test is as follows: If the points of intersection are all formed by *even* numbers of lines, or if there are not more than *two* such points involving an *odd* number of lines, the puzzle is soluble; if otherwise, it is insoluble.

No. X.—The Balanced Egg. Another Method. Solution.

The difficulty in balancing an egg arises from the fact that the yolk, which is of greater specific gravity than the white, lies in an unstable condition about the middle of its longer axis, and so makes the egg, in familiar language, top-heavy. If the egg be well shaken, so as to break up the yolk and mix it thoroughly with the white, the whole contents become of uniform specific gravity, and the egg may then be balanced on its larger end without difficulty.

No. XI.—Solitaire Problems. Solutions. No. 1.

Starting with hole No. 1 vacant, to leave the last ball in hole No. 37.

The moves are as under:—

No.	From	to		No.	From	to
1.	3	-1.		18.	29	27.
2.	12	2.		19.	18	31.
3.	13	3.		20.	31	33.
4.	15	13.		21.	34	32.
5.	4	6.		22.	20	33.
6.	18	5.		23.	37	27.
7.	1	11.		24.	5	18.
8.	31	18.		25.	18	20.
9.	18	5.		26.	20	33.
10.	20	7.		27.	33	31.
11.	3	13.		28.	2	12.
12.	33	20.		29.	8	6.
13.	20	7.		30.	6	19.
14.	9	11.		31.	19	32.
15.	16	18.		32.	36	26.
16.	23	25.		33.	30	32.
17.	22	20.		34.	26	36.

No. 35. From 35 to 37.

No. 2. The Curate and His Flock.

The moves are in this case as under:—

No.	1.	From 6 to 19.	No. 10.	From 24 to 26.
	2.	„ 4 „ 6.	11.	„ 27 „ 25.
	3.	„ 18 „ 5.	12.	„ 33 „ 31.
	4.	„ 6 „ 4.	13.	„ 25 „ 35.
	5.	„ 9 „ 11.	14.	„ 29 „ 27.
	6.	„ 24 „ 10.	15.	„ 14 „ 28.
	7.	„ 11 „ 9.	16.	„ 27 „ 29.
	8.	„ 26 „ 24.	17.	„ 19 „ 21.
	9.	„ 35 „ 25.	18.	„ 7 „ 20.

No. 19. From 21 to 19.

No. 3. The Triplets.

The moves are in this case as under:—

No.	1.	From 6 to 19.	No. 11.	From 21 to 19.
	2.	„ 10 „ 12.	12.	„ 7 „ 20.
	3.	„ 19 „ 6.	13.	„ 19 „ 21.
	4.	„ 2 „ 12.	14.	„ 22 „ 20.
	5.	„ 4 „ 6.	15.	„ 8 „ 21.
	6.	„ 17 „ 19.	16.	„ 32 „ 19.
	7.	„ 31 „ 18.	17.	„ 28 „ 26.
	8.	„ 19 „ 17.	18.	„ 19 „ 32.
	9.	„ 16 „ 18.	19.	„ 36 „ 26.
	10.	„ 30 „ 17.	20.	„ 34 „ 32.

No. XII.—Skihi. Solution.

For the formation of the Skihi designs nothing more is needed than a modicum of the constructive faculty, supplemented by a good stock of perseverance. The cards must be coaxed, not forced, into position. If this caution be borne in mind, and the diagram carefully studied beforehand, the execution of the most elaborate design becomes a mere matter of time and patience.

We will take, by way of example, the Maltese cube (Fig. 464). Though so simple in appearance, it is by no means one of the easiest to construct, no less than eighteen cards being employed, and some little skill being needed to join them neatly together.

First take the card which is to form the top of the central or "solid" portion, and with this combine, by means of the slots, the four cards which are to form the uprights of the upper portion. Slot must be inserted into slot, and each card pushed well home. We next add the four cards which form the four sides of the cube (only the upper portions of which are visible in the diagram). These duly in place, we insert the four cards which form the horizontal platform in centre; and this is a more difficult task, for each such card has to be worked into one of the angles of the cube. When these four are in position, the next thing to be done is to join together five cards as we did in the first instance (four round one centre card) and when joined, unite these to the figure already made. Our cube is now complete; and by following the same method of construction it will be easy to put together either of the other figures.*

No. XIII.—A Card Puzzle. Solution.

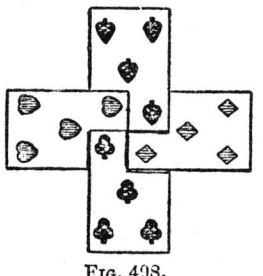

Fig. 498.

The four cards are arranged as shown in Fig. 498, one pip of each being hidden by the overlapping corner of the next.

No. XIV.—Another Card Puzzle. Solution.

First take the four aces, and with them form one of the diagonal rows, beginning from the top left-hand corner. We

---

* A little powdered French chalk rubbed into the slots will be found very useful to diminish friction. The cards when new are apt to go somewhat stiffly.

will suppose that their order is ace of spades, ace of clubs, ace of hearts, ace of diamonds. Next take the kings, and with them form the second diagonal, bearing in mind that the two centre kings must be of the opposite suits to the two centre aces, viz., in this case the king of spades and king of diamonds. Next place the four queens, beginning with the

Ace of Spades	Knave of Hearts	Queen of Diamonds	King of Clubs
Knave of Diamonds	Ace of Clubs	King of Spades	Queen of Hearts
Queen of Clubs	King of Diamonds	Ace of Hearts	Knave of Spades
King of Hearts	Queen of Spades	Knave of Clubs	Ace of Diamonds

Fig. 499.

two squares next the top right-hand corner, and then filling the corresponding squares next the left-hand bottom corner. A very little consideration will show you which queen should occupy each space. Then place the four knaves in the remaining spaces, duly bearing in mind the conditions, and you will finally have the arrangement shown in Fig. 499.

The arrangement will, of course, be subject to variation according to the cards with which you elect to commence.

No. XV.—The Floating Corks. Solution.

If the corks be taken singly, the feat is impossible; but if they be gathered into a bundle, and in that position grasped with both hands, held under water for a moment, so as to get well wetted, and then brought *slowly* back to the surface, the bundle will float upright, as shown in Fig. 500, the several corks which compose it being held together by a sort of capillary attraction.

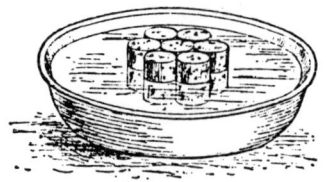

Fig. 500.

No. XVI.—The Obstinate Cork. Solution.

On first trying this experiment the cork will be found to be forced out of, instead of into the bottle, and the more vigorous the "blow" the quicker will be its return. This arises from the fact that the act of blowing drives a certain amount of air *round* the cork *into* the bottle. This compresses the air already contained in the bottle; the cork goes in a little way, but the moment the compression ceases, the air expands, and in so doing forces the cork out again.

And yet, to any one in the secret, the feat is perfectly simple. Take a quill or other small tube, and blow steadily through this against the centre of the cork. The quantity of air in the bottle is now not increased, and the cork goes in without the least resistance.

No. XVII.—Fixing the Ring. Solution.

Let the lady hold the cord at about three inches from the upper end. The gentleman passes the ring over it, then takes hold of the upper end of the cord, and draws it through the lady's fingers to within an inch or two of the opposite end. The cord is held slack, the ring hanging in the centre of the bight. The gentleman then passes the end he holds round the opposite portion of the bight, draws it through the loop thus formed, and the trick is done.

No. XVIII.—The Treasure at Medinet. Solution.

See Fig. 501 for the proper arrangement of the cards.

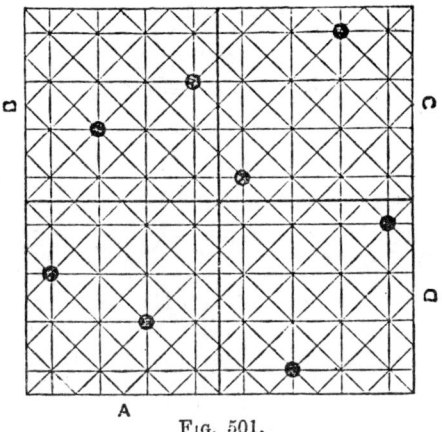

Fig. 501.

The position of the letters shows which way the original *top* of each card (see Fig. 468) is to be turned.*

No. XIX.—The Four Wine-Glasses. Solution.

Place three of the wine-glasses on the table so as to form on equilateral triangle, each side being equal to the height of a single glass. Then place the fourth glass upside down in the centre.

No. XX.—One Peg to Fit Three Holes. Solution.

It will be observed that one side of the "square" is just equal in length to the diameter of the "circle." Cut the cork to this length, as *a* in Fig. 502; and if inserted sideways, it will then just fit the square hole. It already fits the circular hole. To adapt it to fit the triangular space also, draw a straight line across one end of it through the centre, and from such line cut an equal section in a sloping direction

---

* For two other problems of a very similar character, see PUZZLES WITH COUNTERS, Nos. XXIV. and XXV.

down to each side of the circular base. The cork will then

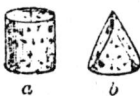

Fig. 502.

assume the shape of *b* in the same figure, and will fit either one of the three holes.

No. XXI.—The Balanced Pencil. Solution.

Stick the blade of the penknife (which should be a small and light one) into the pencil near the point, in the direction of its longer axis. Then partially close the knife. The pre-

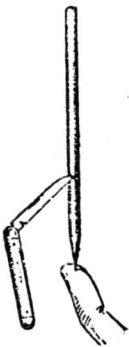

Fig. 503.

cise angle must be ascertained by experiment, as it will vary with the length and weight of the two articles. When you have discovered it, the pencil may be balanced, as shown in Fig. 503, on the tip of the finger.

No. XXII.—To Balance an Egg on the Point of a Walking-Stick. Solution.

Have the egg boiled hard.* Thrust the two forks into

---

* It is said that the feat is possible even with a raw egg, but it is in this case much more difficult, the contents of the egg being in a condition of unstable equilibrium.

Key to Miscellaneous Puzzles. 383

the cork, one on each side, so that they shall form an angle of about 60° to each other. Hold the stick, ferule upwards, firmly between the knees. Place the egg on end upon the

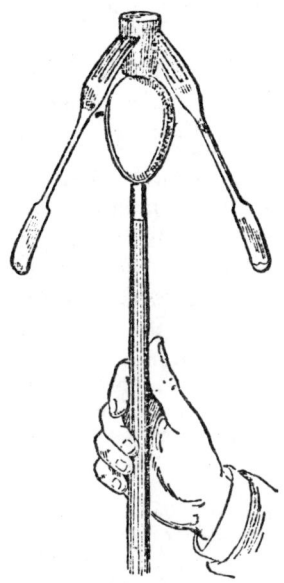

Fig. 504.

ferule, and the cork on top of it, as shown in Fig. 504. After a few trials you will be able to balance the egg in an erect position.

No. XXIII.—The Ashantee Horseshoe. Solution.

Pass the second piece of wire between the first piece and the horseshoe, and raise the latter so that the first wire shall fall just inside the curve, the two viewed edgeways forming an X, though with the upper arms very much shorter than the lower. Now raise the second piece of wire into the angle thus formed, and all will be lifted together.*

---

* See Fig. 426, which shows the method of performing a similar feat with four lucifer matches, the fourth lifting the other three.

No. XXIV.—A Feat of Dexterity. Solution.

With the left hand take hold of the hanging portion of the handkerchief and raise it to a horizontal position, in as straight a line as possible. Then with the right hand make a quick downward "chop" at the cloth at about six inches distance from the table. The cloth will be drawn away with a jerk, but the glass will remain undisturbed, the *vis inertiæ* of the latter overcoming the very slight friction occasioned by the removal of the cloth.

A neophyte, attempting to solve this puzzle, endeavours to pull away the cloth by a fraction of an inch at a time. In such case the glass inevitably comes with it.

No. XXV.—The Divided Square. Solution.

The converse of this problem has been dealt with under the head of Dissected or Combination Puzzles (No. XXI.), but many persons who are well acquainted with the method of forming a single square out of five smaller squares would be quite at a loss if they were asked to perform the opposite process. It is, however, extremely simple *when you know how it's done*.

Suppose $A B C D$ (Fig. 505) to represent the square to be divided. Find the centre of each side, represented by the letters $E F G H$. Draw straight lines from H to B, D to F, A to G, and E to C. Cut the cardboard through the lines thus marked. This will give us nine segments, which we

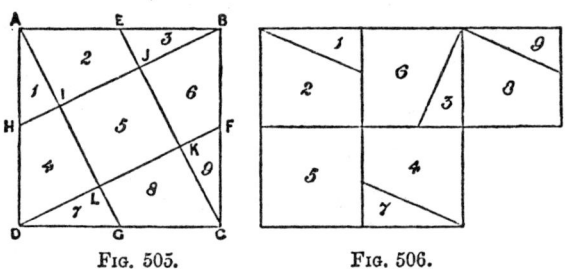

Fig. 505.   Fig. 506.

will distinguish accordingly by the numbers 1 to 9 inclusive. We proceed to rearrange the various segments as shown in Fig. 506, and the problem is solved.

Key to Miscellaneous Puzzles. 385

No. XXVI.—The "Oval" Problem. Solution.

Roll the paper into the form of a cylinder, and then proceed as though you desired to describe a circle upon it. When the paper is unrolled, you will find that, instead of a circle, you have an oval.

No. XXVII.—The Floating Ball. Solution.

Just as the lips touch the ball, inhale vigorously, and the ball will be drawn towards them by exhaustion of the air. Maintain the exhaustion till you have fairly lifted the ball, and then let it fall from the mouth to the hand.

No. XXVIII.—The Cut Playing Card. Solution.

Fold the card down the centre, and cut through the line

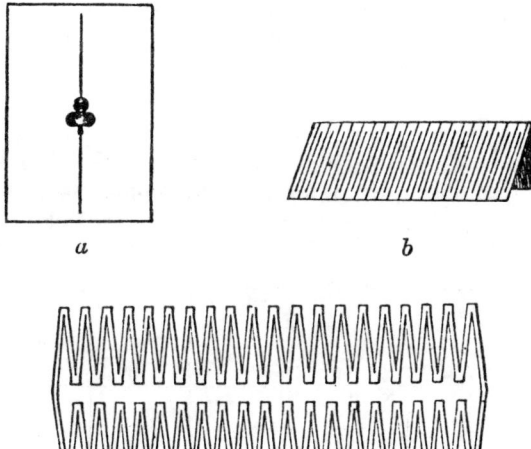

FIG. 507.

thus made to within a quarter of an inch of each end. The card will then be as *a* (Fig. 507). Next, with a sharp penknife, cut through both thicknesses, alternately to right and left, but each time stopping within a quarter of an inch of the edge, as *b*. The cuts should be about an eighth of an inch apart. The card when opened will be as *c*. Open it out still further, when it will form an endless strip, of such a size as to pass easily over a person's body.

No. XXIX.—The Mitre Puzzle. Solution.

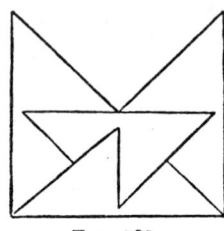

Fig. 508.

Divide as indicated in Fig. 508.

No. XXX.—The Five Straws. Solution.

Interlace the five straws after the manner shown in Fig. 509, the shilling forming a sort of wedge, locking all to-

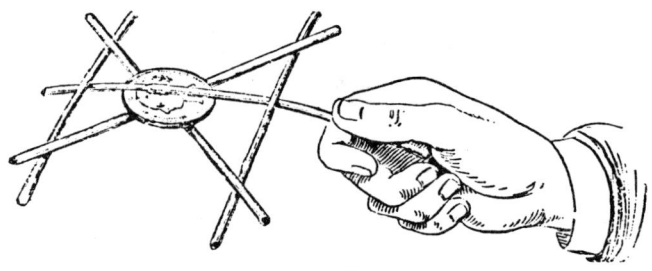

Fig. 509.

gether. They may then be lifted by the end of one straw as required by the puzzle.

Key to Miscellaneous Puzzles. 387

No. XXXI.—The Three Fountains. Solution.

This, though at first sight perplexing, is really a very simple problem. Fig. 510 represents one method out of two

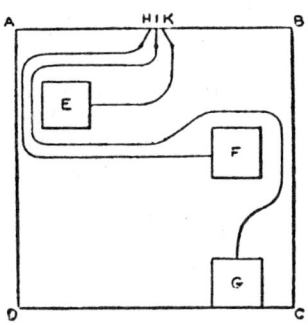

Fig. 510.

or three, either of which would answer the conditions of the puzzle.

No. XXXII.—The Two Dogs. Solution.

Add lines as shown dotted in Fig. 511, and turn the picture partially round, so that what was originally its side is

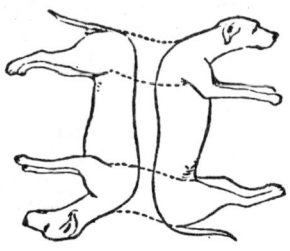

Fig. 511.

now its top. The dogs will now appear not only to be alive, but to be running at full speed.

No. XXXIII.—Water Bewitched.

Fill a wine-glass with water to the brim. Lay a piece of card flat upon it, and turn it over, keeping the card meanwhile in place with the hand. When the glass is inverted the card will not fall, though the hand be removed, neither will the water run out, being kept in position by atmospheric pressure. Place the glass thus inverted on a smooth wooden table, near the edge, and cautiously draw away the card. The water will still not run out so long as the glass is not moved, but the moment any one lifts it the whole will be spilt.

No. XXXIV.—The Balanced Halfpenny. Solution.

The first step is to bend the hairpin into the form shown

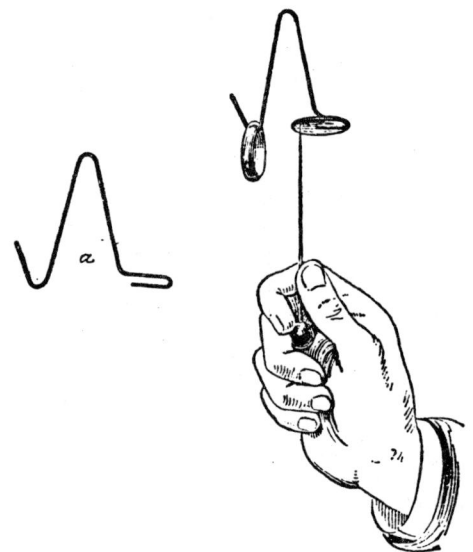

FIG. 512.

at *a* (Fig. 512). Use the narrow loop of this as a clip to

hold the halfpenny, bending the wire closer and closer till you have the coin secure. Hang the ring on the hook at the opposite end of the wire, and then proceed to balance it as shown in our illustration. A good many trials will probably be necessary before you are able to ascertain the precise point to which to apply the pin; but, this once found, you may even set the coin spinning (by gently blowing upon the ring) without destroying its equilibrium.

No. XXXV.—The Balanced Sixpence.

The first step is to fix the needle, point upwards, in the cork of the wine-bottle. The next, to cut a slit, a quarter of an inch deep, across the top of the smaller cork, and to press the sixpence as far as it will go into the cut so made.* Holding the cork with the coin downwards, thrust the two forks into it (one on either side) in an upward direction,

Fig. 513.

at an angle of about 30° to the centre of the cork. Now bring the edge of the coin carefully down upon the point of the needle (see Fig. 513), and, if the forks are properly adjusted, it will remain balanced, and the cork may even be spun round at considerable speed with little fear of displacing it.

---

* The diagram is hardly accurate in this particular. The slit in the cork should be deep enough to admit about one half the diameter of the sixpence.

No. XXXVI.—Silken Fetters. Solution.

This is a very simple matter, though, like a good many of the puzzles contained in this book, it is perplexing enough till you know "how it's done."

Let the gentleman pass the bight of his own ribbon (from the arm outwards) through the loop which encircles one of the lady's wrists, over the hand, and back again, when it will be found that they are freed from the link which united them. Their individual bonds must, of course, be removed by untying in the ordinary way.

No. XXXVII.—The Orchard Puzzle. Solution.

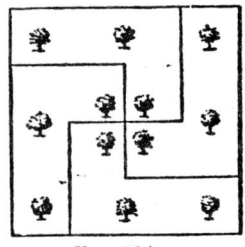

FIG. 514.

The orchard was divided as shown in Fig. 514.

No. XXXVIII.—The Cook in a Difficulty. Solution.

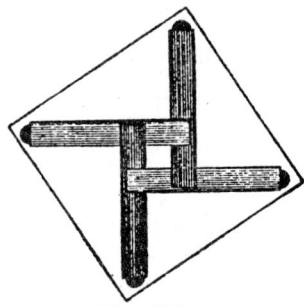

FIG. 515.

The four pieces are arranged as shown in Fig. 515, when they will mutually support each other. The small black

Key to Miscellaneous Puzzles. 391

semi-circles seen in the diagram represent in each case the visible portion of the upper end of the supporting pillar.

No. XXXIX.—The Devil's Bridge. Solution.

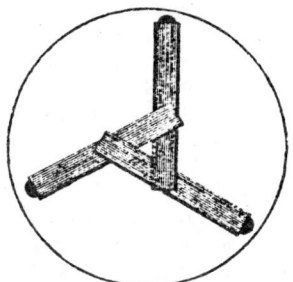

Fig. 516.

The three pieces are arranged as shown in Fig. 516.

No. XL.—The Two Corks. Solution.

The secret lies in the position of the hands as they are brought together. The uninitiated brings them together with the palms of both turned towards the body, with the consequence we have described. To solve the puzzle, turn the palm of the *right hand inward*, and that of the *left hand outward*, in the act of seizing the corks. They will then not get in each other's way, but may be separated without the least difficulty.

No. XLI.—The Divided Farm. Solution.

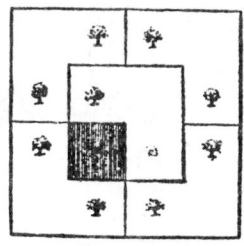

Fig. 517.

The farm was divided as shown in Fig. 517.

No. XLII.—The Conjurer's Medal. Solution.

Starting with the ring in the hole a, turn it round till the gap in it is next to the opening through which it passes, and slide it down to the opening b (Fig 481.) Turn the ring half round, and pass on the cut part to c. Thread the ring into this hole, and out of b. When it is once fairly in c, you have only to turn it once more half round, and it will be free.

To re-insert the ring in a, the process must be reversed.

No. XLIII.—The Maze Medal. Solution.

Insert the ring at the point A, and slide the open portion along into the space marked 1. Now turn the ring round till the opening comes outside the medal; pass it in again at the point B, and slide it along till the opening reaches the hole 2. Turn the opening back to 1, and thence slide it into the hole marked 3. Turn the opening back to 2, and thence slide the ring into hole 4. Turn the opening back to 3, and slide it on to 5. By turning the opening back to 4, next turn the opening back to 5, work it into 6, and thence out at A, to the outside of the medal. Work the opening back to 6, and thence pass it, along the dotted line, into the final hole—HOME.

To extricate the ring, proceed in precisely reverse order.

No. XLIV.—The Puzzle Key-Ring. Solution.

To clearly explain the construction of the ring, it will be

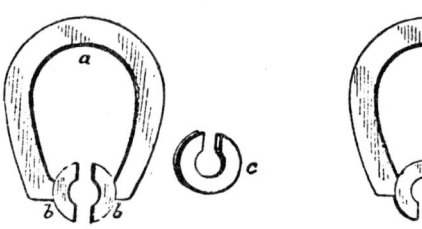

FIG. 518.   FIG. 519.

needful to illustrate its two portions separately. See Fig. 518, in which a represents the larger horseshoe, or ring proper; and *c* the smaller horseshoe, which fills up the opening. This latter is grooved all round, and revolves freely between the two arms, *b b*. To place a key on the ring, *c* is turned round so as to bring its opening outward, as in Fig. 518. The bow of the key is placed within the opening, and *c* is then again turned round, as in Fig. 483, when the key will fall within the ring.

To remove the key, reverse the process.

No. XLV.—The Singular Shilling.

Take hold of two diagonally opposite corners of the handkerchief, with the thumb on the upper surface of each, and stretch vigorously. The handkerchief will be found to form a tense fold, or "overlap," on either side of the coin; and if the handkerchief, still in this condition, be lifted into a perpendicular position, the shilling will remain gripped in the fold, and will not fall.

No. XLVI.—The Entangled Scissors. Solution.

Pass the loop through the opposite bow, and over the ends of the scissors, when they will be free.

No. XLVII.—The Penetrative Penny. Solution.

Fold the paper exactly across the centre of the hole; then take it in both hands, and ask some one to drop the penny

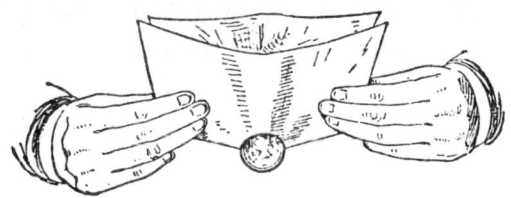

Fig. 520.

into the fold. Let it rest just over the hole, its lower edge projecting below. Bend the corners of the paper slightly upwards, as indicated in Fig. 520. This elongates the opening, and, if the movement be continued, the penny will, after a second or two, fall through by force of its own weight. The paper remains uninjured.

No. XLVIII.—The Packer's Secret. Solution.

As the reader will doubtless have guessed, the secret lies in a sort of starlike arrangement of the counters in the box.

Turn out all but seven of the counters, and of these place one in the centre of the box, with the other six round it, as Nos. 1, 2, 3, 4, 5, 6, 7 in the annexed diagram (Fig. 521).

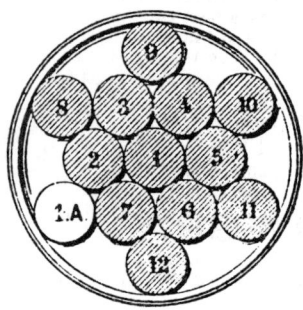

Fig. 521.

Keeping these steady by pressing the fingers of the left hand upon them, proceed to place the remaining counters as indicated by Nos. 8, 9, 10, 11, 12. But you are still one counter short. This you supply by removing the centre counter (No. 1), and placing it in the spot marked 1*A*.

The whole are now securely wedged together, and the open box may be turned upside down without any fear of displacing them.

THE END.

HAMLEY'S GRAND MAGICAL SALOONS

The Talking Hand causes roars of laughter, very clever, 2s. 9d., post free.

Boxes of Conjuring Tricks, 1s. 3d., 2s. 9d., 6s., 11s. 3d., 16s., 22s. 6d., post free. Larger sizes from 42s. to 10 guineas.

Cabinets of Card Tricks, 2s. 9d., 6s., 11s. 3d., 22s., and 43s. 6d. per box.

Boxes of Puzzles, 2s. 9d., 6s., 11s. 3d., 22s., and 64s. 6d., post free.

Ventriloquial Figures, from 15s. to 10 guineas.

Heads for Ventriloquial Figures, from 5s.

Sets of Punch and Judy Figures, from 5s. 6d.

A Large Variety of Marionette Figures.

Price List post free on application.

Superior Lessons given in Conjuring, Sleight of Hand, and Card Tricks.

A large assortment of Books on Conjuring, Ventriloquism, etc., etc.

SHADOWGRAPHY,

as performed by the celebrated M. TREWY. Complete Box of Apparatus, with Book and Full Instructions, price 3s. 9d. post free.

CHAPEAUGRAPHY;

Or, 25 Heads under One Hat.

Just published, with 50 Illustrations. Price 1s. 3d., post free.

A Complete Set of Apparatus, Book, etc., etc., for **Chapeaugraphy.** An immense success for Public Entertainments, Private Parties, Bazaars, Penny Readings, etc., etc. Price 11s., complete, post free.

"TROUBLEWIT."

A novelty for Public and Private Entertainments. Lectures, Schools, Penny Readings, Drawing Rooms, Smoking Parties, After Dinner, Bazaars, Winter Evenings, etc., etc. Unending amusement, gaining unqualified applause. Easily learnt, beautiful effects. Feats of dexterity. Novel! Interesting!! Surprising!!! With this latest and greatest Novelty, from a piece of specially prepared paper, fifty different articles can be made in a very few minutes, such as a Fan, a Muff, a Hat, a Bonnet, a Window-blind, a Couch, an Epaulette, Ornaments for Table, a Boat, a Tumbler, etc., etc., and about forty other different articles all from the same piece of paper. The "Troublewit" is packed up in a handsome box, complete, with full illustrated directions.

Price 2s. 6d., or post free, 2s. 9d.

It will be the Leading Feature at every Entertainment of the coming season.

PUZZLES from 6d. each up to 7s. 6d. can be seen at

HAMLEY'S GRAND MAGICAL SALOONS, 229, HIGH HOLBORN.

MR. J. BLAND'S MAGICAL PALACE OF
CONJURING WONDERS AND PUZZLEDOM.

BOXES OF PUZZLES.

These Puzzles are specially got up in boxes by MR. BLAND, containing a splendid assortment, in handsome box, covered with leatherette and hinged lid, at a very much cheaper rate than if they are sold separately. Customers seeing the grand selection, and the absurdly low price charged for one of these boxes, at once decide upon purchasing one. The Puzzles are all made by first-class workmen, and are all highly finished and nearly impossible to find out. Full Instructions are given with every Puzzle in each box.

Box of Puzzles—
No. 1—2s. 6d., post free, 2s. 10d. | No. 3—10s. 6d., post free, 11s. 3d.
No. 2—5s. 6d., ,, ,, 6s. | No. 4—21s. ,, ,, 22s.
No. 5—63s. Carriage to be paid on receipt.

MR. BLAND has nearly every Puzzle mentioned in this book, most of which are illustrated from his patterns. He will be pleased to quote for any particular one not seen in his list, as he has nearly every puzzle ever invented.

'MR. BLAND'S CATALOGUE OF PUZZLES, ETC., is post free 6 stamps.

BOXES OF CONJURING TRICKS, 1s. 3d., 2s. 9d., 6s., 11s. 3d., 16s., 22s. 6d., 31s. 6d., 43s. 6d., and 64s. 6d., post free.
CABINETS OF CARD TRICKS, 2s. 9d., 11s., 21s. 9d., and 43s. post free.
CABINET OF COIN TRICKS, 6s. 9d. post free.
VENTRILOQUIAL FIGURES, at 15s., 21s., 30s., 40s., and 60s. each, carriage to be paid on receipt.
VENTRILOQUIAL HEADS, at 5s. 6d., 7s., 11s. 3d., and 18s. 3d. post free.
MARIONETTES and **PUNCH and JUDY FIGURES** in great variety, 5s. 9d., 7s. 4½d., 11s., 15s. 9d., 22s., 43s., and 6 guineas a Set.

Mr. J. Bland is the oldest and best Maker of Magical Apparatus in the trade, and everything is sent out in perfect working order.

BOX OF DRAWING-ROOM FIREWORKS, 1s. 3d. post free.
TRICKS from 6d. to £50.
BLAND'S BEST SPRING FLOWERS, 6s. 6d., 10s. 6d., 14s. 6d. per 100.
COILS FOR HAT, 5d. each, post free 8d., or 4s. 6d. per doz., post free 5s. 4½d.
    ,,   ,,   Small Size, 1s. 9d. per doz. post free.
SMALL FLAGS, 1s. 1½d. per gross, post free.

Illustrated Catalogue of Conjuring Tricks and Puzzles, post free, 1d.

SUPERB ILLUSTRATED CATALOGUE of Conjuring Tricks, etc., post free, 6d.
NEW LIST OF NOVELTIES JUST PUBLISHED, ALL THE LATEST PUZZLES, CONJURING TRICKS, SLEIGHTS, ETC.
Mr. Bland gives Superior Lessons in Legerdemain, from 3 guineas the Course of 7 Lessons. Entertainment provided for Evening Parties.

BLAND'S MAGICAL PALACE, 35, NEW OXFORD ST., LONDON, W.C.